"Now if you ever reach the women, really reach them in a book—"

Kate made a gesture to express endless possibilities.

"There's only one way you're ever going to understand about women enjoying sex. We're going to do it. Hey, you all right?"

"I'm fine."

"Get this through your skull. I am as horny as hell and will get hornier as I talk about it. Understand?

"Now I am going to describe every one of my sensations, and you remember them, concentrate on every sensation, every detail. You're going to describe it for your readers, they'll flip."

She let her jacket fall to the floor...

Rich Dreams

BEN AND NORMA BARZMAN

WARNER BOOKS

A Warner Communications Company

WARNER BOOKS EDITION

Copyright © 1982 by Ben and Norma Barzman
All rights reserved.

Warner Books, Inc., 75 Rockefeller Plaza, New York, N.Y. 10019

Ⓦ A Warner Communications Company

Printed in the United States of America

First Printing: April, 1982

10 9 8 7 6 5 4 3 2 1

For Luli, John, Aaron, Daniel,
Paulo, Marco, and Suzo

PART I

*"More people read me than the yellow
pages of the phone book."*

—Arnold Elton

PART 1

1.

Arnold Elton and Oscar Brenner were the only human passengers in the first-class compartment of the 707 and they were spending hard time. During the five hours of flight Arnold, in a so-it-shouldn't-be-a-total-loss frame of mind, had sprawled in at least four different rows of seats. In that same period Oscar had socked away most of the Cutty Sark he'd bought himself at Kennedy duty-free; at that rate he would never make his self-imposed one-bottle-a-day limit.

Arnold pressed the button on his eight-thousand-dollar 18K solid gold Pulsar. Blue digits flashed on the watch's electronic face.

"It is now exactly sixteen hundred hours twenty-two minutes thirty-two seconds Zulu time," Arnold announced accusingly.

"Zulu time?" Oscar asked, knowing that Arnold wanted to explain.

11

"Airline talk. It's what the airline people call it when instead of saying a.m. or p.m. you add twelve hours."

Across the aisle Oscar cradled his Cutty Sark. With considerable effort he managed to hoist one large flabby leg up over the seat next to him so that he too was occupying two seats.

"Like one p.m. becomes thirteen hundred hours." Arnold held up the custom-made Pulsar again. Oscar dutifully made a pretense of peering at the watch with his faded blue eyes. He refused to wear glasses except for reading contracts. Then Arnold got back to the main point. "We'd've been there by now if Arnel had its own plane."

"Don't think I don't know, Arnold." When Oscar got that far down on his Scotch, words came stenciled out of his mouth. "But with crew, maintenance, insurance, interest, depreciation, a private jet comes to minimum, bare minimum per annum." Oscar reached for the miniature calculator that he kept permanently attached to his vest by a long heavy gold chain and let dangle down his pants leg. As far back as Arnold could remember, Oscar had never been without a calculator. In the good old days he had carried one in his pocket. When he bought the first one with a chain, he adopted the peculiar habit of letting it hang down his leg inside his pants, making a peculiar bulge at the crotch. As time passed and the calculators became more and more miniaturized, the bulge diminished. This latest calculator, the width and thickness of a playing card, was one of the trivial spin-off benefits of Arnold's Japanese paperback deal. You had to hand it to the Japanese, the way they miniaturized everything! Miniature trees, cars, computers, calculators . . . Arnold let himself speculate idly about the possibility of miniature cunts.

Oscar's fingers moved with surprising deftness over the calculator squares.

"A private jet," Oscar announced the results, "would cost you, a bare minimum, One—Two per annum."

"Totally deductible even with the new shit tax regulations Congress has just passed," Arnold said impassively.

"Not totally, Arnold."

Arnold decided to give Oscar an argument to reassure him that he was still being taken seriously. "Totally," he therefore said with the monumental certainty that was his most distinguishing characteristic. "Not to mention the exquisite pleasure it would give me of fucking the Internal Revenue Service of the United States of America out of another one million two hundred thousand dollars." Oscar was looking appropriately solemn. He sighed and let the calculator slide back down inside the leg of his pants. "Besides," Arnold continued, "the manna from *Let Me Count the Ways* will more than cover it."

"I have to hand it to you, Arnold"—over the years Oscar had refined ass-kissing into a minor art. "Nobody else in Arnel, including me, caught that one."

"Think about it, Oscar," Arnold said. "Just think about it. They could have made a second picture from my book without paying another fucking penny when there it was in the contract: *'any further motion picture made from the aforesaid literary work shall be paid for under the identical terms and conditions as for the first . . .'* One million dollars—"

"Plus ten percent of the gross," Oscar added dutifully.

"And if *I* hadn't read the contract . . ." Arnold shuddered slightly. "The Studio might've gotten away with it."

"Some one of us would've caught it."

"No, Oscar. That's not good enough. I'm hurt. It's one thing if the other side doesn't read contracts, but when my own people aren't reading contracts—to me, if Arnel is anything it's people who read every letter, every comma of contracts."

13

"Arnel people must read contracts," Oscar said solemnly.

Arnold ran Arnel like a close-knit family. Higher-echelon employees kissed each time they met, even the men—Arnold had introduced that from Europe—then performed the American ritual: *How the hell are you? You're smoking too goddamn much. You've put on weight, watch it, Buster. How are the kids?* The difference was, unlike family, if you screwed up you were chopped so fast your severed head was reputed to do a delayed take as it rolled off the block. Arnold was scrupulously polite to all Arnel personnel as a matter of policy, from the cleaning woman all the way up to Wacszinski and Reilly, but when Arnold was dissatisfied he fired, boom like that; the ax could fall out of nowhere, at any time. To make it crystal clear, despite the anguish it had cost him, Arnold had once fired a top-level executive on Christmas Eve. You performed or you were lopped. That was Arnel Enterprises.

Oscar of course was the very special exception. Arnold needed him the way every family needs a pain-in-the-ass relative to whom no one really listens.

"We're entering a new phase."

Even as he spoke Arnold felt his penis slowly harden, and he gave the incipient erection an acknowledging fond caress. All his life he'd felt an excitement when he worked on big deals, and with the Big One coming up he understood the nature of that excitement clearly. The Deal was going to be the biggest in Arnel history, and last week, when he'd spoken to the Texas moneyman and realized that The Deal really was within the realm of the possible, he found himself quivering with a full-blown erection.

"I've been doing some heavy thinking, Oscar. Have we really faced up to the possibility of a triumph? Do we really have faith in ourselves? Right now we're thinking only about achieving the take-over. But what happens when we have control of the studio? Have we got people who can grow *big?*

14

Does Arnel have the muscle for ongoing responsibility?''

Oscar sensed that Arnold was prepared to begin bitching about practically every executive both in Arnel East and Arnel West, and who could tell, the mood Arnold was in it might even get around to him. Oscar scrambled to safer ground.

"We got the muscle, Arnold, and we got the people. But it's not the money."

Arnold was momentarily baffled until he realized that Oscar had done some fast fancy footwork and was now back to the discussion of private ownership of jets.

"Private jets have more accidents than commercial aircraft."

"You ever check out why?"

Oscar allowed himself another hefty slug of Cutty Sark.

Arnold sighed.

Less than a month before, the two of them had subjected themselves to their annual three-day-down-your-throat-in-your-nose-up-your-ass checkup at Mount Sinai.

Most of Oscar's liver was gone. With his daily bottle of Cutty Sark he was giving himself what the Italians call the *sweet death*. But close as Oscar was to him, Arnold didn't intervene. Every man has a right to choose his own poison. Arnold respected that.

"Like this morning, the delay at Kennedy. Weather. No commercial airline would risk taking off, but you take a private jet . . ."

Arnold felt his erection recede. Sometimes when negotiating, Oscar would lose the thread of his thought in the same sodden way, invariably reaching for and playing with his calculator as the adversaries waited breathlessly. Several times they'd waited so long they'd panicked and upped an offer. As a result, Oscar had gotten the reputation of being a deceptively tough negotiator.

"Private jet"—Oscar had miraculously managed to catch

15

the elusive thread of thought—"crew stands by for weeks getting paid regularly, not moving their asses. Boss Arnold Elton suddenly says, 'We take off for the south of France this morning.' The pilot captain says, 'No problem, Mr. Elton,' and you take off, weather or no weather."

Sri Lanka, a magnificent Afghan hound puppy with a fabulous mane of copper gold, who was almost as restless as Arnold, moved down the aisle making sounds. He was trying to tell them something.

"With my own jet and crew I'd go over the weather myself," Arnold said.

"You know *weather* too, Arnold?"

"Shit, Oscar, you know I sailed the merchant marine during the war."

"Even after all these years I keep finding out things about you." It was a touch of in-depth ass-kissing, but said with a bit of alarm. Ass-kissing always had to be credible, and Oscar had heard many times the story of how Arnold had shipped out in the merchant marine in World War II even though he had been too young.

Sri Lanka's movements—the puppy was practically dancing—made Arnold very nervous. He took it out on Oscar. "You know I have a pierced earlobe, and that every now and then I wear a gold earring? because a sailor who's been shipwrecked is entitled to wear a gold earring—two if he's gone down twice."

The gold earring was incongruous on a man who prided himself on the correctness and elegance of his attire—of his Saville Row suits, his Via Condotti shirts, his Lanvin ties.

Oscar nodded Live and Learn, took another shot of Cutty Sark and went back ponderously to being the father-uncle-pain-in-the-ass relative. "Still I can't let you do it, Arnold. All right. If anything should happen to you—we've got to be realistic, things happen to people—we got umbrellas for all of them, financially speaking. Heavy trust funds for Robbie and

16

Jennifer. But. *But*." He suddenly discovered he was onto a good thing. "Krystina's pregnant. The kid that's on its way is going to need you, Arnold, and even though Robbie's thirty and Jennifer's thirty-two."

"Thirty-one."

Gently chiding, "Two. Don't you remember for her thirty-first birthday you had me buy her a complete set of that whatchamacallit Louie Vooton luggage, nowhere in the world can you get a discount, cost an arm and a leg four thousand dollars American?"

Lately Oscar had taken to talking like a professional currency dealer: dollars American, D-marks for German marks, francs Swiss, once he even mentioned Algerian dinars.

"Yes, but did you hear what the air hostess at Kennedy said they're paying in Japan for my *Louis Vuitton* duffle bag? A duffle bag, for Chrissake. Eight hundred dollars."

Oscar hauled up his calculator. "Eight hundred dollars American, comes, at the present rate of one point nine one zero five yen for the dollar, one thousand five hundred and twenty-eight yen and"—with an airy gesture—"a little something."

"Make a note," Arnold said, although Oscar never even pretended to make those notes—"remind me to send Marcel into Italy. The Italians are making counterfeit *Louis Vuitton* for one-fifth the French price. I want Marcel to buy up as much as he can smuggle across the border." Arnold sighed. "You're right, Oscar. Jennifer is thirty-two."

"That's my point," Oscar went on. "The young stay young longer these days. They still need you. Kids." Oscar got lost but managed to come back fairly rapidly. Even with brains ninety percent whiskey mash Oscar still knew how to worm his way up Arnold's gut. "You know I always keep an omnipresent eye on Robbie and Jennifer." Oscar let a wide beam take over his wide face, with a slight touch of teasing mystery. "And I can report that those kids may have a nice

17

surprise for you." He lifted one heavy arm. "Which I promised not to give away so don't ask. Besides it would spoil the suspense." Oscar tried a mischievous grin, but it emerged as if he was reaching deep into his digestive tract for an elusive belch.

"Suspense is for the schmucks who buy my books."

Thoughts of Robbie and Jennifer always brought Arnold waves of pain and guilt, for he and the kids loved each other with that kind of crazy turbulent love that only those who really love know. He understood how murderous it was being the children of a rich and world-famous father. Over the years, Arnold had watched other millionaire Beverly Hills parents grapple with the problem, although he thought most of what they did was pure horseshit. One of Arnold's neighbors, a man of sturdy old New England stock, loved California but regretted that there was no snow for his two young sons to shovel off the driveway and that he was obliged to think up other odd jobs he could pay them for. Some parents made under-the-table donations to summer camps so their kids could be "hired" as counsellors. Despite the pain it had cost him, Arnold was convinced that he had succeeded where a mixed bag of psychiatrists, psychologists and therapists had failed.

Love, Arnold had decided, had no real value for you unless some of yourself went into it. Dr. Spock, with "kiss 'em and love 'em no matter what," had forced a whole set of parents to overcompensate for an older generation that had been so distracted and frightened by the Depression that it hadn't been able to love at all.

Not that you didn't have to invest time and love. But there was a measure. If you gave love mindlessly, the child would never know what love was. Love had to be earned, achieved. That's what he had done. He had forced his kids to confront reality.

18

And if what Oscar was hinting was so, Arnold's toughness had worked.

It was six months ago that Arnold had tried to make Robbie's thirtieth birthday very special. He wanted it to be memorable, a token of his thoughtful love. It must not be marred by bickering. No matter what, he'd keep his cool. He would stay sweet and gentle but firm, especially with Jennifer. He must not let her get away with anything.

For the occasion Arnold dressed in his best Via Condotti tailored raw silk jacket and fitted slacks, laid on the company limousine and insisted on Tory, the coolest, most competent and most fun chauffeur.

The kids dressed too. They looked great. You had to give that to them. They knew how to look wonderful—Robbie in a navy cashmere jacket, soft gray slacks, naturally open-collared shirt, all effortlessly chosen and elegantly casual; Jennifer bare-shouldered in a frilly white gown with a large floppy romantic hat was something for candlelight. It was going to be a lovely evening.

They were all leaning back in bemused silence, lulled by the limo's almost noiseless purr. Arnold was slowly ridding himself of the tensions he unaccountably built up on these occasions.

"Impressive," Arnold said as they glided down what they were now calling the "Wilshire corridor," with its dozens of gleaming new high-rise condominiums.

"You can say that again," Robbie said with an edge of challenge. "You know what penthouses on one of those things goes for?"

"No." Arnold was willing to be impressed.

"Oh, come on." Jennifer nudged Arnold with a sharp elbow so roughly he winced. "Of course you know. It was a dumb-head sensation for a couple of weeks. Every dumb-head in the world knew how they were selling the penthouses to

Iranians or Arab sheikhs for eleven to thirteen million."

"With a Rolls-Royce thrown in," Robbie said. "One of the buyers—Iranian, I think—turned it back, said he had three Rolls already."

"No kidding?" Arnold realized Jennifer was not buying any of the sincerity his tone was dripping with.

Tory slowed down and was actually negotiating a left turn when Jennifer barked out, "No! No! Straight! Straight!"

Tory, momentarily confused, tried to straighten.

Arnold had completely forgotten—or blacked out—this little habit of Jennifer's. No matter who was driving she gave sudden, precise and authoritative directions, insisting she was the only one who knew the shortest, the easiest, the most pleasant way of getting from one place to another, no matter where they were, Pacific Palisades, Cannes or Hong Kong.

Arnold called out as sharply, "No! Tory! Left! Left!"

Tory had to swing wide, there were screeching tires. He barely avoided a collision.

"What's the matter with you?" Jennifer shrilled at her father. "Don't you know the way to Chasen's after all these years?"

"You almost got us killed," Robbie said sullenly.

"We're not going to Chasen's," Arnold said in a heavily conciliatory tone when they were all able to breathe again. He had managed to smother his first blaze of anger.

"Why the hell didn't you say so in the first place?" Jennifer snapped at him. "He wants to get us killed," she explained to Robbie.

Arnold's mental typewriter clicked out the rest of the scene, his raging at her that *she* was the one who'd almost got them killed. If she had kept her wise-ass mouth shut, there would have been no near miss in the first place and just because she was his daughter didn't give her the right to talk to him that way. There was no one else in the whole world she'd dare take that tone of voice with or who would take it from her. After a lifetime of care and love he'd poured on her, the lousy rotten little bitch, to be so stinkingly stupidly ungrateful and ill mannered. For two cents he'd crack her across her big mouth.

"I thought we'd make it a really big night," Arnold said in sweet calm paternal tones. "I thought we'd go to *Ma Maison*. You know about *Ma Maison*?" Would they ever know, the little bastards, what an effort it cost him to make it sound playful and festive when it was all he could do to suppress an impulse to seize her—Robbie was only her shadow—and shake the living daylights out of her.

"What's so special about *Ma Maison*?" Robbie asked sourly.

"Well gee, fellas," Arnold said, "it's so exclusive it has an unlisted phone number. Imagine a restaurant with an unlisted phone number?"

"Big deal," Jennifer said. "I like Chasen's better."

"But you've never been to *Ma Maison*." Arnold bled big drops of sweet reason.

"I like the fresh cracked crab at Chasen's," Robbie said.

"You can get cracked crab at *Ma Maison*," Arnold offered.

"Fresh?" Robbie asked.

"Fresh," Arnold affirmed.

"Then why didn't we go to Chasen's in the first place?" Jennifer demanded.

Arnold had another image this time, of throwing himself out of the limo, of being run over by the heavy dinner traffic, wheel after wheel flattening him.

"No." Arnold swallowed a quart or two of bile. "We're going to *Ma Maison*." He needed a couple of seconds before he could say, "You can't tell. You may actually like it."

Jennifer made a movement miming vomiting to show how improbable that was while Robbie contented himself with a grimace.

21

"D. V. O. P.," Jennifer said.

"What's that?" Arnold knew it was a mistake to ask even while he was asking.

"Dog vomit on plate," Jennifer explained.

The rest of the evening was like that, only more so.

The two young people barely noticed *Ma Maison*'s lavish décor nor the dozens of other celebrities nor the deference with which the headwaiter greeted their celebrated father, nor the elegant wristwatch Arnold presented to Robbie. Robbie glanced at the watch, handed it to Jennifer, who didn't even bother looking at it as she handed it back to Arnold. By now irritated, Arnold gave it back to Robbie, who mechanically handed it back to Arnold. This time Arnold almost slapped it into Robbie's palm. Finally the boy accepted it with a shrug while Arnold took out his anger and frustration on the iced crab which Robbie had insisted on ordering.

"Hey, now wait," Arnold had protested. "They have a great French cuisine here. Look. Marvelous mousse of salmon, pâté de foie gras, duck à l'orange—"

"None of that fancy junk for me," Robbie had said doggedly. "I like fresh cracked crab."

So Arnold cracked it for them as if they were still kids and they waited mutely for him to crack it for them. He usually got none for himself. He cracked. They ate. And the waiters removed the pile of debris before Arnold could snatch a morsel. It was so expected, the kids didn't even say thank you. Actually, you could consider yourself ahead if you got through a birthday without a major fight.

"You don't order crab at a French restaurant no matter what," Jennifer lectured reprovingly. Arnold searched his mind for a time when she hadn't been critical or hadn't tried to teach him a lesson.

"Okay, okay," with great effort, Arnold made himself sound playful. "What did I do so wrong in taking you guys to one of the world's great restaurants and giving my son the latest Seiko computerized wristwatch—one of the first of its kind by the way to come to the U.S. . . ."

"Latest Seiko Computerized," Jennifer mused, then it hit her. "Say, Robbie, I'll bet you a kick in the ass he got that as some kind of spin-off benefit on that Japanese paperback deal of his."

Arnold cracked crab furiously. As it happened, he *had* gotten the wristwatch that way, but what the hell, for once in her life she could have been gracious.

"Something's eating you guys," Arnold said as he handed Jennifer a neatly cracked claw and began work on one for Robbie.

Usually, Jennifer was the one to speak first—she was the aggressive one, like her mother, and just as Arnold hadn't been able to face up to Kate, so he was incapable of standing up to Jennifer, even though he felt some part of Robbie was now at stake—but it was Robbie who spoke up. "It's one of those things basically you can't talk about," he said.

"There's something *we* can't talk about?" Arnold asked.

"I hate it when you use that face," Jennifer said. "I know you think it's funny but you look just plain dumb. Just because you've been able to talk to us about kinky sex—I mean how could you avoid it with your books and all?—it doesn't mean that there aren't *some* things in life it's not easy to talk about?"

Arnold slowly realized this was going to be something he'd have to handle. He had some kind of unexpected situation on his hands. "You're right," he conceded to Jennifer.

"Okay," Jennifer said as if she'd established an important advantage. "Robbie was hoping since after all he's now thirty, you might come up with something special, and not just, if you'll excuse the expression, another shitty wristwatch he doesn't need."

"Special like what, goddamnit?" Turning up her spoiled nose at a fifteen-hundred-dollar watch.

23

"Like how come you never thought of offering either of us a vice-presidency in Arnel?" Jennifer asked.

Those two infuriating young faces turned on him, blinding him with their injured looks because he hadn't made them executives of the organization he'd fought for for decades, struggled, wheeled, dealed, isolated himself in a writer's utter loneliness for weeks, months, years, living with that forever fear that one day the words would stop coming, pounding out one best-seller after another, always plowing the money back into Arnel—the mountains of shit he'd eaten, the finagling, the waiting, the conning, until Arnel had emerged . . . What did they know about any of that?

"I should have known," Arnold flared at her, "every time you see your mother it takes at least a week for the shit to dissipate itself."

"Okay, Dad," Jennifer said grimly. "You're a big man for straight talk. Well, okay. Frankly we analyzed, Robbie and I, we worked it out objectively. The way people get to the top in Arnel, is to *suck* their way up." Arnold needed a moment to get control of himself. "We both hope you can take that as merely our honest opinion," she added solicitously.

"Suck their way to the top?" Arnold exploded. "What kind of crap is that?"

"See," Jennifer said with a tolerant sigh to Robbie. "I told you he'd take it that way."

"But, Dad," Robbie said with the gentle, slightly patronizing Wasp manner he'd inherited from *his* mother, "let's be realistic. How else can you explain—I don't know, maybe I shouldn't go on—"

"You can't stop there," Arnold snapped at him.

"All right. How else can you explain those assorted assholes you've got in executive spots? I mean, let's take Reilly. *Reilly*, for God's sake. Reilly is basically an asshole."

24

"Sexy though," Jennifer conceded, "but that's neither here nor there, we're talking about executive material. Look, Dad, you've taught us to be completely open with you, and never to hold anything back. If you don't want us to tell you what we really think, okay, we'll dummy up."

"And Wacszinski," Robbie added, "now there's a crew-cut asshole if I ever saw one. And Oscar Brenner. Holy jumping horseshit! What is Oscar Brenner?"

Arnold had listened to this exchange with dry-ice fascination, at one point even bracing his legs against the table. "All right, now you tell me something," Arnold said when he felt himself able to talk. "What in the hell have you two characters ever done that makes you entitled to top slots in Arnel Enterprises Inc.?"

"That's a fair question," Jennifer said unhesitatingly. They'd obviously rehearsed. "One. Robbie and I are nuts about making movies, which not one of your Arnel jokers really gives a shit about. Secondly, we've grown up in the business. We took filmmaking with our mother's milk, right?"

Arnold stifled an impulse to tell Jennifer that he'd fought like a bastard with Kate to breast-feed. "Breast-feed?" Kate had flung at him, "and get my knockers pulled all out of shape?" Arnold merely nodded.

"Thirdly, we've fooled around with cameras and in labs, we've watched dozens of pictures shot, we've read stacks of screenplays, the shit we've waded through—which I think makes us highly qualified. And come on, Dad, wouldn't it look ridiculous if your own son and daughter at our ages started at the bottom? Robbie and me, gofers. Stop and think how stupid we'd feel and look schlepping coffee or buying stamps for those poops you got yourself there. Now you tell us something. What's wrong with our starting with top slots?"

They were both good-looking kids, and they were his own,

and how the goddamn hell could they have drifted so far from reality? Arnold cracked another crab, and he felt his heart curl up like a small animal looking for a place to die because no matter how much he loved them he knew with everything he had in him he was going to have to hit them, and hit them hard; reality was reality, and he had to let them see what it was like, the gut-breaking, power-fighting, throat-cutting world of filmmaking into which they wanted to move.

"Besides"—Robbie obviously felt this was a clincher—"you *know* us. We're a hundred percent honest. We would never rob a production blind. We're full of ideas. We learn fast. We're perfect executive material. We can't understand how come you never thought of it yourself, Dad."

"Okay." Arnold realized he had spattered himself and the immediate vicinity with crab guts and bits of shell, but the two young sat before clean place settings. It seemed symptomatic. He came down hard and cold. "It's my turn now, and I want you to listen and not interrupt. My first studio job, before I began to write, was as a messenger boy, and whatever you may think, there are very special qualities men like Reilly and Wacszinski bring to Arnel." They waited for him to elucidate, but he wasn't about to do that. "I built Arnel with my own guts and blood. It's a big part of my life. You two guys want in, then goddamn it you're going to have to prove to me you're worthy of it. I'll give it to you proudly then and don't ask me how you're going to do it, because that's part of it. I want you to work it out for yourselves so I'll know—and you'll know—it's something you made on your own."

He looked from one to the other then, expecting a fight or childish anger, but to his surprise both had dropped their blasé expressions. In fact, they looked suspiciously pleased with themselves.

26

"Basically what you want is for people to prove they've got it before they can expect to move in, right?" Robbie asked.

"Right," Arnold repeated, grateful to have been understood. "Right. Right. Right."

"Okay," Robbie glanced at Jennifer, who nodded encouragement. "What if we set up a feature film—Jen produce it, me direct it—would that prove we're not some poor jerks who happened to be born lucky?"

"If you could set up a feature film," Arnold said quietly, with deep sincerity, "promote it, develop the project and get it ready for distribution, you would prove even more than I asked."

"Good. Because we have got ourselves one hell of a project," Robbie said then. "In fact it's all lined up. We're on our way."

Arnold felt a flush of pride. Was it possible? Had these kids actually persuaded a money interest to take a chance? Maybe. Maybe the Arnold Elton name had helped. That was legitimate. It would be a miracle, but look at Stallone. *Rocky*. It could happen. Out of nowheresville. Arnold was excited.

"We've got ourselves a package," Jennifer said, her voice brisk and businesslike. Arnold was amazed at his elation. His own kids, on their own, pulling off something like this. "All the elements. Cast—we're taking a lot of faces who've had big exposure on TV and other media, faces you know, like the romantic soap chicks, the macho cigarette cowboy you see in all the magazines, the detergent ladies, you name them. We're putting together a sizzler—"

"Wait." Arnold tightened. "Sizzler like in porno? X-rated?"

"We're not comfortable with the designation porno," Robbie declared, "even though basically we're explicit. We've studied the figures on *Deep Throat*. Over twenty-two

27

million paying customers domestically; we didn't bother with foreign figures; we'll be satisfied if we approach that, huh, Jen?''

"Right," Jen said, "and we figure we should with what we've got. Our idea's real. The explicit hard-core material is justified, like in *Last Tango*, only the story's funky funny, you'll bust a gut, now here's the way the story lines up..."

Arnold had had it done to him dozens of times, hundreds of times really, by a guy who happened to live next door (in Bel Air that meant practically an acre away,) or a guy who went out of his way to run into him casually, or a clerk at Gucci's on super swanky Rodeo Drive—before he knew it, someone was rapping a story at him: everybody under thirty wanted to be a filmmaker, and the ones over thirty had a story a million times better than the shit they'd been seeing on the screen, and surely he would buy it for several hundred thousand dollars.

"I don't listen to story." Arnold stopped her mechanically. That was the hard bottom line of Arnel policy—no matter who, even with his own flesh and blood, Arnold couldn't listen to stories. Story was told to the hired story editor who was paid for that. Even the story editor would only listen when the story came from an accredited agency with the guarantee that the client wouldn't screw around with nuisance plagiarism shit. "All *I* need to know is—what are your bankable elements?"

"We have ourselves a real hot bankable element." Robbie was underplaying it, and effectively. Arnold's curiosity was certainly aroused.

"All right," he said. "I'll listen."

"We got ourselves a jim-dandy, Dad."

"A what?"

"A jim-dandy," Robbie repeated with peculiar insistence.

"What's a 'jim-dandy'?" Arnold asked in all innocence.

Robbie, who had been toying with his fork, let it fall to the table. "Jeez, Dad, you were the one who dropped it on me, and it made a hell of an impression. You said every man was looking for *the* jim-dandy, a legendary wet-dream woman, cunt written all over her without her even trying—quote, a dame who could take her right tit and throw it over her left shoulder and squirt milk down her ass. Unquote."

Arnold remembered it then, a session years before when he had felt particularly close to the adolescent Robbie—they'd indulged in some rough playful man-talk.

"You didn't take that seriously?" Arnold asked. "It was a kind of old-fashioned joke."

"It didn't sound like a joke," Robbie said stiffly. Apparently he had been banking on that to strike some real chord in Arnold. "It had the ring of something basically true. You said every man spent most of his life looking for the jim-dandy. Well, I found one, Dad. At work."

"You call making snatch-shots for *Playtime* work?" Arnold tried to stall for time. Time to find a way of handling this.

Robbie flashed his boyish, musing grin. "Yeah, I know," he said. "Most guys would give their left ball to do what I'm doing and I get paid besides. Anyway, the jim-dandy's a Plaything, a *Playtime* Centerfold. Wait till you see her, one look and you'll *know*. She can do things you won't believe."

"Like what?" Arnold asked apprehensively.

"Like for example," Robbie said, "she can bend over backward and put her head between her legs and you can kiss her on four lips, if you know what I mean."

"Of course he knows what you mean," Jennifer said tartly. "According to Punko here"—Jennifer shot an affectionate thumb at Robbie—"she can screw with her head between her legs and also have an orgasm that way. Visualize that if you can in big-screen glorious color with an eight-channel sound track."

"Not on a legitimate screen, I can't," Arnold was deeply disturbed. Had the kids for Chrissake been looking into his

29

bedroom when he was with Krystina? "How much of this do you think they'll let you show?"

"Enough to send zippers skittering," Jennifer said. "I saw her. Listen. That kid doesn't have to move. She's a human Kama Sutra. Just looking at her you imagine everything you ever wanted to happen to you in sex and never dared hope."

"Fellas," Arnold said as gently as he could. "When you get down to it, what you're telling me is that you've got an acrobatic big-titted unknown."

"You're not listening, Dad," Jennifer said sharply. "This is just about the most grabassable human female I've seen around."

"Nobody's grabbing now," Arnold said.

"What we're telling you, Dad," Robbie said patiently, "is once they see her on the screen, everybody'll grab." Then Robbie took a deep breath and carefully got to the weenie. "Of course, we'll need a beginning push from you. Nothing big—like Two from you would do it, wouldn't you say, Jen?"

" 'Two'? Two what?" Arnold demanded.

"Gee, sorry, Dad," Robbie sighed with a big show of relief. "I forgot that with you 'Two' can mean two *million*. But all we need is *two hundred thousand* seed money for screenplay, options on actors—"

"Yeah," Jennifer confirmed. "Two would get us off the ground and airborne."

"Wait a minute," Arnold said. They were snowing him, his own kids, even though they probably didn't think they were. "What the hell kind of bankable element do you think you got for yourselves if you can't raise Two on it?"

"We can raise everything except the *first* Two," Robbie corrected him sharply.

"That's not a bankable element," Arnold said. "A bankable element is something you walk into a bank with so you can walk out with enough bread to make a film. Redford's bankable. Burt Reynolds is bankable. Clint Eastwood's bankable. Jack Nicholson is bankable. Richard Dreyfuss is bankable. Streisand's bankable. Faye Dunaway," Arnold made a wavering gesture to indicate how uncertain even Faye Dunaway's bankability was. "Let's talk *toches* on the *tish*"—that was another holdover from Kate—"bare ass on the table. What you've got so far is *bubkes*. Peanuts. Nothing."

"What do you mean '*bubkes*'? We've got the rest of the money lined up, for Chrissake," Jennifer snapped at him, "all you have to do is come in with the first Two."

They'd never get anywhere with what they had, no matter what their story was, Arnold was dead certain of that. Not with legitimate money, anyway. He hardened himself with a surge of cold determination. He had to say no.

Over the years Arnel Enterprises had developed a technique for saying no. They'd had several seminars on it, all the top people, and they'd decided something that seemed obvious but really wasn't. The best way was to say no, just like that. No ifs or maybes (who was famous in the industry for saying "I can now give you a definite 'maybe' "?), no screwing around, no bullshit about thanks, it's good, but it doesn't fit into our program at the present time, just no. Out.

But this was going to be the hardest no he'd ever had to utter. There was a lunatic inside of him screaming, *Write out a check for two hundred thousand dollars for Chrissake these are your kids okay so they'll make a semiporno and pornos are on their way out but give 'em the two hundred thousand let 'em find out for themselves it can even be a legitimate tax write-off.* But he fought the lunatic down savagely.

"You *won't?*" Robbie's voice cracked. They'd been so sure it was all cut-and-dried, wrapped up. "You won't, Dad?" Arnold nodded. "But why won't you?" Robbie had dropped the Wasp charm. He was straight pugnacious now. Jennifer was looking at her father, her face a bubbling mass of furious disbelief. "It's our future."

"That's exactly why," Arnold said.

31

"Exactly why what?" Jennifer demanded. "Here you keep telling us how much you love us and what's a lousy two hundred thousand dollars to you? If we fall on our asses you could write it off—"

"Wait a minute," Arnold relented. "I'll tell you what I'll do. You get the first hundred thousand and I'll guarantee the second. You can use *that* in your hustle."

"But the whole idea of the deal we talked was that you would come in with the first Two," Jennifer said angrily.

"You shouldn't have talked that kind of a deal," Arnold said, "not without consulting me first."

"Jeeesssuuus!" Robbie howled. "Here we've got ourselves a Centerfold who's really something, I mean she can and will do anything I ask her to and we've budgeted the whole script carefully and we know we can bring it in for less than six hundred thousand. Six. What the hell's Six these days. Shit. And we'll bring it in for less."

"Get the first hundred thousand yourself," Arnold said. "Come on, you guys. Don't look like that. It's not as though I turned you down. I told you I'm in. But I want you to come in with something you got for yourselves, don't you understand that? Not something that was built on me. Listen. You hustled yourself some of the elements. Hustle yourself the rest. That's where it is today. *Hustle*."

2.

"I just figured out one of the reasons a plane ride is so boring. It keeps making the same sound over and over."

As he said it, Arnold realized he'd left himself open to Oscar's saying "And a goddamn good thing it keeps making that same sound over and over." But that was no longer Oscar's style. Arnold speculated about an Oscar lump-session as a means of making the time go faster, but abandoned it. There was no real sport any longer in handing out lumps to Oscar.

"Seventy-seven minutes twenty-two seconds," Oscar announced, "and we land at Nice. Just visualize what's waiting for you."

"Yeah, okay." Arnold half shut his eyes, visualizing. "They'll be there in the back garden, Robbie and Jennifer." He gave Oscar an opening to say something more about the kids, but Oscar didn't open his mouth, so he let himself think about Krystina. "Krystina's carrying my child. No matter what they say that's something, your woman carrying your flesh and blood. And Sarita and Telly will be there, too—all of them at Villa Lou Soleillou waiting."

"Go on," Oscar mumbled encouragingly.

"Villa Lou Soleillou," Arnold murmured. No matter what else could be said about Oscar, it was especially good talking to him. You could say whatever was on your heart, tell him anything and you could be sure he wouldn't repeat it, because (a) he probably didn't hear half of what you said and (b) he probably would never remember. Besides, you could tell him things he'd heard a dozen times before and he would still listen with that somnolent look of deep and sincere interest. "Soleillou. That's Provençal for sunshine. Krystina wanted to call it Villa Amour. She 's got a streak of the cornball in her. Maybe that's why I love her. They all know how much I enjoy seeing them together. Even Sarita my hot Mexican secretary and Telly my cool Aussie secretary. They're part of it too. I come home after an absence, it's like a family photograph. Question is should I tell them, touch wood, about The Deal? Or should I wait until it's finalized?"

"Share with them the anticipation, that's family. Only seventy-one minutes left. Believe me even though admitting a private jet could save a few minutes, Arnold, I couldn't let you."

The game of "not letting" him had become almost pathetic, as if Oscar could prevent him from doing anything. But Arnold felt a twinge of regret. He'd miss Oscar when that last forlorn piece of his liver crumbled away. The visualizing hadn't made the time drag less. Maybe giving Oscar lumps *would*. Arnold reminded himself that Oscar had screwed up on the delicatessen.

Each time Arnold came back to the Riviera from New York it was Oscar's responsibility to arrange for a huge package of Jewish deli, none of it available in the south of France, to be

34

delivered to the plane. It was a big part of the pleasure of returning, bringing the bagels, pastrami, smoked Nova Scotia salmon, Philadelphia cream cheese, and especially the Jewish salami, to Lou Soleillou. All the flabby sonofabitch Oscar had to do was call Zabar's. They did the rest. Arnold looked forward to those great brunches with Krystina—and this time there'd be Robbie and Jennifer, who'd been persuaded to visit probably largely because they wanted to hit Arnold again with their project, but anyway they were coming, even though it was obviously not their idea of how to spend a hilarious summer. And Arnold got a real zetz out of offending Michel and Germaine, their elderly butler and cook, who believed that smoked salmon was to be eaten only on toast with a dash of lemon and pepper, instead of on toasted bagel with cream cheese.

"How come you fucked up on the delicatessen, Oscar?" Arnold had decided on an Oscar lump-session after all.

"The delicatessen?" He'd been hoping with all his soul that Arnold wouldn't bring it up. "The delicatessen, Arnold?"

One quick glance at Oscar's mouldy-looking face and Arnold knew he couldn't handle it. But time was still heavy.

"Never mind the delicatessen," Arnold said. "I want to talk."

Oscar leaned back, relieved. Every now and then Arnold "talked" to Oscar, letting it all pour out, saying whatever lay buried within him, secret feelings people would be surprised to know Arnold Elton harbored.

"Sure, Arnold," Oscar mumbled in gentle half sleep. "You talk to me. Tell me what's on your heart."

"If there's one guy in the world who can say 'I came from nowhere,' it's me. Did I ever tell you I have a half-brother exactly my age, even born the same week—Myron?"

"Born the same week?" It was too heavy for Oscar. "From the same father? How can that be?"

"The old man," Arnold said, "you'd never believe it to

look at him, was boffing two broads at the same time. And with leaky condoms.''

"Leaky condoms?'' Oscar was stupefied. "And how did you find out?''

"When I was fourteen and ready to leave home, my father didn't try to stop me. He just gave me twenty bucks and a piece of advice, 'Never use a condom more than once,' he said. 'I did. Washed them and then found both of them leaked.' So then it all came clear to me—the real reason why I had a half-brother—we had our bar mitzvahs the same week—You listening, Oscar?''

"I'm listening.'' But Oscar didn't have to listen too closely. He'd heard the story a hundred times. Arnold loved to keep telling it.

"Imagine—banging two women at the same time—with leaky condoms yet. So he married Myron's mother and my old lady disappeared. But he must've felt guilty and forced Henrietta to let him adopt me—I guess you can say I only half know who I am. The old man never told me who the babe he knocked up and who gave birth to me was—''

"So maybe she was from some fancy family. Maybe she was a Rothschild.''

"There weren't any Rothschilds in America,'' Arnold said shortly. "My old lady was probably a striptease queen, or a fan dancer, whatever in hell they had in those days.''

"Yeah,'' said Oscar heavily. "Maybe that's how come your books are so sexy.''

"There's always that possibility.'' Arnold felt lighter when he talked of his past. "If we pull this off, the reality is I'll be a real power in the industry, in the same studio where I started as a messenger boy, the asses I had to suck—and here I am, a beautiful wife waiting for me, two beautiful kids, a baby on the way, and I can say modestly I'm the most successful writer and one of the greatest of all time, the biggest moneymaker ever made money out of words and in a little while I'll be in bed with

Krystina, you should see the body on that girl and it's something else when we fuck, and there's this thing clutching at my heart I'm thinking thoughts I haven't thought since I was a kid, What is Life? Eat, crap, work, fuck and die, I'm thinking of the past and death. Oscar? Are you listening to me, Oscar?"

Oscar's eyes were glassy. Lately Arnold had begun to suspect that Oscar had learned to sleep through these talk sessions with his eyes open. "What is Life?" Oscar repeated to prove he'd been listening.

"Scott Goldman," Arnold said. "He's that writer came to interview me a few weeks ago. You know I never give any interviews. Jesus, I don't know what got into me—I let Telly talk me into it. I shouldn't have and this guy really got to me. Maybe for me he's the symbol of all those fucking literary critics who tear me apart. Oscar, never in my whole career did I give one good shit what they said about me. My philosophy has been, Let 'em, who gives a goddamn? Every day all over the world thousands of people buy a book of mine. You know how many, Oscar—"

Oscar shifted and nodded his head automatically.

Arnold continued. "The day Krystina told me she was pregnant, I was talking to this character, Scott Goldman, and while I'm talking, he suddenly writes something on a little piece of paper—he's always writing on little pieces of paper, which he rolls up and sticks in his pocket. I asked him, 'What did you write there?' and he reads to me, 'For all mortal creatures, no matter how long they live, death always comes as an unpleasant surprise and always too soon.' He's the kind of guy, if he heard somebody else say a line like that he'd say 'I wish I'd said that,' only me, I know fucking well a line like that won't sell even one paperback, then I remember what they said about Scott Goldman in *The New York Review of Books*, they called him 'a cult figure' this 'novelist' who must have sold a grand total of ten thousand books his whole

37

career, listen, there's something about this schmuck when he's with me, he does it without trying, I can't tell you what it is but he gets to me—and I remember something else. This Scott Goldman once wrote about me 'Arnold Elton, the writer who proved the penis is mightier than the sword,' so I suddenly said to myself 'What if I disappear without a word, leave him hanging?' I thought he'd take off after a few days, but no, he's still waiting for me to come back and finish his interview for a few hundred bucks living money. At least he'll know he's been hit by life as it is, you know what I mean, Oscar, listen, Oscar, are you awake?''

"I'm awake," Oscar's words were sleep-slurred.

"Okay," Arnold said, this time really testing Oscar for some sign of life, "so I said to this French hooker 'You're supposed to be special, do something original.'" Arnold waited. Oscar nodded heavily. "So she took out her glass eye and I fucked her in the eye"—Oscar nodded approvingly—"and you, Oscar Brenner, now have the honor of sitting across the aisle from the only man who ever fucked a woman and made her actually see stars when he came. What did I say, Oscar?''

"She saw stars."

Sri Lanka, who had been pacing madly, crapped on the aisle carpet, then came over to Arnold proudly as though waiting to be thanked for having pulled off something great.

"Ring for the stewardess," Arnold said.

But she was there before Oscar could lurch back into action. Joyce Humboldt, a slim sexy Angeleno, bent over and made picking up dog shit in the First Class section seem the most natural thing that could happen. She rolled the dog turd in a paper towel, whisked it off to the First Class toilet, and came back with a wet rag and a special spray that made the place smell like a pine forest. This time she bent over with her back to Arnold so that her buttocks shifted under the

Cardin-designed skirt like marvelously crafted precision instruments.

"Ever stop to think what a wonderful word 'fuck' is?" Arnold asked Oscar while watching Joyce.

"I know it's a wonderful feeling," Oscar said tentatively, not sure yet where this would lead.

"I'm talking about the *word,*" Arnold said. "I'm proud I was one of the pioneers who brought it back into common usage. Even my worst detractors will give me that."

"Absolutely," Oscar said glassily.

"A man 'fucks' a woman," Arnold went on as he watched Joyce scrub the spot Sri Lanka had dirtied. "And it's the greatest. What in life can compete with that? Then there's the equally marvelous 'fuck you!' How else could it be said? 'Don't fuck around,' meaning don't waste time. 'Fuck off,' meaning get the hell out. And you can say 'he's a fucking genius,' meaning he's the greatest; 'don't fuck with me,' a warning; 'not worth a fuck,' meaning not worth a shit. The more I think about it the more I'm convinced that *fuck* is the most useful single word in the whole English language."

Joyce made an especially vigorous movement, which caused her buttocks to move suggestively, then straightened.

Oscar got up suddenly. "Excuse me, I've got to go to Economy Class," he said, and staggered off before either Joyce or Arnold could stop him. Arnold wondered vaguely if this was delirium tremens.

Joyce glanced uneasily at Arnold. Several times during the flight Joyce had sent subtle woman signals, which Arnold was an old hand at decoding. A sexual aura preceded him like advance publicity for a show on the road. When a woman met Arnold, she was meeting a man who had described for millions of readers, vividly, explicitly, lyrically, the images and sounds of fellatio, cunnilingus, anal, oral and every other conceivable variety of sexual acrobatics.

Looking at Joyce, Arnold let reels of erotic images flicker through his head: the cabin lights turned down, under a blanket with Joyce Humboldt on the floor between a row of seats, as frantic hands pulled off her Cardin skirt, groping, feeling, grasping for breasts, belly, thighs, buttocks, pubic hair; sliding into her, pumping, rolling, gasping, the remote possibility that someone might blunder into First while he and Joyce were at each other giving it an added zest—although at the same time Arnold knew goddamn well an experienced airline hostess like Joyce would never in a million flight miles let herself in for anything as stupid as that. Still, that was what was so convenient about fantasies—minimal credibility was demanded, logic was suspended, almost anything went. It lasted about ten seconds and left Arnold vaguely depressed and tired.

He wondered idly about the connection between flying and fucking. Was it because being up in the air, cut off, knowing the slightest error, a bolt missing, a door not properly closed, meant certain death? Death and fucking. Arnold made a note to think that out for a future book. Every one of his books had been a combination of fucking and a special background or institution. That was the secret formula of his incredible success.

"Sorry about the dog shit," Arnold said, although he knew his voice had not the slightest intonation of apology. "He's only a puppy."

"He's certainly beautiful." *That* couldn't be an easy admission. Sri Lanka had peed six times and crapped four during the flight and each time Joyce had valiantly maintained the same professionally smiling, indulgently casual manner through the cleaning up. "Heavenly."

"He's a gift for my wife. He's exactly the color of her hair."

Joyce shot the puppy a quick look and made an appreciative moue at the color of his mane. "Now that's what I call thoughtful, Mr. Elton."

It had been played out. It was over.

"I can't imagine what got into Mr. Brenner to go into Economy," Arnold said. "Would you mind leading him back into First?"

"Yes, of course," Joyce replied uneasily.

Arnold permitted himself to watch the play of her buttocks as she walked off, speculated again on what they might look like without her skirt and panties on and was saddened—it was strangely a time for inexplicable sadness—by the thought that if he followed up on only ten percent of the offers women tossed his way, he'd spend most of his waking life fucking.

Oscar was piss-green when Joyce brought him back.

"You were all tensed up, and she looked like she was available, you know what I mean, Arnold," Oscar said when Joyce left.

"In the plane, Oscar? A man in my position fucking an air hostess? You kidding?"

"Who knows?"

"Well now, Oscar. Let's say I was schmuck enough even to consider humping the hostess on the plane and she was stupid enough to go along—don't you *know*? Haven't you noticed?"

"Noticed?"

Oscar reached for the Cutty Sark. There were still a few drops left. Arnold stopped him, which meant it was serious. Oscar was supposed to *notice*. That was one of his functions.

"I want this marriage with Krystina to be my last."

"Sure, Arnold," Oscar was panicky. "It's a good marriage. It works."

"Before I come back to Krystina, I lay off. It's hard when so much pussy is thrown at me I could go into the fur

41

business. But Krystina always knows I save up for her so that when I get back there's a charge, Oscar, a real charge.''

"That's good, Arnold.''

"So I lay off. I wouldn't have touched Joyce if I could've. I'm surprised you never put it together before.''

"One thing and another, Arnold,'' Oscar apologized.

Sri Lanka now deigned to come close enough so Arnold could pat his beautiful silky head. "The Afghan breed is famous for being a one-man dog'' the vet had said, "and it looks to me like you're already it.'' From the very beginning the puppy had attached itself to Arnold and slept on the floor alongside Arnold's bed. When, during the night, he whimpered, Arnold had only to reach out and touch the puppy's mane for him to be reassured.

"What's the matter, Oscar? You look like you put your hand into a bucket of cold shit.''

"Wade Vernon,'' Oscar mumbled, and Arnold sat up like a sudden erection. "He's in Economy.''

"Vernon's on *this* plane?'' Arnold said, not daring to believe it. "On this plane?''

"You invited him to your Fourteenth of July party,'' Oscar said, "and to get from Dallas to Nice on time, you take a plane on the thirteenth. We are today the fourteenth.''

"He's on the plane,'' Arnold said. "He came, goddamn it, he came!'' He didn't even try to calm himself down. "I knew it. I had a hunch. Remember, Oscar, I told you I had a gut feeling?''

"Yeah,'' Oscar said dully. "You told me.''

"I knew it,'' Arnold suddenly looked over at Oscar. "What's the matter?'' Oscar stood sodden, white. "But he's on the plane! A guy like that doesn't make a trip halfway around the world to see Fourteenth of July fireworks. Goddamn it, Oscar! The deal's wrapped up.'' He moved suddenly over to Oscar, shook him. "What's the matter?'' Oscar just stood there like a huge lump. "You talked to him?''

42

"Yeah," Oscar said, and a sick chill ran down Arnold's spine. "You wouldn't believe it. A big businessman like that. For a triviality—"

"What triviality?" Arnold shouted at him. "Come on, talk!"

"He saw me come in from First," Oscar mumbled. "When I opened the curtain he saw First was practically empty." Oscar hadn't even had the sense to pull the curtain closed. "Economy is jammed. One on top of another. He asked me were you in First." A helpless gesture. "I had to tell him."

"You had to tell him."

"He asked me was anybody else in First."

"You had to say no."

"I had to say no."

"Then what did he say, Oscar? Tell me, Oscar."

"First he burned. Wade Vernon burns like dry ice, you know, Arnold? Looks cold but burns. In a very quiet way he went bananas. Then he said one thing he doesn't stand for is being euchred by a commercial airline. He said he was told First had been reserved for a special party."

"What'd you say, Oscar?"

"Nothing. Then he said his ulcer was bothering him and he was going to spend the night in Nice and then fly back home."

"Going back? He's not coming to the party tonight? He can't go back. We've got to talk..."

"Yeah," Oscar mumbled. "He said anyway on the plane he'd been thinking. Maybe Arnel and his organization are not in the same class."

"Not in the same class?" Arnold reeled.

"He said they don't operate the same way, he said maybe they can't operate the same way. And that's all he said."

"He didn't say he wanted to see me?"

"No, he didn't say he wanted to see you."

"And then what?"

"Joyce arrived. Then we came back."

Arnold looked around desperately. His eyes fell on Joyce, who was standing close enough to overhear and understand what had happened.

The airline had been antsy about selling the whole First to Arnold. They must have instructed Joyce to make goddamn sure nobody in Economy found out. Oscar's blunder could mean her ass too. She was supposed to know how to prevent situations of this kind from happening. That's why she was in First Class.

"I'll tell you what you're going to do, Oscar," Arnold said. "You're going to go into Economy and don't ask me how but you're going to bring the dry-ice sonofabitch back into First."

"How'm I going to do that?" Oscar backed away from Arnold in fright. "I've never seen a man so burned. You'd never think to look at him. Maybe that's why he's got an ulcer, he doesn't let it out, it doesn't show, he keeps it inside—"

"Oscar," Arnold said quietly, "you are going to go back there"—Arnold extended his arm full length, pointing in the direction of Economy—"and you are going to come back with Mr. Wade Vernon or you better find out how they open these emergency windows and throw yourself out. If you don't, I'll do it myself."

Oscar's eyes fixed on Arnold so long they looked like grotesque distortions of the glass button eyes Arnold had once sewed back on Jennifer's teddy bear. She had come to him mutely and with chubby four-year-old arms held up the one-eyed bear to him, showing him the loose eye, which lay in one tiny palm: she looked as if she'd made some appalling discovery about mortality. Arnold had sewed it back and proved to her that it was as good as new, the sun was in its heaven, all was well with the world. Jennifer had hugged the

44

now two-eyed bear, then hugged Arnold tightly with an intense passion.

Oscar lurched off, his heavy legs moving with drunken slow motion, and a sickening revelation hit Arnold with skull-crunching force.

A big part of the special excitement about this homecoming, the so-sweet anticipation, the pleasure in handing out the gifts, the love, were all tied to The Deal. For some reason he couldn't understand, all his fabulous successes in the past didn't count. If he wasn't able to pull this one off, he wouldn't deserve the hugging, kissing, touching, laughing, fucking that was waiting for him.

It was like the movie world. You were only as good as your last film. Nothing else counted. If your last one flopped you were wiped out.

His whole life was on the line. Everything rested on making this goddamn Deal a reality.

Arnold turned. Joyce had been standing in the nearby aisle all this time. She had the look air hostesses have when they demonstrate how to use emergency life jackets.

"You heard—didn't you, Joyce?" Arnold was studying her speculatively.

"Some," she answered uneasily.

"Right now we're both in a crock of shit," Arnold spoke rapidly. "You included. There's a fucking temperamental Texan in there"—he pointed towards Economy—"who's going to raise holy hell with your airline—and with me—because he thinks he was screwed out of a First Class reservation. Your airline may lose a customer and get some small bad publicity, you may get your ass chewed out by your supervisor, but for me it could be close to fatal. I need this man—not just on my side, but with me all the way—so much with me that he'll stake a huge chunk of money on me. If he doesn't it'll be the pits for me and my company."

"You can count on me, Mr. Elton," Joyce said anxiously, making the standard airline employee offer. "I'm ready to help any way I can."

"All right, Joyce," Arnold said quietly. "In a few minutes, if we get lucky, Oscar Brenner will come back with the Texan, will get him here in First."

"Good," Joyce said. "What if I break out the champagne and caviar?"

"Champagne's a great idea," Arnold said, "but it's not enough. There's only one surefire way *I* know to win Vernon over in the time left before this plane lands."

"Which is?"

"You can get him to fuck you," Arnold said.

Joyce dropped the air hostess politeness. "Now wait a minute. I'm a member of a flight crew."

"You're a beautiful woman," Arnold said, "and sexy as hell. Now don't go getting angry with me." It was goddamn maddening. He could tell from the way she was looking at him that there was some way he could persuade her. It was a question of finding that way quickly. "What's at stake here is what in the old days would have been called an Empire. History is full of women who fucked for diplomatic advantage, or for influence. You help me on this, Joyce, and I'll—"

"Make me a duchess?" Joyce said with a kind of grim amusement.

"The equivalent," Arnold said. "I'll cut you in on our share of the deal. One-tenth of one percent, and our share will be over the hundred million mark. Figure it out for yourself. It will be a lifetime annuity."

She was shaken. She stared at him.

"Nobody will bother you," Arnold said. "You're in the First Class cabin of a commercial airliner. We've got well over an hour of flight time left." Behind him he could feel someone approaching the curtain from Economy side. "If

46

anything happens I'll cover you. You've got my word. You know who I am."

Who would have thought, relaxing on a sleepy south of France hillside six weeks ago, that he would be on top of one of the biggest deals in motion-picture history—if a fuck worked.

With regard now to the Sodium vapor, experiments ... the ... ...

3.

Arnold, Krystina, Gina and Alfredo had sat peacefully having a late afternoon drink on the terrace of Villa Lou Soleillou, which overlooked the entire serene Mougins hillside and the Mediterranean directly south. It was drowsy fragrant May. They were enjoying a lull in the hectic Cannes Film Festival.

In the distance the harbor was churning, with cutters bringing tourists from an Italian cruise ship lying white and green a mile offshore, and clusters of sailboats, their sails slanting and many-colored, competing in the spring regatta.

The four sat in contented silence. Down below on the barely distinguishable roadway Arnold caught a glimpse of a small Renault. Scott Goldman drove a Renault, which was the cheapest and most efficient French car. Scott was the kind of guy who knew about things like that.

"I'm leaving tomorrow," Arnold surprised himself and the others by announcing suddenly.

The Renault didn't even stop. It hadn't been Scott after all. Maybe if it hadn't passed, Arnold wouldn't have blurted out that business about leaving.

" 'Leaving'?" Krystina didn't even try to dissemble her utter dismay. "Tomorrow?"

"What's wrong with tomorrow?" Arnold asked blandly.

Gina turned to Krystina, "But surely he is only talking—"

"But you enjoy the Festival so." Krystina was still in shock. Her words tapered off as she saw the look on Arnold's face.

It was not very *in* to enjoy the Festival. You were supposed to watch the mad crush for tickets for the evening showings with distant amusement (who wanted to get into a dinner jacket just for a goddamn film?). Besides, ninety percent of the films at the Festival were exploitation products or arty-farty movies about a farmhand falling in love with a female pig. And the parties the producers put on were so stale sometimes you saw the same people at three different cocktail parties all on the same day.

Arnold's features remained distant, pensive, and it gradually sunk through that he had really decided to leave. Krystina looked completely distraught: her hands fluttered helplessly in the region of her belly—a reminder of a pregnancy that was not yet visible to the naked eye.

"Oh, I'll be back in time for the baby," Arnold said dryly.

"Usually I can tell a few days beforehand when Arnold is getting restless," Krystina was upset. "But not this time." With visible effort, as though wriggling into a too-tight sweater, she tried to pull on her sweet, serene persona, her answer to Arnold's utter unflappability.

"Scott's nowhere near the end of his interview with you," Krystina said in anguish. "How long will you be gone?"

"You know how it is," Arnold's face was blank.

Krystina should have known by now he'd never tell her anyway. He never knew himself how long he'd stay away.

Krystina looked around as if for help. Gina and Alfredo were fascinated spectators. They battened on these little domestic cross-currents. Baroness Gina and Baron Alfredo (or the organ-grinder) as Arnold has spoken of him to Scott Goldman, who had replied, "I guess you'd call any Italian an organ grinder—even Julius Caesar." It was an echo from Arnold's archaic childhood in Boston when there had been ambulant Italian organ-grinders with monkeys to collect coins after the concert).

Arnold had checked Alfredo; surprise, surprise, he was a genuine baron. Every Italian outside of Italy with a little money or good looks claimed nobility, but Alfredo's family was old Sicilian nobility now no longer landed. What it boiled down to was unpaid back taxes of some kind on the title, something like ten thousand dollars, which Gina, the attractive, wealthy young woman Alfredo had managed to marry, immediately put up to reestablish the title. She was now a full-fledged baronessa, and Krystina Elton's closest friend.

Alfredo was vaguely connected, Arnold knew, with the Sicilian Mafia and the Italian motion-picture industry. He was the one you called to help you straighten out the incredible paperwork when you planned an Italian coproduction.

"After coming all the way to the south of France," Krystina said anxiously. "Scott'll want to wait till you come back and finish. What'll I do with him while you're gone?"

"Fuck him," Arnold said amiably, then when Alfred and Gina looked disapproving, added, "I've got a better idea. Let Gina fuck him. Then Scott could brighten up his interview with something like, 'That was the night I fucked the Baronessa G.'"

"What a pork!" Gina gave Arnold what was supposed to be a playful punch but Arnold scored it as effective enough to leave a bruise on his arm. "Frankly, this Scott Goldman is not my type and even if he were, Alfredo and I are always so

51

much occupied during the Festival, I would simply not have the time.''

"Well, you two ladies work something out between you," Arnold said amiably, then turned to Krystina. "If Scott asks when I'm coming back, say like you always do, 'You know how it is when the spirit moves the Boy and he gets the urge to write, there's just no telling.' "

"How long *will* you be gone?" Gina asked.

Arnold didn't answer. Krystina sighed and donned a slightly troubled look like an old-fashioned bonnet with ribbons under her chin. "It's true. When the spirit hits the Boy, there's no telling." She managed a brave smile.

The four sipped their drinks and, bemused, watched the distant harbor.

Twenty-four hours later Arnold was ensconced in their Central Park South duplex, drapes drawn and windows sealed against the noise of the traffic and the disturbingly young spring air. The atmosphere was soon appropriately stale and sour with tobacco smoke. The conditions were optimal for him to start writing. Twinges of guilt, small ones but twinges of guilt nonetheless, plagued him when he recalled Krystina's little-girl hurt face when he'd announced his abrupt leaving. He had to work when the urge hit him.

How else to explain it? He loved being in the south of France in May, he really enjoyed the scramble and the color of the Festival, and Krystina had become more sexually exciting to him since her pregnancy.

But this time there he was sittting before his twelve thousand dollar word processor—and nothing. Each time in the past, the split-second he settled in, the drapes drawn, the world cut off, words spat out of him like machine-gun fire, he lost himself to time, place, hunger, sleeping, fucking, all the pulls of his ordinary life . . .

He finally had to admit it. Shit. The real reason he'd left was to get away from Scott Goldman. There was absolutely no reason this guy should bug him the way he did. He wasn't, by the remotest stretch of imagination, any kind of competition. Scott was a practically unknown scribbler. Okay, a few obscure critics here and there hailed him as a really fine writer. But the poor schmuck had made the trip, expenses hardly covered, all the way to the south of France to do one of those in-depth interviews. And Scott Goldman bugged him in a way he'd seldom been bugged before in his adult life. Everything the guy did. The way he was always making those notes on tiny bits of paper even while you were talking to him, then rolling them up and slipping them in a small pocket in his jeans. And the way he talked. It was all calculated to make Arnold feel that he wasn't part of the real literary world, that he wasn't really a novelist.

"What are those fucking little notes you're always writing?" Arnold had tried to make it sound offhand.

"Oh, those," Scott replied casually. "Things. Observations. I get two thousand words a day this way."

"Any of them about me?"

"Once in a while." Scott sucked in his belly while he rummaged about his jeans pocket, pulled out and unrolled a few notes until he found one about Arnold. " 'Elton,' Scott read, without hesitation, " 'has never learned how to play. Everything he does has some kind of underlying purpose, inevitably leading to writing, fucking or a deal. It's inconceivable for Elton to just idle away forty-eight hours, doing nothing more than watching the clouds or the waves or the sea gulls or lying in the sun—just enjoying.' "

"You get a jolt out of watching fucking sea gulls?" Arnold asked.

"When they come my way," Scott replied.

"What do you mean, 'just enjoying'?"

"That's my point," Scott answered.

Even more infuriating was the utterly effortless way Scott had been totally unimpressed by the millions of dollars

Arnold kept telling him he was making; nor by the astronomical number of Arnold's books people were buying. Nor had it seemed particularly interesting news to Scott when Arnold revealed that he was getting three million dollars for the paperback rights to his *next* book, as yet unwritten (what Arnold didn't tell him was that it was a paperback company owned by Arnel Enterprises and that the three-million-dollar figure was an advance worked out by a corps of tax experts).

Scott had listened intently and made absolutely no comment. Desperate to get a rise out of him, Arnold resorted to describing Krystina and some of their sexual acrobatics in physical detail. Arnold felt mildly ashamed, and irritated that he felt ashamed. In the past, whenever Arnold had been challenged about the erotica in his writing, he would calmly cite the Supreme Court of the United States, which had declared there was no part of the female body a description of which could be held to be obscene. In that spirit he saw no reason why he should feel guilty when talking about his wife's vaginal muscles, and how she responded to sexual stimulation and other intimate details.

Nor had Scott reacted to that. He simply interrupted Arnold, "I can't visualize that last one. You say you're flat on your back, she's in the opposite direction. She arches her back, her feet and hands flat on the floor, her head backward, then is able to lower herself exactly over your erection, then raise and lower herself *ad* orgasm?"

"That's it," Arnold said calmly.

"Gee," was Scott's only comment, "she must have a hell of a set of neck and thigh muscles."

As Arnold thought about it alone in the hermetically sealed Central Park South duplex, he finally admitted it all to himself for the first time. Yes, he had screwed off suddenly from the south of France, where he'd been eminently comfortable, and had been enjoying himself, because he had wanted to lay one on Scott.

54

Let Scott hang in at Cannes waiting, spending his pitiful advance money—not knowing when Arnold would come back.

Having admitted all that to himself, curiously enough not only was Arnold able to work, but he worked like a bastard. The words flowed, the characters fell in love without his intending them to, they fucked in odd and satisfying ways and abundantly, they killed, pulled brilliant deals, startled him constantly by their unexpected behavior and gave Arnold extra satisfaction because that particular sudden leaving was now justified.

Oscar knew the routine. He was responsible for food. He'd see to it that there was a never-ending supply of onions, pickles, relish, catsup, hamburgers, spaghetti and meatballs, salami, omelets, bagels, lox and cream cheese (Arnold assumed it was Sunday when the lox came up), chili, celery tonic, tequila with clam juice, cigarettes, Maalox, asthma relief inhalers—in short, his basic life-sustaining essentials.

It was with considerable surprise that Arnold looked up and realized that it was not the young Puerto Rican waiter who ordinarily delivered his supplies who was hovering over him. It was Reilly.

"Jesus," Arnold said after a moment, "has it been that long?"

With gentle solemnity, "Ten whole days," Reilly said, "and nights."

Arnold made a quick mental scan of his body, the sweep beginning slightly below his chin and descending to his balls. His body answered with such a surge of seething excitement Arnold was obliged to give his testicles a reassuring squeeze urging them to patience, help was on the way.

Of course Reilly was right, it was well known that Arnold's absolute limit was ten days' abstention. If Arnold didn't get laid, previous experience had demonstrated it would affect the whole of Arnel Enterprises. Not only would he not be able to continue his work, but he would indiscriminately throw the shit around. No one was safe—from the three Arnel East and Arnel West vice-presidents to the executive secretaries and subsidiary staff. A call would go out to Reilly. Reilly knew how to handle it.

There was a special routine. It had to look as though the call girl Reilly would invariably send up to him was a secretary who was excited by Arnold's reputation, or a married woman looking for excitement. It was never to look as if it had been paid for. Arnold had open contempt for the schmucks who had to pay for it.

And this time Reilly came through big. He presented Arnold with one of the most extraordinary specimens of femininity he'd ever seen, a six-foot Louisianian named Clover.

"Really something. She's in some kind of special circumstances made her available."

Clover looked excitingly familiar, but Arnold couldn't place her, which was odd. She was not the sort of woman you failed to remember.

Clover came in wearing a light spring coat and, underneath, something reminiscent of the late miniskirts; on closer examination, it proved to be well-tailored, obviously expensive, beige raw silk shorts. They gave a caressing parenthetical emphasis to a generous and beautifully sculptured ass and encouraged the eye to revel in an unbelievable expanse of the most mouth-watering thighs Arnold had ever fantasized. They were topped by superb breasts, a long graceful neck and glistening black hair.

He shuddered in anticipation before this embarrassment of sexual riches and tried again to recall where he'd seen her. It must have been with someone he knew.

"Champagne?" Arnold was able to ask finally.

"Thank you"—Clover seemed reassured that he was actually able to speak—"I'm not thusty."

"You don't need to be thusty for champagne," (he tended to take on the accent and speech mannerisms of people he was talking to), "in fact, you *mustn't* be thusty when you drink champagne." She looked around quickly and seemed to sense where the bedroom was, glancing at him impatiently. "Champagne's for taste and sensation."

"I only drink when I'm thusty," Clover said firmly. "Coca-Cola does the trick for me. But if you-all need it," Clover said, "go right ahead. I'd just as soon we got right down to the business at hand."

"Which business at hand is that?"

She scrutinized him intensively and frowned.

"Now don't tell me your Mr. Reilly got me up here jist to type some letters? He mentioned I should say somethin' like that, but seems to me you're a big boy and we don't have to play games." When Arnold didn't budge, she added grimly, "Well, mister, believe it or not I *can* type." She glided over to the word processor, sat down and typed furiously, with her two index fingers. Arnold peered over her shoulder. What flashed on the word processor screen was: *It is hereby understood that the party of the first part agrees to furnish the party of the second part the following: one gasoline station on the outskirts of Shrimpsville Louisiana, presently known as Skoogs Sure Fire Service; one (1) part in a major motion picture; the sum of fifty thousand (50,000) dollars in cash, tax free.*

Arnold realized it was some kind of a settlement she'd made or was hoping to, with one of her lovers.

"But if I read them eyes of yours right," she said, her voice sensually deep, "it ain't letters you want."

"We've seen each other before," Arnold said.

"Well, mebbe. Now could we git goin'? When I know I'm

57

goin' to fuck, I like to git right to it I don't hold much with this fohplay they been talkin' about I think the main thing about fuckin' is fuckin'."

"So say I." Arnold wondered where the hell that came from, besides he'd delivered it straight. She rose suddenly and in her platform shoes she was taller than he. She started to move, then stopped as if bothered by something.

"Mebbe we just better get ourselves squared away here," Clover said, "I ain't lookin' for love, I'm kinda in love and he loves me even though I'm through with him at this time. If ever I do want love he's there any time I say, so don't get any fancy ideas. here's the way it is. Fuckin's fuckin', and that's all they's goin' to be to it between you and me."

"That's fine with me," Arnold said hastily, and added sincerely, "I'd like very much to fuck you."

"What in hell we waitin' foh, then?"

Before he could answer, she reached over grasped his penis and testicles and gave them a trial squeeze. His penis stirred to a slow erection. Reassured, she dropped his genitals, and took off her clothes.

She was beyond doubt the most perfectly made woman he'd ever seen. Unending lengths of delicately tanned skin swirled over the marvelous curves of her breasts, which were indeed firm and in scale; a startlingly tiny waist flared out to graceful generous haunches; her belly swelled slightly, meeting her pubic triangle. Having thus permitted him to get a full look at her (he realized she had been deliberately posing for his pleasure), she turned and with a sure instinct found the bedroom.

By the time he got there she had already installed herself on the bed, her long legs were drawn up, her knees spread generously making a great yawn with the pubic juncture.

She followed his undressing with a certain interest, her eyes focused on his middle.

The moment he was within reach, she again sought out his

58

penis and lifted it up for scrutiny, nodded noncommittally, let go. It threw Arnold for a moment; there was the vaguest hint of disappointment. But then she called out cheerily, "Now you jes' jump right in! The water's fine."

He did everything he could think of under, over and around her. Every now and then he would pause slightly and steal an anxious glance at her. He invariably caught her looking off somewhere thoughtfully, totally unaware of him. He plunged his head between her extravagant thighs and worked doggedly over every even remotely erogenous area but when he surfaced, she still had that distant reflective look.

Exhausted, he got on top of her. Her body made the slightest motion of accommodation as he penetrated, pushed, pulled, rubbed, bounced. The most he got, once when their eyes met and he was attacking in full force, was a fleeting smile of acknowledgment but it was more like a friendly greeting to someone you know vaguely. He gave up, spurted himself out, lay on her panting. His body was soaked and his underbelly glistened with various sexual moistures but even Clover's coiffure was unruffled.

In the days that followed, they developed a routine. Because he was so serious about it, she was as helpful as she could be; she would thoughtfully move to any position he preferred, on her back, her belly, standing or bending and always patiently reflective until it was over.

He bought her more and more expensive gifts. It was a standing tradition for all Arnel executives: Tough in negotiations but never stint with women. Arnel Inc. mustn't be known as cheap. For Clover he began with antique gold, then went to emeralds, which looked fabulous on her deep tan. She thanked him profusely and immediately forgot them. He pressed her once when she seemed particularly pensive. She told him she'd simply been thinking that her lover had never bought her gifts like that.

She became an obsession with him. He dragged out old

and long unused Scandinavian manuals on sexuality. He even reread *MacDougall's Guide to Good Fucking*. He cut down on his smoking, took deep-breathing exercises hoping to improve his wind, so that in fact he did last longer. All he noticed was a slight impatience on her part. Once, sweat-drenched, panting, he looked quickly and caught her stifling a yawn.

No woman, Arnold told himself fiercely, had ever left him without having at least one orgasm.

She allowed him to position her as though she were an actress and he a stage manager.

"You mean you'd like me standin' on my head," she asked, "with my legs spread out wide." She stood on her head and spread her legs wide. "Like this?"

"Wider," Arnold directed.

She strained her legs apart. He then tried slowly kissing his way down one thigh, getting to the pubic area, teasingly skipping it, kissing his way down the inside of the other thigh.

"Well now," she said from the floor, "I ain't sure I'm goin' to hold up my legs much longer."

She was finally obliged to lower her thighs and him with them, with a sigh of relief.

"Guess I should of told you sooner," she said. "Not that I don't appreciate yoh efforts in mah behalf—"

"Something wrong with you?" he asked, outraged. "You can't have an orgasm? Goddamn it, here I've been busting a gut for days and what's worse I haven't been able to work—"

"Well, ahm real sorry," Clover said, not sounding sorry at all. "But there ain't nothin' wrong with me. When I'm with Lover Man I have me a five-alarm bell-ringin' orgasm would knock your ears back. 'Course he's special—"

"What's so special about Lover Man?" Arnold asked.

"Well, ah'll tell you what's so special about Lover Man," Clover said hotly. "That boy's got him a real hooked dong."

"A what?" Arnold asked.

"A hooked dong," Clover said, crooking a pinkie so it formed a hook.

"A hooked schlong." Arnold was taken aback.

"Really hooked," Clover said wistfully. "When that man gets his hooked dong in me I like to have conniption fits, like no other dong before it or after it has been able to do for me."

Naked as he was, Arnold got off the bed. There was only one man *he'd* ever known who had such a dong. "Doctor says it's a condishun that's got a fancy name," Clover prattled on, "says it don't hurt nothin'. Hurt! If only that old doctor knew! Then he says he can operate to straighten it, but I said, 'Boy, you jes' tell that doctor of yours to keep his cotton-whackin' surgery knives off your dong. I would'n have it no other way for all the oil in Texas.'"

Suddenly it hit Arnold. He remembered when he'd seen Clover before and where.

With Dennis Hume. At Vegas, one night right in front of the Roman Palace. This very same statuesque Clover with Dennis Hume. Arnold had just paid one of his rare courtesy calls on his old friend, Uncle Millie, who owned the Roman Palace. Handsome Uncle Millie, who got his start in life as a piano-wire Mob hit man.

So Clover's ex-boyfriend was Dennis Hume, who had confided to Arnold at one of their monthly poker games when the conversation turned to schlongs and the reputed ratio between length and pleasure brought to women, that he was one of the few men who held the answer. It was the shape that counted. His, which was of modest length, when in an erect state, curved, hooked (Arnold remembered that Denny had made the same gesture with his pinkie that Clover had) and he had said that every woman he had had occasion to use it on had freaked out.

Dennis with Clover. Dennis, a graduate of the Wharton

61

School of Business Administration, one of the new breed of filmmakers who knew how to use computers and market research. A rare combination of talent, shrewdness and taste which had paid off. At thirty-five, head of Associated Artists. Before Hume, Associated's listing on the Big Board had been a lowly $8.00 per share of common stock. Less than a year after, one of the films Dennis fought for was a big hit: Dennis followed with two more blockbusters. The stock had soared close to a fabulous $18.00 per share. Fox with all its prestige and real estate and successes was at $28; the venerable powerful MGM $38; all of which added up to making Dennis Hume one of the sudden powers in the film world. Two hits in a row was fantastic. Three in a row, in times when the profits of a hit reached outer space, were enough to cause a man to be deified.

Arnold began to recall the details of the night they had crossed paths at Vegas.

"Clover Carlin," Dennis introduced her to Arnold. Clover snuggled her head into the luxuriously abundant collar of her ermine coat. Arnold had noticed Dennis's sheepish little-boy loser's look. Arnold remembered that look from the poker games. Dennis was a goddamn good poker player with one important reservation—he would never quit, he kept on playing until he lost. He lost so often that sometimes Arnold thought it was deliberate. It was well known that every addicted gambler had an unconscious need to lose.

Arnold had assumed Clover was a Vegas showgirl out with Dennis for the evening, and was ready to forget about her. Vegas showgirls were spectacular but were rarely more than a one-night thing.

But Denny had held Clover's ermined arm close to him and murmured, "Clover's my good luck charm, my Lady Luck."

"Not with that silly old wheel he keeps playin'," Clover said petulantly. "Why anybody in his right mind wants to throw his money away on that old roulette wheel I'll never know." She turned to Arnold and became very deep Louisiana in her indignation. "They jest ain't no smart way playin' that wheel, 'cause they jest ain't no way of knowin' wheah that crazy lil ball's gonna stop."

"Clover's power doesn't extend to roulette unfortunately," he had added with a rueful smile. "But I don't mind as long as she keeps on bringing me this kind of luck on films. We've had a trial showing on *Claws II*." His voice sank to an awed whisper. "The projected take on it is the biggest yet."

"Four in a row," Arnold said with reverence. "That's an all-time record."

"It is," Dennis said, clutching Clover with a gambler's superstitious fervor. "She's one superstition I'll never let go of."

Arnold remembered thinking, Christ, he's serious but why not? Nobody knew why a film was successful and she was as good a reason as any; better than most because you could fuck her besides.

"You'll be the all-time white-haired golden boy," Arnold said. "It'll be all yours. You'll do anything you goddamn please."

"I do already," Dennis had reminded him quietly. "They've just renewed my contract. Three years, options only on my side, bigger percentages, a nice chunk of stock, complete autonomy, the works."

"The dream contract." Arnold had been annoyed. That fabulous success was just too much to take even though Denny was his friend and it couldn't happen to a nicer guy. *Claws II* had been released and more than fulfilled the projections. It was a bigger hit than its predecessor. Associated stock had zoomed to an unbelievable $20 a share.

Clover was watching him peculiarly. He'd been fondling her nipples, which were now erect.

"What's eatin' you?" she demanded.

63

"Why nothing. But I know your boyfriend. He's a friend of mine."

"How come you know him from the description I gave you?" she asked suspiciously.

"I saw you together in Vegas," Arnold said, "right in front of the Roman Palace."

"Yeah," Clover said slowly. "You're pretty sharp. That's him all right."

"You keep saying 'Lover Boy,'" Arnold said, perplexed. "Does that mean you're in love with him?"

"Well, I guess it does," Clover answered with a sigh. "I'm in love with that boy."

"And you think he's in love with you?"

"Love with me?" Clover exploded. "Why that boy is jest plain obsessed. Calls me three four times a day," Clover said. I came out East to git away from that, and when I stopped answering, he sent me one of them expensive telephone answerers. Each time there's a call for you at home that thingamajig beeps." She extended a long graceful arm across him and down to the floor, found her huge bag, fumbled in it, flicked on a battery-sized beeper which immediately started beeping. "That's him. Damn thing keeps beepin' once it's turned on till you answer."

"I don't understand something," Arnold said. "Why aren't you two together?" He remembered a rumor that even Denny's wife had accepted another woman in his life—it could only have been Clover—on the grounds that she brought Dennis his fabulous luck with films.

Clover sat up with a movement both sudden and violent.

"I gave that boy over three years of mah life," Clover said with passionate intensity, "and he kep' promising me that part."

"Part?"

"The nice big fat part in a movie every girl dreams about," Clover said heatedly. "In the beginnin' I went right along figurin' when he got to be in a position he can get me a *fat* part in some super-dooper production, I wasn't settlin' for no walk-on in some asshole two-bit production no sir ma'm, then he has one hit after another and keeps puttin' me off tellin' me, now you just keep your shirt on, honey girl, you are one speshul girl and it ain't gonna be easy findin' the part, well I'm nobody's fool I know I'm speshul but I ain't *three whole years* speshul, when finally finally finally up comes the dream part, a kind of all-woman sexy star-war, a small planet where all the men get killed off the women have to go fightin' for male studs, nacherally I'm the head lady—''

"Why didn't they make the picture?" Arnold was excited, Now he knew he was on to something.

"Well, you just said it," Clover said indignantly, "why didn't they? I never knew what hit me, I been waitin' so long gittin' my hopes up and there he is stallin', well thing about stallin' is, you can stall somatha people somatha time but you can't stall all the people all the time." She looked hurt, as if Arnold were a surrogate Denny Hume. She shifted emotional gears from hurt to grim, "Time came when much as I hated to, they was jest no way out for me, it was Honey Boy you been sittin' on that pot a mighty long time, you shit or git off. That's when he tells me. He's got them big black circles under his eyes. 'Honey child, you gotta give me time. Nothin' better I'd like but no way. They cancelled that picture on me.' My mind ain't exactly a bear trap but I know when it just don't figger, how come he cain't make any goddamn movie he pleases. He like to bust a gut almost got down on his knees beggin' me not to leave him. I jest kept lookin' down on him like he was dirt and said, 'How come they cancelled out *my* film on you?' and he says, 'Baby they cancelled out *all* my films on me; don't ask me why, I cain't tell you but they got me on freeze—'''

"What?" Arnold demanded. "Dennis Hume on freeze?"

"You said it," Clover said grimly, "and him beggin' away,

sayin' over and over I mustn't leave him he'll lose his luck in films and me sayin' jest come across with my part like you promised, and he sayin' he needs more time. Once my mind's set thére's no budgin' little Clover.''

"You any idea of the nature of the trouble he's in?" Arnold asked, playing it offhand, but Clover got suspicious.

"No, happens I don't," she said. "How come you're so interested?"

"Nothing, only I hate to see somebody like you in trouble. I thought maybe I could help."

Clover studied him carefully. Her attitude toward Arnold had changed visibly, possibly because of Arnold's expression of sympathy.

"Ah'm sure," she said. "But if Denny cain't do it, nobody can. But I'm mighty sorry you been bustin' a gut. Now you jist lean back and fergit all that. You jes put yourself in mah hands and ah'm goin' to show you what a man and woman can really do together when they both put their mind to it.''

Arnold fell back. His head was still buzzing with Dennis Hume. He was sure there was some possibility there some-where if only he could grasp it.

Slowly he began to forget Dennis Hume and Associated and himself and was aware only of Clover, who was working on him with a subtle sensuality that built itself slowly until they were both swept into a frenzied abandon, arms legs torsos tossing and heaving, her timing so perfectly attuned to his that she came when he did, then collapsed on him moist and panting.

When Arnold was able to think, he realized he felt wonder-ful, he hadn't felt this way for years. Clover was magic: he could understand why Dennis, or any man with whom she let herself go, would think she brought him luck.

He got rid of her quickly with an expensive jewel. She left without any fuss and he immediately called a meeting of the two top executives of Arnel East—Oscar and Reilly.

66

* * *

Each time Arnold saw Reilly, even if he saw him several times the same day, he experienced a mild irritation. Reilly was too good-looking for ordinary use. Arnold felt absolutely convinced that Reilly was spending a good part of Arnel Enterprises' time fucking. And Reilly walked, reacted, held himself as though he were in a daytime soap serial. He stood a beat too long looking thoughtful when you asked him a question, as though giving the busy housewives a chance to absorb the full import of his profile.

But Reilly, Oscar and Arnold had one quality in common. They had no set rhythm. Oscar lived in a permanent state of jet lag. Arnold imagined Oscar's Estelle tapping him on the shoulder when night came and telling him it was time to go to sleep.

Arnold deliberately tried to live outside the normal rhythm. In his books, most of the scenes took place at night. The people who excited him did what they did best at night.

As for Reilly, at three in the morning he was showered, obviously freshly fucked, clean-shaven, smelling of a lime aftershave, impeccably tailored and looking younger than his thirty-four years.

But it was Oscar who took the floor first. "The answers to your questions regarding Associated Artists stock are as follows: A. Arnel Enterprises Inc. owns 50,000 shares acquired at $8.50 a share, now worth $19.85 per share. B. It is generally agreed that this gain is due entirely to the aggressive leadership of the present vice-president in charge of production, Dennis Hume. There has been a slight fluctuation in the stock's value these last few weeks, it's gone down a fraction or two, but nobody can explain that, because Dennis Hume is still in charge and his announced plans for the future look very good."

Oscar put the report on what he evidently thought was the

table but was actually empty space. Reilly and Arnold followed the paper's spiralling descent to the floor. Reilly picked the paper up and gave it back to Oscar, who couldn't understand where it came from.

"It would be foolish for Arnel to sell," Oscar concluded.

"I checked the stock out." Reilly was able to make it sound as though Oscar had not spoken at all and was not even there. "AA is as happy as any stock these days. Shelley, Getz and Littell, our brokers, give it a clean bill of health, although when I said I caught a little hesitation on their part, they immediately said no, there was no reason to be nervous but *they* also mentioned that there had been a small point loss. I finally got the sense that they were feeling *me* out to see if *I* knew anything; but it was only my instinct Ar, nothing specific. What's up, Ar?"

"I don't know yet." Arnold was very excited but not showing it. "I got an idea buzzing in the back of my head but it'll only work if it's what I think it is and if it stays in the strictest confidence—within Arnel Enterprises—or it's dead. But if I'm right and we pull it off . . ." Arnold paused for a deep breath which he needed badly. "Then we stand a chance of something so big I won't even talk about it."

The two others greeted this with appropriate silence. Reilly nodded solemnly. Oscar looked more like an owl than ever.

"Oscar, did you understand me?" Arnold demanded.

"My lips are sealed," Oscar said, slightly hurt that there was any doubt.

"Okay," Arnold said slowly. "I have good reason to believe that for the last few weeks Associated Artists has put the freeze on Dennis Hume. All Dennis Hume projects are for the time being suspended; and that's why the stock's been a little jittery. Rumors must have seeped out."

"Dennis Hume on freeze," Reilly said in awe. "If this really got out, AA stock would nose-dive." Then, eyeing Arnold skeptically, he asked, "Where did you get this, Ar?"

"From an unimpeachable source," Arnold said. "The best there is. I got it straight from cunt."

Reilly whistled, then he too got up in excitement and started to pace.

"Then it must mean Hume pulled something so heavy even AA can't cover for him. But what could that be? What could a guy who's had four sky-shattering hits in a row do to get himself in that kind of shit? Murder, rape? Christ, Dennis Hume could assassinate the President of the United States right now, and AA could cover for him, he could be caught his hand elbow-deep in the till they'd cover. Do you realize what it must mean for them to put the freeze on their top asset?"

Reilly stopped pacing suddenly. "Say-ay," he said slowly, "I just remembered something. I didn't pay any attention at the time, but a while ago I heard a rumor that Hume was in some kind of trouble in Vegas. At the time I asked my friend Michael Saintsbury, but he hadn't heard anything so I forgot about it."

"Dennis Hume's got to be in bigger trouble than we think," Arnold said thoughtfully. "I know two places I can go to find out. One is L.A., where Don Wacszinski is asshole buddy with top law people there. I'm like you Reilly, I can't imagine what Dennis Hume could have done and you know me—I can imagine anything. The second place I can go to find out is Vegas—I've got a friend there and I've got a funny feeling that that's where it's at."

In Las Vegas they seemed to have made a major breakthrough in agronomy. They had learned how to plant and grow slot machines even in tiled floors. At the Vegas airport men's room where Arnold had taken time off to pee (he'd been too busy on the plane going over figures), there was a slot machine planted near each urinal. The man next to Arnold was holding his dong with one hand, directing the stream

69

while he worked the lever with the other hand. As Arnold watched, the golden rope of urine was cut off as the machine whirled. When the man hit three cherries, the urine gushed in accompaniment to the rattling coins spewing out.

A slave girl was waiting for Arnold at the Roman Palace just as he entered. She smiled, took his briefcase, led him away from the Niagara of sounds, the machines' zing, the murmur of the blackjack dealers, the whirling roulette wheels, the click of the dice, shushing sounds of hundreds of voices. An air of profound concentration hung over the game room, a concentration Arnold had almost forgotten. He hadn't been to Vegas for months.

The slave girl, attired like all the female personnel of the Roman Palace in a minitoga of gauzy fabric, accompanied Arnold up a heavily carpeted staircase, paused before what turned out to be Uncle Millie's office, smiled and said, "If there's anything you need, Mr. Elton, don't hesitate to call me. Just dial room service and ask for Lynn."

Arnold slipped her a twenty-dollar bill. It paid to stay in good with slave girls.

Uncle Millie's office was a haven of silence and tranquility. Uncle Millie looked like a handsome corporation president in his old-fashioned leather judge's chair with its tall back and comfortable arms. It was hard to realize this soft-eyed, silver-haired grandfatherly type had once been the top hit man for the most important mob in the East.

Arnold settled back and puffed dutifully on one of Uncle Millie's finest Havanas.

"Too long no see," Uncle Millie said. Every word Uncle Millie utttered was weighted. He was pissed that Arnold, whom he considered a sort of protégé, had been in Vegas several times without coming to see him.

"I've missed you, Uncle Millie," Arnold said, "but you know how it is with my life. You can tell who my best friends are. They're the ones I almost never get to see."

70

"People are close to you because they're close to you, and them you make time for," Uncle Millie said. "I read every one of your last books. It's a good product."

"Thanks," Arnold was nettled by having his books designated as product. "How is it with you, Uncle Millie?"

"Like you see," Uncle Millie made a slight gesture. There had been a struggle within the Mob as Millie worked his way up. It had wound up with Millie surviving, but with half the back of his handsome silver head shot off. Peace had prevailed and Millie was now an important part of The Boys. "I command a certain respect." Unconsciously he touched the scars on the back of his head so artfully concealed by his silver hair. "Things are quiet. There's more than enough for everybody. No need to push. What can I do for you, kid?"

"I'm sorry we didn't see each other more often, Uncle Millie," Arnold said.

"Cut the shit," Uncle Millie said evenly. "I know exactly how many times you been in Vegas over the years without stopping even to say How are you."

"I was in and out, doing research for a book."

"Come on, kid," Uncle Millie waved the ribbon of fragrant smoke under his nose. "Each time you came here you divided your time equally between crap tables and hamagoochery. What's on your mind?"

"What can you tell me about Denny Hume?"

Uncle Millie's face shut a little. "I hear he's doing great. Why?"

"He's into me big, and not paying."

"What you do? Loan him money?"

He bought the movie rights to my last two books." Arnold held the gray eyes fixed on him without flinching.

"I read some big outfit bought the movie rights to your last two books, kid."

Now Uncle Millie was lying too. The movie rights to

Arnold's last two books had not yet been sold to anyone.

"No. Hume's got the movie rights, personally."

"Yeah? Funny. His contract forbids him making any outside personal deals . . ."

"I didn't read his contract, and he outbid the studios. He asked the deal be kept on the QT but I didn't think anything of it. We were dealing with Dennis Hume. Never in a million years would it enter our heads to worry about payment."

Uncle Millie didn't elaborate on how it happened he'd gotten hold of Hume's contract. Something *was* up, and Uncle Millie knew what it was. "We figured he was getting ready to break away from Associated Artists and set up on his own."

Uncle Millie puffed on his fine cigar reflectively. "Tell me about the kids."

Arnold whipped out his wallet. Usually he carried only a picture of Krystina, but he'd specially prepared two wallet-sized photos of Jennifer and Robbie.

Uncle Millie put on old-fashioned gold pince-nez with graceful black ribbons; they looked chic on him as he clamped them on the bridge of his nose and studied the photos. His face softened.

"You mean this darling young woman is our little Jennifer?" Uncle Millie sounded exactly like a well-to-do Jewish grandfather. "What is she now, twenty-one?"

"Thirty-two."

"Thirty-two!" He gave a heartfelt sigh. "Time-time-time, slips between your fingers like sand. Cute as a button. Still takes no shit from nobody?"

"Can't get away with a thing with that one."

"Like her mother," Uncle Millie said.

Arnold, caught in the communal emotion, now stood directly behind Uncle Millie and because of the chair's unusually high back, had to lean over and accidentally touched the older man's shoulder. At the touch of Arnold's hand, the gray eyes moved away from the photos, the silver head turned slowly, the eyes slid down to the hand resting on his shoulder and held there. Arnold, almost with a jump, straightened, withdrew his hand hastily. He'd forgotten—it had been so long— Uncle Millie couldn't stand anyone standing behind him and didn't like being touched. The gray eyes went slowly back to the photos; the doting grandfatherly look returned. "And Robbie. Will you look how tall . . . That California . . ." He gave up the photos to Arnold. "Well, kid, they both sure as hell got you stamped on them." He sighed wistfully. "That's gotta be a good feeling."

"They're the center of my life," Arnold said.

"You know I got me a godson?" Uncle Millie asked with distant pride, pointing to a portrait in a leather frame standing on his desk, the only photograph that he had anywhere. It was an artfully casual portrait of a dark good-looking young man in his late twenties. Arnold, who had taken a fleeting glance, stopped in surprise to look again. "Of course it's not like having your own, but Michael is like a son to me."

"But I know Michael," Arnold said with the excitement of discovery. "Michael Saintsbury."

"Why sure you do," Uncle Millie said. "He told me he met you a few years ago."

Michael Saintsbury, Reilly's friend. As a matter of fact one of the reasons Arnold had hired Reilly was a rumor that Reilly had contacts with the Mafia. Arnold had not put it to Reilly directly, but Reilly had as indirectly implied that it was true.

At the time Arnold had been banging a kooky actress who had the throughly mistaken idea that she'd make it in the movies through Arnold. She'd been busted for driving while spaced on hash. Oscar had tried a clumsy payoff, which had only gotten them deeper in shit.

"Okay," Arnold told Reilly, "here's your chance. I hear

you have friends in the Mob. Get them to fix this up."

Reilly, with big mystery and a show of confidence such that Arnold would have sworn it was all bullshit, within twenty-four hours arranged a lunch at the Four Seasons with his buddy Mike Saintsbury, a young man Reilly's age, who was good-looking, a product of Harvard Business School. The Saintsburys, by common consent, had been designated to handle the legitimate side of Mob business. They'd changed their name from Salvatore, which was practically the Italian equivalent of Saintsbury. Mike, in one generation, had become enough of an inverted snob to be able to order *spaghetti bolognese* at one of New York's finest restaurants.

"I'll see what I can do for you, Mr. Elton," Mike said, "we have friends who might be helpful." The way he said it at first you might have thought it was as simple as arranging tickets for an opening.

"We'd be very grateful," Arnold said, reconciled to Reilly becoming a permanent part of Arnel. Actually, he was very pleased. Now they'd be able to let the word circulate, discreetly of course, that Arnel Enterprises had real weight with the Mob.

"Glad to be of help," Mike said, then his manner changed as he leaned close to Reilly and hugged him in a way that recalled images of mafiosi kissing their victim full on the lips with the kiss of death. "I'll go a long way for my buddy Reilly. There's something about classmates in parochial school together. There are few relationships in life that can touch that." Reilly seemed a little wary of that expression of devotion, in fact he was scared shitless. "Only don't ever contact me again for this kind of petty thing, understand?" Arnold caught a glimpse of what the Saintsburys must have been when they were Salvatores. "That doesn't mean never call on me. I'm still your classmate." He searched for the most economical way of putting it. "Imagine I'm a priest. You come to me only for extreme unction."

* * *

"You heard anything about Dennis Hume made you come to me?" Uncle Millie asked as if in passing; it was then, Arnold knew, that Uncle Millie was on the red phone alert.

"You hear things," Arnold tried to sound equally casual, but one look at Uncle Millie's gray eyes fixed on him made Arnold drop it. "Two and three make five," Arnold tried to make it sound significant when he knew basically it was shit.

"I won't stop to figure that out," Uncle Millie said. "I owe you a favor. I've owed you one for years. Uncle Millie doesn't forget. Now you sure you want to use it for this? Once I do you this service you're no longer into me. We're quits, kid."

Arnold had a brief hesitation. He hadn't realized Uncle Millie had considered the service Arnold had rendered him years ago as a personal favor. Using that up for this was a matter that he might have given more thought—but he quickly decided that it was worth it.

"Okay," Arnold said, "I understand that."

"I can only tell you what goes on in Vegas," Uncle Millie cautioned. "There may be trouble he's in in L.A. that I don't know about—"

"Okay."

"One," Millie said. "Dennis Schmuck Hume owes it to Uncle Millie he didn't get his head blown off. Two. This whole business here is strictly a question of hamagoochery. You know Nadelman?"

"I know Nadelman." Arnold shivered a little. Nadelman was reputed to be the deadliest of the Boys in Vegas, with the desert littered with the unmarked graves of his victims.

"Well, Nadelman has a *meshugass*. Every now and then takes it into his head that he's in love—would you believe it? Nadelman? Me, at my age all I ask is for a clean good-looking girl who hamagooches me regularly once a week for my health's sake. After, it's good-bye good luck God bless

75

you. But Nadelman decides this lady—I hear she's from the South, a first-class hamagoocher, even maybe special—he pays no attention she's no longer free-lance, being more or less with Dennis Hume for some time. Suddenly Nadelman makes a big announcement she's his private exclusive hamagoocher, everybody else keep out. Dennis Hume forgets this is Vegas and as much as tells Nadelman to go fuck himself, keeps seeing her. Between you and me and the lamppost Nadelman does not give one real shit about her, but once all Vegas knows he's sent word out and Dennis Hume defies him, Nadelman figures he's lost respect. Now Arnold you know one thing here in Vegas, you lose respect you're finished. Nadelman is like a wild man—he's actually going to put a hit on a personality like Dennis Hume. Luckily I find out in time, I say to Nadelman. 'Are you crazy? It's a new ball game. We live here in Vegas, we got roots here we got our image to protect.' Nadelman raves and rants, 'I want the sonofabitch Hume should be taught a lesson.' I said orright teach him a lesson but no violence. Right now Dennis Hume is Hollywood's Golden Boy, the sun rises and sets in his ass, I try to warn Dennis Hume. But would you believe it, this Wonder Boy has a *meshugass* of his own. He really believes this Southern lady is his Lady Luck, his pictures will fall on their ass if he loses her. Even though I understand about these superstitions—personally I still pull my left ball before each major decision—who better than us in Vegas to know what shit this Lady Luck business is? On the other hand who can argue with this hot-shot Wonder Boy when four times in a row his pictures hit big? On one side we got him, on the other we got Nadelman a raving lunatic. Besides, we've got to do something to protect Nadelman's respect. You follow?''

"I follow," Arnold said, listening in fascination. "What did you do?"

"We ruin Dennis Hume plain and simple," Uncle Millie

76

said. "We spread the word that Dennis Hume is hooked up with the Mob, that the Boys have control of him. He's their baby. We have ways of spreading that word, people believe it."

That's it, Arnold thought excitedly. The one thing they couldn't think of that could ruin Dennis Hume. Once the word is leaked that you're linked to organized crime, no matter who you are, what your track record is, you're poison. Nobody will go near you. Respectable big money—*any* big money—will drop you, cut you off; they will sever all connections with you, quietly, stealthily, without fuss, they'll push you out, away from them, away far out in the cold.

"I don't know if the L.A. law's got something on Dennis Hume. I don't think so. But it's well known that Dennis Hume is a big gambler. So the story we put out is that he got so deep into us we took him over. And this is now working. The Wonder Boy's got problems—has he got problems! Nadelman is satisfied, and we operated in a dignified way. I'm sorry if you got hurt by this, kiddo, but that's the way it is from here, like Walter Kronkhite says."

"Now it's all over?" Arnold asked.

"Over. Finished." Uncle Millie said. "Nadelman's made his point. As for the hamagoocher—anybody can have her now. The affair Dennis Hume is closed."

"I'm glad to hear that," Arnold said gravely. "It's of big personal help for me to know this." Uncle Millie was looking at him strangely. "Naturally I'll treat this in the strictest confidence."

"Naturally," Uncle Millie said quietly. "Give my love to the kids."

"Without fail," Arnold said with deep sincerity.

Millie surveyed him a full moment, then nodded. The two shook hands and Arnold left. It dawned on him slowly that he had lucked into the greatest opportunity of his lifetime.

The motors of the Vegas–L.A. DC-10 had just been killed, the passengers were beginning to disembark, when a movement on the tarmac just outside the plane caught all eyes that had the advantage of a window seat. Arnold bent down as the others did to see what the excitement was.

It was Don Wacszinski driving up in an official-looking limousine complete with uniformed black driver. That was Don; knew everybody, even the people you had to know to get special permission to get a limousine on the runway.

The most important experience in Wacszinski's life had been landing from an amphibious craft in the attack at Okinawa and seeing three-fourths of his fellow marines get their heads blown off. He managed to stay a marine afterward all through civilian life. His walk was as brisk as it had been when he was in boot camp on parade; the only real difference was that now he walked like a colonel, with unerring sureness as if he had an important order and knew exactly how to carry it out.

"We're going right straight to his office," Don said, "if that's okay with you. I didn't sound him out too much but I don't think we need to worry. Tatum and I go away back—to Okinawa as a matter of fact."

"We've been counting on that, haven't we Don?" Arnold was annoyed, for Don had made it sound like an arrangement newly achieved. "What'd you manage to pick up?"

"Little vague whispers here and there," Don said as they crossed to the limousine. "That your friend the Boy Wonder is in some kind of trouble with Vegas."

"So what else is new?" Arnold asked dryly. "How widely known is it?"

"It's at the Hey-have-you-heard-what-they're-saying-about-Hume stage," Don said. "Kind of uneasy rumors."

"We keep it that way for now," Arnold said. "Do you know if Tatum has anything else on him?"

"Remember we're dealing with a tight-lipped conservative lawman."

"You just said you were asshole buddies."

"I have close friends who are also tight-lipped lawmen." Don was sweating. He leaned over to the driver. "Hey, Tory. You forgot to turn on the air conditioning."

"I didn't forget," Tory said without turning his head or taking his eyes off the tortured summer traffic clogging the road. "You told me last time you didn't like it."

"You're right," Don said. "But this time I like it." Tory turned on the air conditioning.

The air conditioning began to cool them off. Arnold was best able to concentrate in the limousines going to and from airports or to and from anywhere. He almost never looked at the surrounding scenery, no matter how exotic. It made very little difference where he was—Hong Kong or Argentina. When he needed to describe backgrounds for his novels, he went to guide books and postcards.

"I hope there's nothing else on El Jerko Hume," Arnold worried aloud. "For all we know he may have been fucking minors or Christ knows what. . . ."

"We can rule that out," Don said grimly. "Tatum is murder on morals infraction—he wouldn't have played along even with me on a rap like that."

"You're probably right," Arnold said. "A man with a curved schlong doesn't need to molest children. He'd have to spend all his free time beating off adults."

Tatum looked like a football coach and his office was decorated with sports trophies. He resembled Wacszinski so much you could have said it was a cloning job that had gone a little off.

"I'm not sure I know just what you fellas expect." Tatum studied a sheaf of papers before him. "Wachie"—this was the first time Arnold had ever heard *that* nickname for Don—"didn't tell me much."

"What would you like to know, Mr. Tatum?" Arnold asked pleasantly.

Tatum shot him a glance, made a grunting sound, consulted a couple of the pages. "What I'd like to know first is"—Tatum glowered, Arnold braced himself—"exactly what is *your* capacity in this situation, Mr. Elton?"

"I think you'll understand why the Associated people can't afford to be directly connected with this affair," Arnold said.

"Frankly I don't," Tatum said slightly less pleasantly. "We've had this information around here for some time. We've been wondering why you people didn't get in touch with us long before this."

Arnold was only now beginning to realize how carefully he'd have to play this.

"Associated," Arnold said, "has a public image as the most successful and the most active of the remaining studios. We're smaller than people imagine. We don't have huge reserves. Despite our backlog of hits, any scandal involving our most valued executive could hurt us badly."

"Mr. Elton," Tatum said after a moment, "I don't know what you're pussyfooting around for, but that's not my style. If you weren't a friend of Wachie's, I'd conclude you were hiding something important. Now, I'm going to tell you precisely what we have so far on your most valued executive. Nothing but a bunch of vague allegations that he had—or has—tie-ups with organized crime. I was about ready to throw them out as unfounded and make a public statement to that effect when you walk in sniffing around. I now get the definite impression that you people at Associated have some reason to be worried that those allegations had substance—"

"I can give you definite assurance, Mr. Tatum, that that's not the case," Arnold said.

"Let's get this clear," Tatum said. "What are you assuring me? That your people are one hundred percent sure that Hume has no tie-ups with organized crime?"

Arnold took his time thinking that one out and knew Tatum was aware he was taking time. This man was dangerous. Wacszinski should have warned him.

"Obviously," Arnold said at last, "nobody could give one hundred percent assurances of that kind unless he himself had ties with organized crime. That's why these allegations are so insidious. That's why this situation is so bothersome."

Tatum now took his time. "Okay," he said. "There've also been complaints from prominent film people that Associated had promised them profit participation. Now, we know very well you film people do what you call 'creative bookkeeping,' but when you've had four history-making films bringing in so much profits that even an armored truck would blush for shame trying to pretend there haven't been profits, we have to look into it."

Arnold felt a sudden elation. It was all he hoped for.

"This certainly has nothing to do with Mr. Hume?" Arnold pointed out.

"Nothing," Tatum said. "I'm only trying to explain why we in this office couldn't just disregard these allegations."

"I understand," Arnold said, but the mood had changed completely. He was in control now. "How much time will your office need before you'd be willing to give Mr. Hume a complete bill of health?"

"That's hard to say." Tatum was not a man who could be sucked in easily.

"You've known Don Wacszinski a long time," Arnold said.

"I have," Tatum said.

"He's vouched for me," Arnold said.

"You wouldn't be here otherwise," Tatum said.

"I've known Mr. Hume for twenty years," Arnold said. "If I personally were to vouch for his integrity, would your office then make a public statement clearing him?"

"If our investigations continue to show no evidence of tie-ups," Tatum said, "of course we would."

"How much longer does your office intend to continue its investigations?"

Tatum thought that over too. "Seventy-two hours," Tatum said finally. "And that's it."

Arnold put out his hand. After a little hesitation Tatum took it.

"Some years ago," Tatum said, "a big Wall Street firm sent three of their brightest young men West to see if they could make some sense out of Hollywood. They stayed for months. One of them committed suicide, the other went into the shoe business and the third made a report to the effect that all ordinary rules of business or logic don't apply to motion pictures or the people who make them. It's a world with laws unto itself. I think I'm glad to have made your acquaintance, Mr. Elton."

"Thanks," Arnold left, floating on a cloud of euphoria.

"Now here's what's going to happen," Arnold said as he and Wacszinski sat in the backseat of the limousine, heading for LAX. "You are going to find a good hot outlet for leaking word that Dennis Hume has been investigated by the local law people and there are strong suspicions of ties between him and the Mafai. That he's one of the Boys' boys."

"Poor bastard," Don found it necessary to say, and when Arnold looked puzzled, "I mean Dennis Hume."

"Dennis Hume?" Arnold said impatiently. "This isn't aimed at Hume. This is an operation. Relax. Dennis will

come out of this smelling sweeter than when he went in."
Don was silent. It always came as a shock to be reminded that
Don had scruples or had to be permitted to believe he did.
The fact was that Arnold's special hold on Don and Reilly
was that nowhere else could they get the kind of pay Arnold
was dishing out to them—if indeed they'd ever be hired
anywhere else. "The stakes are enormous, Don, but we could
lose too. That would mean the end of Arnel. I'm counting on
you, Don."

"You know I'm with you," Don said. "You know in the
crunch I'll always be there."

"Sure you will," Arnold said. Once that was out of the
way, he became sharp, businesslike. "You've got to be
careful about that outlet. It has to be indirect. We can't have
it traced back to us."

"Put your mind to rest on that," Don said. "I've set up
the fastest and widest coverage in the West, your pal Armand
Harris. I've got a date to meet him in the Polo Room in an
hour. The news about Dennis Hume will reach New York
before you do."

"Armand Harris?" Arnold asked dubiously.

"This is the kind of story Armand thrives on," Don said.
"He'll spread the word fast. And he loves to make you
believe he's the horse's mouth itself. He would never credit
any other source if it killed him. No. He's perfect. And he is
jealous as hell about Hume. Sure you don't want to see if we
can catch the kids? There's another flight for New York in
two hours or so . . ."

"I don't want to risk being seen," Arnold said, "even for
that. The slightest connection with me and we've blown it."
With a rueful grin. "Anytime I don't hear from the kids it's
good news, and listen, I'll be seeing them soon."

Arnold knew it was Reilly even before he opened his eyes;
Reilly's aftershave lotion walked a good three feet ahead of

83

him, and even drowned out the smell of the coffee he'd brewed for Arnold.

"This better be good, Reilly," Arnold mumbled, his face in the pillow, "the plane was delayed by mechanical trouble. We didn't get in until three. I didn't get to bed until four-thirty."

"It's two in the afternoon and I've got today's *Hollywood Reporter*," Reilly said. "It must have come on the flight right after yours." Arnold's eyes snapped open. " 'Long-simmering rumors of trouble in the Associated Artists paradise,' " Why in hell did Reilly have to use that newscaster voice every time he read something out loud? " 'came to a boil late yesterday.' " Reilly even paused dramatically. " 'A major industry puzzle for some weeks has been why Associated Artists has thrown Topman Dennis Hume's entire program in a deep freeze. The word now is that that situation is not temporary. It's being taken so seriously an emergency meeting of the board has been called in crisis haste by its chairman, Norman Bentley, who would neither confirm nor deny.' " Reilly stopped. "Well, Ar, it's out."

"Get me Oscar," Arnold reached for a cigarette. It took him a couple of seconds to see Reilly was not only offering him one but was holding a lighted match in the other hand. "Come on, come on," Arnold said tensely. "Get me Oscar, goddamnit."

Reilly handed Arnold the cup of coffee he'd put on the night table, then hastily dialed Oscar.

"Anything happen?" Arnold asked as he burned himself on the coffee.

"Where?" Oscar's voice was very clear. He was only about a quarter bottle into his Cutty Sark. It was the best part of the day for him.

"Where? for Chrissake? On the New York Stock Exchange," Arnold spat out from burn-stinging lips, "Associated Artists stock."

"What happened is the following," Oscar's voice lumbered over the phone. "Associated Artists fell a little over three points . . . it's now down to seventeen and a quarter."

Arnold's heart pounded so he could hear it in his ears. It was under way.

"Okay—how's the trading?"

The surface level of the coffee he was holding was swaying. If it had been California he would have tried to blame it on an earthquake.

"Light, nobody's buying," Oscar said. "Getz, Littell and Shelley think it'll go down at least another two points before it finds its level. You've got a date at eight o'clock at Twenty-one. Heavy money from Texas. Name of Wade Vernon, flying in late this afternoon." An uneasy pause. "Did I tell you about him?"

"You told me," Arnold said.

"He is it. Wade Vernon. Read about him?"

"I don't read the papers," Arnold said.

"Yeah," Oscar said. "He's the guy tried to pull a take-over lately, that West Coast airline that had that terrible crash. Remember? You must've seen that on television."

"I don't look at television."

"One of the worst crashes in history," Oscar said. "Don't know how you missed it. I guess Wade Vernon figured he would just walk in because of the crash and grab. Big proxy fight. Well. He lost. So listen, Arnold. He's hungry for a take-over. And you know what, Arnold?"

" 'What, Arnold?' " Arnold mimicked Oscar's voice. It was a game they played when they were riding high. It always broke Oscar up.

"I'll tell you what, Arnold," now Oscar was mimicking Arnold mimicking him, and doing a lousy job, but having a hard time not breaking up because it was so funny, "I know this man. I've had contact with him. He's been in touch with me. He's got the hots to get into the movie business." Arnold could hear the unmistakable gurgle of the Cutty Sark being poured. Normally he would have jumped on Oscar for that. But Oscar had done good. At least it looked like it, very good, and must have known Arnold felt that way, he was making so free with pouring the whiskey. "He's what the doctor prescribed. He's our man, Arnold. He'll play ball with us. We're in like Flynn, Arnold."

"Okay, Oscar," Arnold looked around frantically for wood to touch. It was his one heavy superstition. "From now on it's timing. Nothing can go wrong. Every goddamn detail has to work on precision."

"It will," Oscar said. "I've got a very good feeling. I'll see you this evening." He hung up quickly.

"Things are breaking for us, Ar." Reilly seemed to be searching for something. "Shit, a man has to look all over hell to find real wood in a modern apartment." He touched the arm of a chair fervently.

"That chair's plastic, for Chrissake," Arnold said. Reilly, who was nearsighted, peered down at the chair and nodded. "But you've been walking around with a piece of wood in your hand."

Reilly saw he was still holding the match. "Oh. Yeah." He touched the match fervently. "I found your Princess Alexa— and she's quite a dame. Anyway I got you a date with her today—at five o'clock. I told her you wanted to see her on a matter of great urgency. Which related to Associated Artists' situation."

"You said 'situation,' you didn't say stock?"

"Situation. I was very careful, Ar." Reilly handed Arnold the wooden match. "Maybe you want this for luck. From the way the Princess sounded, maybe you'll need it."

Arnold pretended not to see the match but took it anyway.

Princess Alexa's East Sixties mansion was made up of two brownstones, not one, in order to house the large art collection she had gotten from one of her four husbands, the studio head, all of whom she'd outlived.

As he was ushered in, he recalled that, like most of the business-minded princesses, she was lending her name to everything from household linens to eyeglasses, which she was supposed to have designed. He noticed that the drapes and wallpaper matched.

"You did them," he guessed, "with your usual flair."

Alexa, a thirty-looking fifty, was seated in an elegant couturier version of a sari which flowed over her knees and over the fragile Madame Récamier couch she was half reclining on. Her fine features, Limoges complexion and delicate blondness gave her beauty a slightly old-fashioned indoor quality. She acknowledged the compliment with a nod.

Then Arnold looked over the paintings dutifully, and, emboldened, he said, "That's a lovely Renoir."

"It's not a Renoir." Alexa had more British accent than he remembered her having in her first films when she arrived from England. "It's a Matisse. They're a far cry."

"Of course, Matisse."

"Frankly I don't care much if you know a Renoir from a Matisse." Her sharp manner was a *far cry* from the softness of the classic beauty who had been the last of the romantic postwar superstars. "And neither, I suspect, do you."

"Now I don't."

"Good," Alexa said as if they'd established something. "Will you have some tea?"

"I don't drink tea, I don't drink anything before seven."

"One of *those*," she said. "You won't mind if I do?" She poured some black tea from a silver teapot into a delicate porcelain teacup that matched her complexion. "When your man called me," she stirred although she hadn't put in any sugar, "I couldn't for the life of me place what I remembered of you together with anything that could be of remote interest to me, then he mentioned Associated. I've agreed to this meeting because I assume you're in some way related to the current trouble—are you?"

"If you mean am I responsible," Arnold replied, "the answer is no."

"From what I know of you, there's something in it for you. What is it?"

"I'm a stockholder. I want to protect my holdings."

"Oh, come," Alexa said wryly, "I know all the major stockholders. You, Elton, are not one of them. You don't hold enough stock to explain," she gestured their meeting together, "all this."

"My first job was with Associated," Arnold said. "I have a feeling about it. I happen to know it's in danger. I'd like to help. I was sure that you as the widow of the man who founded the studio would also have a feeling about it—"

Alexa finished the last drop of her tea and put the delicate porcelain cup delicately back on the silver tray. She had long, slim, beautiful hands.

"Look," she said sweetly, "I have a suggestion to make. Shall we, as you Americans say," (she was still making with the 'You Americans'), "cut the crap and get down to bare-ass essentials?"

Before Arnold knew it his mind grabbed her, undressed her, lifting the elegant sari high, feasting on the long slim thighs underneath, remembering from years back the boys saying even though a woman had wrinkles around her face and neck (and that wasn't even true of Alexa), it didn't mean that the rest below her chin didn't remain soft, smooth and voluptuous and—

"Surely you weren't anticipating a late afternoon quickie, Mr. Elton?" Alexa called him back as she observed him with distant curiosity.

"Not that that would be bad." He forced a boyish grin.

"For whom?" she asked.

Arnold squashed the grin on his face like a squirming

insect under his heel. "I happen to have information that leads me to believe Associated Artists' stock is going to continue to go down."

"What information?"

"Information."

"I'm a major stockholder." She was on the defensive now, scared.

"Then you should have sources. Go to your sources."

"I have. I expect you know what I'm talking about. They've reassured me."

"They're full of shit," Arnold said, "and as long as they stay in control, it'll keep on going down, maybe to where it was before. Eight dollars a share for the common, counting inflation, ten maybe eleven—and maybe that's Associated Artists' true level. Maybe that's all it's worth."

"As long as they stay in control," she repeated, getting to her feet. She was a smaller woman than he had imagined but she still had a great body. "You're trying to frighten me into something. Into selling, I should think."

"Not selling, giving me your proxies."

"Why on earth would I do that?" Alexa asked. "I happen to be on the board, yes. My late husband did build that company and I will not be party to some group of hucksters moving in and making a shambles, using Associated as some tax gimmick or worse . . ."

"I'm going to make you an offer . . ." Arnold began.

"One that I can't refuse?" Alexa was far less in control than she pretended.

"One you shouldn't refuse," Arnold slapped on his plaster face. "An offer, like they say, for a limited time only. You give me power of attorney to vote your shares, that is, proxies. In return I will transfer the sum of a quarter of a million dollars to a numbered account in Geneva in your favor."

"A *quarter of a million dollars*?" She was stunned. "In

Switzerland—why that's money you won't be able to account for..."

"We're not kidding. It's earnest money for you. The reason I'm doing it is because I know I can put Associated back on its feet..."

"It's hardly doddering on the edge of ruin," Alexa said shaken.

"Do you know what's going on there? If I don't come in, that bunch of fatasses who are supposed to be in charge will run it out of existence. You know how sure I am I can put it back on its feet? I'll guarantee to buy all your shares at yesterday's price anytime within a month, providing you give me the proxies within the next week. What can you lose?"

"That's what I'm trying to work out," Alexa was looking at him with a fascinated absorption.

"What you can't figure out is what I'm going to do once I get in," Arnold said. "That's my problem, not yours. Think it over."

"Obviously I will," she said carefully, "especially if Associated continues to drop."

"Good enough. By the way, you don't happen to have a numbered account in Switzerland, do you? It's the kind of thing I don't like transmitting on the telephone or in writing."

"Zurich," she said after a moment, "not Geneva. Crédit Suisse. Four five nine four."

Arnold had given the question of where they would meet Wade Vernon a great deal of thought and had finally decided on Twenty-one. It exuded an atmosphere of established security. It was the favorite New York eating place of many nationally known figures and had been for decades. Former President Nixon had dined there whenever he was in New York. Even on an ordinary week night like this one with a little luck you would glimpse at least a half-dozen recognizable celebrities.

"Conservative, that's the image," Arnold had told Reilly.

So Reilly came in his most sober summer suit, a lightweight classic soft gray, a blue shirt and a simple solid-colored dark blue tie. The trouble was Reilly looked dressed up. You were aware of his clothes and how well they looked. The net effect, Arnold decided, was to make you look around for a salesclerk, while he, Arnold, wore his simplest five-hundred-dollar Gucci suit with a simple hundred-dollar Gucci tie, both of which seemed to belong to him even though he couldn't remember if he'd ever worn them before.

Despite the unostentious air conditioning, Reilly was sweating. They were on their third drink. A waiter was hovering alertly, eyeing Reilly's glass. The moment it got within an inch of the bottom the waiter would be there with a fresh whiskey sour.

"Don't have a fourth," Arnold said.

"They're almost forty minutes late," Reilly said. "I knew I should have gone with Oscar."

"He's Oscar's baby." Arnold was having a hard time keeping the uncertainty out of his tone. The one thing they absolutely had to convey to Wade Vernon was assurance. "Oscar knows the man, Oscar's had contact with him."

"Forty-three minutes late. I told you that Wade Vernon's going back tonight."

Arnold decided to get rid of a little of his annoyance on Reilly. "Don't keep telling me the same thing over and over, Reilly."

"It's just that we're going to have so little time to do so big a job on this guy."

"We're not going to do a job on this guy, we're doing him a favor. We're letting him in on a terrific opportunity."

Reilly started to protest, thought better of it. "Got it," Reilly said.

"Turn your motor off," Arnold said. "I don't want the Texan to see you this way. The image for tonight is we're calm, in control. We know what we're doing. If you've got any questions, for Chrissake ask them now, or hold them until after the meeting. Never ask questions *during* a meeting with outsiders. You almost fucked up the Japanese meeting with your questions . . ."

"I thought the Japanese were impressed," Reilly was so wound up he actually fought back, "by a kind of honest questioning. I was beating them to it, there were honest doubts they would have raised . . ."

"I don't want any honest doubts raised tonight," Arnold said. "We don't have any."

He stopped.

The Maître d' was escorting Oscar and Wade Vernon. The Maître d' was being unusually obsequious, and he was a man Arnold had never seen obsequious before, Arnold had seen him show Nixon to his favorite table as if showing presidents of the United States to their tables happened every ten minutes at the Twenty-one. Not only was the Maître d' obsequious, but little circles of silence, from the chattering tables, followed Oscar, Vernon and the Maître d'. Oscar of course was dressed in one of the three identical dark gray suits he had bought ten years ago. As long as he didn't change weight he saw no reason to buy new clothes. Every two weeks he sent one to the cleaners. He managed to look like a meticulously dressed bum.

Wade Vernon was a man of medium height who seemed taller because of his Texan boots. He had a lean functional look, neither smiling nor unsmiling as if he saw you electronically. There was a half circle of a hat welt around his forehead. Obviously he was a man who wore a hat a great deal. In fact he now carried it, a custom-made ivory-colored Stetson with its rim flat against his chest, curiously near his heart, the way men who were sitting for their photographs in the eighties held their hats. He looked straight ahead of him, paid absolutely no attention to the other guests nor to the ripples of curiosity he caused. He seemed not to need to know where he was or who the others were. It gave him a peculiar disquieting quality of authority.

"Your guests, Mr. Elton," the Maître d' said to Arnold and Reilly.

Arnold nodded, dismissing the Maître d', "Of course," he said with a smile, holding out his hand. "I'm Arnold Elton."

"Vernon," Wade offered his hand to Arnold the way he would have offered an official document, say a contract, "Wade." He had a faint carefully controlled Texan accent. "We're runnin' late because I wanted to see Mister Brenner's office." Oscar smiled. He was high. "When he informed me our meetin' was at a restaurant, I wanted to see your headquarters." Arnold shot an instant-kill look at Oscar. Whenever he could, Oscar steered anybody who would go to his office so he could show the wonders his Estelle had wrought in decorating it. For Arnold's money, there was nothing wonderful about buying the most expensive Early American antiques and lining the walls with incredibly priced oils and signed lithographs. "I like to get an idea of the people I am considerin' doin' business with."

"Sure," Arnold said dubiously. "Mr. Reilly, our vice-president in charge of all East Coast Arnel operations."

Wade turned, focused on Reilly, permitted his automatic lenses and shutters to arrange themselves properly, committed Reilly to his archives, shook his hand, as they all sat down. He gave no indication of being impressed by the man who was in charge of all East Coast Arnel activities. He promptly refused drinks.

"I have an ulcer," Wade announced. He spoke a little more loudly than might have been necessary, "Which requires immediate feeding."

Arnold studied Wade intently. He had counted on at least twelve or fifteen minutes' bullshit time over the drinks. To make matters worse, the Maître d', perhaps because of the impression Wade had made, was hovering within obvious earshot, for he was with them even before Arnold could signal him to come; he bent over Wade solicitously as he offered him a huge menu. Wade promptly handed it back to him, and ordered three lean, well-grilled lamb chops with boiled squash and no salt or seasoning on anything.

"That sounds good," Arnold managed a bright enthusiasm. "I will have the same." The Maître d' looked at him incredulously.

"I don't mind what anybody else eats," Wade announced. "It doesn't bother me one bit. I just stow away those damn lamb chops like a real trouper."

"I see there's *boeuf bourguignon* on the menu tonight," Reilly said, "I'll have it."

"Do you realize what *boeuf bourguignon* is?" Arnold asked Reilly severely. "The spice and the fat..."

"Love it," Reilly said. Arnold shouldn't have let him have that fourth whiskey sour.

"Mr. Elton?" the Maître d' gave Arnold a second chance. "You still wish lamb chops and boiled squash?"

"Of course," Arnold said. "Mr. Brenner will have the same."

Oscar looked at Arnold reproachfully, then nodded sadly as the Maître d' bowed and withdrew.

"Now I'd like to put something straight, especially if we may be workin' together." Arnold braced himself. He'd never met a character like this before. You couldn't tell what to expect. Wade indicated his gut. "Because of my condition once we start eatin' we don't talk business. What it amounts to, whatever we have to say to each other in business sense we say before. Doctor's orders."

Even Oscar looked solemn.

"We'll be talking about a multimillion-dollar deal," Arnold said.

"It's been my experience," Wade pronounced (Arnold realized vaguely that this was the only person he'd ever met—in the last years anyway—who seemed to be as certain as Arnold always was that what he was saying was absolutely right), "that the amount of the deal doesn't matter. If it makes sense, it can be put together in three minutes flat, a hundred million dollars or a hundred dollars. I've heard it said that all good stories can be told in approximately the same time."

Arnold was calculating fast. With luck he could count on eight or ten minutes at the outside before the food came. And Oscar was high. You never could tell what shit he would kick up.

"I think you should know there's a special situation at Associated Artists, which I'd like to tell you about," Arnold began.

"I know that," Wade cut him off. "I think we should deal with the basic essentials at this meetin', I'll be askin' you the necessary questions when the time comes, I'm confident you'll bring me the necessary answers."

Out of the corner of his eye, Arnold saw their waiter heading toward their table with the customary appetizers Twenty-one provided for its clients to help them through the wait between ordering and being served. Appalled, Arnold wondered if Wade would count that as eating.

"Maybe it would help matters," Wade also had seen the waiter approaching, "if I tell you exactly what I need to know."

"Maybe it would." Arnold was at that point where he figured nothing much would make any difference. He had counted on a long build-up, then on the conversation flowing naturally to their venture.

Wade Vernon didn't need any buildup. He really got right to it. "What are you-all bringin' to this deal?" Wade enunciated carefully. "What do you-all expect in return? What do you expect us to bring, and what will we get for what we bring?"

The waiter arrived and immediately began arranging garlic toast, iced celery, radishes and olives. Wade was studying the appetizers dubiously. Reilly and Oscar watched Arnold. They'd move only when he indicated.

"Arnel Inc. will bring nine percent of the voting power," Arnold said, "five percent in proxy, which we have in our possession." Reilly turned pale. Reilly knew goddamn well it was not yet in their possession, but Reilly was a schmuck. Either they got it from Alexa or there was no ball game anybody would play.

"You now control five percent of the total votin' power of the Associated Artists common stock?" Wade wrote something in a small notebook.

"We do," Arnold said. Wade added a word or two to his notes. Oscar watched him sourly. Oscar didn't like things in writing, especially statements like that. But what the hell, in the situation they found themselves the lie had come big and fast and without hesitation. "And when the common stock slides to thirteen—"

"You anticipate another drop of four points?" Wade asked.

"We are confident of it," Arnold said. Wade made another note. "At that point Arnel Inc. will acquire four percent of the common stock, which will give Arnel nine percent in voting power. Now. We will expect you, at that same point, when the common stock is at thirteen, to acquire seven percent—"

"Why seven percent?" Wade asked.

"So together we will have sixteen percent of the total voting power," Arnold said. "Which is the amount we've determined is needed to have total control over Associated Artists. That will cost you, on a fifty-percent margin, four million four hundred and forty-five thousand dollars."

Reilly absently reached for a garlic toast. Arnold, who was

sitting next to him, stayed his hand. It would be impolite to eat something Vernon could not eat. It took Reilly a few seconds before it sank through.

"Our first action when we're in control," Arnold said, "will be to vote out the old board and vote in a new one. I will be on that board, and so will you, Mr. Vernon."

"Those are also details," Wade had stopped writing. "When I inquired about why you suggested my organization acquire only seven percent of the vote, Mr. Elton, I was asking whether or not you meant by that that in our association you expected Arnel to be in control?"

"Yes," Arnold said. "We've worked out a plan of action that we are confident will bring Associated stock back to its highest point, that is, twenty dollars a share."

Wade, in the heavy silence that ensued, wrote something in his notebook.

"I don't mind tellin' you," Wade said quietly, "that normally my organization does not enter into any situation in which it does not have control." The other three had stopped doing anything not vital to maintaining life. "How confident are you, Mr. Elton, that your strategy will cause that stock to attain its previous high point?"

"So confident," Arnold said, "that if within one month after Arnel takes over management of Associated Artists the stock hasn't risen to that point, we'll yield total control to you."

Wade thought about it for a long time.

"Well," Wade said finally. "We would be fools to fight for control with a management that was able to enhance stock value by almost one-third in the space of a month. You understand part of our objective is for me to learn somethin' about the film business."

"Certainly," Arnold replied so fast he almost stuttered.

"My doctor," Wade went on, and somewhere there was the faintest possibility of a smile, "has suggested for health's

97

sake I get into another field. Somethin' less stressful than oil.''

"You'll be the only man in living history," Arnold said, "who came *into* the film business with an ulcer."

Reilly laughed a little too loudly, as he always did at Arnold's jokes. Oscar barked once or twice.

"I may be deludin' myself but I had an idea motion pictures," he looked at Arnold with his full electronic stare, "might just be more interestin' "—there *was* the faintest hint of deference, even a touch of hope, "than oil . . ."

"One thing's for sure," Reilly had gone through a fourth whiskey sour, "there's got to be more succulent pussy wandering around the Studio back lots than you'll find in the oil fields."

Wade looked up from his notebook and over at Reilly.

"I'll get myself back home and discuss this with my colleagues," Wade said, as if Reilly hadn't spoken. "I can give you an answer in ten days."

" 'Ten days,' " Arnold repeated, then on the principle that no first offer should be accepted, everything should be negotiated, "that may be too long. We may have to act fast. Now I have a proposition to make to you. On the fourteenth of July I'm going to give a party on my yacht." (If he could get Wade on his yacht, Wade would have a better sense of who Arnold was.) "Why don't you join us, Mr. Vernon? A trip to the south of France might also be just what the doctor ordered."

"Exactly where in the south of France is your yacht berthed, Mr. Elton?" Wade asked.

"Cannes," Arnold said.

"Now isn't that the place," Wade had a definitely speculative look in his eyes, "where they have those beaches where the women . . ." He caught himself. "No. I guess I was thinkin' of Saint-Tropez."

"Why *that's* caught on in Cannes too now," Arnold said

carefully. "Miles of beach where the women go topless. And when we take the yacht out we pass dozens of out-of-the-way beaches where they go everythingless."

"In public?" Wade asked gravely.

"In bright sunlight," Arnold reassured him, "they love it when we cruise near them. They wave and smile . . ."

"I'll talk it over back home," Wade said, "if we are interested, why I will meet you in Cannes. But we may not be. You will be takin' a seven-day chance on us, Mr. Elton."

"We'll take that chance," Arnold said.

Wade nodded.

They had an agreement.

This sonofabitch's coming in, Arnold told himself, we're going to pull this goddamn deal off. We're going to take over the whole goddamn Associated Artists, and Arnold Elton, who was once a messenger boy on that lot, will be the head of the whole fucking Studio.

He made a mental list of the hotshots he'd fire the minute he got himself in the top slot.

4.

Someone was drawing the curtain. Joyce moved forward swiftly. Her face lit up with a big fat air hostess welcoming smile as she whipped the curtain back so fast that Economy would see no more than they had to.

Oscar had come through.

Wade entered, with Oscar right behind him looking as though he'd been in a bad traffic accident. Joyce gave Wade a quick once-over, and Arnold knew she wouldn't reject him on looks. Wade was not a bad-looking guy, even though he was wearing the same dark unremarkable but obviously expensive and well-cut suit he'd worn when Arnold had first met him, with the identical black string tie at his collar; he carried the identical custom-made ivory-colored Stetson and his eyes had the same electronic gaze. But the expression on his face reminded Arnold of one of those fancy new alloys, heat resistant, cold resistant, shock resistant, logic resistant—

everything but warm-pussy resistant, Arnold said to himself hopefully.

"Mr. Vernon!" Arnold hoped his voice sounded as if this meeting was the nicest thing that had happened in a long time, and by way of emphasis, made a warm welcoming gesture, his arm sweeping over the sixteen empty seats, inviting Wade to sit in one of them—any one of them.

Wade's eyes rested on Joyce, who was standing a little too close for an ordinary air hostess-passenger relationship. She had a peculiar look about her, as if she were keeping up a good front while preparing her passengers for what, with a little luck, would be a survivable crash.

"My reservation for First Class was unaccountably canceled at the last moment," Wade's seductively soft southern speech could chop you up as quickly as Cuisinart could make hamburger out of raw steak.

"Not 'unaccountably,'" Arnold said. "This is Miss Humboldt, our lovely stewardess. Mr. Vernon..." Wade looked at Arnold, puzzled. Normally stewardesses were not presented—not that way. He nodded to Joyce.

"There was a reason?" Wade asked with polite interest.

"Carrying an animal in a passenger compartment on a transoceanic flight is against flight regulations," Arnold said.

Joyce looked at Arnold with fascination. By now she was almost objectively curious as to how Arnold would work it all out.

"So I understand," Wade said.

"I've been away from my wife for several weeks," Arnold said. "I wanted to bring her a special gift." Sri Lanka, as if knowing it was his cue, came condescendingly, conveniently down the aisle. Arnold caressed his beautiful copper mane. "He's it."

Wade did not bother to look at the dog. His manner, which had been that of one who had dropped in for ten seconds to find out what was going on, changed. Now he was also curious about what would happen next.

"You tellin' me, Mr. Elton," Wade said evenly, "that you convinced the airline to reserve to you the entire First Class cabin on this flight so you could bring your wife an Afghan hound as a gift?"

"Yes," Arnold said. "I am. I did."

Wade looked at Arnold, then at Oscar, then at Joyce. She smiled and quickly withdrew to the galley, where Arnold and Wade could watch her.

"By the way, Mr. Elton"—Wade made it sound like an exit line—"I happen to know a little about dogs. I've got me somethin' of a kennel back home. It's only the pug-nosed breeds that suffer when shipped in the unpressurized baggage compartment—the Pekingese, the boxer, the bulldog, the Lhasa. Your Afghan would have done real fine as ordinary live freight."

He made a movement as if to go.

"The vet in New York said practically the same thing," Arnold said, and that stopped Wade. "But he also said there was some small risk. I didn't want to take even that small risk."

"And it's because of that negligible risk you bought the whole of the First Class compartment for this flight?" Wade asked.

"Yep," Arnold said calmly, "that's it."

Wade thought about that for a moment, then decided he wanted to know more after all. "You could have shipped the dog on a freighter," Wade said.

"I like to be there when I bring a gift," Arnold said. "I'm piggish that way." He was once again in possession of that outrageous confidence for which he was famous. "Especially when it comes to my wife and children. I want to see their faces and hear their voices when they get the gift—from my

103

hands." From his wallet he pulled out a lock of hair tied with a bit of green ribbon. "This is my wife's hair." Arnold hoped Wade would not reach out to touch it because it happened to be a lock of Krystina's wiry pubic hair.

Arnold held the wisp of hair next to Sri Lanka's exquisite mane. They were exactly the same color, a perfect match.

"My wife's pregnant."

Wade put on his Stetson, leaned back, took a very good look at Arnold, Sri Lanka, Oscar, and at Joyce in the galley, who stopped what she was doing and flashed him a bright smile. He took off his custom-made Stetson. He looked better without it.

"Well now, Mr. Elton," Wade finally conceded, "it must have taken a certain amount of doin' to convince an airline to cancel all other First Class reservations and sell it all to you."

"It took a little doing," Oscar admitted modestly. Wade again briefly took on an electronic look. His built-in computer was whirring away trying to figure it out, but it was impossible. He was not programmed for data like Arnold and Oscar.

"There's some surprisingly fine Dom Perignon on board," Arnold said, wondering if Wade's ulcer took champagne. "I would appreciate the opportunity to compensate, even slightly, for the inconvenience I've caused you."

Before Vernon had thought out his answer, Joyce arrived with an ice bucket that held the Dom Perignon and a tray with glasses and a bottle of Cutty Sark, which she handed to a grateful Oscar.

"Funny you-all should mention Dom Perignon," Wade said, openly watching Joyce, who was holding the long phallic neck of the champagne bottle suggestively between the palms of her hands and whirling it sensuously in the ice bucket. "That's just about the only alcoholic beverage my ulcer has signed a nonaggression pact with."

She smiled at him—Wade was clearly pleased with the attention—then judged the Dom Perignon sufficiently chilled and passed it quickly on to Arnold. Arnold and Joyce worked rapidly and well together, with the oiled coordination of a carny team. The champagne popped, the wine gushed, Joyce, flushed with excitement, was there with two glasses to catch the overflow.

She handed the first full glass to Wade, the second to Arnold.

"May I break another regulation?" Arnold asked. "Miss Humboldt's been most gracious. May I invite her to join us?"

Joyce looked over at Wade, who shut down his computer for the day, and with it his electronic look.

"Why, it's your cabin, Mr. Elton," Wade said. "I think I'm a little like you-all. I got where I am by refusin' to take some regulations seriously."

Joyce sat very close to Wade and eyed him openly. Arnold was still nervous. Wade was withholding some final acceptance; he was willing to take whatever delights they offered him, but he would give them what they wanted only when he decided they were worthy of it. They still had some sweating to do.

To fortify himself, Oscar poured himself a huge slug of whiskey.

Arnold kept the champagne flowing.

By the third glass Wade was slightly more at ease; maybe the fact that Joyce now had one leg pressed against his helped.

"Something bothering you, Mr. Vernon?" Arnold asked casually.

"Well, yes there is," Wade said. "I don't mind tellin' you that my colleagues and I have done a great deal of talking about you. When you're thinkin' of associatin' yourself with someone you look everywhere for some kind of slant on what they really are. I've always found how people make their money a pretty good indication. So, would you mind if I ask a personal question, Mr. Elton?"

"Not if you call me Arnold."

Wade hesitated a long time. "Personal relations don't come easy with me," he said.

"Maybe that's why you have an ulcer," Joyce said in a low voice, moving closer and putting an arm around Wade's shoulder.

Idly he caressed her cheek.

"Are you going to ask me if I've done all the things I've written about in my books?" Arnold suggested.

"Well, no," Wade said thoughtfully, "I wasn't thinkin' of askin' you about that . . . Arnold . . . although I should warn you I've read several of your books since we met." He paused. "Would you mind telling me how much you get a word for what you write? We've heard all kinds of stories . . ."

"They're all true." Arnold gave the nod to Oscar and refilled Wade's glass.

"How much per word is hard to say," Oscar began solemnly, "but if you want an idea—some professor somewhere came to the conclusion that if you figure how many trees been chopped to make paper for all the books written by Arnold Elton, you're looking at something like ten thousand trees." Arnold shrugged. He wasn't sure he liked that particular tidbit. Oscar pulled himself together. "On his last book per word it'll come to—" Oscar went into one of his trances so long that Arnold was convinced he was gone, but he came back at the last fraction of time that was still within reason, yanked up his calculator, fiddled with it for a moment, looked up. "My educated guess would be ten dollars a word."

Wade sat up and tried to digest the fact of ten dollars for every word a person wrote. "What would that come to a page?"

"Twenty-five hundred dollars a page," Oscar said, "more or less. And of course the book's career is not over. Serial rights, movie rights . . ."

"But then you-all write many pages before you get *the* page?" Wade entreated Arnold.

"Yes, I rewrite," Arnold gave no quarter, "but it doesn't matter. Sometimes I do a whole book in a few days."

"My ulcer is givin' me a hard time on that one," Wade said, and the other three burst into delighted laughter, which surprised and also delighted Wade. "Let's get serious here. You're telling me you sit down and type away at ten dollars a word, twenty-five hundred dollars a page as it rolls out of your typewriter—in a few days?"

"It doesn't roll out of my typewriter," Arnold said tersely. "It rolls out of me."

Wade nervously finished the last few drops of champagne in his glass and Joyce quickly refilled it. "Nobody else would ask," she said gaily, "but I've been dying to." She turned directly to Arnold. "Have you done all the things you've written about in your books, Mr. Elton?"

Arnold smiled enigmatically. Joyce was okay. She knew how to steer the conversation into turbulent sperm-filled waters. In fact he found himself mildly excited by the question, as he always did when a sexy woman asked it. He looked over at the others. "I'll bet there isn't a person in this cabin who hasn't." There was an icy silence. "You've read my books, Joyce?"

"Oh, yes," Joyce said cheerily.

"Well?" Arnold challenged.

" 'Well' what?" Joyce laughed.

"Have *you* done all the things I write about in my books?" Arnod asked.

Joyce hesitated a long time. "Yes," she said heartily. "Except for the dope stuff."

"*All* of them?" Wade said.

"Let me put it this way," Joyce said, "I can't remember reading anything Mr. Elton described that was new to me."

"Do my books excite you?" Arnold kept at her. It was obviously titillating Vernon.

"Sure. Just the way they do any woman who's honest with herself." She turned to Wade, who was looking at her in absolute fascination. "Arnold is one of the few men who writes for women. He understands what goes on inside a woman."

"You mean like right now you're excited talking about it?" Arnold asked.

Joyce lifted her head as if sampling herself.

"Yes," she said at last, "I am."

"Very excited?" Arnold asked.

"I don't think that's quite a gentlemanly question to ask," Wade protested.

"You're sweet." Joyce touched Wade as if to make sure he was real. "I didn't think they came like you anymore." She kissed him on the cheek. "Why shouldn't he ask me that?"

"It seems to me it's your own business," Wade said. "Nobody else's."

"I'd feel that way only if I was with people I didn't like, and don't you think," she added in a teasing whisper, "that I know it's exciting to you, too?"

Arnold got up. "Come on, Oscar."

Oscar who was very comfortable where he was, didn't move. Arnold kicked him in the shin.

"You and I, Oscar," Arnold announced, "are going to sit ourselves right there in the last seat in front of that curtain. You and I will stop anybody who tries to intrude from Economy dead in their tracks. We've had enough embarrassments for one flight, haven't we, Miss Humboldt?"

"Aye, aye, sir," Joyce said. "We have, sir."

"You sure nobody from the crew ever comes in during the flight?" Wade said.

"Dead sure," Joyce said.

Oscar finally lifted himself up, grabbed the bottle of Cutty

108

Sark and moved down the aisle alongside of Arnold. They sat themselves down in the row before the curtain. There was a silence, then a sound of slight rustling from behind them, then Joyce murmuring something.

"Funny how the sounds of foreplay carry over even the noise of the plane," Arnold said.

"What?" Oscar said.

"Nothing."

Oscar drank silently for a few minutes, then he got nervous. "What are they doing back there?" he whispered thickly.

Arnold got up and looked.

Four feet protruded from the back row into the aisle.

"Mr. Wade Vernon," Arnold said to Oscar as he sat down, "is fucking Miss Joyce Humboldt."

"That's good," Oscar said heavily, "very good."

The sounds from behind became more pronounced, unmistakable, intense whispers, rustling, gasps, soft moans, bodies adjusting themselves—

"My assessment," Oscar pronounced in low tones as he sipped his Cutty Sark contentedly, "is that you handled a difficult and very dangerous situation like a master."

The sounds behind became more urgent, insistent, incoherent.

"My assessment," Arnold said, "is that we should make a heavy gift to Miss Humboldt."

"Stock, Arnold?" Oscar asked.

"Sure," Arnold said. "I've already promised her that, when it hits thirteen, put one-tenth of one percent of the stock in Miss Joyce Humboldt's name. But when you get back to New York, buy her a jewel, too. An emerald, I think. It's cheap for the lesson we learned."

"Lesson, Arnold? What lesson is that?"

"Even with a multimillion-dollar Texan conglomerate oil man with ulcers"—and the moment he said it, Arnold made a

note to use it as a snapper for one of his chapter endings—
"it's impossible to overestimate the power of cunt."

The lights flashed on announcing they were to fasten their
seat belts, the plane began its descent to the lovely flowered
sea-encompassed Nice airport.

Customs passed Arnold and Sri Lanka with a quick nod at
Arnold's passport and the vaccination papers a dog needs for
entry into France. Arnold was so well known to the entire
Nice airport personnel that an airport hostess immediately
took Sri Lanka's leash, whisked dog and master past the
long line of docile passengers waiting at immigration.

Vernon, looking flushed and happy, stood in the line
directly behind Joyce. They both waved to Arnold; Vernon
mouthed silently, as he pointed to Joyce's back, Could he
bring Joyce to the party tonight? Arnold raised both hands
over his head in a congratulatory gesture, and nodded enthusiastically. He was delighted that Wade was bringing Joyce—who
at that moment, feeling some activity behind her, turned, saw
Arnold, who stopped the dumb show with a grin. She flashed
a smile at him, took Wade's arm in a loving possessive
gesture.

Arnold sighed. Maybe a romance was going there. He
hoped fervently that it was. It would do everybody good
and what's more, if Joyce snagged the kind of money Wade
represented, perhaps there would be no need for Arnel Inc. to
show its gratitude. Arnel might save itself one-tenth of one
percent of whatever Associated Artists common stock would
be worth in the next few days.

Arnold felt very good, the highest he could remember
being on a natural nonchemically assisted high. The world
was a pretty goddamn good place to live in when you got down
to it.

Michel was at Baggage and Customs waiting for him as
expected.

Four years earlier, when Arnold and Krystina had bought the Villa Lou Soleillou in Mougins from the Vicomte and Vicomtesse de la Porte *(de la Porte*—all that meant was "of the door," for Chrissake), Michel and Germaine, who had served the de la Portes in the Villa for thirty years, were elegantly dropped on the Eltons. Arnold admired the job the Doors thought they were doing on him. The elderly couple should have been pensioned off. Instead the Doors made them a subtle condition of the sale of the Villa.

"Ah, but I have read your books," the Vicomtesse said with an indulgent smile. "You are a man of the world." In Europe that meant you were supposed to understand and accept lying, cheating, bribes, tax evasions. "We have never declared Michel and Germaine with the Sécurité Sociale, of course it was they who preferred it thus." Michel and Germaine had neither medical insurance nor retirement fund. All they had was what they'd saved and pilfered, although that last must have been meager. The Doors kept all their wines and liquors under lock and key and knew intimately each vegetable and every ounce of meat in the Villa. But naturally, Michel and Germaine must have had a kickback, the standard ten percent from the local butchers and grocers. "So you will understand why we could not think of selling Lou Soleillou without them. I may say they are the heart of the Villa. They know it like the inside of their pockets—the plumbing, the electricity, the repair men for the machines— and of course when you entertain, they are without parallel."

Arnold checked around quietly and worked out a simple but ingenious way of getting back at the de la Portes. In all openhearted innocence, he registered Michel and Germaine as his employees and made scrupulous payments to the Sécurité Sociale, which had immediately investigated, given the ages of the two elderly servants. The Doors had to pay back social security payments for thirty years and a good-sized fine as well. Even better—that was Arnold's style—he practically forced the Vicomte and Vicomtesse to continue to give every outward sign of being the Eltons' dear friends. There were other tax-dodging tricks the de la Portes had indulged in and which they knew Arnold found out about, so the de la Portes not only came to the *crémaillère* (French for housewarming) when Arnold and Krystina moved into Lou Soleillou but screwed their aristocratic smiles on, submitted to the greeting kisses from Arnold and Krystina and appeared dutifully at every Elton cocktail party from then on.

Arnold might have just gotten rid of Michel and Germaine a respectable time after that but he felt a curious distant affection for them and liked the image of them as the faithful old family retainers, and besides, Krystina was still ill at ease in what she thought was Riviera High Society and felt the elderly couple would steer them to the right thing and the right people. Krystina had the hots for titles. Her dream was to give a garden party for Princess Grace of Monaco. After all, Krystina reasoned in her innocence, they were all Americans, and Arnold was from Hollywood too.

With a subtle subservience Michel and Germaine took liberties Arnold was sure they would never have dared with the Vicomte and Vicomtesse.

On an evening when Arnold and Krystina were looking forward to a feast of the Greek goodies Krystina made so well, Germaine in the kitchen, Michel in white jacket and gloves served tiny portions of the *taramá* and *dzadzíki,* and *moussaká*—noodles, chopped meat and eggplant, as a beginning dish. Then he came in with a *gigot*, a whole leg of lamb done in the French style, pink almost bloody inside (either because that was one of Michel and Germaine's favorite dishes or because lamb was so expensive and they wanted to run up their 10 percent cut of the butcher bill—or both). Neither Arnold nor Krystina had ever eaten bloody lamb before. Krystina managed to stow it away with apparent gusto and to keep telling Michel how delicious it was. Arnold had to force himself to eat one mouthful; later on in their bedroom, Arnold took out a long New York kosher garlic salami that he'd kept hanging in the closet hidden under a bathrobe so Michel would never see it, and gobbled almost a fourth of it before Krystina made him stop.

Every day when Germaine did their black and gold bathroom, she would put Arnold's Water-Pik carefully out of sight. He was sure Germaine thought it was some kind of forbidden apparatus from a sex shop. On the other hand, Germaine would invariably find the set of phallic vibrators Krystina hid carefully, wash them and set them up neatly on top of Krystina's night table—even the latest vibrator Arnold brought, the one that looked unmistakably like an erect penis and which, in operation, extended and retracted.

And Michel managed to convey his disapproval of the way Arnold overdressed, the expensive custom tailored silk underpants, the formal Via Condotti suits for lounging—a tie when everyone else wore a sport shirt and, above all else, that incongruous incomprehensible earring.

Now Michel tried to look at Arnold without too much disapproval as he greeted him and grabbed his one small bag. Arnold had complete wardrobes in all his residences. When he traveled he needed no luggage, only the Louis Vuitton duffle bag in which he carried several packages of his favorite ribbed multicolored condoms, a few paperback editions of his novels so he could hand out autographed copies, notes for the book he was working on and an extra set of porcelain caps just in case.

Michel took Sri Lanka's leash from the hostess with evident distaste and led the way to the car park. Like the de la Portes, Michel and Germaine were cat lovers, but Arnold claimed he was allergic to cats, so cats were out at Lou Soleillou. Michel hated dogs, he was worse than Germaine. Dogs upset the quiet orderly comfort the old couple dedicated themselves to providing. A small part of the reason Arnold

113

had bought the dog was that he knew it would bug Michel and Germaine and they would have to pretend they loved it. The Afghan, a nervous breed, could jump fantastic heights and the kind of surveillance it needed would certainly tax an elderly couple to their physical limits.

"Monsieur intends the dog for the Villa?" Michel asked nervously as Sri Lanka pranced uneasily at his side, pulling at the leash trying to get over to Arnold.

"Of course. He's a gift for Madame, so she shouldn't feel so alone when I'm away."

"He's a beautiful dog, but Monsieur can be reassured, Madame never feels alone." The old bastard was able to give almost everything he said some barbed meaning that was impossible to nail, and now, with the same ease with which he wore a white jacket and white gloves when serving, he slipped on a look of impassive dignity.

They spoke French in spite of Michel's fluency in English. It was another of Michel's ingratiating tricks, for it implied that Arnold's French was *that* good, which it was not.

"It's good to be—back." Arnold had been about to say "home" but he was not really sure which was home, the New York duplex penthouse on Central Park South, the Villa Lou Soleillou in Mougins or the big house on an acre and a half in the heart of Bel Air.

"Monsieur will want to go to the house and refresh himself before the party." "Refresh himself" was Michel's way of saying "fuck Madame." Arnold felt a surge of sexual excitement, very different from outside banging. Only with Krystina did he have the feeling of utter security when he had an orgasm. Braunschweig, the Beverly Hills analyst, with his Austrian accent, had told him, "You feel exposed when you ejaculate, no? It is classic, especially with your traumatic experience in childhood. You are afraid of anal rape." "Me? Anal rape? Ecch..." Arnold said with revulsion. "You are over-reacting," Braunschweig continued, "it does not mean

114

that much. I have known British officers who indulged in anal intercourse with their subalterns and would not even speak to them afterward.''

Oscar's Estelle, ample-haunched, everybody's mother, the seat of her dress as always when there was the slightest suggestion of heat, sticky crumpled, planted a wet kiss on Arnold's lips. She still had not *piged*—caught on—as the French would say—to the niceties of the Continental greeting. The only people you ever kissed on the lips were people you happened to be fucking. She'd been away from her Oscar a little less than twenty-four hours. She'd gone ahead to make sure their accommodations at the luxurious Port Clubhouse were in order even though it was one of the most impeccably run hostelries in the world—and one of the most expensive (paid for of course by Arnel Enterprises). But that was Estelle. ''When it comes to Oscar's well-being, I trust no hotel in the world''—even if there wasn't a chance in a million that she would find the slightest thing wrong. Not only was it so well serviced and appointed, but also it was so close to where the *Delphi* was berthed, that the odds were good that Oscar would stagger on his own to the yacht without falling into the Mediterranean.

Estelle was so flustered by their arrival that they were outside the airport building and halfway to the parking lot before she remembered. She rummaged through a huge, messy but very expensive handbag and pulled out an envelope.

''A telex that came on the boat,'' she explained, ''that Captain What'shisface—your Captain Australian what's his name—thought maybe it was too important to wait till you got down to the yacht.''

She finally relinquished the envelope and because the sun was very hot, decided it would be wiser to get her Oscar poured into the station wagon she had rented for their stay.

Wartime buddy, the telex read, *can't keep lid on any longer*

115

*too much pressure will blow in next forty-eight hours have
convinced the menace Riviera vacation good for his health he
will contact you on arrival tomorrow July fourteen if he
doesn't you can reach him Eden Roc Antibes regards Wachie.*

So Dennis was arriving today. Arnold would have to figure
out some way of getting him to stay put. As Arnold remembered,
Dennis, like all real gamblers, was a restless sonofabitch.
Maybe Arnold would send him to the local hookers. Arnold
had spotted a couple on the Croisette who looked promising.
Of course Clover was a hard act to follow, but tomorrow
Arnold would look over the current crop. Maybe he'd find
one that had some really kinky specialty—it might be good
enough to keep Dennis occupied for a least forty-eight hours.

Up ahead, Oscar waved a triumphant good-bye as Michel
impassively led the way through the car park to Arnold's
tomato red Monteverdi. Arnold's great good feeling was
whipped away by a storm of anger.

It was one of the house's unwritten rules that no one else,
Michel especially, was ever to drive the car. Of the twenty
Monteverdis made by hand each year, Arnold's was the only
convertible. What's more, the Monteverdi people had given
Arnold permission to redesign his, nothing radical, but Arnold
had exaggereated its low-slung look by lowering the outside
door handles and he'd given it a larger rear window. He
hadn't understood then how important the car would become
to him.

Just a few months after he and Krystina bought Lou
Soleillou, Arnold had climbed the electronically activated
ladder to the dovecote, which had been converted into his tiny
work area, shut the trapdoor and sat down to work.

At first he hadn't understood what he was experiencing, it
was so unusual. Gradually, with a sense of panic, he was
forced to admit that, for the first time in his life and for no
reason, he didn't feel like working. It took him a long time to

realize he was face to face with that basic dread he'd lived with for years—that one day the magic excitement that inevitably shot through him, when he sat down to work, surging from his balls upward, so that his fingers flew over the keys, making words spill out like boisterous tumblers— might fade away. He talked to himself persuasively, saying how much his writing would bring—the paperback rights, movie rights, serial rights, foreign rights, TV rights. Nothing worked. He got up at least ten times and each time forced himself back, but then he remembered the first book he'd read about writing years ago, how the lady author had sternly admonished that when you couldn't write, you were to move away from the typewriter immediately so you would not associate the machine with the dread Writer's Block. He had fled, barely giving the ladder time to complete its slow descent, jumped the last couple of feet, and landed with a thump that must have alarmed Krystina.

She was sitting in bed holding a sheet in demure agitation above her breasts when he burst in. She slept nude unless they were going to fuck, in which case she wore Frederick's of Hollywood trick lingerie—frilly panties with exposed crotch and curved cut-outs to leave the buttocks exposed.

Arnold pulled his clothes off so fast he didn't give her time to pick a Frederick's number. They fucked intensely. At first his urgency bewildered her. Naked, his penis only half erect, he threw himself on her, grabbed frantically at breasts, buttocks, hidden places. She mistakenly attributed his wildness to an impetuous burst of passion that finally excited her enormously. He, although consciously noting her orgasms and dimly proud of them, fought desperately to still a persistent, barely audible voice that kept repeating, "This is not the cure for your Writer's Block."

Another voice snarled back, "Fucking's the cure for anything. It always has been."

He tried a dozen different positions and when he finally came it was with the dismal knowledge he still didn't want to work.

Silently, depressed, he had left Krystina half asleep, basking in the afterglow of an unexpected deeply satisfying sexual experience, blissfully unaware that he was close to terror.

He had let the Monte seek the Esterel superhighway. The silky purr of the motor brought him none of his usual pleasure. But he had become consciously aware of something he'd never paid any particular attention to before. Practically every Provençal male driver on the highway (they had to be the most aggressive drivers outside of Italy) considered the Monteverdi a mortal threat to their masculinity. No matter what cars they were driving—one actually pulled it on Arnold in a two-horsepowered Citroën, popularly known as a yogurt pot—they would pass him, then swing back over too soon in what the French called contemptuously, "the fishtail." Slowly, Arnold began to feel himself come tinglingly alive.

He had hung back, waiting for his prey. He had not long to wait. Some macho joker, perfectly cast, bald, bespectacled, in a dark suit and tie, a respectable briefcase visible on the seat next to him, gave Arnold a whopper of a fishtail.

This time, Arnold slowly, with apparently great effort, swung out, came alongside, kept even. His quarry reacted beautifully. He almost broke a gut trying to pass Arnold, who for a fraction of a moment let him, then inched up on him. Arnold kept it up until he had the sonofabitch screaming wild insults at him; he then turned so he could get the full enjoyment of the contorted face, made the obligatory triumphant middle finger Up Yours and surged away.

Light-headed, elated, he had swung back home, and when he seated himself before the typewriter, the keys clattered at an unusual speed and he felt he was writing at his best.

The next week Arnold had had the Monteverdi painted

flaming fire-engine red, on the grounds that the color would be even more provocative. It turned out to be completely true. When Arnold took to the highway for what he now thought of as his "therapy" with the red Monte, the percentage of victims was even higher, the choice greater. Practically every male driver was sucked in. His preferred choice was some young putz about Robbie's age.

And each time afterward, after having left them raving in frustration on the highway, he had been able to work like a bastard.

Michel prided himself on being a good driver and had actually taken the Monteverdi on several emergency occasions, always irritatingly justified.

But now the idea that Michel had sat in the driver's seat of this marvelous piece of machinery with its gleaming steering wheel, its tortoiseshell dashboard and alligator fittings was unbearable.

Arnold played with the idea, What if I turned on Michel and just said, "Fuck off. You're fired, both of you." A small scenario played itself out in Arnold's head, Krystina's shock, "Oh, but Arnold honey—the party—and Germaine! What will I do without Germaine?" Krystina's utter helplessness. It wasn't worth it. It would spoil the homecoming.

"Madame felt you would enjoy driving the Monteverdi home," Michel explained but without apology. "Monsieur will of course wish to drive?" Michel had the gall to make it sound as though he was offering something.

Arnold was so pissed off he had to give Michel some kind of small kick in the ass, "Will you mind sitting in the back seat, Michel?" It was really not a question at all. Michel knew he was too old to look around for other spots. "Sri Lanka must sit in the front alongside of me. He gets carsick in the back."

Bleakly. "But it is really not a seat, Monsieur. I am not certain I can get in. My legs are a bit stiff."

119

"You, stiff?" Arnold said heartily. "You're like a young boy."

"*Oui*, Monsieur," Michel yielded dubiously. "I did not know dogs have the carsickness."

"But of course. They're only human." Another small resentment. Michel never laughed at Arnold's jokes. "Sri Lanka vomited all the way out to the airport in New York, until we put him in the front seat."

Michel, long and thin, a cross between Jacques Tati and General de Gaulle, went through elaborate contortions jack-knifing himself into the small back space really intended only for packages—the Monteverdi was strictly a two-passenger car. Finally, Michel was below window level, where he couldn't see or be seen. Arnold led Sri Lanka to the front seat alongside the driver, which the puppy occupied as if it were his birthright. Michel tried a tentative groan or two hopefully but Arnold totally disregarded them, revved up the motor, held his breath as he listened. The motor was smooth as silk, Michel's driving hadn't hurt it.

Sri Lanka sat proud and tall in the death seat alongside Arnold not in the least disturbed by the car's motion. His marvelous mane rose high enough so that when Arnold pulled to a stop to pay for the parking, the busy attendant called out, "Messieursdames," a greeting used only for a man and a woman; he'd mistaken Sri Lanka's copper mane for a woman's hair. When they came to a stop on the parking lot, one of the armed airport security police, holding an automatic rifle—the Nice airport had had its share of hijackings—saluted and because he knew Arnold and Krystina, he too smiled and said "Messieurdames," then leaned over startled, "*Mon Dieu*, a dog! Pardon me, I thought it was Madame." Arnold enjoyed it hugely, smiled broadly and said in French, "Well, that's part of the idea." "What a dog," the security cop said, "with his mane, he looks exactly like a woman. One would think it was Madame, that color." Arnold, glowing with pleasure, said, "Well that's the rest of the idea—" then whizzed around the circle that took you out of the airport and onto the highway leading to Cannes.

Perhaps because of his experience with the Game, he was immediately aware that a macho driver was behind him in a Peugeot 604, looking as though he might want to play. The 604 was the most powerful motor Peugeot made and ordinarily Arnold would have loved the challenge. But now was not the time. Besides, he was still savoring the parking attendant's and the cop's mistaking Sri Lanka for Krystina. Who else would have had the idea of giving his wife a dog that matched her hair so perfectly?

But the 604 picked him up right outside the airport. Arnold had a fleeting mildly disturbing impression that the moment the 604 had seen the Monte, he'd suddenly swung out from the airport parking as though he'd been lying back in wait.

It would be a few minutes before they would hit the superhighway, until then Arnold couldn't have let the Monteverdi out anyway. It was not only the height of the tourist season but the eve of the Fourteenth of July, France's national holiday, and the roads and beaches were jammed. The 604 was still behind him but that could have been simply because he also was on his way to Cannes.

For a while there was a persistent feeling that the big white car was tailing them, then Arnold forgot about him, and the feeling that the world was good again took over. Actually these impulsive periodic absences were good. It was the only way a marriage could work.

He felt a glow of warmth as he thought about how they'd worked out a really good setup with the U.S. Internal Revenue people. What made it even more enjoyable was it hadn't been easy. Arnold had played a crazy long shot.

A bare ten days before, Oscar and Arnold had been summoned to the New York IRS office. They'd faced a bright blond young man in his ambitious thirties who might have been a dentist instead of one of the IRS's top operators.

"Do you mean, Mr. Elton, that you want all your living expenses in France deductible?" The IRS man had consulted some notes. "A villa on the Riviera, a cook, a housekeeper, a butler, a yacht with a captain and an able-bodied seaman, a ship's cook, two secretaries,"—Sarita as well as Telly was on the payroll as a secretary—"a gardener—"

"It's a life-style," Oscar said ponderously; he'd probably thought that one out in advance and sprang it as a little surprise for Arnold too. It was a mistake to bring Oscar along.

"That's some life-style," the IRS cookie replied sardonically. "We're allowing you deductions for your New York apartment and a fully staffed Bel Air house." The IRS cookie raised the stainless steel ax high over their heads, then chopped. "I see no justification at all for your place in the south of France."

Oscar looked dimly dismal. Almost all Elton family life had been predicated on that deduction. Shutting the Bel Air house, arranging for Margaret, their black housekeeper, to sit the house, packing, the flights, a hundred and one irritations— all this for nothing unless it was being paid for by the United States Internal Revenue Service.

Oscar sat there like a goddamn lump.

"Then may I explain it to you?" Arnold himself said, his voice surprisingly icy calm.

"By all means, Mr. Elton," the IRS man said with the pleasant anticipation of a guy who looked forward to a nice little free-for-all. He was sure he wouldn't lose.

"It's the way I am, I have to move. I can't stay in one place too long," Arnold explained with earnest simplicity. "If I do, I get stale, I can't write. We're talking about the creative process, at least the way it works for me."

"The creative process," the IRS cookie was in no way

122

fazed by that. "Well, Mr. Elton, I'm afraid your creative process is going to need a slight taking in hand."

"I have an income of three or four million dollars a year from my writing alone," Arnold said, without batting an eyelid. "I know myself. If I can't have the setup I need, I won't even try to write. There'd be no point. I simply would not write. Not a word. You'd not only not have to worry whether my expenses in the south of France are deductible, you wouldn't have to worry about a three- or four-million-dollar income for the IRS to tax."

Two days later Oscar puffing with excitement had called Arnold and told him the Internal Revenue Service had accepted all Arnold's French expenses except the yacht, which he hadn't expected anyway—as legitimately deductible.

Arnold pulled out of the crowded slow-moving traffic and onto the Esterel superhighway between Nice and Cannes. He let out the Monteverdi, not too much, just enough to make absolutely sure Michel's driving hadn't screwed her up. It hadn't.

He hit a hundred and forty kilometers an hour when he spotted the 604 behind him but he still gave it no special significance. He was glowing with physical pleasure, almost exaltation, from the feel of the Monte. She was a rare, beautiful animal. She gave him a jolt as solid as the cocaine would later on. This was better than "speed," which he no longer touched. He chuckled a little at the weak pun, then saw that the 604 was unmistakably moving up and was directly behind him.

"Another one of your Provençal champions!" Arnold shouted joyously to Michel, who, because of his position, couldn't see, and because of the roar of the wind at that speed, could barely hear. "A 604 who wants to play!"

"A 604 Peugeot!" Michel shouted back and the wind couldn't cover his fright. "Careful! Careful!"

"What? Of a 604?"

"No, no, no!" Michel tried frantically to hoist himself upright. "Don't fool with the 604!"

"Fuck him!" Arnold had observed that when he wanted real feeling he could get it only in English. There was no satisfying French substitute for good old heartfelt "fuck."

Arnold was beginning to feel really good. This 604 was just what he needed after Oscar's screw-up and the tension of the trip and The Deal. If the bastard wanted to play, he was about to get a real run for his money.

He slowed down just enough to make sure the 604 was looking for action. The Peugeot immediately swung out left, doing a hundred and sixty but curiously didn't try to pass, stayed momentarily even with the Monteverdi.

Great! The sonofabitch was really asking for it! Because of the speed, Arnold couldn't take his eyes off the road but he had a peripheral picture, nothing clear, a fleeting image of a man slumped over the steering wheel driving with a scary concentration: then with a terrifying suddenness, the 604 zoomed over to the right.

That was not the way it was done—The Game—even with the wildest drivers, was never played like that—the crazy bastard was whipping over, obviously to sideswipe them off the road—it took a fraction of a second too long for it to sink through to Arnold. He whipped the steering wheel wildly, the Monte bounced crazily out of control on the soft shoulder. The bastard was insane. He was trying to kill them.

There was a splinter of an image as the driver tore his eyes off the wildly swaying 604 to glance at them, a fraction of time that could have been measured only electronically. Then the hulk in the Peugeot unaccountably shot wide to the left, freeing them at the very last second, and tore away. Arnold fought the Monteverdi back on to the concrete-topped highway, subdued it, brought it to a shuddering halt.

Michel in shock heaved himself to a sitting position.

"We could have been killed." Arnold was barely able to speak. "They should be shot these lunatic Provençal drivers."

"No—no—all over France—" Michel spoke with the strangely calm voice of a man who had brushed death. "There's been an epidemic—road madness—I tried to warn you—604 Peugeots are forcing cars off the road, no one understands it. A family of five was killed."

"Road madness?"

"Mostly with stolen 604s. They usually pick on old small cars, force them off the highway. For sport . . ."

"Sport? This one looked to me like a typical local driver—"

"No. This was not French, this one. I saw him—"

Michel had given him a small outlet for his compressed rage.

"Let's forget the chauvinism, he looked like one of those fucking rugby players you breed here in the south of France—"

Some of Michel's hostility came out of hiding, "I had an impression, you know how one thinks in moments of life and death, I thought, 'It's an American—'"

Arnold made a disgusted sound, swung the car onto the highway. They'd suffered no damage. The Monteverdi was also tough.

At the toll booth, Arnold shouted to the worker whose only responsibility was to see that the drivers had the proper change for the toll basket. "A white 604—just pass here?"

Unexpectedly, the toll worker was interested.

"A 604, white, has just rolled by a few seconds ago. Did he aggress you?"

"Aggress? He tried to kill us!" Arnold shouted. "Did you get his license number?"

"No. He had the exact change."

"What did he look like?"

"He wasn't young—in his forties . . ." the attendant caught

himself. "Ah no, monsieur," the toll worker rejected it, "if you have ideas of personal vengeance, it would be best to forget it. I will notify the police there has been an accident." Cars had piled up behind Arnold and were honking. "Now be good enough to move on at once."

"As I thought—one of those 604 madmen," Michel called as they pulled out, grimly pleased that he'd been right. "604 fever."

Arnold, irritated again, hoped they'd catch another glimpse of the 604 but as they got well along on the Esterel, it was evident they would not. It took him a long time to decide it was just as well.

The afternoon heat faded, the highway was dazzling with flowering oleander. Arnold finally let himself be lulled, sloughed off the raw emotion of the 604 incident. By the time they were near Mougins and the Villa Lou Soleillou, his crotch was vibrating and aglow.

He swung the Monteverdi up the almost perpendicularly steep driveway, pulled the hand brake. There was an iron grille gate halfway up. Some friends thought the gate just there was crazy but it made sense. Arnold himself had worked out the layout when they had redone the Villa. People driving up had to stop, get out, identify themselves, then if Germaine was satisfied, she pressed the electric button, the gates opened, the driver had to get back in the car, drive through the gate, stop, get out again, then close the gate behind him. Crime was growing in France but the only way to Villa Lou Soleillou was through that spiked gate on that steep driveway. They had to park the old car on the street below, then puff their way up, which also pleased Arnold. Only very intimate friends were invited to growl their cars up the steep driveway and use the limited parking space at the upper Villa level.

Michel had to push himself out practically under Sri

126

Lanka, then speak into the gate microphone; Germaine buzzed, Michel flung the gate open, there was a yell of joy from up above; Arnold shot up the driveway, letting Michel shut the gate behind him and make the rest of the steep climb on foot.

5.

They were waiting for him on the back terrace as he had pictured.

It was deeply satisfying, the garden in full flower, Krystina, her fabulous copper hair flowing, running toward him radiant with her fecundity but, as she had told him on the phone a few days before, "You'd never know I was pregnant. Dr. Jean-Louis says there's no doubt about it, I've got a little Elton in me and very well attached this time—," as Germaine touched her apron to her eye in a very Mediterranean gesture of being overwhelmed with gratitude that the gods had made it possible for the Master to return from far places.

It was a marvelous moment, one of the ~~best~~, you wouldn't think it would come at forty-nine, pushing fifty (okay, so he bullshitted himself about a few years).

Arnold held Krystina to him, felt her breasts, her haunches pressed hungri~~ly~~ against his.

The first time he'd seen Krystina he remembered thinking

129

he would vote her the real estate agent he'd like most to fuck. He'd decided he wanted finally to get away from the Beverly Hills house he and Kate had bought, and he and Beejay had lived in.

Krystina, petite, curvesome and with that fabulous copper-colored hair, had showed him houses in Bel Air. After the fourth house, Krystina said she had a theory. You couldn't really get the feel of a house until you'd had a drink in it.

The next day when Krystina showed him the fifth house, Arnold brought a bottle of champagne. When they'd put away half of it, Arnold said Krystina was absolutely right but that you couldn't get the *real real* feel of a house until you'd also fucked in it.

Krystina gasped, then burst into her cluster of soap bubble giggles. The next thing, they were fucking and in that marvelously crazy first time they made it together, Arnold whispered in awe, "Why—it's the same color as your hair!"

Krystina—what a wonderfully supple body—bent over backward so far she was able to thrust her head through her crotch from behind, the way circus acrobats do, her incredible copper tresses mingling with her pubic hair as she trilled in her sweet girlish voice,

"Look—collar and cuffs to match."

It was that combination of ostensible innocence and ferocious sensuality that had wiped him out. He had bought the house and asked her to marry him.

Arnold turned and saw Robbie standing uncertainly in the background, as Krystina whispered, "And Baron Alfredo's waiting for you inside—"

"Good—was there a message for me from Reilly?" Arnold whispered back, tickling her ear.

"No, nothing," Krystina murmured.

Arnold looked around. "Where's Jennifer?"

"On the *Delphi*," Krystina said, bright as flashing needles.

"She's been darling about helping now that I mustn't do too much. Jen really wanted to be here." It was a big effort for Krystina to be fair to her stepdaughter. "She knows how much you love everybody to be together when you come home but somebody has to be on the *Delphi* for the party. It's going to be immense."

"I'm pleased Jen is helping out." What he meant was that he was pleased Jennifer had at long last agreed to become part of the Elton family setup.

Although it hadn't been that long since they'd seen each other, Robbie seemed to have made one of those subtle jumps in age that happens around thirty. Arnold felt a special twinge of love, pride; the boy had come to resemble him even more. Before thirteen there'd been strong indications of Beejay's soft golden features in the adolescent unformed face: it seemed Robbie would be his mother's child. Now Beejay was being imperceptibly superseded. This was Arnold Elton's son even though his hair was very blond like his mother's and not black and curly like Arnold's. And Robbie was even taller than Arnold, with the slim grace of youth. Still he had that agitated quality of the young out to make it, a state Arnold understood so well. Arnold wanted to tell him to relax, not to let his ambition consume him. If only there were some way of squaring what he wanted his kid to be with the urge to just say, "Forget it, drive your cars, live it up, fuck everything in sight."

Arnold went to him, Robbie never came to you, hugged him hard and affectionately, kissed him on both cheeks, felt a slight hint of Robbie's discomfort at the emotion his father was attempting to convey. Beejay had been like that, but with mocking style. She'd always kept a part of herself inviolable, utterly separate even in the most intimate moments, and then in those terrible moments the worst he'd ever had to live through. Was Robbie's new assurance because he and Jennifer

131

had pulled it off? If they had, *they'd* tell him. Never in a million years would Arnold ask, no matter how much he wanted to know.

Arnold stopped short. One step behind Robbie stood a fascinating human female, a product of hormones and special highly selective breeding. Was this Robbie's bankable jim-dandy? None of the other Playthings Robbie had photographed was as remarkable as this one. If anything, Jennifer had been miserly in her description. Without even moving, this girl was able to conjure up illustrated books like *Uninhibited Sexual Intercourse, MacDougall's Guide to Good Fucking, The Joy of Sex, Ninety Positions You May Not Have Tried . . .*

"She's the Centerfold," Robbie introduced her. "You separate her in the middle. Thirty-nine–twenty-five–thirty-six. Our jim-dandy. Boobs all hers and would you believe it, she's just turned seventeen."

The Centerfold Plaything jim-dandy (if anybody ever could have thrown a left tit over a right shoulder and squirted milk down her ass, it was this girl) knew she didn't have to say anything, nor was she expected to. Out of habit, Arnold lost himself as he mentally ripped what clothes she had off her, quickly went through oral, anal, vaginal fucking, sighed—at which point she came to him. Arnold backed away slightly, kissed her on both cheeks prudently.

She startled him by saying, in a voice that went well with the rest of her, sweet perverse, "Hey now, that's no way to kiss," and planted a wet kiss warm and sucking full on his lips. The others laughed uncertainly as Arnold hurriedly unstuck himself from her lightly sweaty contours.

Krystina giggled with a kind of sensual tension.

Michel finally puffed his way up, making gasping sounds to dramatize the cruel effort climbing the steep highway had demanded of him.

"I hope you didn't mind Michel driving the Monte." Krystina was always worried about something or was convinced she'd done something wrong. "Sarita thought I shouldn't let Michel take it but *I* thought you'd enjoy it so driving it back. And Michel is such a careful driver."

Arnold nodded curtly, kissed Germaine's cheeks, was kissed back very respectfully.

"I brought you a gift," Arnold said to Krystina. The optimal light was going fast and Arnold, who wanted them all to see the fabulous matching colors he hoped they would be—after all he had only a snip of Krystina's hair to go on—opened the Monteverdi and Sri Lanka made his entrance. The hound had built-in showmanship. He moved with supreme assurance, proud, elegant, aloof.

Krystina opened her mouth wide and gasped at the dog's tall slim beauty. She was the most marvelous person in the world to give a present to. Even after four years of marriage, Krystina hadn't yet realized she was the wife of a rich man and was staggered by the lavishness of his gifts. She still made gasping sounds and clapped her hand to her mouth in delight. Now she was deeply moved, for it was evident that Arnold must have given this time and thought. She undid her hair, lowered her head, let her hair spill all over Sri Lanka. They were all stunned. The puppy's coat and her hair really did match so perfectly you couldn't tell where the woman ended and the dog began. She stayed bent over low, her head snuggled against the Afghan's mane, her huge eyes dramatic as though challenging anyone to deny that Arnold was the most wonderful husband any woman ever had.

"Hey, but they're exactly the same color," excitement made the Plaything's childish voice more childlike.

"I had a sample of Krystina's hair," Arnold flashed a conspiratorial grin at Krystina. They were the only ones who knew where the snip of hair came from. "So I matched it."

"I call that real neat," the Plaything said. It was the highest praise she could bestow on anything.

Arnold and Krystina had been in their black and gold

bathroom on that May day when Arnold had made that crazy, wildly lucky decision to take off for New York. Krystina stood naked on the rim of the huge bathtub so that her pubis was level with his face. She was ostensibly looking at herself in the full-length wall mirror directly opposite—with that perfect body she had a right to look. Arnold buried his face in her pubic hair, clasped her buttocks so she wouldn't slip off the wet porcelain rim. Even after a series of clutching orgasms, which she had worked at so hard in the forlorn hope that he might change his mind and stay, it still aroused Krystina. She made groaning appreciative sounds, and when he came up for air, she whispered, "Don't stay away longer than you have to."

Without having thought it out beforehand, Arnold suddenly took a small scissors off the dressing table behind them, snipped off a good-sized cluster of her pubic hair. That impulse was a little like his writing, which popped up suddenly, mysteriously from nowhere, it would all come together in a flash. The perfect gesture—and he'd even topped it with the perfect touch.

He'd noticed a bit of green ribbon on the dressing table—green was Krystina's favorite color, naturally with her copper gold hair and green eyes. Arnold skillfully tied a perfect knot about the wisp of hair with the ribbon, then trimmed the hair to an appropriate length, making like a fancy hairdresser. Krystina had giggled in delight.

"I'll keep it with me always, right next to my heart," Arnold mimed, slipping the beribboned wiry copper gold wisp of hair with reverence into a wallet, holding the wallet next to the heart side of his naked chest.

"It's real neat that color," the Plaything said to Krystina. "Who does it for you?"

Robbie looked at the girl indulgently. "Nobody does it," he explained almost paternally, "that's her very own color."

"Wow!" the Plaything exclaimed.

134

"You want her, Dad?" Robbie asked half seriously. Krystina giggled uneasily.

The Plaything laughed uncertainly. She hadn't been able to decide whether she had been insulted or flattered.

"I've got something for you too," Arnold said to Robbie, as he went over to the Monteverdi and pulled out the latest model Nikon. "It's a prototype," Arnold said, "it hasn't come out on the market yet, fully electronic with built-in filters you can control. One of the top Nikon guys got it for me—for you."

Arnold could have kicked himself for blurting all that out. After that Seiko quartz wristwatch—Robbie would easily guess Arnold hadn't had to pay for the camera.

But Robbie took it and manipulated it the way those who really knew cameras would, whistled appreciatively. "They'll never improve on this one. It's got to be the end."

He passed it to the Plaything, who handled it in a way that made it seem like some kind of foreplay.

"Maybe I'll take a few shots tonight on the yacht—" Robbie said.

"I've got a surprise for you too," Krystina interposed, and Robbie's face shut like an undersea plant that felt itself menaced.

When Arnold didn't move immediately, she showed signs of impatience. Was it true she manifested impatience only when her stepchildren Robbie or Jennifer were the center of attention? "Come—" Krystina, practically dancing with impatience, held out her arm imperiously.

"I may have another surprise for you in the next couple of days," Arnold said quietly. "The biggest of all time—"

Krystina dropped her arm.

Michel, still puffing from the steep climb, leaned forward to Germaine, who poured a liquid awed whisper in his ear. They must have been trying to translate the biggest surprise of all time into its French equivalent, and decided it had to be

135

something astronomical. They and the others looked at Arnold as though he'd descended from another planet.

"A deal, huh?" Robbie asked. "How much?"

"Big," Arnold said quietly. "Very big. Don't ask me more. I can't say now."

A cathedral silence. They seemed suddenly like people at church.

"Well, like she would say," Robbie indicated the Plaything, "like Wow!"

"Is it like a billion dollars?" the Plaything asked excitedly and decided it was. "How much is a billion dollars? Is it a million million dollars or a thousand million dollars or what?"

"It's a thousand million dollars," Arnold explained gently. "But it's nothing like that—"

They obviously all decided it *was* something like that.

"It can't be film," Robbie said, "there's not that kind of bread in films, no matter what."

"Now all I'm going to tell you is it *is* films," Arnold said severely. "Nobody's to try to guess and we're to keep it to ourselves—is that understood?" They remained mute. Arnold took it as a pledge.

"Look," Robbie said, when it had reached the point at which somebody had to say something, "a silent shutter," he pushed a lever, and there was a barely perceptible sound, "and all she needs is available light. With this baby, you can shoot practically in total darkness. Nobody sees you or hears you—I'll bet I get me some sensational shots of your friends tonight. You'd be surprised," to the Plaything, "even at their age what they do in dark corners at those parties—"

"Watch it, Buster," Arnold tried to accompany his apprehension with a chuckle, "you just be careful what you shoot on the *Delphi* in available light when people don't know—"

"Don't worry," Robbie said, "I'll get signed clearances. With that surprise of yours it looks like we'll be really sueable."

136

"Never do business with any man who hasn't got enough assets so you can sue him," Arnold had taught Robbie. "Two words these days, if you want to make it in films—*bankable* and *sueable*." "Bankable" had long ago sunk in and now here was "sueable" already part of Robbie's vocabulary.

Robbie went off suddenly with the Centerfold, without saying good-bye. Arnold had a disturbing feeling that the boy had forced himself to wait for Arnold's arrival and that he had fled the first moment he could, extricating himself from—well, from what? The family that was forming about Krystina? And why hadn't he mentioned anything about his and Jen's project? Had Arnold's announcement of a big surprise made him ashamed to talk about his little project? If that were so, it was a shame—

"Now come," Krystina said with finality. The preliminaries were over. The main event was coming up. "Come."

She actually pulled him. Michel and Germaine remained immobile, their eyes as blank as those on Roman statues—they were probably still trying to convert the big surprise into what it might mean to them. So far they seemed to have concluded it would mean nothing.

Inside the house Krystina skipped with impatience.

"Baron Alfredo's thataway," like a silent films actor Krystina pointed toward the front garden, and then in a mysterious promising whisper added, "As for you, Mr. Elton, I'll be seeing *you* upstairs."

She danced her way across the living room, twinkled up the staircase carrying sensual promise and a teasing whiff of mystery, gesturing him to hurry. But he stopped long enough before the bookcase in their huge living room to glance lovingly at the one hundred and ninety-seven leather-bound copies of his eleven novels. Most had been translated into twenty languages. Several had gone into Hindi and Swahili; that last told you a lot about what was happening in Africa.

He moved over to the bookcase, slipped in a leather-bound

copy of *A Dream of Love* (his last book), picked up the telephone and, making sure Alfredo wasn't trying to listen, called Don in his Laurel Canyon house in Los Angeles.

Even though it was barely eight o'clock in the morning Don was up and alert.

"The Menace will be arriving at Nice in an hour," Don told him.

"Today?" Arnold demanded. "Your cable said tomorrow—"

"Yeah, but listen, Arnold," Don said calmly. "That leak made all hell bust loose. The poor bastard is locked up in his house with phones that don't stop ringing, free-lance photographers are hiding on his grounds, he's become a one-day sensation here—we finally decided we'd better get him out, which we did in the limo with him on the floor. It was practically a 007 operation and I figured he'd be better off at the Colombe d'Or because it's nearly all French film people, Eden Roc for Chrissake you're bound to run into Swifty Lazar—"

"Okay, okay," Arnold said hastily. "You did well. Colombe d'Or's better. Will he give me any problems, I've got this big party tonight—"

"I know that," Don said. "I did everything I could to impress upon him the necessity of his staying the hell away until you give him the signal to emerge. He won't bother you—"

"And were you able to get a promise from him to stay away from the casinos?" Arnold asked. He spoke in low tones so Alfredo, who hadn't moved, couldn't possibly hear. "I don't want the sonofabitch getting into trouble here."

"He swore on his wife's head he'd stay away," Don's voice came crisp no-fooling around, "but guys like Dennis—I wouldn't take his left ball, not to mention his wife's head, as guarantee when it comes to gambling. You'll just have to keep him away from those high-class gambling dens they've got on the Riviera. He offered to go to Shrimpsville,

Louisiana—what's in Shrimpsville, Louisiana?—but I figured we needed him under your eye. Incidentally, AA took a real dive this morning right at the market's opening. It's down to nine—Tatum made an announcement to the press last night that as far as his office was concerned they made no distinctions. All wrongdoers, no matter how important, could expect to feel the full weight of the law—"

"Jesus. Are you sure we've got this guy under control? That's a little more than we needed."

"Arnold," Don said patiently, "I drafted that statement. We want those stocks to go down."

"Okay," Arnold said dubiously, then told himself Don was handling it brilliantly. Scare the shit out of everybody. Drive the fucking stock down, down. "How was the Menace's morale?"

"He was almost in tears when I drove him to the airport," Don said. "He thinks the sun rises and sets in Arnold Elton's ass. He was blubbering he had you all wrong, how he'll never forget what we're doing for him. I gave him your number—he'll call you the minute he gets in. And listen, Arnold, he's got no bread on him. I told him we would take care of all the bills like hotel, car rental, et cetera. I figure he's less dangerous with no money. But I think—I wouldn't bet on it though—he'll stay away from the casinos for at least a week. He's worn out from the strain. He's been hit hard by all this, needs a rest."

"Good going. Keep an eye on the stock market and keep in touch."

"Relax," Don said, "everything's under control. Have a good time. The world's ours—Arnold, listen, I've got another call urgent. You'll hear from me."

There was a click. Arnold hung up. He was glad he'd made the call. It was beginning to roll the way it was supposed to.

The Baron waited in the open door, looking moodily out at the lights of Cannes and of the cluster of villages about

139

it. Pearls popped up in the harbor as if strung together by invisible hands. Arnold saw himself typing the words.

"Alfredo!" Arnold had the trick of uttering your name so that you would think it was the most wonderful surprise of all that you were there and that you were his friend.

"Ah, Arnoldo," the Baron handed him two small boxes, his manner tight and solemn. The kind of man whom you could rely upon to arrange the details of your funeral, who would tell your widow not to worry, he'd take care of the grotesque business of getting rid of what was left of you. "One is coco, the other is *amies*."

"I'll take them both, although coke's enough for me these days. I don't go the *amie* route."

Arnold felt he had to get upstairs to Krystina immediately, he couldn't hold out another second. And she'd said Surprise— some mysterious secret she had waiting for him—a crazy kinky object from the Cannes Sex Shop? although Christ knows there was no need for that. It was enough—man and wife, prick stiff and hard, cunt moist and avid, Arnold tried to remember if he was quoting himself, decided he probably was and that he wouldn't worry about it.

"I must speak with you," Alfredo startled him by stopping him with morose urgency.

"Oh sure, Alfredo," Arnold moved away, called out, "later—"

Alfredo grabbed him.

"No! Now!" Alfredo said, actually holding him. "It is an urgency."

Arnold yanked his arm out of Alfredo's grasp and looked at him with distaste. "I'm in a hurry." Arnold glanced upward, but Alfredo made another even more vigorous restraining gesture.

"I tell you it is important."

Arnold pushed Alfredo's hand off with what was almost disdain. What could the organ-grinder possibly have to say

140

that could be of any real interest? Arnold continued to walk away, disregarding totally Alfredo's high-pitched shouted frantic, "Arnoldo! life and death!"

Arnold was already three steps up the staircase. Alfredo actually had a foot on the staircase when Arnold turned to him with such outrage that Alfredo fell back sullenly, and watched Arnold, taking the steps two at a time, disappear up the staircase.

In their enormous bedroom Arnold expected to find Krystina stretched out on their emperor-sized silk-sheeted bed all decked out in a new Frederick of Hollywood open-crotched black number. The bed had been turned down but she wasn't there. She often played a sexy hide-and-seek, which he pretended to enjoy. He tiptoed to the closets lining the dressing room, whipped them open, certain he would find her in one of them.

Only her dresses, dozens of them.

"In the bathroom," Krystina's voice called. Had he heard a suppressed giggle? "Only no admission for people with clothes on. *Nudo*. Naked. Nude." Then in her fractured French, "No-compris?"

"Compris," Arnold zipped out of his clothes, but kept his shorts on. He wasn't crazy about the way his body looked and even a well-muscled man walking with his balls dangling was not the most prepossessing sight in the world.

The bathroom door suddenly swung open. Arnold caught a swirl of black and gold bathroom fixtures, of silver mirror, then a cluster of giggles like soap bubbles children make, Krystina's freckled creaminess of which there was just a hint more than when he'd left.

Sarita, who had been hiding, stepped from behind a shower door, flung her arms wide like a magician's assistant and accompanying herself by a simulated roll of the drums and a large orchestrated *da de dah*, presented herself as the major attraction of the evening. Her bronzed Aztec body had tiny slashes of white around the breasts and haunches. She'd sunbathed with a string halter and a thong bottom.

He looked at them in dismay.

Their giggles became convulsive.

Two naked women with him, one his wife. He'd always kept wives out of this kind of scene. A wife was family. This kind of fucking was something else. He was offended, hurt, upset.

Sarita sprang toward him, he recoiled in a silly movement, realized vaguely Sarita had shaved off all her pubic hair—with these thong bikinis, you've gotta shave—well—Krystina hadn't shaved her pubic hair. She never would. It was rock-bottom proof that the fabulous color of her hair was real.

Sarita, pointing to Arnold's shorts accusingly, burst into spaced-out laughter. The gold coke spoon dangled crazily at the end of a gold chain about her neck, swaying back and forth between her breasts, as she said with heavy mockery of maternal pride, "Now isn't that sweet! He's shy!" Sarita tugged at his shorts persuasively but Arnold backed away so violently she stopped, momentarily thrown.

"But I thought you would love it," Krystina said apprehensively. "You see, Dr. Jean-Louis—"

Sarita cut her off with an impatient gesture, "Screw that frog doctor of yours," snatched the small box out of Arnold's hands, then, still playing the magician's assistant, "and now, Ladies and Gentlemen, the magic powder—" filled her gold spoon with the cocaine, sniffed it avidly, sighed in deep satisfaction, grabbed Arnold's coke spoon, which he'd been holding, filled it, handed it to him.

"Now just a minute," Arnold tried to sound authoritative, clutching frantically at his shorts. Sarita had by now gotten them halfway down his belly. Spinning a little because of the coke, she yanked so hard they almost tore. "Sniff!" Sarita jabbed the full coke spoon under Arnold's nose so suddenly that Arnold involuntarily inhaled a nostrilful. He quivered a little as the hit covered him like a vast caress from head to toe, but he still clung to his shorts. Sarita groped inside, squeezed his balls. She was searching for the vulnerable part of his underpants, found it, ripped hard and his genitals tumbled out.

"I've seen everything," Sarita said, for Arnold had made an involuntary gesture to hide his balls. "Arnold Q. Elton, Mr. Chief Cocksman of the Universe, a shrinking violet, now you just take your hands away from there you nasty boy, all we're going to do"—the coke had really sent her—"is f-u-c-k . . ."

"Dr. Jean-Louis—" Krystina started to say but was interrupted by Sarita who, holding Arnold's penis and balls in her left hand, pulled him close to Krystina, then held a full coke spoon with her free hand almost under Krystina's nose. "You know I'm off it," Krystina said reproachfully, making a quick gesture of avoidance. Then with pride to Arnold who was having difficulty appreciating the full measure of Krystina's sacrifice, for Sarita was now really squeezing, "I've even quit smoking. I mean just plain cigarettes. Dr. Jean-Louis says they've found it's bad for the fetus."

"Fuck Dr. Jean-Louis for the second time," Sarita said.

Sarita rolled Arnold's rapidly expanding penis as though it were a cylindrical twist of pastry dough. Krystina shouldn't have been so openly avid in watching. What further irritated him was that, in utter disregard of the feelings of the man it was attached to, his penis stood martially erect.

Not that he had actually ever hidden anything from Krystina. He simply hadn't gone out of his way to tell her, but of course she knew. When Arnold was absent too long, she cheerfully explained that he was doing research for his books. And she knew about Telly, too. As Sarita intensified the two-handed message, Arnold grew angrier. Krystina should have been aware he was not big on more than one woman at a time even though in all his recent books there had been an obligatory scene of a threesome. But for him there was enough variety in one woman's body. It annoyed him even more that his own wife was sucked in by what he wrote.

"What's wrong with you?" Sarita asked petulantly, for Arnold had pulled himself from her violently.

"Well you know how careful Dr. Jean-Louis is," Krystina apologized. "He said I sort of could. But he says it's a kind of dangerous moment for the pregnancy so," hoping the coke had relaxed Arnold a little, she tried the playful approach he usually loved, she wagged her finger at him as if he'd been naughty, "no penetration if you please, Mr. Elton. Everything else but. Dr. Jean-Louis is so understanding." (The way French doctors put you on a no-alcohol diet but let you have a glass of red wine, never white, with each meal because, Who can live without wine?) "And you always keep saying you don't like your potatoes without meat, so just for the present, Sarita and I thought I'd be the potatoes—and first—" She spoke rapidly, enumerating the delights like a child at a party. "We'd take a bath together." The black and gold bathtub had been filled with warm water and foamy bath oil. "Then—"

"Then catch as catch can," Sarita cut her off, "play it by ear, or mouth, ass or cunt," Sarita effervesced. Then mimicking Michel's and Germaine's subservience, "Perhaps Monsieur would prefer to have his cock sucked first?" Before he could move away, she was on her knees, her head darted, her mouth engulfed his penis like an animal seizing its prey.

That excited Krystina.

With a mighty effort, Arnold pulled himself free.

Sarita rose, looked at him incredulously.

"It's all right, Love," Krystina said hastily in a soothing whisper, "it turns me on."

"Turns you on?" Arnold said angrily to Krystina. "You're my wife, goddamn it!"

"But, lover boy," now Sarita mimicked Krystina's tones.

"Krystina and me, no secrets we've talked about it. She knows—"

"Who the hell told you to talk about it?" Arnold raged. "I'm here for the woman I married. Understand?"

The look on Arnold's face had Krystina really frightened now. "Oh, Sarita darling," Krystina said hastily, "why don't you just slip out by the back way? Michel and Germaine are dolls but you know how servants are. They don't have much to talk about—You'll dress fast won't you, darling?" Arnold was forced to admire the way Krystina was handling it. "You know the other staircase, the back one?"

Arnold scurried toward the huge tub, slid into the bubbly scented water. He had a vague glimpse of Sarita dressing, heard the closing of a door.

Krystina came in, creamy, pink and copper, stood a moment so he could admire her, then carefully, with an exaggerated sound of sensual anticipation, slid into the water, curled herself next to him.

"Sweetheart is not angry with his Sugar?" Krystina whispered, her breath tickling his ear as her hands caressed his body. "Sugar just doesn't want to take any chances with Sweetheart's," she brought his hand to her stomach, "little bumpkin."

The warm water, the cocaine, the trilling words were beginning to work. It was getting close to what he'd hoped it would be. Their lips touched.

"You're my wife," Arnold said sternly.

"And you're my husband," Krystina said softly.

They kissed again, then she got out of the tub, towelled herself quickly.

"Not to move until Sugar says so," Krystina waved an admonishing finger at him.

Arnold languished in the water, lifting himself slightly so that the flushed pink head of his erection protruded above the bubbles. He eyed it with irritation, which in no way seemed

145

to affect its arrogant autonomy. He half hoped it would wilt. That would teach Krystina a lesson, but no, it continued stubbornly pointing to the ceiling.

She called him softly. He pulled himself out of the tub, eyed his erection glumly but the more he looked, the harder it seemed to get. He attacked it with a splash of cold water, to no avail, muttered at it, but the erection defied him with its mindless rigidity.

Krystina was on her back stretched out on the emperor-sized bed, a cushion under her. Arnold studied her position with an expert eye; Krystina slipped another cushion under her buttocks and spread her legs even wider apart, then beckoned seductively.

Arnold yielded, got on the bed on his knees as she directed, gently moving his head so that his mouth was full over her, then positioned himself so that her head was between his thighs.

Heads moved, hips pumped, bodies writhed, until, in a surprisingly short time, they were both rocked by a series of violent upheavals, about seven on the Richter sexual scale, he judged. She yelled piercingly. Arnold gasped. They collapsed panting and drenched.

"Love you," Krystina whispered, breathing hard.

Arnold lifted his head out of the moist hair long enough to mumble the expected "Love you."

They lay there that way for a long time, then Arnold moved his head enough so that his lips were free.

"I thought Sarita was making out with Scott," he said drowsily.

"She keeps saying he's gay," Krystina murmured languidly from somewhere. "Sarita thinks anybody's tactful is gay."

"Maybe he is," Arnold felt a touch of resentment that Krystina was defending Scott.

Krystina lifted her head slightly, "Oh no. He's not gay at all." She kissed his belly soothingly.

146

"How would you know?"

"Why he's having a thing with Telly."

"With Telly?" Arnold asked in shock.

"With Telly."

"You sure?"

"Oh, absolutely," Krystina edged her belly ever so slightly closer to Arnold's mouth. "Telly told me."

"Jeesus, you women tell each other everything. Telly told you—Why the Admiral's daughter doesn't know the difference between her cunt and a hole on a putting green." Arnold moved his lips, playfully chewing on Krystina's hair, "I feel guilty about Scott—keeping the poor sonofabitch dangling for six weeks. Did he deign to accept our hospitality?"

Before Arnold had left for New York, Scott had even refused a drink from the Eltons.

"An in-depth profile for *The Review*," Scott had said. "That means to me, in-depth."

"What that 'in-depth' bullshit means," Arnold said casually, "is you want to feel free to tear the shit out of me. What the hell. Be my guest. It's all been said, anyway. I don't pay any attention."

Scott interrupted, "But Krystina says you read your reviews carefully—"

Krystina. Sometimes he could kick her in the ass with her big mouth.

"I didn't say I didn't read them. I read them. Sometimes I even learn from them." He paused. "Another thing 'in-depth' means is you'll be here for quite a while. Let me put you up at a comfortable hotel."

"I am comfortable."

"I know that quaint joint you're shacked up at. Doubles as a whorehouse."

"Only the first floor. And the girls are pleasant. We talk and they don't bother me."

147

"Hundred-and-fifty-franc hookers, I know them."

"Not that I invited it, but they talked about you. So many of them know you." That last seemed to impress Scott.

"That's our good old Arnold Elton," Arnold said.

"Not that I'll use any of *that*."

"I told you," Arnold said impatiently, "use what you like . . . Scott Goldman. That's quite a mish-mash of names . . ."

"My mother's maiden name was Scott. She's English-English. And of course my father's Russian-Jewish."

"How'd that combo work out? English-English-Russian-Jewish. The chemistry doesn't seem right."

"The biggest difference is that wherever we lived, no matter for how short a time, my mother planted roses. My father would say we'd never be there long enough to see the roses bloom. And of course each time we moved, my grandfather, my father's father, who lived with us and whom my mother loved, would sing an appropriate Russian folk song. He taught us all, including Mother, enough Russian to understand. So it went. Mother planted roses and Zaide kept singing. When did *you* change your name?"

"I never did." Arnold wasn't even sure that Scott meant the name-changing crack as a jab. But there was that irritating quality of effortless privacy about Scott that Arnold found particularly challenging. No matter how intimate the questions he threw at Arnold, all of which Arnold answered, Scott kept that place Arnold would never enter.

Krystina made a slight movement, his head was getting heavy on her thigh.

"I suppose I should have called him except, what do I owe him?"

Krystina reached over and stroked Arnold's hair. "Nothing, only he did burn when he realized you'd left without even warning him and I didn't know what to say, I didn't

148

know how long you'd be, I kept saying you'd be back, but not to worry—I finally convinced him to move into the Club. You would never think he was so outdoorsy and he's really handsome in his swimming trunks, and it really agrees with him, especially the waterskiing every day—''

Arnold sat up so suddenly she almost fell off the bed. "Don't tell me we've been paying for him all these weeks at the Club?"

"Oh, but I was sure that was what you wanted," Krystina was upset again. "And besides," her voice became young-girlish, "it's all tax deductible—"

"Goddamn it, Krys, not everything is tax deductible, and sure I invited him but not for six weeks..."

"Oh, but, Sugar," Krystina snuggled up to him, "it was four weeks and then he moved in with Telly..."

"Only four," Arnold said curtly. "You know what it costs at the Club per day? And I hope he's been pumping Telly in only one way, everybody knows I don't like intimacy among Arnel personnel."

"Oh, but Scott isn't Arnel personnel," Krystina said as she stroked his genitals lovingly.

"If he's lived the good life off me for four weeks, in my book that makes him Arnel personnel."

"But Telly's *so* discreet, and Scott has been really sweet, on Michel and Germaine's day off, he helps me with the marketing. Imagine a famous writer like that carrying a market basket..."

"He's not famous."

"He loves the French markets. He showed me the Cannes Marché Forville, where I saw Roger Vergé himself doing the marketing for the Moulin de Mougins, you know, and that street that's blocked off, full of shops, marvelous cheese places, I never would've known about it, it's so lovely in the morning, fruits and vegetables, and as Scott says they look

149

like the dew is still on them, fish they've just caught."

"Did he ask you anything?" Arnold asked. "Did you tell him anything?"

The spell was broken. It was over. Krystina reluctantly let him go.

"All he did," Krystina answered, "was ask about how you work. I showed him the Pigeon Coop. He didn't believe it at first."

On the top of their Neo-Provençal villa there was a *pigeonnier,* just like on the old farmhouses of southern France, a traditional small coop on the roof for pigeons to nest. Arnold had it converted into his work cell. He needed the most minuscule possible space in which to work but there could be no distractions, not even a window, which would have given a fabulous panoramic view of the lower Alps to the north and the Mediterranean to the south. Only a skylight high up in the ceiling permitted a glimpse of an occasional bird flashing by.

There was barely space for Telly but the tools of the trade were there, the word processor, the tape recorder, intercoms, photocopiers, switchboards and teletype, which made it possible for him to be in touch with any part of the world at will. And of course the electronically controlled ladder. It was the only way he could produce those ten-dollar words, page after page of them. His work was sacred. No one could get near him when he was at work. Room had been made for a couch, which was for impromptu sex if the mood should hit him.

Arnold and Krystina allowed themselves a last drowsy moment. She washed his face, dried it gently, spread a fragrant cream over his mouth and cheeks, rubbing her scent away.

He dressed slowly. The coke had hit but still he felt cheated. It never came off the way you imagined.

Krystina puckered her lips to Arnold. "Love you."

"Love you."

Madame Germaine was waiting for him directly at the foot of the stairs. Arnold was annoyed. She knew the Eltons didn't like anybody loitering even remotely within hearing distance during the bedroom sessions.

"The Baron is still here," Germaine whispered. Authentic or not *she* had never accepted his title.

Alfredo was standing before the picture window of their living room, a brooding silhouette against the faint light of the Mediterranean evening.

"The Baronessa must be down at the *Delphi* by now," Arnold observed dryly.

"She is." Ordinarily Alfredo would look intently at Arnold as if worried about his health. Now he made Arnold feel like the carrier of an infectious disease.

"Then she must be worrying where you are." In two minutes Arnold would kick the organ-grinder in the teeth. What was he playing?

"You treat me like I am a fool." That Italian tendency to imply a vowel after every word was intensified by Alfredo's nervousness. "Why do you keep me waiting? I tell you I must talk to you and you oblige me to wait."

"You got something better to do?"

"You see? You don't believe I can have urgent matters to say to you."

Arnold started to protest. Alfredo made an imperious downward Italian gesture, his right hand like a sharp instrument slicing everything in its path.

"Listen to me and you listen very carefully."

Well. This was a new Alfredo, tough, angry, apprehensive.

"*Primo*," Alfredo said in careful low tones. "I am your good friend no matter what you treat me like, I forget that."

Alfredo tapped his temple. "You just keep remembering I am a friend."

"Alfredo is my friend. Alfredo is my friend." Arnold memorized dutifully.

Alfredo refused to be swerved, his tone stayed hard, spiteful. "I now tell you what I can. You must not ask me question. You must listen with great care."

"I must listen with great care."

For a moment Alfredo seemed to be considering simply walking out, then thought better of it, for which Arnold was grateful because by now Alfredo had managed to convey a clammy fear to him.

Although Alfredo spoke quietly, he couldn't keep a slight tremolo of panic out of his voice, "Somebody is trying to kill you."

"Somebody is trying to kill me," Arnold repeated in the same childish mocking tones, then caught himself sharply. "What are you talking about?"

"Somebody plans to assassinate you."

The dark had jumped upon them with the sudden leap of a black cat pouncing on its prey. There was no real twilight on the French Riviera. Alfredo was barely discernible.

A familiar icy clutching like frozen hands clawed Arnold's gut. *You know of course that these sudden cramps and the asthma are psychosomatic,* Dr. Braunschweig the analyst had told him, *triggered by a panic situation, or one you judge to be panic. You might consider psychotherapy.* "Fuck psychotherapy," Arnold had replied, "that's for the kids. After what I've lived through, I can stand on my own."

"Now shall I tell you why I was chosen to bring you this message?"

"Tell me," Arnold said numbly.

"Because I am always up here when you return," Alfredo said. "I am the one you're sure to see you before you go out."

After a moment's silence, Arnold said, "In other words I'll confront this danger the moment I leave here. So they needed to warn me immediately."

"That is my assumption."

"So the danger is immediate?" Arnold's lips and mouth were dry.

"That would be my guess," Alfredo replied shakily. "Although I know no more than what I have told you. And now I must leave."

"Now you must leave?" Arnold asked harshly. "What is that?" Alfredo really started to go, Arnold had to lunge and grab him by the jacket. "Alfredo, who's trying to murder me? And why . . ."

This half-ass Italian baron who'd hung around the periphery of the film world hoping some crumb would fall his way, if he hadn't married Gina would still be discreetly pushing dope here and there, making promises to arrange matters with bureaucrats who stood in the way of complicated Franco-Italian coproductions. Not one of Alfredo's projects, to Arnold's knowledge, had really come off.

With rigid, surprisingly strong fingers, Alfredo swept Arnold's hand from his lapels.

"You did not listen. I told you three important things. *Primo*. I am, no matter how you treat me, your friend. *Secundo*. I cannot tell you more. *Terzo*." (At this point Arnold suddenly realized Alfredo was scared shitless.) "Somebody wants to murder you. *Ecco*—"

"Ecco, my ass," Arnold said, but Alfredo put up one palm, then the second in the gesture of a French traffic cop stopping traffic dead. "Come on, you're going to tell me more. How did you find out about this? Who told you? You've got to know *that*." Then when the Italian still wouldn't budge, Arnold grabbed Alfredo's elegant lapels, shook him violently. "You bastard, let's say I believe you—which I haven't made up my mind about—what about my wife and kids, goddamn you, are my wife and kids in danger?"

Alfredo hit Arnold on the shoulder so hard and unexpectedly that Arnold let go.

"You think I wouldn't tell you more if I could?" Alfredo, breathing hard, asked contemptuously.

"Wait a minute, goddamnit." The fear was beginning to seep through his whole being. "Who contacted you? Somebody dropped this information on you—Right?"

Alfredo wouldn't even affirm that. "How? Was it by telephone?" Alfredo forced his shirt and jacket back into place. "Then maybe they'll contact you again—"

"Surely not if you do anything stupid against me. And even then maybe not." Alfredo seemed offended, as though he was the injured party. "I have regarded you as a man of intelligence." With passionate scorn. "You are behaving like a woman. Now do not touch me again and think out for yourself what must be done."

"Like what?"

Alfredo made a gesture he must have inherited from Pontius Pilate, washing his hands of it all: there was nothing more he could do.

"Hey now. Man. Alfred. Friend. Is this for real, for Chrissake?"

It was Alfredo's turn to mimic. "Is it real, for Chrissake? We are grown-up men, we are talking seriously."

"If you know that you must know more."

"No! No!" Alfredo said, his voice shrill with fear—he was covered by a sheen of moisture, Alfredo's silk sweat. "Nothing. No more—" This had to be the Mafia. There had been rumors about Alfredo and the Honorable Brotherhood. But why? And why were they retailing it to him this way? They must have some purpose? But what? No wonder Alfredo was scared shitless and there was something he, Arnold, was expected to do. He'd been told the danger was imminent, immediate. They expected a next move from him. But what?

154

And if it was money they wanted why hadn't they been explicit? Not only had he been told but shown, that crazy incident with the 604 Peugeot must already have been part of it and what else could it be but money if it came from the Mob.

Probably big money.

But why right now? What had made them suddenly decide on hitting him for a big chunk of bread? And why had they already started in on him with the Peugeot? If he'd been knocked off, there would obviously be no money they could have collected. Maybe they had pulled the Peugeot business just to make sure he believed the menace was real—a warning.

Well, he believed them. He believed Alfredo's warning. The danger was there and now it could come from anywhere. The soft balmy Riviera atmosphere was charged with danger. A shot on a dark road, a knife plunged into your gut in some isolated corner—a knife you never saw.

Alfredo almost ran. Arnold realized if he wanted to stop him it would have to be by physical force. Besides, Arnold was now convinced that Alfredo, if he knew anything more, wouldn't tell even under torture.

There were sounds.

Krystina slowly became perceptible in the blossoming light—they had special dimmers in the living room—in a picture hat and soft romantic taffeta gown, radiant with before-the-party anticipation. Or after-fucking glow, take your pick.

"But, darling, you were standing in the dark." Then as though to reassure herself, "I've never known anybody like you who can get *so* tied up in his own thoughts—Aren't you going to tell me how I look?"

"Sure I'm going to tell you how you look. You look gorgeous—"

"Who were you talking to?" Krystina's dress whispered as she moved to him.

155

"Why, the Baron. I was just paying him off." Krystina was not reassured. He managed a bantering tone, "Although why the gini bastard still pushes dope with all the bread his wife's brought him I'll never know."

Krystina, with a touch of mild indignation—she rarely had full-blown emotions, there was always a tinge of pretend, like a child playing at grown-up feelings, until her real self-interest was involved. Then she could be as tough as she needed to be. "Oh, Alfredo doesn't do it for money, you know that. He does it as a favor." The Baronessa Gina was Krystina's only real girlfriend. "Sweetheart, you look funny—"

"It's The Deal."

"All those millions of dollars, well, that must be something. I know you like to think of yourself as a big tough boy, but really, Arnold. Maybe this is out of your depth."

"I never get out of my depth," Arnold said.

Krystina gave him a quick scrutiny, then did last-minute pulling and straightening in the long mirror.

"That kind of water must be full of sharks." Then, delighted by something she remembered, "Sarita told me—do you think it's true? There's a kind of shark that goes straight for a man's balls." She made a hissing sound, then a playful biting movement with her mouth. "*Whsst*, like that. No balls." She moved up so close he felt the cool of her dress, caught her fragrance. "What would I do with a man like you without balls?"

"The French call a man's balls *les bijoux de famille*, 'the family jewels.' I take good care of the family jewels."

"I'm glad. I don't want any sharks stealing our family jewels. Come, Love. They're waiting for us."

"Why don't you have Michel drive you down in the Rolls? I'll be along in a few minutes."

Krystina didn't drive. Not that she couldn't. She drove when he first met her. But now she simply hid the fact that she could so she wouldn't have to do the eternal chauffeuring of hotshot guests to and from the Nice airport—insecure film executives who might consider it a deliberate insult or that they were slipping if neither she nor Arnold met them personally at the airport.

"Krys, I've got a couple of calls to make. I won't be long." She gave him a long soul-searching stare, the one she used when she felt he was coming down with something. "Let's face it," he said lightly. "Our male guests won't give a shit if I ever turn up once you get there. Probably some of the female ones, too. Tell Michel to drive carefully."

"What *is* the matter with you? You know Michel drives like it's a horse and buggy."

"This crazy Fourteenth of July traffic. Tell him to watch it. Especially the 604 Peugeots."

"Oh, them." Apparently she knew about the 604 madness. "I'll tell him." She glanced at herself for an admiring moment in the ornate mirror and saw his reflection.

"I've laid out your shirt, the one that matches my dress, I mean it's made from the same material. Do you really like it?" She whirled, then lifted her dress chin high ostensibly so he could judge the material, but she was completely nude underneath it. "Don't forget to wear that shirt," she said teasingly, then burst into giggles of laughter.

Arnold stared at her creamy belly and the coppery pubic triangle and thought wistfully how good life would have been then if the goddamn organ-grinder hadn't tossed that bomb at him.

"I won't forget," he said.

"Love you."

A quick feathery kiss. He was able to manage a furtive playful caress of her crotch before she dropped her dress, then holding her floppy hat in place with two hands and looking like a commercial for Palmolive, Balenciaga, Pucci and Joy, and giggling soundlessly, she danced her way out.

He watched the Rolls descend the steep driveway, its twinkling red taillights dwindling into the gloom.

Arnold stood in the vast solitary dusk, now alive with menace.

Kill *me,* warm, generous, loving Arnold Elton?

You've got to be kidding.

Okay. So I can be tough as the next guy when it comes to making a sharp deal. But that's business.

And talent. More people read me than the Yellow Pages of the phone book.

I've got three residences, a yacht, my own paperback publishing outfit, a motion-picture producing unit, I'm in the middle of the most important deal of my lifetime. I'm about to take over a studio.

To wind up a corpse in some dark alley? No way. Not now. Not me.

Nobody writes endings like that for guys like me.

I'm a phenomenon. I became an important element in American life. I rid a nation of its sexual hangups. A nation? Maybe the whole Western world.

And I came out of nowhere. What am I saying? Worse than nowhere.

I was a mistake. My half-sister Shirley, my half-brother Myron, my stepmother Henrietta—it wasn't even that they hated me. They just made me feel unwanted. Except maybe my father Nathan. Not that he loved me. He felt guilty about me.

The only one who really loved me was my grandmother Adelheid.

And if you think about it, you can see the beginnings of my talent. There were those "whoppers" I started telling when I was about eight years old. It was Henrietta who called them "whoppers" but anybody with any understanding could have seen a kid with imagination, a born storyteller.

PART II

*"The greatest single word
in the English language..."*

PART II

1.

It was Henrietta who called them "whoppers" and punished him for them. But his eighth birthday, that was the worst.

It was the middle of the Depression but the Eltons went once a month to the Loew's Orpheum Saturday matinee, where a Fanchon and Marco stage show played along with an MGM picture. (Henrietta decided they could afford that one luxury, since Nathan was a bookkeeper and, as she put it, "Only bookkeepers are making a living, figuring out the books on bankruptcies.")

So far Arnold had not been taken along even once to the Orpheum. Henrietta would let him believe he was going, then would stop him at the very last moment.

"I'm asking you," she would address Nate, Myron and Shirley. "Do boys who tell whoppers deserve a Fanchon and Marco?"

But for the first time Arnold was really excited. He

couldn't believe Henrietta would keep him from going on his birthday. He went so far as to get dressed up and vaseline his hair. He was actually going to see a Fanchon and Marco (Boy! It must be really something the way Myron described it, the color, the flashing lights, the half-naked girls in glittering sequined costumes). Arnold had vowed to himself no more whoppers but finally it was Shirley who egged him on—

"Didn' somepn happen to you yesterday?" Though she was only six, Shirley was an accomplished egger-on.

Myron, his hair shiny with Vaseline as always for Fanchon and Marco, was a pretty good prodder himself. "Come on, Arnie, somepn's always happened to you."

"Well, yeah," despite himself he couldn't resist. "There I was coming home from school yesterday, when this Pierce Arrow car, brand new, black and gold with this chauffeur all in uniform sitting out in the open in front—"

"Get to the exciting part," Myron urged, for there was always an exciting part to Arnold's stories.

"Just hold your horses," Arnold loved the way he could keep them spellbound. "Well, see, all I was doin' was crossin' the street, and the chauffeur wasn't lookin', or somepn, but bango! I get knocked down—"

"Run over?" Myron, bug-eyed asked.

For proof Arnold showed a skinned elbow he'd gotten playing stickball.

"Anyhoo" (Arnold got the "anyhoo" from Henrietta), "the nice lady was so sorry, she took me in the car. Lissun, you've never seen the insides of a car like that—full of silver and gold."

"*Real* gold?" Myron breathed, entranced.

"Nacherally real gold," Arnold said. "In a *Pierce Arrow?* Then they took me for a ride around the Common, then they took me to this real fancy ice cream place,

Brailey's, or something, and I had a enormous chocolate sundae—"

Henrietta and Nathan, all dressed and ready for Fanchon and Marco, caught the tail end of the story.

"What kind of whopper is he telling now?" Henrietta demanded.

Myron clammed up. Arnold could punch him in the nose. But Shirley blurted out, "Well, there was some kinda Indian, who shot a fierce arrow at him and hit him in the elbow, and then bought him a chocolate soda."

"I don't want to hear no more," Henrietta said icily and fixing on both Arnold and Nathan at the same time, "what kind of terrible stuff is that to fill a little girl's head with? No wonder she keeps having nightmares." Henrietta didn't even give Arnold a chance to defend himself. She whacked him hard and focused on Nathan.

Arnold still didn't believe Henrietta would keep him from Fanchon and Marco, seeing it was his birthday, but she was relentless.

"I hoped to God for once, now he's eight years old, he wouldn' tell those whoppers, but tell me, Nathan, does a boy who invents whoppers like that deserve a Fanchon and Marco, eighth birthday or not?"

Arnold clung to a forlorn tatter of hope that Nathan would not yield, but no. Nathan, his face grim, went over to the telephone and called Grandmother Adelheid.

Arnold decided once and for all that there were two kinds of people in the world, shtummelwees and the other kind. Shtummelwee was a word that meant nothing but which Adelheid invented to use "in front of the kids" when she didn't want to use a dirty word to express her full contempt for foolish people. Now Arnold knew a shtummelwee was someone who believed there was justice.

163

When the others were gone, Arnold began prudently to tell Adelheid a whopper he judged easy to swallow:

"There was this hole, see, and there was this blind man walking right into the hole only I saved him at the last minute like." Adelheid made no comment so Arnold figured she was ready for headier stuff. "I was walkin' past a factory building—"

"What kine factory building?"

"Oh, just a plain building," Arnold took it in stride, "and suddenly a small suitcase falls out a window drops right next to my feet. So I pick it up and it turns out to be full of money, you never saw so much in your whole life." Adelheid watched him with unusual seriousness. "Some stealers were stealing and the police caught them. And everybody said I deserved to have my picture in the papers."

"I didn' notice your picture in no newspaper," Adelheid commented.

"There was nobody there had a camera," Arnold answered promptly. "Just my luck. Wouldn'tcha just know that?"

Adelheid stopped him. "*Zu viel ist ungesund*," she said. "Today is serious. In the old country people believe eight years is when you can use your *Kopf* and think and reason." She gave him two silver quarters. "I'm goin' to try to teach you somethin' about what is life. Like you ain't rich enough to buy cheap," she began. "Cheap falls to pieces before you get your use out of it. You need something? You wait till you can buy it at the right price. It'll last a hundred times longer. Only the rich can afford cheap they use it twice, three times, okay even six times, throw it away. You can't afford that. Now, you take presents. Presents is something you give, nobody really needs." Arnold listened solemnly, believing he was absorbing real wisdom. He loved Adelheid. She was the only one he trusted. "Henrietta she gives kids sweaters, gloves for presents. That ain't a present. That's clothes.'' Arnold nodded. Adelheid as always was a hundred percent right. The only present Henrietta had ever given him was a made-over pair of Myron's mittens, she'd wrapped in left-over party paper. "Also remember when you got to give a present, keep your eye open, sooner or later you'll find just the article, when it's on *speshul* it's somethin' nobody needs, sometimes it'll come down to half price, I can swear I even saw one speshul like twenty percent of the original price. Then you buy. Like the weddin' present,'' with a slight grimace, "I brung Henrietta and Nathan.'' She pointed to a crystal figure of a nude woman holding a torch high and standing for some reason or other on her tiptoes. "Dreck, but it's the kinda dreck Henrietta likes.'' Arnold loved to sit and stare at that nude figure, and when no one was around, he would walk behind and trace the crystal buttocks with a forefinger. Henrietta caught him at it and called him a dirty boy, and did she make him see stars!

"So now we come to your birthday which is now,'' Adelheid went on. "You know the Greek baker around the corner?'' Arnold knew him well. The Greek was getting really old. "So what do I see, as I pass right now, in his window? A birthday cake *speshul,* like never your whole life you seen, who knows what he first marked it? But now, it's twenty-four cents. So here. One of these two silver quarters is for you to keep—your present. With the other you buy the speshul and bring me back a penny change, you and me we'll have a party.''

The bakery, also a candy store, was full of cakes, cookies and candies. But finally Arnold spotted it, the fanciest cake he'd ever dreamed of, the "speshul.'' The more Arnold looked at it, the more he figured it must of sat in the window a long time, nobody was going to buy a cake like that, it scared people.

"I'll buy it for fifteen cents, you throw in a few jelly beans and a licorice whistle," Arnold said to the weary elderly Greek.

"For fifteen cents," the outraged Greek said passionately, "I'll throw the cake away and you with it."

Arnold held fast. People who screamed never whacked.

"Seventeen cents, I ain't got no more."

"Twenty cents," the elderly Greek said.

"Seventeen," Arnold said stubbornly. "That's all I got." The Greek accepted resignedly, even giving him the candy. Arnold pocketed the eight cents.

"So where's the penny?" Adelheid asked him. He had hidden the jelly beans and licorice in a coat in the hall closet.

"I got a twenty-five cent speshul. The Greek said it was better," then backed away as Adelheid rose in righteous wrath. "It's only a penny, Granma."

Adelheid, the redoubtable Adelheid, stared at Arnold for a long time, but he could even outstare her, and she'd stood up to some well-to-do relatives who'd paid her fare over from Hamburg and expected her to be their house slavey for the rest of her life. Oh no, they didn't do that to her. She'd upped and walked out on them the minute she'd paid them back her fare.

"I'm going to tell you something, Arnold, you ain't going to have an easy life." Arnold understood she was expressing a truth he'd suspected for a long time. He wasn't having an easy life already with the Eltons. The business with the enemas was the worst.

When he had to go to the toilet, Henrietta would come in and stand over him so he couldn't go. So for his own good she took to giving him enemas.

Once on a bitter cold winter day she filled the bag with ice-cold water to clean it of the soap she'd used the last time she'd given him an enema. Adelheid telephoned. Henrietta went off to answer the phone. When she came back, there was the enema bag high on a nail with the rubber tubing and the nozzle attached and naked Arnold lying patiently on the bathroom floor with his ass up. She just stuck the nozzle in Arnold's rectum, pushed it well in and snapped open the metal clamp.

Arnold gasped when the ice-cold water hit but then he always did, only this time he writhed and screamed. It took her quite a while to remember the water was ice-cold, she quick pulled the nozzle out but was so flustered she forgot to squeeze the clamp shut so that the icy water sprayed Arnold's naked back and behind and legs and splashed her good too before she caught the wriggling rubber tube and clamped it off, Arnold was making such a noise you'd think he was being killed.

Later when she reported the incident to Nathan, Myron and Shirley, the latter two listening in fascination, she made it seem like Arnold's fault, he couldn't believe it, and she didn't say anything about the terrible icy pain in his gut.

"There I was trying to give him an enema, ecch, you know how much I hate fooling around down there and he wouldn' hold still I got my self good and soaked. That boy . . ."

Arnold looked up at Henrietta, remembered the icy clutching at his intestines, and for the first time was able to formulate it to himself.

"She don't want me. I ain't really wanted."

Henrietta was looking at Arnold and it was then he developed his plaster expressionless stare. He got so he could outstare anybody in the house, all he did was imagine his face was plaster. It would drive Henrietta nuts.

Arnold was very good at school. (Myron was not.) Nobody made a fuss over Arnold's skipping a grade; when

Myron plain ordinary passed you'd think he'd flown the Atlantic like Lindbergh. And when Henrietta taught them how to type "touch system" she learned at Business School, it was Arnold, not Myron, who became a speed demon, but she never praised him.

"You are going to have to fight," Adelheid went on. "Now come here to me."

Arnold trustfully went to her. He thought she was going to kiss him. After all, it was his eighth birthday but when he got close enough, she grabbed him and hit him with her calloused hand across his face. "I mean you should know what a penny is," Adelheid kept hitting him so hard his lip bled. "That's what a penny is," and kept on even when her hand was stained with blood. "A hundred pennies make a dollar," slap slap slap, stunning, blinding—"a hundred make a hundred dollars, ten times a hundred dollars make a thousand dollars," the passion in her voice accumulated, "twenty times a thousand dollars," this with a particularly hard blow, "*twenty thousand dollars, five percent interest from twenty thousand makes a thousand dollars a year you live like a prince, you schiess on everybody, you don't have no worries, twenty dollars each week the rest of your life.*"

Breathing hard, Arnold understood vaguely she was expressing some kind of dream she'd nurtured for years (If only I had twenty thousand dollars in the bank).

"That's what a penny is," she stopped hitting him, took him to the bathroom, wiped the blood off his mouth.

Then she made Arnold put on his worn coat, they left the house, she took his hand and they walked. She stopped suddenly.

An old man was assiduously going through a garbage can, looking at each stinking object he pulled out, every now and then putting one in his pocket.

"This is what is waiting for you," Adelheid pointed to

168

the old man. "Never forget him. Never. Never. This too is what a penny means."

For a long time they stared at the old man and the garbage can.

Arnold understood that money had a meaning and a power much beyond what it seemed to have, and that of all the people around him, only Adelheid really loved him and wanted him to know how to protect himself.

The next Saturday to everyone's surprise Nathan announced he was taking Arnie to the Orpheum, just the two of them for his birthday.

"His birthday was last week," Henrietta was shocked.

"So we'll celebrate it a week late."

"You already seen the show," Henrietta's voice rose.

"Pretty girls you can look at twice. Go get dressed, Arnold, comb your hair." Nathan, for once in his life, stood firm.

Nathan massaged some of his own Brilliantine into Arnold's hair, then combed it out carefully, not the way Henrietta would yank the comb through the knots in his hair, half-tearing his scalp. It was the first time Nathan had made any kind of intimate gesture, and Arnold had a hunch there was something shtummelwee coming, but he forgot all of that once they were actually inside the Orpheum.

Oh, the unforgettable, never-to-be-rivaled excitement, the buzz of expectation as he and Nathan walked down the carpeted aisle. Arnold had never seen anything like it, the lavish curtains, the lights on the walls, the soft seat, the lights dimming slowly, the awe-inspiring moment when the organ rose magically out of the pit, and the man at the organ played "Blackbird, blackbird, Singin' the blues all day," and wound up with the joyous "Happy Days Are Here Again." Then the curtains slowly parted and the stage burst with a glory Arnold could never have imagined. All those girls, *really* half-naked, Myron and Shirley hadn't even begun to do justice to the glittering colors, the plumed sequined costumes, the fairyland whirling lights as the girls danced and sang with practically no clothes on.

It was then, entranced by the song and dances and the half-naked girls, that Arnold knew that when he grew up he would become part of that world. And with that came a strange conviction. He would show people he had something in him, he didn't know what, but one day he would be somebody and everybody would say "that's Arnold Elton."

After the show, it was like five in the afternoon, Nathan and Arnold stumbled out of the magic Orpheum and into the harsh reality of downtown Boston on a Saturday afternoon, the roaring noise, the cold, the people coughing, men selling apples on street corners.

"Now I'm going to buy you a salami sandwich, with root beer," Nathan took him over to one of the few Jewish delicatessens in Boston. Then Arnold *knew* there was something shtummelwee coming.

"I got something to tell you—you ever wonder how come you and Myron are the same age? You gotta know the truth. The time has come—Arnold—" Nathan belched, he was having difficulty with his pastrami sandwich. "Momma Henrietta is not your real mother and I'm not your real father." The resemblance between the boy and himself was striking, the same small bland gray eyes, the black curly hair, the nondescript nose, the set of the shoulders, Arnold even walked the way he did, characteristics that Myron did not have. (Adelheid, looking at Myron with an open grimace of distaste, "One thousand percent his mother.") "So you see," Nathan mumbled, his collar wet with sweat, "we like adopted you when you were a baby." Henrietta must have briefed him on what you were supposed to say in cases like this, "We *picked* you." Nathan had to answer the question that stuck out like a child putting his fingers to his nose taunting, *Why* had they

170

adopted Arnold when they already had a boy? "I always wanted twin boys, so when Myron was born, I went to the hospital, and what do you know, there you were, born the same day. So we picked you."

Arnold knew that was shtummelwee but he was so deep in enjoyment of his salami sandwich he didn't say anything. (Henrietta had found out he loved salami so they never had salami around the house. "It don't make sense to keep a salami around that boy," Henrietta would say, "leave him for ten seconds with a salami and good-bye Charlie-salami.")

"Who's my real mother?"

"Real, real. They never tell you. I ast when we adopted you, and it's like a rule. It's the people who love you like Momma Henrietta and me who're your real mother and father."

"My real mother jist had me and then went away?"

"Like I said, they don't tell you," Nathan belched again. "Maybe she didn't have the money, maybe she had troubles, who knows?"

"She left me at the hospital. She didn' want me."

"You mustn't think like that of her. Maybe she couldn't help it, Arnold, listen, maybe she couldn't keep you."

"No. She didn' want me. Kin I have another salami sandwich and a Coke?"

Normally Arnold would never have dared ask for a second sandwich. And a *Coke*. Cokes were out. Cokes were an idea of how serious it was. Nathan bought him a second salami sandwich and ordered him a Coke.

After that Henrietta dropped even the pretense of inviting him to their once-a-month Orpheum outings and neither Nathan nor Arnold even bothered to insist.

Besides, something Arnold enjoyed almost as much (of course, not the same) started happening. Adelheid had taught Arnold how to play pinochle. Each time when she came over

171

to sit they would immediately start a game. The way she played either pinochle or hearts with him reinforced the idea that she was preparing him for the future.

Unlike the way Henrietta played war or slapjack or some other kid card game (not like pinochle or hearts, which were real grown-up games), Henrietta always made sure Myron and Shirley won. She even bawled the shit out of Nathan right in front of Arnold one night because, despite his best intentions, Nathan couldn't avoid beating Shirley at casino, she played so lousy. It brought Shirley to loud lamenting and tears. Adelheid, when she played Arnold, was out to win. Period. Gambling was Adelheid's only vice. Twice a week she went for a little "pokerel" with the "girls." She would make Arnold kiss a fifty-cent piece, sometimes a whole silver dollar, for good luck, come all the way to the house for that, claiming Arnold brought her luck (something, which by implication, Shirley and Myron did not). In the beginning when Adelheid first taught Arnold pinochle she invariably beat him, then each time would patiently explain what he'd done wrong.

Arnold learned to watch the cards, then Adelheid's face, and how to figure the odds. He began to beat her at first intermittently, then often enough to put her in a bad humor, although he knew she was also pleased and proud of him—such a kid beating her like a veteran.

She eventually shifted to gin rummy on the grounds that that was a game where he couldn't rely so much on his luck. He would have to think more and she implied he would win less.

One afternoon it dawned on her that he was not only beating her most of the time, but he was now playing to let her win, so she wouldn't be so upset. When she realized that, she reached across the linoleum-covered kitchen table and whacked him so hard she knocked him off the chair.

She said, "When you play cards, you show no mercy."

From then on it was really for blood. He beat her more often than not, and she bragged to Henrietta, "A regular killer, that boy."

Adelheid shifted to two-handed poker with the twos, threes, fours, fives removed, and forced him to play with his own money, explaining that real gambling was only when you played for more than you could afford to lose. For some reason or other neither one saw any contradiction between that and the way she'd impressed on him the value of a penny. To lose at gambling was different. At first she won back the birthday silver quarter, and then some other odd change he'd managed to amass, but then, he not only won back his money but several dollars, pennies at a time.

The Eltons didn't even report it when Arnold, barely fourteen, ran away from home. Henrietta didn't want the police poking around what she called Nathan's "shame."

It was Adelheid who wept and remembered that on his so-called Bar Mitzvah—it was just a quick ceremony in the synagogue (Henrietta didn't want to call attention to two nontwin brothers having their thirteenth birthdays in the same week), Arnold said to her, "You know that speech they made me memorize *Today I am a Jew Today I want to thank my mother and father and my kind teachers Today I am a man and from now on will strive with all my might to be a good man?* Well. I was really thinking about you, Granma, what you told me, I was thinking I'm going to make twenty thousand dollars and never have to worry and if I don't have to worry you won't neither, you'll never be like the garbage can man and so won't I, that's what I was really thinking."

When Arnold left Boston, he had on him twenty-three dollars in paper money, which he carefully hid in his shoes, one dollar and thirty-six cents in coins, which he sealed with a large diaper pin in a pants pocket, and the conviction that nothing terrible would ever happen to him, he was special.

His immediate short-range objective was to get as far away as possible from Henrietta, Myron, Shirley and let's face it, the salami sandwiches notwithstanding, even Nathan. One clear determination was to make Adelheid's twenty thousand dollars; another was to find that something inside himself that was going to make him stand out from everyone else.

He'd hopped what he thought was an empty freight car in the Boston freightyard and was disturbed to discover the car full of bums but they let him get in and asked no questions.

Most of the bums said how the Depression was almost over. One bum said sarcastically it took a war in Europe to pull us out of the Depression, then some other bum said how they were really taking anybody on in the airplane factories on the West Coast, and how it was California Here I Come for him.

Then after that most of them talked fuck of various kinds.

The jokes went on and on. A couple of hours out of Albany, when night fell, the old hobo next to Arnold tried to trick him into some kind of fuck thing. Arnold didn't really understand what it was but when he discovered it meant the old bum sticking his prick up Arnold's ass, Arnold reacted so violently that the old bum moved away from him as though he'd been burned.

No sir, that wasn't for Arnold, nobody was ever going to touch his asshole again that was for sure and the moment the freight car slowed down, Arnold jumped off.

By now it was Cleveland, which to Arnold looked like a city that never took its pants down. A guy who talked like a preacher gave Arnold a job as a soda jerk. The ice cream parlor was in the center of the red-light district and the girls from the neighboring whorehouses sneaked out for a couple of minutes to have an ice cream soda and talk about their work. They barely noticed Arnold except one who went by the name of Agnes (they all had made-up names) and she was

174

small, blond and kind of pretty. Once when the boss wasn't around, Arnold made Agnes a banana split with twice as much ice cream, syrup and banana as he was supposed to use.

"Now that's some fancy banana split," Agnes said, "could choke a horse, ain't sure I can get it all down."

"I just figgered you work so hard," Arnold said, "that maybe you need extra nourishment."

"You wouldn' bulieve what a girl sees, it's an eddication. I could tell you things make your piss turn sour. There's this trick comes up to the joint with a live goose." Agnes practically leaned all the way across the marble counter to deliver that one. "Why even some of the other girls wouldn' bulieve their eyes, and bulieve you me they jist about seen everythin'. Well this goose trick comes walkin' in, the goose squawkin`, all the trick wants is me just standin' there watchin', while he slits that ole goose's throat, then jerks off while the blood is spurtin', then the gism comes spurtin' outa his cock so hard I gotta get outa the way." Arnold was not shocked by that, he just nodded his head wisely as if he knew about such things. That's the way it goes. "There's this other trick comes up carryin' baby clothes in a valise." Arnold liked the professional way she revealed these secrets to him. "Then he dresses himself in them baby clothes lays hisself down ass up, then I got to whop him with a whip, boyohboy a real horsewhip." Agnes got a little bit excited by that. "He gets real fussed if I don't whop him hard, I mean big red marks on his ass, red, then they turn blue. Course when I was a kid I got me strapped across the ass but they never turned blue. Hey, I like talkin' to you anybody can see you're real intelligent." At that, Arnold felt a rush of warmth from his balls up. "Then there's this trick Madame Ella makes me take on, he's real scary, but Madame Ella is kinda around I hope I hope because he ties me up, then I gotta play like he's rapin' me, fight him off and all. He don't ever really hurt none but I kinda prefer the whip man, yeah, and even the goose man. Hell they don't go poundin' away at my tubes and frankly I prefer Frenchin' a trick for the same reason, it saves wear and tear on my tubes.''

For years after that Arnold had the vague notion that women had a kind of rubber tire inner tube in their vaginas.

"Main thing I learned,'' Agnes once confided over a huge pineapple sundae, "is you can't go by looks. You see the goose trick, the whip trick, the rape man on the street you would think they's ordinary guys. It don't show.'' Arnold made a note of that. Something told him it was important. *You couldn't tell by looking at people.*

Agnes looked around, leaned all the way across the marble counter again, a sure sign there was something particularly juicy coming up. "Now you take your boss for example, church-goin' and all, I know you been keepin' books here for him, didn'cha notice?'' As Arnold shook his head, "Why, hells bells, he brings a coupla cases soda pop regular up to the joint, takes it out in trade.''

Arnold was so shocked by that, Agnes hastened to add, "Course he's a normal trick half and half, French and then straight.''

From then on he watched the boss like a hawk and when Arnold caught him taking two cases of soda pop out, carefully noted it in the books under the Expenses column. The next time the boss went through the books, he took one look, fired Arnold, such firing to take effect in the next seconds. Arnold learned another important lesson, that despite what Adelheid had taught him that you mustn't lie, cheat or steal *sometimes it didn't pay to stay too honest.*

Arnold headed west and by the time the war broke out Arnold found himself in Hollywood, where he tried dozens of times to get into one of the movie studios but each time the studio guards would say, "Sorry, Buddy, you gotta have a pass to get in.''

Arnold peered through those gates and couldn't get himself to believe it, but there they were, all those extras dressed in strange exotic costumes and once he actually caught a glimpse of Gary Cooper and his heart pounded. It was the most exciting, glamorous, colorful place in the world, like a thousand Fanchon and Marcos, and he vowed someday he would work there, there was no other place in the world for him, if only he could figure out how to get in.

Arnold finally gave up and got himself a job in an aircraft factory in Burbank.

Lockheed was the first place he worked for a long time that he heard no fuck talk at all. There was the noise, and everybody talked about the war when they had a break; they were mixed, men and women working together, most of them riveting. What with the masks there was almost no chance for any kind of talk at all or really getting to know anybody.

Eventually Arnold met an asshole from Oklahoma whose name was Jimmie-Lou, who added a few details to Arnold's sex education about how if you pulled your prick out in front of a sucking calf and called *suckee, suckee, suckee,* you could get the calf to suck you off. What was more interesting, he told Arnold, if you enlisted in the merchant marine, you could make a shitpot of money. Of course you had to convince them you were over eighteen. The goddamn ships were getting blown ass-over-elbow all over the North Atlantic as fast as the Nazi submarines could torpedo them.

Arnold recalled the only really intimate feeling between Adelheid and Henrietta was when they both discussed how Hitler should be treated when he was caught. Henrietta was for putting him in a cage and displaying him all across America and maybe keeping him starving like the prisoners in the concentration camps, whereas Adelheid was for chopping his head off and throwing all that was left in a garbage can, but Henrietta held out for at least having him run over by a subway train.

When Jimmie-Lou got a distant relative to swear he was eighteen, Arnold, feeling Adelheid would be pleased after all he was going to fight Hitler, picked up a wino in downtown Los Angeles, gave him twenty bucks and the guy swore he was Arnold's father, and that Arnold was eighteen.

The merchant marine enlistment officer looked slightly puzzled when he ran his eyes over Arnold who was barely sixteen. But the confident way Arnold carried himself won the guy over and Arnold was signed on. Besides, the merchant marine was losing more men than they were replacing.

A few weeks later Arnold and Jimmie-Lou found themselves on a Liberty ship part of a North Atlantic convoy, heading for Murmansk.

The regular merchant marine guys played all the standard jokes on the younger guys. They sent Arnold for buckets of steam. They put him on the mail buoy watch—bullshitted him into sitting watch after watch looking at the gray foggy dreary empty ocean searching for a mail buoy, which would have their mail on it, until Calvert, a tall handsome young regular naval officer (one of the two regular navy men each merchantman had on board as gunners), befriended Arnold.

Arnold told him he'd been sitting for hours watching for a mail buoy.

Calvert didn't even laugh. Maybe because there was too much danger around from the Nazi submarine wolf packs that were hounding them, but Calvert explained there was no such thing; that port was left and starboard right; and that the worst thing you could do was throw garbage in the ocean. That way U-boats would pick up your trail. Calvert showed Arnold how when he took his watch in the unbearable heat of the boiler room, you could cook potatoes on the pipes. Since there was no hot water for washing yourself, Calvert taught him to stand upwind to avoid the body stink.

But mostly Arnold saw that the moment the guys had any

time off and more than three got together it was the same as everywhere else across the U.S.A. Shit-scared as everybody was—they all knew by then if their Liberty ship got hit you lasted less than a few minutes in the freezing ocean—they talked fuck. In the morning when they huddled over coffee, in the afternoon, in the evening, during the night watches.

Jimmie-Lou suddenly became a great cocksman with his story about the girl he screwed on the Lockheed swing shift.

"Didn' nobody notice?" some jerk asked in awe.

Jimmie-Lou created unbelieveable whoppers; and this was the asshole who'd confided to Arnold he'd never worn real shoes until he'd started working at Lockheed. And they believed him.

"Noise of all that rivetin' so loud," Jimmie-Lou explained calmly, "nobody paid no attention. Best old humpin' I ever done was right under a wing of one of them B-17s . . ."

Schmidt, an asshole from Minnesota, picked up the talk. "Limey broads sometimes they give it to you for nothin', kind of a patriotic gesture."

When Schmidt told a cockamamy story about getting it for nothing, Arnold was startled how much status it got him. "We're up in her bedroom and I didn' even haf to ast, she comes right out and says, 'What's your pleasure, sailor? Arf and arf, straight French or round-the world?' " Then suddenly to Arnold whom he thus consecrated as the ship's official pain-in-the-ass, "You know what 'round-the-world' is?"

Arnold knew. Agnes had told him. But Schmidt didn't give him a chance. "Round-the-world is you begin with the usual, she sucks you, then you stick it in her ass."

They wanted all the details, they gloried in them. All they asked is that you make them remotely believable.

There they were, sleeping with life-jackets on, Calvert explained to Arnold and the others why the convoy was moving so slowly—they were like sitting ducks because the

179

speed of the convoy was determined by the speed of the slowest ship, and what to do in case they were hit (nothing). Still they wanted Schmidt to go on.

"First I let her suck me a little," Schmidt began. "You kin come too fast, that ain't smart you'll never make it round-the world."

There was a flash from way behind them, then a moment later a booming sound—one of the ships had taken one. "Then I said 'ne'mind the straight, we had the potatoes," Schmidt said, and they all laughed hysterically. "Gimme the real meat, then she spreads some o' the butter I brung her on my dong, boy they ain't seen real butter in years."

"Real butter, whaddya know," Jimmie-Lou said appreciatively.

"Then she turns over on her belly, so's I can shove my cock in kinda slowlike, ram, all the way up her ass," Schmidt made a gesture with his two hands indicating how deep he'd gone, "and boy I kep' shovin' and pullin' until I spurted so hard her back teeth musta been afloat."

Jimmie-Lou, his voice high and cracked with excitement, "Oklahoma gals jes' don' seem to favor that. Tried once, barely got it in, gal kinda yelled and farted."

"Tighter'n pussy. Ain't no comparison, best there is."

There was a moment of silence, which Arnold misinterpreted. They were savoring the images Schmidt had evoked.

"Well yeah," Arnold jumped in, "there was this girl in Cleveland, girl by the name of Agnes . . ."

There was a lightninglike flash and a soft boom, and they all knew the submarine pack was after them for real. Calvert and the other regular navy guy manned the two guns and watched for something nobody would ever see.

Arnold quietly drifted over to Calvert crouched behind the gun. It so happened not only was Calvert from California but he was from Hollywood, the only child of a banker who financed films. "Know my life ambition?" Arnold asked.

"From the way I've seen you take the guys in the crap game—to be a gambler." (Arnold had won several hundred dollars from the boys. He loved craps. He could figure out the odds in his head with lightning speed as the dice changed.)

"Nope—Hollywood."

"Hollywood? What in Hollywood?"

"Anything. As long as it's Hollywood."

They were now zigzagging furiously, as if that did any good.

"You look young. What kind of experience have you had?"

"I was fired out of a meat-packing house in Chicago, couldn't stand the smell of blood—I was walking in twenty below without a dime—and there was this girl named Agnes—"

"I didn't mean that kind of experience."

But the fuck talk kept Arnold's mind off his fear. "Then this convertible drives up there's this blond in it with the top down. She asts me to get in, I can't believe it at first." And suddenly Calvert was listening, deeply absorbed, not questioning, "turns out she's sadlike, her boyfriend was killed at Pearl Harbor, she asts me up to her place, girl by the name of Agnes, did I tell you that? Anyway, she's got this real nice apartment." An excitement Arnold had never known before took over and strangely, communicated itself to Calvert. "I don't tell her I never been with a woman before, tell you the truth, that was my first time, she turns the lights down low, turns the radio on . . ."

Actually Arnold's first and only sexual experience had happened one day when Agnes came running into the ice cream parlor all excited.

"Say, Arnie, there's this one-dollar lay you can buy yourself. But you gotta move fast, she ain't goin' to last long, they're going to beat the shit out of her, run her ass out, she's cuttin' in on business, selling it for a dollar."

There was a long line but finally his turn came.

181

The one-dollar hooker was dumpy and fat and old, at least thirty, and she was all naked when he walked into the trick room. Arnold had never seen a naked adult woman before; Shirley had occasionally teased Myron and him by allowing them sly, ostensibly accidental glimpses of what Myron called her slit.

Arnold was taken aback by the whore's bush of black hair, there was so much of it her crotch was practically square.

"Say," she said after about thirty seconds, "you-all never done this before?" (The legend that hookers were excited by taking a guy's cherry exploded. She was annoyed.) There were at least ten guys waiting. "Come on, boy, you get them pants off." She got on the bed and spread her thighs wide, revealing a pinkish dark vaginal interior, "Now you jes' climb up on top o' me and put yo' dicky-thing raht heah." When Arnold hesitated, she grabbed a banana from a nearby bowl of fruit, "Now watch. Like this," she jammed the banana into her vagina, then pushed and pulled. She forgot about Arnold—kept moving the banana back and forth while Arnold's eyes bulged—breathed hard, made a gasping sound, opened her eyes.

"Fust tahm in a montha' Sundays got me mah jollies off," she confided to Arnold, who by this time had his pants off and had an erection. "Come on here, boy."

Arnold was surprised at how good it felt once he was in her and got going. Finally he ejaculated and it was one of the most exciting experiences of all his life all in all.

"She had this long white dress on, we kissed, then she took her dress off slowly and then our naked bodies rubbed together with the music playing and she kinda shivered and kissed me—"

Calvert was fascinated. "You were lucky," Calvert sighed wistfully. "My first time was with a broken-down New Orleans whore."

The next time there was a lull, the boys let Arnold talk,

and they, too, were fascinated. He retold the story he'd slipped to Calvert. To his utter amazement, details poured out of his mouth. He had no idea where they came from. He described in glowing terms how she'd undressed slowly, and they loved the music idea. He made another important discovery. Romance and fucking went over bigger than just plain fucking, and what was more, once you established the romantic mood, all the details about breasts and buttocks and cunts and how you kissed and slipped it in held them absolutely spellbound.

He became the most popular guy on the ship, the boys kept urging him to tell his Agnes story—even the Oklahoma asshole Jimmie-Lou who knew it was a crock of shit. They couldn't get enough of it, Arnold must've told it about ten times before they got hit.

Among the missing were Calvert, Jimmie-Lou and Schmidt. Arnold and five others were picked up within seconds by a destroyer which had been heaving to almost alongside. But even the seconds were too many. The icy water got to his left hand. From then on, the fingers of his left hand were curled and he couldn't type at the tremendous speed he had had when he was eight.

The first thing Arnold did was to head straight for Hollywood. The next thing he did was to buy himself a whole New York Jewish garlic salami. After that he went to see Mr. and Mrs. Calvert who greeted him like a strange part of their family. Mr. Calvert made a phone call and said to Arnold, "You have an interview for a job at the Associated Artists studio in the Valley."

2.

There was a manpower shortage because of the war and the studios were hiring anybody. Not only was Arnold a war veteran but the Calverts put in a good word and Arnold was taken on as messenger boy. He nearly died when he realized that Hart, the Studio head, knew he was the torpedoed Boy Hero and always greeted him when he passed.

The Studio up close, with all those glittering sets and costumes and girls and Stars—the Scandinavian Blond who was boffing the Studio head—skating in a snowy wonderland next to the swaying coconut palms of the *White Tornado* jungle, where the dark Mexican Star was doing some kind of hula with a volcano spitting fire behind her—once Deanna Durbin asked him to post a letter for her—she was as glamorous as he'd dreamed. No matter how he tried he couldn't figure an angle but he knew that somewhere in that exotic world there had to be a place for him.

It was great being a messenger because you could get to all

the far-flung corners of the studio. If you didn't actually have something to deliver somewhere you wanted to go, you could turn up there and say, "Was there a package to go from here?"

And he ran his ass off hoping somebody would notice him, he wasn't sure for what. That was how he met nice, patient Bernie Zuckerman, head of Accounting; McCabe, head of Publicity; Geisy, the executive producer; Armand Harris, the gangsterish writer with his streets of Chicago wisdom and Larry Blake, the writer who looked like a movie star.

Once, when he delivered a memo to Accounting, Bernie Zuckerman was on the telephone.

"You got nothing to worry about," Bernie said into the telephone, "You get yours *pari passu* with the producer—"

Arnold listened fascinated. Another language. Bernie motioned him to sit down.

When Bernie hung up, Arnold asked, "What's '*pari passu*'?"

"If a star or some other high-priced movie personality wants to gamble on a film," Bernie loved explaining, "he or she defers part of his fee. Once the film is out, '*pari passu*' means that the receipts from the film are distributed to all who risked money in equal parts as it is collected. If the star deferred say five percent of the total cost of the film, the star collects five cents of every dollar the film takes in, the moment the money starts coming in. That's '*pari passu*.' " Bernie should have been a teacher. "The star gets an extra percentage of the profits for taking the gamble. Or sometimes an aging star *has* to defer—when nobody really wants him—And sometimes the star or director—or even the writer—defers because it's a project they have their hearts set on—but the Studio considers it risky. Some of the sleepers got made that way—you know—the big hits the studios didn't believe in and made for peanuts."

Every trip to Bernie Zuckerman's office yielded some more

186

motion-picture technology. When Bernie didn't offer new knowledge, Arnold asked.

"Listen, kid, I'm glad you ask. If you're going to be in this line of work, you've got to know. '*Above the line*' and '*below the line*'?" Arnold nodded, yes, he wanted very much to know. "'*Above the line,*'" Bernie said, "refers to expenses incurred for the creative personnel—actors, directors, writers, producers. '*Below the line*' is all other expenses— like for rental of sound stages, technicians, carpenters, electricians—y'see. I'll tell you what, Arnold, glance at these—" Bernie tossed him some studio contracts to read. "You'll learn more from these than from anything else."

Arnold studied the contracts, and then he asked Bernie more questions.

"How come in the Writers' contracts," Arnold asked, "the studio which buys the Writer's work is 'hereinafter known as the Author'?"

"Copyright laws," he said tersely. "But don't ask me to explain how a studio can be an Author."

"It also says that not only does The Studio own the Writer's work forever, but they can use his writing in films—okay—films—television—who knows when that will be? But, Bernie, they can use his work in all possible devices known, or for Chrissake, as yet *unknown*—"

"You look for logic in the movie world," Bernie said complacently, "you're dead."

Arnold worked hard anticipating services he could perform for the people he thought might be helpful to him, but there was the simple biological fact that he was not boffable—most of the other messengers were pretty girls who were being boffed by one or another of the Studio hierarchy—and there was even some innuendo that Arnold was cutting the boff supply down by preempting a messenger job.

Despite an instinct that told him he was being a jerk,

187

Arnold went to Peter Gorham, who had the vague title Studio Personnel Supervisor, and who'd officially given him the job in the first place.

"I want somethin' better'n messenger. Last time I ast, you said studio policy wouldn' let you give anythin' better to anybody liable for the draft. I just found out, they ain't never goin' to take me. Because if they do, they'd have to go back about me bein' sixteen, in the merchant marine and—"

"I know your story," Gorham cut him off. "Okay. You're a hero. So we gave you a job. There's no other opening for you."

Arnold should have listened to his instinct. Not even instinct, just plain ordinary horseshit sense. For he knew Gorham's background. (Arnold was the kind of kid who picked up all the Studio gossip.)

At a Studio party one of the Studio executives had raped a fifteen-year-old girl. That the executive thought she was eighteen was no excuse. To make matters worse, in an excess of passion he had bitten a nipple off one of the girl's tits. It wasn't anything the Studio could hush up or pay off. Gorham, who'd been at that party (as a drink-pourer), was offered a lifetime job if he took the rap. The girl had been drunk and wasn't sure who it had been.

Gorham had talked it over with his wife. He was twenty-eight and a 4-F on account of diabetes. Three years in the slammer, maybe less. Time off for good behavior and special treatment because of his diabetes. He and his wife had decided it was not too high a price to pay for lifetime security.

He had done two years and three months. The Studio had kept its word scrupulously. They manufactured that Studio Personnel Supervisor job for him but he was stuck. With the motion-picture industry boom, guys no better than he were being made executives but he was permanently fixed in his spot. And he began to have a strange reputation. The top people took him seriously only when he would say "Strictly no talent . . ." But they paid no attention when he recommended anyone. What could that jerko Gorham, who made it only by doing time in the can, know about what was good? So he became known as a guy who could only do you harm. Most people, even the screenwriters over whom he had no immediate power, avoided him. Gorham would have loved to stop in on a screenwriter and throw the shit but they clammed up whenever he came near them. It irritated him that the punk kid was accepted where he was not.

Gorham summoned Arnold to his office.

"Listen, Hero," Gorham said to Arnold, "I'm your boss. You want something you come to me. Don't go sneaking over or under or around me." Gorham sounded like a guy who had done time when he talked that way. "I got half a mind to throw you out on your ass."

Arnold was petrified. Everybody knew the war was practically won, the boys would be coming back and as veterans would be given first priority on all jobs.

"I'm sorry," Arnold said (and when he thought about it later he was again impressed by his strange inborn ability, whenever he was in a really tight spot, to come up with some fast talk that would extricate him, often he'd come out of the ordeal better off. Talk fuck to him and fast, his instinct told him). "Only reason, I got desperate. Listen, Mr. Gorham, I'm in trouble."

"What kind of trouble?" Gorham asked suspiciously.

"There's this babe I been boffing." Immediately there was a flicker of interest in Gorham's eyes. "I won't hide it from you," Arnold realized his whole biology was working for him, he was actually sweating. "She sucks my cock." Gorham practically spasmed to alert attention. "Girl by the name of Agnes. She likes it that way." Gorham was nodding encouragement. "I know she likes it because sometimes when I got my cock in her mouth she pops."

There was a student nurse named Marta who was Norwegian

who occasionally let Arnold make love to her but never in anything but the strictest missionary position. And before each boff she would examine his penis with a professional expertness, nod and make him wash himself thoroughly and she would personally test the condom by blowing it up like a balloon.

"She pops?" Gorham's excitement was growing, then the old suspicion came back. "How do you know she pops if you got your prick in her mouth?"

"She makes sounds like this," Arnold made some buzzing sounds, which were the closest he could come to the sounds of a woman having an orgasm. "And sometimes grabs my hand and shoves it way deep in at the psychological moment, you know, I can feel her."

Gorham was hooked. "You can feel her? She pops from just taking it in her mouth?"

"Convulsions like."

"She knocked up?" Gorham asked hopefully.

"Yeah," Arnold grabbed at that avidly. "Like a horse's ass. I couldn' let well enough alone, I slipped it to her, just couldn't resist, seemed like I was gettin' only potatoes, wanted some meat . . ."

"Yeah, yeah," Gorham encouraged him.

"Came inside of her." Arnold was amazed at Gorham's excitement.

Gorham sighed. "No condom?" Arnold nodded, made a helpless gesture. "Should always use condoms." Then grew a little suspicious. "You say she's a nurse? Nurses ought to know what to do."

Arnold overcame a momentary panic, but then the marvelous inner mechanism came through brilliantly. "Nurses, it's the worst for them, they got to be overcareful. They're watched like hawks, you know—?"

Gorham bought that too.

Gorham gave Arnold a doctor's number and told him to say Sidney sent her.

"Okay, Sidney," Arnold said with a big show of gratitude. "How can I thank you?"

Gorham patted him on the shoulder and said with deep emotion, "If you need anything, kid, don't hesitate."

"Thanks, Mr. Gorham." Arnold was choked with emotion and a gratitude he almost felt, it was so close to the real feeling, it was amazing, even though he was bullshitting, he could feel so deeply. "You've helped me a lot. You've lifted a stone off my neck. Thanks again, Mr. Gorham."

"Don't mention it," Gorham said, also quite emotional now.

Arnold lived for weeks on that, reported almost daily to Gorham. Arnold would go into details, always giving it a slight variation. Then one day Arnold told Gorham that he and Agnes had split up.

What had actually happened was that Arnold had tried to fuck one of Marta's friends, also a student nurse. Her name was Mabel. The condoms widely used then were called the Three Merry Widows, Agnes, Mabel and Becky. Mabel was just as plain as Marta but she had stupendous boobs. Marta had okay boobs, nice ass and cunt hair like corn-fleece, all you had to do was not dwell on her face.

He told Gorham he'd gone from Agnes to Mabel.

"I'm looking for a Becky," Arnold said with a shy grin.

"Say, that's pretty good," Gorham chuckled. He never laughed out loud, the most he permitted himself was a rattle of laughter. "You'll have yourself the three merry widows," Gorham said laughing again, as though he had invented the joke.

Arnold was able to vary the Gorham fuck talk enough so it rode him safely past VE Day, when the Studio scuttlebutt had it, it was sure, the returning heroes would be given all the available jobs. Fortunately, Arnold was able to keep Gorham fascinated even past VJ Day when the Studio sirens sounded triumphantly, people came streaming out of the sound stages, and the writers out of their trailers, kissing, hugging each other. Everybody was honking horns on the Sunset Strip. Beverly Hills was full of champagne garden parties, anybody passing in a car was invited to join the party.

But Arnold knew he desperately needed a break of some kind, and didn't realize it was a break when it did come.

There was to be a convention of exhibitors at the Studio. It was no longer as easy to sell films as it had been during the war. The studios were wooing exhibitors who were now getting choosy.

Although it was strictly speaking not his fault, Gorham goofed. That night on one of the sound stages there was to be a party for five top exhibitors and Gorham's task was to see to it that there were five girls available for them.

All the other studios were having conventions of exhibitors at practically the same time. The old reliables in Gorham's stable had been spoken for. Even the call girls he didn't have direct connections with and whom he could call in a pinch were suddenly not available. There'd been a jurisdictional struggle between the L.A. and the Hollywood vice squads. The L.A. boys were complaining. A disproportionate amount of the payoff was concentrated in the comparatively small area between Hollywood and Beverly Hills. The L.A. boys moved in, knocked off a couple of stars they caught smoking marijuana (the studios had paid off to the Hollywood boys for protection on that) and also caught a couple of minor studio executives in classy Hollywood call houses. The call girls were not taking calls—only from very longtime clients.

So Gorham, who'd never faced a dearth of this kind before, suddenly found himself desperate.

Pale and in a sweat he called Arnold in.

"Lissen, kid, those nurses you been banging? You really been banging them? How much is horseshit?"

"I been banging them." Arnold was firm as a rock.

"Okay then, now think carefully, this is serious, what do they look like are they for example dogs?"

"Dogs? Why I wouldn' fuck no dogs. They're no dogs. You might even say they're pretty."

"All right, Arnold, now listen. I'm desperate. Those nurses always come in bunches. I need five babes for a Studio party tonight. For really important exhibitors, you understand? Now you been bending my ear for months about what a hotshot you are with those nurses. Listen—those girls'll have the time of their lives. You can promise them that. But you understand, you got to come through for me and that's final."

That "that's final" could only mean that either Arnold came through with five babes or he was out. Forever. It didn't even occur to Arnold to bemoan the unfairness of it. He'd learned not to waste time or emotions on situations you couldn't do anything about. On the other hand, if by some miracle Marta had a night off that very night and he was able to persuade her to come and to bring four other babes who happened to have this night off—oh boy—he would have Gorham by the balls. It would inevitably come out that he, Arnold, had pulled it off. Gorham would then be forced to keep him around.

Marta answered almost exactly as Arnold imagined but the most fantastic thing of all was the yell of excitement, "A studio party? A *real* studio party? Why sure, Arnold." Not only would she come but she would get four other of her best girl friends. Why sure they'd put on their very best party dresses, what'd he think, they'd wear their uniforms to a *studio* party?

Gorham insisted Arnold stay with him on the sound stage,

193

Arnold had the feeling Gorham was holding him as a kind of hostage; Gorham was very nervous and made Arnold nervous.

The huge stage had been partitioned off into corners, and there were flowers and booze and tables full of lobster, smoked salmon and cold cuts, and divans placed in odd places. Arnold was straightening out some of the dishes, grabbing a little smoked salmon on the sly when he saw Gorham look over at the stage entrance.

"Once you know them they look good." Arnold felt the icy grab of panic in his guts. Now that he saw them in the studio against all those flowers and that fancy food, he could have kicked himself in the ass. How could he have ever imagined bringing them to a real Studio party? He must have been out of his head. But what was, was, so he clung on desperately, fighting with all he had. "You got to give yourself a chance. Once you get used to them they're not bad."

"Three with goggles." As the girls got steadily closer, Gorham sweated sourly and more profusely. "Holy shit!" he repeated, then took his eyes off them long enough to focus his hatred on Arnold. "You are a prick, Elton, a stupid prick. I tell you we got top-notch exhibitors, big men, and you come up with these bums, these pure dogs." Out of the depths of his misery, as he watched the girls giggling nervously, Gorham dredged up a gem. "That," Gorham said with heartfelt feeling, indicating the girls, "is a sheer waste of five perfectly good cunts."

McCabe, the head of Publicity (he was directly responsible for seeing that these evenings came off as they should), came running in from another sound stage party, an advance man to make sure all was as it should be, stopped, watched the girls as the Studio driver left them at a nearby table and gestured they were to help themselves. The girls glanced uneasily at

Arnold, who hadn't come to them and at Gorham and McCabe, and munched noisily on celery stalks, which they dipped into Roquefort.

Gorham moved over to McCabe, who by now was walking slowly, his eyes riveted in disbelief on the five girls.

"I can explain everything. It's not my idea bringing these dogs," Gorham stuttered in panic. "Dogs. It's this little schmuck Elton I got workin' for us, him, here, he snowed me, I'm going to throw him out so fast, the little schmuck won't know his prick from his elbow."

"Cut that," McCabe said tersely. Like Arnold he was also a realist. "In this business you got to learn to work with what you got. I've had to sell pictures that were worse dogs than them. The trick is to make the guys coming think they're not seeing dogs."

At this point Arnold was in a I'm-going-to-be-thrown-out-on-my-ass-what-can-I-lose-anyway frame of mind. He could afford to be a little pissed off. "Trouble with you guys," Arnold said almost angrily, "you guys are spoiled. I been bangin' them and I tell you—" He didn't back away from Gorham, who looked ready to pounce physically. "Number one, they're great bangs. Secondly," he spoke more rapidly now because he realized he had no time to spare, "you guys don't know any more what real girls look like. They look like them. That's what the girl-next-door really looks like."

Gorham and Arnold stopped. McCabe had a funny look on his face like in a trance, then snapped his fingers. "Yeah, yeah," he said slowly. "Maybe we got something there. We may-just-have—a little something there. Yes, sir."

Before their eyes McCabe became a changed man.

The sound stage door opened and the five exhibitors came in ushered by another studio driver. The five looked expectantly, hungrily ahead. Two were heavily built substantial-looking men in their late forties, the third was a thin executive type who wore glasses and looked vaguely New York, the fourth was short, gray-haired, very tailored, and the fifth was big, fat, bald-headed and in his late thirties.

"Get as much booze into them as fast as you can," McCabe whispered to Gorham. "I'll do the rest." McCabe slipped a big shiny beam of pleasure over his face, rushed over to the men as Arnold and Gorham, paralyzed, watched from a safe distance.

McCabe and the others clapped each other about the shoulders affectionately, shouted joyous insults.

"They can't fire me, they can't fire me," Gorham was murmuring like a prayer almost to himself, thus convincing Arnold for all time that the scuttlebutt about him was true.

McCabe was now escorting the five exhibitors tenderly, as though they were fragile, directing them to the buffet where the five girls huddled absently munching on celery stalks; at that point they looked to Arnold like a herd of some kind of strange-looking birds standing on one leg in zoos and so nervous they might bolt any second. Arnold's heart was pounding as McCabe and the five zeroed in. McCabe seemed to be telling jokes that were not getting laughs. Finally the five stopped, stared at the girls as if deeply puzzled, turned to McCabe for some kind of clarification.

"Gentlemen, I want you to meet our lady guests for this evening," McCabe said with a flourish, "who we invited specially for you." The five now looked obviously from the girls to McCabe, but McCabe was radiating not only hot waves of confidence but of excitement and promise. Gorham was somewhere behind Arnold. (Arnold could always tell when Gorham was behind him the way you can tell when a gun is pointed at you.) Gorham was trying to destroy Arnold with sheer eye-power, but McCabe went right on. "Gentlemen,"—he would have made one hell of an actor—"not starlets. Not glamour sirens, not high-fashion models. No, sir." With humility, tenderness, "Gentlemen," dramatically,

196

"real one hundred percent American girls—the Girls from Next Door."

Both Arnold and Gorham took another look at the five girls—tall, skinny, pigeon-toed, bad-skinned, short, wide-hipped, lordosic, badly dressed. It trembled for a fatal moment on the lip of the abyss of utter incredulity as the five's heads moved as at a tennis match, from McCabe to the girls, back and forth.

Then in a haze Arnold saw the New York type slowly moving over to Marta, taking her hand, his eyes meeting her faintly suspicious gaze. They looked like a weird kind of romantic close-up as he said in deeply respectful tones.

"Ah'm muddy pleased to make your acquaintance." He wasn't from New York at all. He was from Alabama. "Mahnd ef ah jes' say Mistah McCabe heah is raht." His tones almost quivered with reverence. "You *ah* the girl next door."

It went like a house afire after that. Within ten minutes, by the time Gorham had managed to pour a couple of drinks into them, it was wrapped up, made, done.

The five middle-aged men recognized that these girls were for real, something you could never buy. Moreover, the girls were not that easy, they had to be worked on. There was a great bout of playful pushing and slapping of roving hands, which made it all much more exciting, especially since there was always the comforting assurance that you'd eventually make it. Couples gradually drifted off to where the divans with screens had been placed and where for a moment they could recapture their youth.

Toward midnight when it was over, the five exhibitors were mellow and sentimentally grateful. They had had the time of their lives, it had indeed brought waves of nostalgia for their youth, the days they'd had to fight for it. McCabe, Gorham and Arnold were all invited to visit Mobile, Alabama, Kansas City, San Francisco and Chicago, where the five exhibitors promised they'd show them the town like it had never been

197

seen. The Kansas City type whispered with profound gratitude to Arnold, "Tighter'n a mouse's ear. Could barely get it in."

And the girls were thrilled down to their toes. They'd been in a real film studio, eaten all that food and champagne and were given autographed photos of Clark Gable, Gary Cooper, Spencer Tracy, Ronald Colman, Robert Taylor (all quickly and carefully signed by McCabe and Arnold with great flourishes in a secluded part of the sound stage while Gorham kept the girls busy—photographs not only autographed but with things written on them, "Kindest Regards to Mabel from Clark Gable—it rhymes Ha! Ha!" "Fond Memories to Marta," "Sweet Dreams to a Sweet Lady for Mary-Lou from Guess Who"). The girls could hardly wait to get back to their student nurses' quarters and pin the inscribed photos on the walls behind their beds.

The clean-up staff swiftly obliterated all traces of the evening. McCabe, Gorham and Arnold were finally alone. McCabe tossed off two heavy slugs of Scotch one after another, shuddering as the whiskey hit.

"Well," McCabe admitted, "That was close. I'll never forget the moment when those babes first walked in." He shuddered again, without whiskey. "It all goes to prove what I always say. You can make the people believe they're seeing anything you tell them they're seeing."

"Way I figured it," Arnold was very expansive, he'd had a couple of shots too, "guys like them—exhibitors—what do they want? They've had the expensive hookers up to their balls. What they want is Just Plain Jane."

McCabe now eyed Arnold with special interest. "Just plain Jane."

"And another thing I just learned from you, McCabe," Arnold was encouraged to go on, "in Hollywood you hustle what you've got."

"Kid," McCabe said earnestly, "if you've learned that, you're halfway there already. What'd you say your name was?"

"Elton," Arnold said. "Arnold Elton."

"Well, you've got the gray matter and you've got balls, Elton," McCabe said. "From the looks of you I'll betcha you don't want to stay a messenger boy all your life."

"You can say that again, Mr. McCabe," Arnold said.

"I owe you a favor," McCabe said, "the Studio owes you a favor."

Arnold had already learned that that was the most solemn commitment Hollywood could make. There were dozens of stories of studio heads inexplicably loaning out their hottest stars to competitor studios for no reason that fell within ordinary logic.

"Owed them a favor," Armand Harris had explained solemnly to Arnold. When a guy like Armand Harris accepted any code as sacred, it had to be heavy.

"Christ knows this studio can use brains and balls," McCabe went on to Arnold. "You any ideas what you'd like to do?"

Arnold almost panicked, but then he realized this was one of those moments in life that had to be grabbed while they were there. Arnold was surprised by how clearly he was able to think. His answer was needle quick.

"Accounting," Arnold said.

"A ballsy kid like you?" McCabe asked, not believing it at first. "I had half a thought that maybe I could give you a shot at publicity."

That was a temptation, but Arnold remembered what Papa Nathan had said to him. *It's in the numbers in the books, that's where it is.*

Arnold knew now beyond any doubt that he was going to make his life somewhere in this glamorous business. He also

199

knew he was going to make money here, lots of it and he figured he ought to be in the best place to find out how it was done.

"Accounting," this time Arnold called it loud and clear as though answering a merchant marine roll-call.

"Listen, kid," McCabe said, "accounting is a dead-end street. Publicity, you get to meet everybody. You want to make your way in this business, it's publicity."

Arnold knew he had to decide fast. McCabe had one foot poised as though ready to leave. Maybe McCabe was right. Publicity would give him the possibility of jumping around everywhere, getting to know everybody.

"Okay, Publicity," Arnold said at last.

"Good," McCabe said. "You start tomorrow."

Arnold had a little cubbyhole of his own assigned to him. It had been a storage space for old scripts, quickly cleaned up, and a desk and chair and an overhead light installed.

For the first few months Arnold couldn't see that it was much different from being a messenger. In fact he *was* a messenger. McCabe or one of the other studio publicity men would hand him a story they'd written on one of their stars or contract writers. It was Arnold's job to get himself over to the City Room at the *Examiner,* the *Los Angeles Times* or the *Daily News,* and sometimes the *Citizen-News*. He was supposed to plant the items with the City Editors, get them to print it as a news story, but they would take one quick glance at the mimeographed handout and wave him off to the columnists.

He caught glimpses of the legendary columnists, Louella Parsons, Hedda Hopper, Conchita Pignatelli, but he never actually got to know them. As far as he could ever get was their assistants, who would take the handouts without looking at him. He did get to know Jim Henigson at the *Hollywood Reporter* and Irving Hoffman at *Variety*. They began to notice him, exchange cracks with him, read what he had for them, and most of the time toss it directly into their wastebaskets.

"I need something with a little imagination," Jim Henigson said. "Any goddamn thing, but I can't run this shit."

Then Arnold would have to face the PR men at the Studio, who would take it out on him.

From the way McCabe kept looking at him, Arnold realized it had been a mistake not to insist on Accounting. Arnold would have been very comfortable in Accounting with Bernie Zuckerman. Every free moment Arnold had he'd be there in Bernie's office, reading contracts avidly. He began to see that he was the only one in the Studio who really read contracts all the way through. The top Studio lawyers looked only at the clauses in the contract that had to do with money and length of service, and skimmed through the rest. Several times Arnold ferreted out jokers in fine print that might have cost the Studio money, pointed them out to Bernie, who regretted he couldn't give Arnold credit for having discovered them.

Bernie even took time off to discuss Arnold's problem with Publicity. Bernie warned Arnold that there would be periodic crises in the Studio when the word would be that Dead Wood Is Being Cleared Out. What that invariably meant was that a few of the lowest-paid people, like secretaries and messenger girls, would be fired. Also people like Arnold.

Arnold had to figure out some way he could contribute to Publicity.

"The trouble is," Arnold said, "those pricks up in PR just keep turning out the same dull crap. Stories about how Lenka Schmebouble, their Skating Star, was encouraged to skate by her fourth-grade teacher. How Mrs. Shitface McAllister, the wife of our Western Star, accompanied her husband on every one of his rodeo tours, how Lassyhole, our Dog Star, stopped production when she had pups . . ."

"You gotta have an angle," Bernie thought out loud, "why

don't you study the handouts they do take, and work out why it is they take *them*?"

Arnold studied the columns. Louella Parsons and Hedda Hopper had their favorite stars—maybe those stars paid off. A romance that had been dreamed up by the studio flacks broke up. Hedda and Louella printed it. Stars got divorced. Stars had a fight in public. They printed that. What caught Arnold's eye was when they printed handouts about unknowns.

He noticed that whenever Jed Harris or Herman Shumlin, or some lesser-known English producer mentioned he was interested in such and such a young actress or actor, all the columnists jumped on it.

One day Arnold realized that McCabe was going all out to push a starlet he was fucking. None of the guys, including McCabe, could get her into any prominent column.

Arnold had met Walter Winchell's West Coast legman and had bought him a couple of drinks. Arnold got a sudden idea. He sat down and invented an English producer, Sir Loring Paisley.

"Sir Loring Paisley," Arnold wrote, "the eminent British producer of the Globe's Shakespearean productions, has made a flying visit to Hollywood to persuade Associated Artists, who have Yolanda de Haven under contract, to permit her to play Juliet in Sir Loring's upcoming *Romeo and Juliet*."

That night Winchell reported in great excitement that a young American actress was going to star in one of England's most prestigious productions. The next day the Studio was deluged with queries about Yolanda de Haven. Louella wrote a whole paragraph on her. Hedda did a special interview with her. McCabe called Arnold in, congratulated him, and gave him a ten-dollar-a-week raise.

Arnold was in.

McCabe began to use Arnold as a troubleshooter.

The director of a Tallulah Bankhead film had placed Tallulah on a ladder about four feet above the ground; she neglected to wear panties, and the workers on the set complained. They thought it was disrespectful of her to expose her bare backside where they could not avoid seeing it. The top studio personnel had a hasty meeting. Considering Tallulah's temperament they were sure she'd walk off the set. She had to be handled with great tact. Hart, the Studio head, dropped the problem in McCabe's lap. McCabe called in Arnold and dropped it in his lap. Arnold would be easy to fire in case something went wrong.

Arnold listened to McCabe, knocked on Tallulah's dressing room door. She looked at him with distant curiosity.

"Miss Bankhead," Arnold said, "you know that scene when you're up high on a ladder?"

"Yes, I know the scene."

"Well, you're not wearing any panties," Arnold said, "so the men can see your bare ass. It gets them bothered. Could you wear pants, please?"

"Of course," Tallulah said.

McCabe didn't even thank Arnold. It was supposed to be all in Arnold's day's work.

At Christmas Louella made the round of all the studios and collected gifts and checks from the stars and studios.

At Associated she had a drink with the actors, looked at the check.

"I guess you boys don't care what reviews you get," Louella said.

The actors conferred hastily while Louella picked up her Studio check. When she returned to the actors there was a delay until they managed to scrape up a bigger check.

This time she was satisfied with the amount but disgruntled over the loss of time. When she and her driver got back to her limousine, they found that it had been broken into and all the gifts she had collected on her rounds, two mink coats, a pearl necklace and a diamond brooch the four major studios had given her, had been stolen.

She blamed it on the delay at Associated Artists. McCabe was hurriedly called in by Hart, the Studio head. Again McCabe called in Arnold, who was forced to accompany her driver while they made the rounds of the four major studios. Arnold had to explain each time about the theft. It was almost midnight before the four studios managed to duplicate the gifts. Louella looked the duplicated gifts over and wasn't too happy. She was sure some were not as good as the originals. She bawled Arnold out, then went off in a dudgeon.

McCabe just nodded and told Arnold he could go home.

Every now and then Arnold would report that Sir Loring Paisley had made a hurried visit scouting a starlet.

After the sixth time Arnold used Sir Loring, Jim Henigson published an item in his *Hollywood Reporter: The many friends and admirers of the eminent British producer Sir Loring Paisley will be shocked to learn of his sudden death in his sleep last night. London and New York theatrical circles are in deep mourning.*

McCabe called Arnold into his office. Several newspaper wise-asses had sent McCabe telegrams of condolence. His office was loaded with wreaths. McCabe looked at Arnold sourly. McCabe was not a man to appreciate being the butt end of practical jokes of this kind.

Arnold went back to his cubbyhole and did some serious thinking. He wrote a little blurb, *The many admirers of Sir Loring Paisley will be pleased to know that his son, Loring Paisley, Jr., will carry on in his father's tradition.* When McCabe read the announcement, he nodded in satisfaction. Arnold was back in.

But Arnold was shaken. He realized that he'd been lucky so far in Publicity. It was really too nerve-racking. Besides, he would never make any real money at it. He began to look around in earnest for some top spot he could fit into. He began by eliminating the impossible.

It was impossible for him to be a Star. Let's not waste time on that one, fellas.

And as for being a Producer, nobody could really explain how anybody became a Producer, it was clear that most of them had had years of experience in the film industry or in some activity related to it. Or they seemed to have been exhibitors or owners of chains of theaters or were relatives of Studio heads.

It was also impossible for him to be a Director. Aside from the fact he didn't feel himself a Director, no one could really explain how Directors became Directors. Some of them seemed to have come from the theater or worked their way up after years of making shorts or documentary films, others had been cameramen or cutters, and again a few here and there were distant relatives of Studio bigwigs.

The only top slot in the industry that seemed possible was the Writer. Arnold was fascinated by the Writers. From studying the contracts he began to realize that guys who came out of nowhere, who had had some crappy play produced, or a short story published, or sold original unpublished material to the studios, sometimes got jobs starting at a thousand dollars a week. He wasn't sure why, nor was he sure what screenwriters did.

Marta, whom he was still seeing—she was clean, handy and made no demands, never expected to be taken out at night. She had such odd hours as a student nurse that on her nights off she was glad just to stay in. She would even cook a meal for both of them, then they'd hump. She expressed this ignorance clearly, and put it into focus.

"Say, what does a screenwriter do? I mean there's Cary Grant, he always says those funny cute things, I know there's a cameraman who makes the pictures, but what does the screenwriter do?"

Arnold looked into it and found that of all the creative

personnel, high-priced, too, the Writers were the easiest to approach and the most open about what they did.

"So you wanta know what screenwriters do?" Arnold asked one night after they'd humped. Marta nodded eagerly. Anything about the movie world fascinated her, especially after that Studio party and a Studio tour that had been arranged for her through McCabe. It left her buzzing and humming for weeks. *Actually sitting next to Ronald Colman so close I coulda touched him and all those actors in costume I saw you wouldn' believe it Basil Rathbone dressed like Sherlock what's his name the famous English detective.*

"Writers do everything," Arnold told her, "all those cute things Cary Grant says? It's the Writers who think them up. Abbott and Costello?" Again the excited nod from Marta, she was eating it up. "It's Writers think up all those funny gags and words, it's Writers tell the cameraman what he should do—It's all in the script CLOSE-UP (your friend) RONALD COLMAN, 'If I should be the victim of some affliction or some terrible accident and I should lose my memory, I would forget all else.' PAUSE. 'But never you.' PERIOD."

"Gee," Marta whispered.

"Yes, sir, it's the Writers tell the Director how to move the Actors, *medium shot Humphrey Bogart, Lauren Bacall, she walks to the door stops looks suggestively at Bogart,* 'If you want anything, just whistle.' "

"Oh my goodness," Marta was sounding more American by the week, "how do they do that? How can you just sit and think up all that outa your own head?"

How? If you knew that—Wow—

The Writers, who were notoriously eager for any excuse not to face the blank pages in their typewriters, invited him in to watch them at work. Some paced up and down dictating to a secretary as fast as they could, the secretary typing word for word. They were fantastic, those secretaries, they typed like lightning. Sometimes the Writers would say *Strike all that* when the secretaries read back what they'd dictated—*we'll begin all over again*. Some dictated from notes. Others sat down suddenly and wrote furiously longhand. They nearly all belched a great deal and took antacid pills or had ulcers. Some stared out at the bright palm-lined California sunlight, called in their secretaries excitedly, then sent them away. One important writer sat around carefully inking in pubic hair on publicity shots of bathing-suited starlets, explaining he was waiting for his subconscious to come through for him.

Armand Harris wore a black hat and thick-lensed glasses and if you hadn't known he was a screenwriter you would have taken him for a Mafia lawyer. Armand worked only on what he called his own original ideas, and despite the way he looked was talkative and eager to give his particular brand of advice and analysis.

"First thing to understand business-wise," Armand told him, "is where it is for the studios. It's with the Stars. Studios make a product—movies. They got to have guarantees. Stars give 'em a kind of guarantee. So the studios keep all the Stars under contract. So what happens? The Stars eat their heads off, the Studio has to keep turning out movies no matter what. So they have contract Writers, dozens who have to keep grinding the stuff out for the Stars. They're the poor schmucks who get their guts torn out. They got to work on any old piece of shit the studio hands them. Now I'll tell you my secret. I take an old tried-and-true story in public domain, which means you pay nothing for it, but it's stood the test of time, I don't fuck around, I rewrite modern."

Harris had changed the lead character of a classic American play from a man to a woman and nothing much else. The critics hailed Chicagoan Armand Harris as the first American playwright to create a genuine woman heroine.

"Analyze," Armand advised further, "the way I analyzed the Andy Hardy series. Every Hardy picture. One: Someone almost dies, but doesn't. Two: You have to cry at least four times. Three: The girl loves him but he doesn't realize she does. Four: You add five minutes of moralizing at the end and you got yourself a sure-fire Hardy-type story.'' Armand sighed heavily. ''But even if you analyze and follow the tried-and-true, there's still something kills a Writer. What kills a Writer,'' Armand said mournfully, ''is when he's got to wait around for the fuckers to read what he's written and give an opinion. He dies a thousand deaths waiting. You know what my dream is?''

''What's your dream?'' Arnold asked dutifully, he was fascinated.

''My dream,'' Armand said, ''is to work out a way to write screenplays nobody has to read and approve.''

''Hey now, wait,'' Arnold protested, ''a Writer writes words on paper stands to reason people got to read it, there's no way around that.''

''Never take things the way they look on the surface, you follow?'' Armand said moodily. ''Look deeper, there's always a way.''

''You found a way of being paid for writing something nobody'll read?''

''Not yet,'' Armand said gloomily, ''but I'll find it.''

''Sure I'm not bothering you?'' Arnold asked, poking his head into Larry Blake's trailer.

''Nothing bothers me,'' Larry Blake replied. ''Come right in.''

He was glad of any distraction that would take him away from the grinding terror of his assignment.

Larry Blake smoked a pipe and was surprisingly good-looking—people invariably added ''for a Writer''; on the lot everybody was sure he was an actor, maybe a Star.

Larry had been in the marines and had written poems, plays and a long short story or a short novel—depends on how you read it, Larry said—which had been bought by Hollywood.

The trailer was broken into two compartments. In the minuscule part up front, Miss Tweedy, Blake's secretary, sat reading *Silver Screen* and the *Hollywood Reporter* religiously. The writer's compartment had a couch, a table, a desk, a typewriter and an enormous amount of pads, pencils, erasers, typing paper, carbon. "One of the best things getting an assignment as a Writer," Blake advised Arnold, "is even if you're fired, if you play your cards right, you can take home at least a year's supply of stationery and writing materials when you leave."

"Everything I say," Blake pointed to Miss Tweedy, "she takes down in triplicate." He was stretched out on the couch looking up at the trailer ceiling. "Sometimes I like to lie here and think of all the shit in triplicate the Studio has stored up in some warehouse. Acres and acres of shit." Blake's six-foot frame remained practically motionless on the couch. "In case you don't recognize it, you're now seeing a Writer at work in a movie studio. I'm thinking."

Second after second dragged by, Arnold broke into a cold sweat, the only sound was Miss Tweedy turning the pages of *Silver Screen*.

"What are you thinking about?" Arnold asked in desperation.

"Harem," Blake said.

"Harem?"

"That's right, 'Harem.' One word. They gave me one word, 'Harem.' I crapped myself I could do something about Women's Condition. You know," Blake, suddenly off the couch, paced, "Kemal Atatürk, the reform in Turkey, taking women out and into the world. Geisy, you know Geisy, he's my producer?"

"I know him," which meant that Arnold and Bernie

Zuckerman had gone over Geisy's contract carefully. Two thousand dollars a week. "Why does he get two thousand dollars a week?" Arnold asked. "He's got street sense," Bernie Zuckerman said. "What's that?" Arnold kept on. "Beats me," said Bernie Zuckerman. "All I know is the Studio is willing to pay two grand a week for it."

"Geisy said to me," Blake continued, " 'Larry, you want to take the women *out* of the harem? That's serious. Here we been breaking our balls trying to work out ways to get women *into* the harem and you come busting in here telling me you want to take the women *out* of the harem?' What was I thinking of?" Blake asked rhetorically, "Ever imagining in a Hollywood studio I could show something real about the condition of women?"

The seconds rolled by as Blake continued thinking.

"This the way a Writer works?" Arnold asked, in a sweat.

"Yep." Blake got off the couch. "I scratch my ass, I cut my nails, I squeeze blackheads, I pull out ingrown hairs." Blake held up a huge black object. It was the first generation of electric razors and it was powered by an enormous battery. "This helps. It makes dozens of ingrown hairs, I fuck around with my pipe, I scrape it, I clean the stem, I tamp tobacco in, I scratch my ass." He shouted, "And don't put any of that in triplicate, Miss Tweedy."

"Yes, Mr. Blake," Miss Tweedy who had been half up at the first shout, hopeful for some action, quickly sat down.

Blake lowered himself back onto the couch and thought some more. The minutes dragged by like huge weights you pulled. The way the Volga boatmen pulled barges.

"Wow," Arnold said.

"You said it," Blake said, "My biggest problem is not falling asleep. Like Winnie the Pooh I mustn't think myself to sleep. Gorham comes padding in, he wears rubber soles did you know? Finds me asleep, reports it to Geisy's office, they have my ass in a sling."

Arnold could feel Blake's terror. There was a payment coming up on Blake's car and it looked like his wife was going to leave him. He needed to make it on this job.

Blake got up again, scratched his ass, pulled at nonexistent ingrown hairs with a tweezers, squeezed an imaginary blackhead and tamped tobacco into his unlit pipe.

"Bad day," he said. "Nothing comes."

"Jesus Christ. You do that day after day after day?"

"Day after day," Blake said, "until an idea hits."

"What if an idea doesn't hit?"

"Fucked."

Arnold stood it a few minutes more, then fled in terror.

"They say he's a Phi Beta Kappa," Bernie Zuckerman tried to reassure Arnold. "If that's true, he's a sure loser. They say his agent turned deathly pale when he found out Blake was Phi Beta Kappa, warned him never to wear his key where anybody could see it. The kiss of death here."

Arnold went home and thought about Blake and "Harem." He was convinced that somewhere Blake was wrong. He dropped in on Blake a few days later. The word was now out that Blake was hanging by a thread. He'd be out any day. Arnold was sorry. He liked him.

"Can I say something?" Arnold dared only because the situation was so desperate.

"Help yourself," Blake said.

"I don't know shit about stories."

"Then you're already ahead of the game."

"How about this?" Arnold began timidly. He'd remembered Harris's emphatic advice, "Don't fuck around trying to invent new stories. Stick to the tried and true."

The Agnes story that Arnold had told dozens of times all over the world was tried and true. "How about there's this guy—"

He told Blake the Agnes story but instead of Agnes being a

211

beautiful blond in a roadster, she was a beautiful some kind of Turkish broad.

"A Turkish blond?" Blake asked.

"Yeah, like some kinda slave they captured. There's this American sailor he's alone in this Turk town, what's its name? Constantin—"

"—ople."

"Constantinople," Arnold went on, "there's this blond Turkish broad with the veils, she's being carried through the streets in one of them chairs."

"Sedan," Blake said.

"Chairs they carry," Arnold said.

"Sedan," Blake insisted.

"Okay, sedan. She sees the American sailor boy alone, she orders the chair sedan to slow down she drops a note tells the sailor to meet her. See she's fallen in love with the sailor."

"Why?"

"Why what?" Arnold was bewildered.

"Why does she fall in love with the sailor?"

"Because he's Jimmy Stewart or John Payne or Robert Taylor," Arnold answered.

"Okay, okay," Blake said grimly, "go on."

"The sailor meets her at the place she said . . ."

"The sailor read Turkish?"

"Why no," Arnold was pleased and a little frightened at how nimbly his mind turned, swiveled, avoided obstacles like a marvelous broken-field runner. "The note's in English. The Turk broad's really English! She's been kinda kidnapped and maybe she's been sold to this Turk in the slave market." Arnold got excited. A creative fever hit him. "Maybe you can even have a scene in the slave market where she's sold naked. Say, the guys would like that." Blake looked at him without moving his body, his eyes following Arnold, who was now pacing, Blake sometimes having to look down the line of

212

his nose. "That American sailor doesn't believe it at first, here's this beautiful Turk broad invitin' him off the street for a free fuck."

"I don't believe it, either."

"It happened to me," Arnold said stoutly, meeting Blake's eyes.

"I know you were in the merchant marine but I didn't know you were in Turkey."

"In Cleveland," Arnold said, "a girl named Agnes."

"She was driving a roadster with the top down?" Blake asked.

Arnold didn't flinch. "Yeah, she was driving a roadster with the top down."

Blake got up off the couch and looked out the window of the trailer.

Outside on the lot about fifty extras, young girls dressed in snake costumes, paraded past for the serpent sequence in *White Hurricane*. A few seconds later Sherlock Holmes in his deerstalker and pipe, with Dr. Watson at his side, went past. Arnold came up alongside of Blake as they both looked out the window. Sherlock Holmes and Watson in their Edwardian capes were engaged in earnest conversation with Frankenstein's monster. One of the snake girls stopped practically outside the window and pulled out an autograph book from some-where in that skin-tight snake costume ("Only from between her legs," Arnold insisted, "only place it coulda been with-out showing") while Sherlock Holmes signed an autograph absently, continuing the passionate conversation with the monster and Dr. Watson.

"That's what I love about Hollywood," Arnold said wistfully. "My adopted father took me once to the Orpheum in Boston—Fanchon and Marco. I made up my mind I would some day be in show business. It's the most exciting place in the world."

Blake still didn't answer, kept looking out the window, but

what was for sure, he didn't feel the excitement the way Arnold did. "One of the troubles with Blake," Bernie Zuckerman had further diagnosed, "is that he's blasé." Arnold looked up the word.

Arnold made it his business to pick up at least three new words every day. His lack of even a high school diploma weighed heavily on him. He worked every day on his grammar and studied from Dr. Elliot's five-foot shelf, which he'd bought himself, a full high school course, worked on it faithfully every night no matter what, the only time he broke that schedule was for humping Marta, which wasn't as often as Arnold would have liked. Sometimes Marta had the curse and couldn't hump, sometimes her nursing schedule kept her away.

Blake turned and looked steadily at Arnold, who didn't swerve.

"I'll tell you something," Arnold's tone was aggrieved, "I've told that story—thing really happened to me, about Agnes—a lot of times, you're the only guy didn't believe me."

"I've heard that story in various forms at least twenty times," Blake sighed, "once in the air force mess hall in Alaska, five or six times in England, I heard it in the South Pacific, it's a romantic wet dream, about a GI being picked up by this babe in a roadster—"

"Well, just proves what I'm saying," Arnold said hotly, by now half convinced that Agnes had really picked him up in a roadster, "it just proves it's universal."

"Okay. Now tell me how you make it believable."

"You better start right away, everybody knows you only got a few days left. What've you got to lose?"

"My self-respect," Blake said.

"Can you make the next payment on your car with that? In California a man without a car," (another piece of wisdom

214

he'd picked up from Bernie Zuckerman) "is a man without legs. You can always get self-respect some other way."

"You're a ballsy kid all right," Blake sighed again, then went to work on a version of the Agnes-Turk-Constantinople story, sitting in front of the machine typing away furiously, his nose bobbing up and down each time he punched a key. It took him three days, then he gave it to Miss Tweedy, who typed it up in one day. Blake then sent it up to Geisy.

Arnold happened to be in Accounting when he got the flash that Geisy had asked Blake to come up to his Executive Office the very next morning after he'd submitted the treatment, a surprising speed for a verdict.

Bernie Zuckerman shook his head. On a treatment, not a good sign. Usually, when a top producer like Geisy had to make a decision, lay his two-thousand-dollars-a-week job on the line, he took precautions. "Geisy always asks first his girl friend," Bernie Zuckerman went on, "then his gardener, then he gets one of the grips on the sound stage to read it on the sly, then another girl friend and if *she* understands it and likes it, he reads it over again and then he thinks about it for a long time before he gives an answer."

"Maybe he liked it right away," Arnold suggested.

"Maybe," Bernie Zuckerman was doubtful, "anything is possible in Hollywood, but one thing for sure, if he doesn't like it, he'll throw Blake out but fast. Once Geisy even had his assistant seek out a writer, and found him in the can. He told the poor sonofabitch over the toilet while he was taking a crap that he was fired. My opinion is Blake's out, like that." Bernie snapped his fingers.

Arnold shuffled over to Blake's office and waited, surprised at his own tension. Even Miss Tweedy wasn't reading, she sat in her cubicle like she had a rod up her ass. Blake came in just a few minutes after Arnold got there, the session with Geisy had been alarmingly short, Blake moved about in a daze, picking up his personal possessions, he didn't say a word to either Arnold or to Miss Tweedy, who in the suspense of the moment had actually crossed the frontier of her cubicle. Blake finally noticed her. "Will you excuse us, Miss Tweedy?" he said to her. "I have a few words I would like to say to Mr. Elton in private."

"You'll tell me what happened, won't you?" Miss Tweedy transgressed another Secretary-Writer barrier (at least the Blake-Tweedy line).

Blake said sure, and for the first time shut the door between them.

Arnold was now rigid with suspense. "Geisy didn't like the story?"

"Why no," Blake said, "he loved it." Arnold sank down onto the couch. "Not only did he love it, he's prolonging my contract for eight weeks, he's talking about whether or not I want a seven-year contract with the Studio."

"I don't get it. You look like you've leaving—"

"I'm leaving," Blake said, "and for Christ sake don't try to stop me."

"Your car, your wife," Arnold began, but Blake cut him off.

"My car, my wife," Blake almost snarled. "You and I know Geisy's a full-fledged unmitigated irredeemable asshole and goddamnit I couldn't sleep all last night worrying whether that unmitigated asshole Geisy would like it. But what's worse, far worse, is that this morning when Geisy liked it, I felt like singing with joy—" He packed furiously. "I've got to escape, it's now or I'm fucked forever. And don't try to talk me out of it, you're a persuasive kid."

Arnold felt a new strength, a superiority over Blake.

"You're flat on your ass and you're in and you want to piss all that away?"

"I've got to walk out this minute. It's now or never."

216

"You're a schmuck," Arnold was enjoying the power he had over Blake.

"Goddamnit to hell, millions of people will see that bullshit story. I'll be catering to those silly dangerous phony dreams Hollywood sells, I know it sounds pretentious, but I do have principles, I believe we're responsible to those millions all over the world who go to those fucking movies—"

"If you don't do that story, somebody else will, you won't stop Geisy. I'll keep repeating it even if you try to beat my brains out. You're a one hundred percent horse's ass if you walk out." Arnold used a line he'd picked up from Armand Harris, who'd obviously picked it up somewhere else, "You've got to be pretty well educated to be that goddamn stupid."

3.

More than a year later when *Harem* was already playing neighborhood cinemas, Bernie Zuckerman confided to Arnold, "The one place in Hollywood where the truth shines forth naked and unadorned, *really* is in Accounting. Look," he showed Arnold the figures on *Harem*. "No matter how much phony overhead charges are piled on by the Front Office" (the dread mysterious Front Office, which made final decisions, which answered to no one), "no matter that *Harem's* been double-billed with this year's worst dog, covering up for it, they can't stop *Harem* being a real moneymaker, just no question about it, it's this year's biggest grosser."

Blake was suddenly hot. Since he'd directed several college and Little Theater plays he was signed to a long-term Writer-Director contract, moved out of the trailer and into a luxurious office.

Arnold was unaccountably invited to the top Studio Christmas party.

"Unprecedented," Bernie said. "This is the first time in all history that anybody from Publicity made it to the Big Blowout. Something's cooking, Arnold."

But neither he nor Bernie could figure out what it was.

At the party, Blake, looking morose and lighthouse-lonely in an ocean of seething whiskey hilarity and sex, added to Arnold's excitement.

"Are you here, Elton, as a guest or for some other reason?" Blake was close to drunk, he was having trouble with his wife again. "Of course you may use my office," Blake told Harris, who had a very ripe-looking starlet in tow, "but be careful. Slippery when wet, the floor is littered with used condoms." When Harris and the girl had gone, Blake made a makeshift viewfinder with forefingers and thumb and focused on the direction Harris and the girl had taken. "I can see him clearly, very genial and polite, ordering a hit on one of his fellow Mafiosi, or on anybody."

A Top Male Star who made himself known as a crusader for purity in film staggered over with a bubbling messenger girl so low in her teens she probably still gave her age in half years. The Star, speaking with the same passion he used in films when endorsing fundamental American values, asked if he could use Blake's office.

"She hears America singing and wants to join me in the song," he explained. When Blake told him his office had been booked for the next twenty minutes or so, the Top Male Star said, "Too long," and spread his jacket on the floor directly before Blake and Arnold. "Like our rugged pioneer forebears we must live off the countryside." The Top Male Star and the fifteen-and-a-half-year-old proceeded to fuck enthusiastically at Arnold's and Blake's feet.

Blake disregarded the gyrations of the two on the floor. "No one is invited to this unless it's for a special reason."

"Nobody's told me anything," Arnold said excitedly.

"The most rigidly structured hierarchy in any society is

right here in our Hollywood," Blake said as he observed the two grunting bodies on the floor. "Technicians mingle only with technicians, five-hundred-dollar-a-week writers never speak to two-hundred-and-fifty-dollar-a-week writers, thousand-dollar-a-week writers socialize only with thousand-dollar-a-week writers and five-thousand-dollar-a-week writers give interviews. We are here at Olympian levels, reserved exclusively for Stars, Producers, Directors and Important Writers. The more attractive Secretaries—our Miss Tweedy is not among them—and the more seductive Messenger Girls are here, as you may have noted, purely for the purposes of informal fucking. Your presence, Elton, is a signal, a sign from on high, you're passing a class line." The couple on the floor had a noisy orgasm. Blake sighed. "You're destined for bigger things."

A few days later, just before New Year's Day, Geisy called Arnold into his office. Arnold had never been in an Executive Producer's office before. It had its own toilet, kitchen, refrigerator and was half the size of a basketball court.

As usual Geisy was doing many things at the same time. He was studying clippings, making corrections in his gold-edged address book and answering phone calls. A few minutes after the fourth phone call Geisy buzzed for his secretary. Executive Producers like Geisy had what was the ultimate status symbol for Hollywood—unbangable secretaries. It emphasized the importance and quality of their positions. Writers, Directors, Associate Producers tended to have bangable secretaries. Miss Retz, a woman in her forties, was definitely not bangable.

"No phone calls for ten minutes," Geisy commanded.

"Yes, Mr. Geisy," the unbangable Miss Retz gave Arnold a photographic once-over. A young punk like Arnold Elton, who merited a ten-minute-no-telephone-calls sessions, was someone to remember.

"Obits," Geisy held up the clippings. "During the year Miss Retz clips them, just before New Year's I go over the whole year's collection—people more or less close to me who passed on I cross out of my address book." Geisy held up one clipping. "Not exactly a buddy-buddy but close enough to be an obligation, flowers on anniversaries, shit like that." Geisy tore the obituary, dropped the pieces in a nearby wastebasket, carefully crossed out a name, address and phone number, then got down to only two things at the same time, talking to Arnold and crossing out the names of the year's crop of deceased. "At first I had Blake down as a wrongo, Phi Beta Kappa and shit like that, frankly I didn't really expect much—I took him on because I Owed a Favor to his agent. Then Blake comes through with entertainment. That's the name of the game—entertainment."

"*Harem*'s a good, entertaining product," Arnold wanted to show he'd picked up the lingo, was right in there. "Hefty b.o."

"Yeah," Geisy said, "bothered me for a long time," tapping his nose to indicate flair. "Then I solved the mystery." Arnold tensed. "Miss Tweedy told me—a year late but she told me—said you practically outlined the whole story in one session."

"Well, yeah," Arnold's heart was pounding but he played it modest, reluctant to take too much credit, then took it all. "It's a story kinda happened to me, real life."

"Don't tell me you got picked up by a Turk cunt in Constantinople?"

"Well, not exactly," Arnold had enough sense to say, "but I'll tell you, Mr. Geisy, I sort of developed things based on what happened to me."

Geisy was not a man for horseshit. "You want a job, Elton? I got a good feeling about you." Geisy tossed over a manuscript in the standard studio blue folder. "Read that, get back to me after New Year's. Two hundred a week."

222

"I already get two a week in Publicity."

"You really are a ballsy kid," Geisy said, "I'll check it out and if it's true I'll give you two fifty."

Holy Christ he was going to be a screenwriter! But he was scared; something told Arnold he wouldn't cut it, it grabbed him in the gut so badly he had the runs.

McCabe apparently shared that doubt. "No sweat, Arnie, you're always welcome back here in Publicity. I'll save your slot for you. How's the story they gave you?"

It was called "A Guy A Gal and a Mutt" and was supposed to be romantic and funny. There was a Rich Girl who had a Mutt who kept running away from her palatial mansion and tailing over to a Poor Boy where the Mutt preferred the food—hot dogs and beans. The Poor Boy kept bringing the Mutt back to the Rich Girl and finally all three got together.

Arnold didn't believe it at first, kept reading it over and over but that was it.

When Arnold had the runs again, Blake offered to help him but Arnold had an instinct Blake was wrong for it.

"I'll bullshit my way through," Arnold said to himself bleakly as he went up to see Geisy for his first story conference.

The first time Arnold had been on the third floor, the executive floor, he'd noticed a girl sitting behind a desk, but she had no telephone, no pencil or paper, nothing. He'd wondered about that, but had been too nervous to give it serious thought. The second time he was on the third floor the girl was still there, exactly as before. Later, Blake explained her to Arnold, with great relish—he considered her symbolic of Hollywood. Believe it or not when the top Studio art director had redecorated the third floor, he said excitedly, "Here I see a girl sitting behind a desk." So for years a girl had sat behind a desk with absolutely nothing to do. "The best part is," Blake went on with gusto, "that when that girl goes to lunch Miss Tweedy or another girl replaces her.''

Geisy grabbed a walking stick, which was one of his trademarks and paced up and down. There was a complete change in his attitude now that Arnold was working for him at two fifty.

''Here's how I see the story. There's the Cunt,'' Geisy worked himself up. ''And there's Jake the Plumber'' (Blake had forgotten to warn Arnold that all heroines in Geisy's projects were the Cunt and all heroes were Jake the Plumber).

Geisy went on for twenty minutes. Arnold's stomach began to churn again. He didn't understand one word Geisy uttered.

Geisy collapsed into a chair after all that creative effort, ''How'd you like that approach, kid?''

''I kind of didn't understand you,'' Arnold said numbly. ''*I* read something about a guy and a girl, there's this dog.''

''Dog?'' Geisy asked. ''Aren't you Faster Faster?''

Arnold said, ''No. I'm A Guy A Gal and A Mutt.''

''Shit,'' Geisy said, ''wrong story.'' He got another walking stick, paced back and forth for another twenty minutes talking about the Cunt, Jake the Plumber and the Mutt. ''Go write that up,'' he said when he'd finished.

Arnold staggered out of the room, went to the trailer office (he'd inherited both Blake's trailer and Miss Tweedy), stared at the treatment, sprawled on the couch, scratched his ass, clipped his nails, couldn't even hump when Marta was willing, began to take antacid pills, couldn't sleep.

Desperate, he went to Armand Harris, who tried, you had to give him that, but he couldn't remember ever seeing or reading anything remotely like *A Guy A Gal and A Fucking Dog,* for Chrissake, so he was no help, and finally Arnold (again with the runs) realized it was between him and the terrifyingly blank piece of paper in the typewriter. He bought a book called *On Being a Writer,* which recommended that you write first thing in the morning when you got up even before you went to the can, you just let yourself go, your creative juices would flow, just write, get it started.

What came out was a story about the Rich Babe who was on her yacht with her Mutt, and the Poor Guy who was on a Merchant Mariner as a plain sailor, there's a storm, the two ships sink, the Guy makes it to a small uninhabited island with cases of canned hot dogs and beans, while the Girl makes it to another nearby island so close they can talk. She has tins of caviar and champagne. They fight. There are a few storms and a few wild animals to make it exciting until finally in the big scene the Girl swims over to the Guy, who builds a fire. The Girl undresses completely because her clothes are wet, they fuck romantically, the Mutt starts barking, a passing ship sees the fire and comes just as they finish fucking. They get taken back to a big white yacht and the first thing the Girl asks for is hot dogs and beans and she and the Guy kiss while the Mutt looks on happily and you know they're going to get married and be ecstatic from then on.

Miss Tweedy typed it up in triplicate. Every twenty minutes Arnold moved into her cubicle and tried to read some reaction on her face, but the longer she typed the blanker her face became.

Once Miss Tweedy got up from typing and moved from *her* cubicle into Arnold's side of the trailer and stared at *him*. He even encouraged her by asking "Yes?" but all she said was, "No, no, nothing," and went back to her typing. Three days later the hundred and twenty pages were typed and delivered to Geisy by one of the cute messenger girls.

Geisy called Arnold immediately. In the light of the speedy reaction Blake had gotten, maybe—maybe it was a good sign.

Arnold walked up the three flights, hoping the effort would make him less nervous.

"I couldn't believe my eyes," Geisy didn't even bother with his walking stick, "you been at the Studio all these years and you not only give me a naked Cunt but you have her fucking with Jake the Plumber. We can't have people fucking. Don't you know about the fucking censorship? The Hays Code? Where the hell you been? You're not even housebroke."

Geisy fired him on the spot, Arnold went back to Publicity.

It was Blake Arnold sought out for the ritual commiseration drink. Blake went through the standard consoling-writers routine about how Geisy was a notorious putz as were most Hollywood Producers, and how after all this was Arnold's first try, but it brought Arnold only scant comfort.

"I'm surprised how much shook up I am," Arnold said, "you know what, Larry, I really wanted it, you know what I must of thought—there was going to be some kind of a miracle. Shit, I still want to make it, that's really what I want. I know I got something in me. I know I can make it."

"Hey now, Arnold," Blake said with sudden inspiration, "who says you've got to be a screenwriter? Maybe you should be a *writer?* Who's going to stop you from writing on your own, something you've really experienced? The stories you've told me, how many guys are there who've gone down in a Liberty ship in the North Atlantic? Why don't you write a book about that?"

"What do I know about writing books?"

"What does anybody?" Blake asked. "And you won't have a putz Producer like Geisy standing over you, no Hays Code and, what's more, I'll help you, only whatever you do, write true."

The idea slowly took hold. What was the harm in trying? Besides, maybe he hadn't been wrong and wasn't wrong now in his gut conviction he could write.

"Your train is in the station but it's on the wrong track." Armand Harris was so utterly disinterested in anything that did not affect him directly that his opinion carried great weight. "Fuck that crap of Blake's about writing only what you've experienced, you really want to cook with gas, plunk your ass down, read some of the best-sellers, just pick out what you can use, change a few things, use only tried and true."

The Studio had just bought a big best-seller called *Tiger Tiger Burning Bright*. Arnold got himself a copy and read it all in almost one sitting.

Marta came over the night he'd finished reading it.

"You know something? I think I can write a book like that."

Marta took that as an affront, almost an insult.

"Yah, you think so? People pay fifty thousand dollars for somethin', you think it can be easy?"

Marta grabbed the book from the end table and plunged into it. It was a very sentimental love story and Marta was so absorbed by it that humping was completely out of the question.

For days after that she'd get on his bed and before Arnold could say or do anything, she would be into the novel. He'd never seen anything like it. She would be lost to the world. She would weep and steadfastly refuse to hump.

He tried sneaking up on her as she lay curled on the bed, his hand moving up her thigh. At first she seemed not to notice, but when his fingers worked themselves up to her panties and under the elastic band and downward, she lowered the book. When his fingers moved swiftly into her vagina, she looked at him severely.

"What're you doing, Arnold? What do you think you're doing?"

"You know what I'm doing," Arnold held his arm grimly in place, his fingers stubbornly in the moist aperture.

"I'm asking a question of you, Arnold. I'm asking of you a plain simple question."

Christ, she was beginning to sound like Momma Henrietta.

"If you want to know I thought maybe we'd hump," Arnold said.

"Here I am reading a beautiful book and you come in with your dirty talk." She pushed him away violently. "Hump!"

But on the night she was hungrily reading the very last part, she was so caught up in it, she not only let him get his hand into her panties and into her vagina, she even let him make back-and-forth movements until she was stimulated into dainty spasms, sighed, tears streaming down her cheeks as she read the end.

She then lay on her side slightly curled up, letting Arnold get on the bed and lie alongside of her as she burst into sobs, "So beautiful, so sad."

He took her in his arms and made hushing comforting sounds. She clutched at him, kissed him passionately, her lips tangy with the taste of tears. Still sobbing she let him undress her, his consoling hands roaming over her breasts and belly as he kept whispering, "Yeah, yeah, it's okay." But she sobbed even louder. For a moment, Arnold worried the neighbors might hear, but then they were humping and the sobbing stopped. Marta humped ferociously. She'd never had an orgasm as powerful before.

He thought about that a lot and decided that people liked to cry almost as much as they liked to hump, and then made another, more important, discovery: crying and humping were related. What a great combination that would make, crying and sad, romantic humping.

He knew it was right, then suddenly he was at his Royal portable.

The words poured out of him. The Agnes story, as Armand Harris advised, that was something tried and true. And he took Blake's counsel to tell the story against a background he knew, the merchant marine. He told *that* very true. And he remembered a rumor that had shaken the guys aboard, that Betty Grable had actually personally made a surprise visit to

228

one of the merchant mariners in midocean right smack during the war.

Arnold altered Agnes into a movie star and had a hero, Stevie, sort of based on Arnold in that he was an orphan and a kind of self-effacing guy. The Agnes-Movie Star comes in on a ship-to-ship line unexpectedly to boost morale. To make it sound real, Arnold had one of the boys, the Oklahoma asshole, belittle it all as a publicity stunt. But no, it's for real. She is there to help the War Effort.

Then she sees Stevie.

Right there in the middle of an ocean infested with Nazi submarine wolf packs, something neither one of them expected or understood happens. A magic flows between them and she asks that Stevie be invited to lunch at the captain's table. Everybody on board is dazed. Stevie can't believe it.

Before she leaves, she takes Stevie aside, hugs him and slips him a number in Beverly Hills. The Okie asshole again says it's all publicity, and Stevie would be a jerk to swallow it, but Stevie has faith. Then the ship is hit and all aboard are presumed lost. The Agnes–Hollywood Movie Star makes a sad statement to the press how she knew one of them, a sweet boy named Stevie. But Stevie is miraculously picked up, he and the Okie asshole and Schmidt, it was easy to describe how they talked (he made that part true too), Arnold could hear them, Stevie is taken to a hospital in San Diego. He makes his way to Beverly Hills, calls the number the Agnes-Movie Star gave him and they meet secretly. The Agnes-Movie Star doesn't tell him why they have to meet secretly, but they spend a night together, they hump beautifully, sadly, passionately. In the middle of the night Stevie hears Agnes-Movie Star crying, but doesn't ask why, instead they cling to each other and she keeps saying over and over, in a whisper, I love you, love you, love you, Stevie, then they discover that they are both orphans, they hump again tenderly, passionately. They have a tear-stained orgasm, Stevie, blissfully happy, says he can't live without her and she says yes, yes, and falls asleep in his arms, her soft breasts and nipples cool against his chest, but in the morning when he wakes up, she is gone.

Arnold got stuck for an ending. He told Armand Harris he wanted the saddest, most romantic ending of all time. Armand said without hesitation, Emil Jannings in *The Way of All Flesh*. Bernie Zuckerman arranged a projection of the film. Armand was right. The saddest ending Arnold had ever seen was when Jannings looks through the living room window and sees his love and her husband and their children all together around the Christmas tree so intimate. Even though Jannings knows she is the one love of his life, and he's the one love of hers, he just stands there. She turns toward the window, Does she see him? You never know, that's a heart-breaking moment, too. With snowflakes falling Jannings moves away from his love back to his eternal loneliness.

If it could move Arnold to tears in that crappy studio projection room, it would make anybody cry.

So Stevie, after heartbreaking persistence, searches doggedly, and finds her house.

It's Christmas and the first snow in thirty years in Southern California. Stevie looks through the window from the lawn of her Beverly Hills home, there is snow on the oranges, realizes her secret. She's married and has a child. It's been kept a secret. Studios in those days didn't like their female stars married or even worse, mothers. She'd been married when she was sixteen; he stares sadly à la Jannings through the fantastic snowfall. Then Stevie goes over to an orange tree, tears off a leaf, rubs the leaf, smells it, the fragrance of orange fills his nostrils, his mind goes back to an earlier scene, tender and romantic, when Stevie and the Movie Star were in Palm Springs, he for the first time.

It was based on a scene that Arnold took from his own life. He had driven Marta in his battered De Soto ex-taxi limousine out to the desert to see the cactus in bloom. He stopped the car in amazement.

"Just look at that, Marta" (in awe), "look at that."

"Look at what?"

"There, there—"

"Where?"

"There—" (irritably) "that tree."

"Tree?"

"Tree, goddamnit! *It's got real grapefruits on it.*"

"Well sure, it's a grapefruit tree, why're you so surprised? Where did you think grapefruits come from?"

"The supermarkets, that's where."

A tanned older guy in shorts, who owned the place, watched in benevolent understanding. It must have happened before. "Gee whiz!" Arnold said, "grapefruit on a tree!"

The old guy carefully picked two grapefruit, one for Arnold and one for Marta.

"You young people eat them right now fast before they lose their vitamins and minerals and their flavor, yes sir, while they still got the goodness of the sun in them. You have never *tasted* grapefruit before." The two ate the grapefruit while they were still warm.

"You're right, sir," Arnold said, "I never have."

"Nor me," Marta said.

The old guy, some kind of a sun, dates-and-nuts nut, pulled a leaf off an orange tree, rubbed it in his fingers and said "Smell that," and the air was filled with the fragrance of oranges.

Stevie smells the orange on the lawn of the Agnes-Movie Star's home and walks away from his love to sign up again for the loneliness and danger of the North Atlantic.

Blake was the first person he gave the book to—Blake's wife had definitely left him—he had rented a crazy house on

Beachwood Drive. It had an open study in the backyard with a fireplace and no fourth wall and a tree growing through the roof. It was there Blake and Arnold talked.

Blake kept looking at Arnold oddly. Arnold was so anxious that unlike other writers (Blake had once explained the last thing a writer does is to ask you directly, "Did you like it?" They're too scared), Arnold asked right away, "Did you like it?"

Blake got up, scratched his ass, picked up his pipe, "What do you want, Elton? Why did you write that?"

"You make it sound like I did something wrong."

"Do you want to make money, is that it?"

"Well, sure," Arnold was bewildered by the question, "Doesn't everybody?"

"You will," Blake said, scratching his ass again. "People will read your book, they'll cry, it's one big sob after another and girls who've never read a book before will read yours, cry, sob and maybe even romantically cream their pants."

Arnold was stunned, baffled, suspicious.

"Then what's the matter?"

"The matter," Blake's voice rose steadily, Arnold had never seen him that excited before, "is that some of it is real, true! Some of it is fine writing! You can write, goddamn it! But then the rest of it is a big goddamn lie! That's what the matter is!" He controlled himself. "It makes the mind boggle, you were so fucking young and yet you tell about the guys getting killed, the killing, and it's real. And then, what do you do? You make it sad and sweet and romantic."

"Wait a minute! Wait a minute!" Arnold cut in urgently. "You did say people will buy the book?"

"Yeah, yeah, yeah!" Blake started to yell. "I said they'd buy the book and that's all you want to hear, but you know as well as I do that war is not sad or sweet or romantic! It's blood and shit and pain and screaming and terror, what about the guys you knew, your buddies, you saw them get knocked

232

off? And what about the buddies got blinded or burnt they're now at the Sawtelle Veterans' Home?''

"Nobody wants to know about them," Arnold said with a crazy elation. "It's tough titty for them. But you did say I'd make money."

"You'll make money," Blake said, spent. "I was trying to tell you you had the stuff in you to write a fine novel about the war, about the merchant marine, oh shit, a fine novel." He stopped Arnold's protests. "Okay. Okay. I know. It's tough titty for the losers, nobody wants to hear about them, like Geisy says, That's not entertainment." He stared at Arnold a long time. "Just once more, Elton. You understand this is a kind of crossroads for you? You choose one way and that'll be your way the rest of your life."

"You promised you'd help me."

Blake made a resigned gesture. "I will. Who am I to talk? Don't worry," Blake said quietly. "I'll not only correct the grammar and the spelling, but I'll edit it."

Sirens suddenly went off in Arnold's head. He was having his own VJ Day—a VAE Day, Victory for Arnold Elton Day. Here was Lawrence Blake, Lawrence Blake, for Chrissake, telling him that not only would his book be published, it would be successful. Blake would even help him with it. Arnold didn't want to hear anything else. He tried to calm himself down. There had to be something wrong.

"What will you want for doing it, helping me?"

"Nothing." Blake seemed to be miserable. "After what you did for me on *Harem,* as they say here in Nowheresville I Owe You A Favor. Only—" Arnold held his breath. "I don't want anybody to know I had anything to do with it. Okay?"

"Okay," Arnold said with passionate sincerity. "And I'll tell you what, Larry. I'll put in more tough stuff about the war."

After Blake had gone over the first version, Arnold included several more scenes of warfare, the grim suspense of capricious bloody violence, exploding suddenly, tearing off heads and shattering bodies.

Blake fulfilled his promise and even got his agent Johnny Farina to handle the book.

A month later, when Arnold was in his favorite haunt, Bernie Zuckerman's office, a call was transferred to him there. Only urgent calls were transferred for employees like Arnold Elton.

It was Johnny Farina's secretary. She was crisp and businesslike. Mr. Farina would like Arnold Elton to be at his office at five o'clock that afternoon.

"I don't get off till six," Arnold said nervously.

"Mr. Farina has you penciled in for five o'clock," the secretary said. "You'd better arrange to be here then."

She sounded stern and unrelenting.

"McCabe won't mind," Bernie said, "it must be important. Maybe it's good news about your book."

Arnold refused to let himself get excited. "Stands to reason if they have good news, she'da told me."

"Nothing stands to reason in this business," Bernie Zuckerman said.

Farina's inner office was huge and luxurious. Wood panelling. Bar. The first real fireplace Arnold had seen in California. Most California fireplaces you couldn't burn anything in them, they were just for decoration. There were pictures of stars all over the walls, each one inscribed with love or affection and gratitude to Johnny.

Arnold's heart was pounding like a Liberty ship engine under full steam. Johnny waved Arnold into an armchair, stared at him while he took five phone calls in a row.

Finally Johnny hung up, poured himself a drink, but didn't ask Arnold if he wanted one. Arnold was sure that was a bad sign.

"Well, kid," Farina said, "I got news for you."

He sipped his drink, took his time enjoying it.

"Good news?"

"I would call it good news," Farina said. "I would call it wonderful news. I would call it fantastic news."

Johnny was a sharply handsome black-haired man. "One of the biggest publishing houses has accepted it." Arnold turned pale, leaned back in the large chair.

"Accepted?" Arnold's voice cracked.

"Accepted."

"They're going to publish it?"

"Yep," Johnny said. "They want a few changes but nothing much. In fact we were all surprised how few changes they wanted, especially for a first book. How do you like that?"

"I like it, Mr. Farina."

"You should," Johnny said grimly.

"I do," Arnold said.

"We want you to sign a contract with us," Johnny said. "We want exclusive rights to handle you for the next seven years."

"Okay," Arnold said numbly. "Are they going to pay me any money? The publishers?"

"We managed to get you a five-hundred-dollar advance," Johnny said. Arnold just sat there. "Listen, you're lucky they're going to publish it."

Arnold realized he'd had vague dreams of making a lot of money. Still. Five hundred dollars was five hundred dollars.

"On your next one we'll get you more," Johnny promised.

"Okay," Arnold said.

"Congratulations, kid," Farina shook his hand, "you're going to have a book published."

"I want my picture on the dust jacket," Arnold said.

"I'll see what I can do," Farina said. "Bring a photograph and sign this contract."

Farina slipped a document under his nose.

Arnold started to read it carefully.

"It's a standard contract," Farina said impatiently.

"I always read contracts," Arnold said.

"Okay," Farina said shortly, "take it home and read it."

Arnold kept working in Publicity. He was already working on his second book, even though he and Bernie Zuckerman went through the publishing contract and it was obvious he wouldn't get very much more than the advance from the book sales. If the movies bought it, it would be a different story. And of course if it was a good seller, that would be different. Arnold wasn't counting on anything, but McCabe had promised he would help with the publicity.

When the book came out that fall, Martindale's in Hollywood devoted a whole window to him.

There was a cocktail party given, Arnold thought it was for him, by Marian Hunter's in Beverly Hills. That was really coming up in the world. Bernie Zuckerman said, and went to it.

The only trouble was nobody seemed to know who Arnold was, despite the fact that his picture was on the dust jacket. It seemed to Arnold and Bernie that it was more a gathering of other writers, mostly ladies who seemed to have written sad love stories. As far as Arnold and Bernie could make out, there were no book buyers there.

One of the lady novelists introduced herself to Arnold in the excitement of the evening.

"I am Naomi Swet Winters," the lady said. "I write. What do you do?"

"I'm a dentist from Kansas City," Arnold said, "and this is my uncle, Dr. Zuckerman. Bernard Y. Zuckerman. He's a cat and dog doctor. This is Miss Naomi Swet Winters who writes."

Bernie shook hands with her gravely, and Bernie and Arnold left.

"Don't worry, kid," Bernie said as they stopped at Delhaven's for some cheesecake, "someday you'll be recognized."

Even though it got practically no reviews, it sold surprisingly well for a first novel. The publishers reported that it was extremely popular with lending libraries. As Blake had predicted, the people who read it loved the sad love and humping, thrilled to the terror and violence they could enjoy in comfort and security, and wept at the snowflakes falling in the Beverly Hills scene. Every now and then Arnold's heart leaped as he said, "Jesus Christ, I've got a book published, I'm a writer." He could walk in a crowd and feel superior although they couldn't tell by looking at him he had written a novel. He'd always thought that if he actually got a book published, his whole life would change. He could take it easy, the royalties would roll in. Small royalties rolled in, but it was not like he'd hoped.

So Arnold kept working in Publicity. Nearly everybody he knew expected him to give him or her a free autographed copy.

One day McCabe poked his head into Arnold's cubbyhole.

"Hey, Shakespeare, Geisy wants to see you."

" 'Geisy'? Again? No kidding?"

"Hang tough. That's all I can say," McCabe said enigmatically, "without being disloyal to the Studio. Hang tough."

"I just read your property," Geisy said briskly as Arnold walked in warily. "What's it, again?"

Arnold thought, He sure as hell knows what it is. "*Guns of Love.*"

"I want to make a deal for it." Arnold could barely believe his ears. "Now I'll tell you how I work. You name a price, I say I buy or I say fuck off. That's it, you understand?"

Arnold watched him even more suspiciously. "I don't want games," Geisy went on. "Agents sending properties to all the studios and getting studios to bid against each other, cutting each other's throats. Horseshit. I know Johnny Farina's handling you but I want to do business with *you*."

Farina had had a long and earnest conversation with Arnold after they'd signed.

Don't ever make a move of any kind, especially moneywise, except through the agency, understand, Arnold?

"I'm laying it out on the line for you," Geisy said. "You got a price in mind for your property?"

"I sure have, I don't need Johnny Farina or anybody else to tell me." Suddenly Adelheid was alongside of him, nodding in approval, slapping him, her hand covered with blood. "I want twenty thousand dollars."

"You've never been published before, this is your first—" Arnold got up, started to leave.

"Where do you think you're going?"

"You told me it would be 'yes' or 'fuck off.' "

"Say you're pretty cocky for a first property."

"I just took you at your word," Arnold again started toward the door, hoping the way he was shaking wouldn't show. Farina had had doubts about anybody buying the book for a movie.

"Elton!" Geisy called. Arnold stopped, turned. Geisy held his hand out. Arnold floated over to him, he was practically paralyzed. Geisy shook his hand.

"You're probably the first writer in all time to get twenty thousand on his first property. You want to do the screenplay?"

"Oh no. The twenty thousand dollars is fine with me."

The moment he got out of Geisy's office he broke into a run, first into Accounting, grabbed Bernie Zuckerman, who was short, sturdy, black-haired and blue-eyed, and the last guy in the world you'd grab.

"Twenty."

"Twenty?"

"Twenty thousand dollars. Twenty thousand dollars." He started out of the office, stopped, grabbed Bernie Zuckerman again. "Twenty g's."

"Jesus Christ. Where you running to?"

"Home."

"You quitting Publicity?"

"No, no. I'm going to put in a call to Boston. Granma Adelheid. I want to tell her."

"Call from here. We'll charge it to you later."

Nathan Elton answered the telephone.

"Arnold! How are you, Arnold?" Then shouted to the others, "Henrietta! Myron! Shirley! It's Arnold! He's calling from Hollywood! Come on, will ya!" Then into the telephone, "Arnold? Henrietta and I read your novel, boy, are all the neighbors talking. Hot stuff. Momma Henrietta won't let Shirley read it, but I read it, it's good. Everybody's talking about it, you can imagine."

"I sold the book to the movies. For twenty thousand dollars."

"How much?"

"Twenty thousand dollars."

"What?" Arnold heard him tell the others. "Arnie's sold his story for twenty thousand dollars to the movies." There were cries of shock? delight?

Then Henrietta's voice, "How much?"

"Twenty thousand dollars."

"Oh my God! How much? Twenty thousand. I knew. Such an imagination. The stories you used to make up. I knew all along that something special would be." Nathan must have grabbed the phone from her.

Nathan, savagely, "Arnie, you get a good tax man? You hear me? Get a good tax man."

"It's all taken care of."

"You need a tax man," Nathan was yelling. "Otherwise the government takes it all away from you. You get left with dreck. Arnold, I never said much to you before, but now I'm speaking to you as a father to his son, *Get a good tax man*! If you don't do nothing else, get a good tax man!"

"Writers are allowed to spread it over three years. So I'll keep a lot more than dreck. It's all taken care of, don't worry."

"I am worried!" Nathan yelled. "Without a good tax man—"

"Granma," Arnold managed to get in. "Granma Adelheid. Hello? Hello? Hey, operator, I been cut off—"

"No, you haven't been cut off, Arnie," Nathan's voice came low and slow, "I'm here."

"Tell Granma to come to the house," Arnold yelled. The call was going to cost a fortune. "I'll call like ten o'clock Boston time, later today."

"She's dead." Nathan was crying. "Your grandmother Adelheid died three weeks ago. I wrote you a letter. Didn't you get it?"

"I've changed addresses. I don't live where I lived before."

"Heart attack," Henrietta's voice, "I been after her for months to see the doctor she wouldn't listen, Arnold—"

Arnold had hung up.

"What's the matter?" Bernie Zuckerman looked scared.

"Adelheid," Arnold stared at the mute phone in its cradle. "She was my grandmother. Everybody writes for like one person, you have one person's face in your mind." He put his head down near the telephone. "She's the one I been writing for."

As Arnold sat absently chomping kosher salami, the words surged up from his balls, shot through his gut—hunt and peck, he could knock out ninety words a minute despite his curled left hand. It was hard to keep up, there was so much to tell—places, ideas, wisecracks, gags, emotions.

The second book was kicking, writhing, struggling to be born. "Once I'm working at the typewriter," Arnold had told Harris, "you could shove a red-hot poker up my ass, I wouldn't know it. It takes over one hundred percent, like when you're fucking" (at that Harris had registered a trace of skepticism, but it was true).

Yet now, gradually, he was forced to recognize that his doorbell chimes were sounding.

Somebody was at the front door. There was always somebody at the door, sharp young types who claimed they were working their way through college selling magazines, vacuum cleaner salesmen, out-and-out nuts.

Once again those silly chimes vibrated with sonorous insistence.

The only time he could work on his second book was nights and, like now, weekends. He was still hacking away in Publicity, those twenty thousand dollars were nestling in a savings account in a bank and were quietly working for him night and day, bringing in something like twenty dollars a week every week of the year, as Adelheid had dreamed. Of course it was now far from the guarantee you wouldn't starve that it had been in Adelheid's time but you could bet your ass he wasn't ever going to touch that money.

And he still wondered nervously if he really was a writer, even though his second book was happening all by itself exactly as his first had. It was the mystery of it that got him. Where did it all come from, words, characters, jokes, observations, and how did it happen? How could you be sure it would keep on happening? If a guy knew that, he could control it, he could relax. Nobody seemed to have the answer.

All Blake could say was, "Who the hell knows? The only advice I can give you is never quit a day's work at the end of a scene, always quit in the middle so the next day when you start you know where you're going, at least you've got that first momentum and you can keep on——''

Armand Harris had been openly discouraging. He was probably jealous of Arnold's success with an original work on his first try.

"Just don't get your balls in an uproar, Elton. Ask around you'll see every jerk in Hollywood thinks he's a writer from the mailman to the Jap gardener. My dentist's been trying for two years, finally he gets my mouth fixed so I can't even make a noise, wham he tells me a story. I make notes, who knows someday maybe I could steal a couple scenes? As for you, Elton, you could turn out to be one of those one-shot hotshots—only time will tell, you follow?''

That icy hand clutched at his gut. What if that sonofabitch was right and there was just one book in him? Who knows? Maybe that merchant marine experience was special—Maybe this second book would never be published—Maybe—

The goddamn chimes kept on and on. Arnold finally tore his ass off the chair. At the window he carefully lifted a corner of the heavy drape.

A not-too-bad-looking babe of about his own age had a rigid forefinger stuck in the chimes button. She was dark-haired, vaguely unHollywood in that she was wearing a businessy tailored gray suit. And she wasn't carrying a bag, so she couldn't be selling anything.

Her first words shocked hell out of him even though there was no particular hostility in her tone.

"Don't you ever answer your fucking telephone? I called at least twenty times.''

It was the first time he'd ever heard a girl say *fuck*. Even Agnes and the other whores he'd known had scrupulously avoided dirty words.

"Yeah, well, reason I don't answer my telephone is I

always wonder who's going to telephone me more important than the book I'm working on.''

(What the hell, no harm in dropping on the girl the fact that he was a writer, she had a nice round ass and perky good-sized boobs.)

"If that's what you always ask yourself, here's the answer. Me. I'm from the Johnny Farina Agency with whom—remember?—you just signed a seven-year contract. My name's Kate Sorel. Kate—like *The Taming of the Shrew,* like Kate Cornell—one of the great ladies of the theater. My mother and father were nuts about the theater. And Sorel, like the hero in Stendhal's book *The Red and the Black,*'' moving a doubting eye over him, "that is if you know who Stendhal is. Way back when, I guess the name's French.''

"*French*?'' French had a special meaning for him, hopefully, French sexy—French sex—

"French extraction. Only don't get any ideas. I'm legitimate and I work like a bastard. I did PR on Broadway until Johnny Farina sucked me into coming out to Hollywood.''

Arnold shut the door behind them and they moved deep into the huge somber fake-Spanish living room. She sniffed, wrinkling her nose, which was cute but had the slightly cut-off look most redone noses had.

"Don't tell me,'' Kate inhaled, "Send a Kramer's Salami to Your Boy in the Army?'' She was quoting from an advertising slogan a New York Jewish delicatessen had used during the war. "Three o'clock of a sunny summer afternoon in Hollywood, California, you eat kosher garlic salami?''

"I don't have special times for things. I mean I can do anything anytime.'' Arnold gave it a hopeful emphasis and when Kate looked at him appraisingly, he wondered nervously whether he'd gone too far too fast.

"Yeah. Well. It sure fills a room, that smell. I'm on a diet. I've got to watch my calories, anything I put in my mouth,

243

boom, straight to my ass." Arnold took advantage of that to take another look at her ass. It was an okay ass, all right. "I didn't have much lunch, look just cut me a slice. I can kid myself I'm eating in self-defense otherwise I wouldn't survive in this air, then let's put *toches* on the *tish*."

Although she wasn't Jewish, she'd been around Broadway long enough to pick up some choice Yiddish morsels like "*toches on the tish*," which meant bare ass on the table, let's get down to basics.

She was the first really attractive girl he'd met who talked like a man. He felt comfortable around her. Besides, any girl talked like a man—maybe she would fuck as readily as a man? Maybe?

He cut a chunk of salami thick enough to choke a horse.

She gnawed at the salami with nervous enthusiasm. "I set up a new kind of job for myself. From now on the Agency will render a real service to its clients, especially writers. I make a breakdown." This last as if daring him to question it. "I'll give you a for example. John Garfield, okay?"

"Okay."

"My breakdown is that John Garfield is tough, gentle, good-looking but—*but*—but in a way that every ordinary twat, salesgirl, factory worker, school girl, secretary, can bullshit herself into *You know it's possible I could meet a guy like John Garfield, not like Cary Grant or Clark Gable they're strictly in wet-dreamsville, but Garfield*. Between you and me and the lamppost the ordinary twat has as much chance meeting somebody like Garfield as a fart in a hailstorm. The important thing is they believe it. Now. Once you got yourself that breakdown, all you do is tailor stories to fit gentle tough reachable Garfield and what have you got? A top star, that's what. Am I getting to you or am I losing valuable oxygen which God knows you need in this joint?"

Arnold had been concentrating most of his available wits on whether because of the way she talked she might let him fuck her, but now he began to perceive she was saying important things that could be of great use to him. He could rework the hero of the book to make him like Garfield, "reachable-possible." He'd sort of done that in his first book by instinct, but now he could do it deliberately, he knew exactly how, he was excited.

"I see you're taking notes in your head," Kate observed with satisfaction.

"Oh yeah, I think you're very interesting."

"Because I've got a lot to say to you." A nervous energy exuded from her like heat from a portable electric heater. "Exactly what did you mean Very Interesting—we talking about the same thing?"

"I hope so."

"I'm not sure a salami eater could get my motor whirring, but that's another question. How open are you as a man? For new experiences?"

"Not only wide open but I'm hungering for them."

"Let's put the hunger aside for the moment. Now I'll tell you my breakdown of you. I went through your first book and the pages you've been handing Farina on the new one. I think the potentialities are fantastic, only nobody's realized that yet, including you. *I* know exactly what you should do."

"Now wait a minute, that scares me. I kind of write instinctively. I mean first of all it's got to come out of me naturally. It's got to pour out by itself."

"It'll keep pouring out, all we'll do is direct the stream."

"I got this gut feeling there's something inside of me nobody should fuck around with."

He caught himself, although she'd used the word "fuck" *he* hadn't, it had slipped out by itself. It was the first time he'd used the word "fuck" in the presence of a woman.

"See? See? Look at yourself! You think you say 'fuck' in front of a woman it's a big deal. That's one of the items I've got here on my list, maybe you won't understand how

245

important it is what I'm saying, *the word 'fuck's' time has come*! I've got a lot of other things—"

"Wait a little minute, now wait, that list, what happens if *I* use that list?" Years of working at the Studio and reading contracts and hearing about plagiarism suits and other squabbles had made him cautious. "What will you get?"

"Cut me another slice of that salami. I don't know what I did with the one you gave me."

"You ate it," Arnold cut her another thick slice.

"Anything you write will be strictly by Arnold Elton . . ." Kate went at the second slice just as voraciously. "Johnny Farina Agency will get its normal ten percent take. Period. But I don't mind telling you I've left a copy of this list with the Agency, on file, because if you hit on account of me I don't want to be the patsy who has to run around telling everybody, 'Hey, fellas, it's really me who put Arnold Elton on the map!' I'm telling you beforehand, I want it on record what I did I'm a creative agent. There it is, *toches* on the *tish*."

Arnold thought carefully, finally said a cautious, "Okay."

"Believe me you won't be sorry. Now my breakdown of you as a writer. You are a phenomenon. You've been made possible, you will be possible, because of dozens of circumstances mostly by the hypocrisy of this Puritan duckfucking nation that believes in the bullshit all-in-white-here-comes-the-bride wedding while all that duckfucking goes on behind the bushes."

"So I'm a phenomenon," he admitted cautiously.

"The way I analyze it is that you've come at exactly the right moment. The Hays Code—the ridiculous self-censorship the film industry is carrying on its back, it's okay for a man to hump all over the place—but for the twat if she humps unmarried, before the picture's over *she's* got to be punished, lose a leg, get killed, blinded, *retribution*, that's the Hays

246

Code. For the movies, the most interesting subject there is, namely humping—is out."

"You like a Coke with your salami?"

"No," she said but took it without knowing she had. "And all that crap about how movies are your best entertainment, is crap. Fucking is your best entertainment and don't let anybody tell you different. Now you just happen to be writing a *book*. There's no Hays Code there to stop you. You can write anything you want. Really let fly, I mean shove it in all the way and break it off, and describe *penetration*. Describe the details of how a woman is put together, how she feels." She studied him for a moment. "Okay, so you probably don't know your ass from your elbow in that department, but I'm going to do you a great service. It happens I'm not bashful, I'll tell it all to you, sensations like tingling around the nipples, the steamy twat."

"Like some ice with your Coke?"

"Yes, please. Number Two of my breakdown. Use famous people everybody will recognize. The readers loved guessing who that star was in your first book. More. More of that. They like to know about glamorous people, what they eat, look at Louella Parsons and Hedda Hopper and all the others who got fat barely *mentioning* them, but in your book you're going to go to town, you will not only fill it with glamour people, you'll tell them *who* the glamour people are fucking and *how* they fuck, *how* they feel."

It came to him slowly, spreading until it covered him with a crazy elation, a revelation.

"My God she's right. Nobody's ever done that before. Here I am writing a book about Hollywood I could use the details about Marta and the nurses and the five distributors, only make them into recognizable people, and the Big Male Star who fucked the Messenger Girl in front of everybody there'd been enough whispers about that so people would know who it really was.

What Kate was telling him was not stopping him at all. He felt two compelling urges, one, to get right to the typewriter and put it all down and the second, he could barely wait to fuck her.

"Those famous people, hey? Can't they sue me?"

"I worked that out too." Her manner changed. She'd won him over, now they were working together. She was excited. "Let's say you use Harry Truman as a character."

"*Harry Truman*? What would I do with Harry Truman in my book?"

"Oh I'm only saying him for another for example," she showed her first impatience. "You use a character in the book you describe him exactly like the real Harry Truman and everybody says Ho Ho, he can't fool me that's Harry Truman, and then to prevent yourself getting sued by Harry Truman, in another place in the book you have like a parade, and Whammo, there's Harry Truman. At least you say *he's* Harry Truman: of course everybody knows the other character was Harry Truman but this way you're protected, get my point?"

"Say. That's real good. That's a good trick."

"And use them all, celebrities, playboys, sexpots, no sweat, just pile it on." Kate was pacing. "And now." The way she repeated "Now," Arnold knew she was coming to a crucial point. "There's something you're going to have to learn, it's the most important of all, you're going to think at first it's silly, but it isn't, it's something you don't know, so I'm going to say it clearly. Women enjoy it."

Jesus, she was right. Even Marta, boy, did she enjoy it, the way she moaned and yelled. But she never talked about it. Kate was on to something. Men would flip their wigs when they read how women enjoyed it. So would women, come to think of it.

"How old are you?" Kate asked.

"Twenty-three. I know women love fucking. They don't fool me—"

Kate made a sound of disgust. "Fool you? You still don't get it."

"You think I'm naive or something? I've been around."

"To the wrong places. I'll bet you a kick in the ass you got initiated by a hooker who made you feel she was doing you a big favor and couldn't get you off her fast enough. I'll bet another kick in the ass when you're with a babe and you put it in, you say, 'Am I hurting you, honey?'" It was apparent from the odd look on his face, she had him there too. "Jesus—half the world's more'n half—are women, nobody has ever written anything woman-raunchy. You ever read a book where the woman's *horny* and says so?"

Arnold was uneasy. She almost read his thoughts.

"You see? You see? It's unladylike to be horny. It's all been a man, men. You know of a book where the author describes cocks and balls for the benefit of the ladies? Never mind answering. Now if you ever reach the women, really reach them in a book—" Kate made a gesture, her hand rising over her head to express endless possibilities. "Tell the truth, you ever fucked a woman you absolutely knew really enjoyed it, I mean really, and didn't mind saying so? Just what I thought. You never have. Now listen."

Arnold felt the beginning of an erection and thought, Jesus Christ, all along my prick's known something I didn't.

She spent evenings at his place during the whole of the next week trying to get that one main point across. Finally, the next Saturday afternoon, after a week of his walking around with practically a perpetual hard-on, she tossed down a quantity of Scotch.

"There's only one way you're ever going to understand about women really enjoying fucking let's face it. We're going to kill two birds with one stone. You and I will fuck. Hey, you all right?"

"I'm fine."

"You look half-paralyzed. You can't get yourself to believe maybe I'm horny, that maybe I'll enjoy it."

"Well—"

"It's okay, you've got to throw off centuries of bullshit. Get this through your skull. I am horny as hell and will get hornier as I talk about it. I am going to enjoy the shit out of fucking, just like every *Joe* Schmo does. Understand?"

"Yah." an undeniable erection was there.

"And while we're fucking I am going to describe every one of my sensations, and you remember them, concentrate on every sensation, every detail. You're going to describe it for your readers, they'll blow their tops."

She stopped and they faced each other. Arnold was frightened by the solemnity. There was a sense of ceremony like at a wedding.

"The beginning's going to be strictly for looking. That's an important part, Visual Anticipation."

She let her jacket fall to the floor and the momentous idea seeped through, Jesus Christ we're really going to fuck. He whipped off his shirt and undershirt, his fingers unsure, stood bare-chested attentive. She took off her brassiere, revealing very nice tits, firm with black aureoles about the nipples. Without thinking he reached for her tits but she stopped him. "This is strictly looking time. We'll strip naked, I'll fix on your cock and balls. You should see yourself, even now you're still in shock a woman talks that way, only proves my point. You concentrate on my cunt and boobs."

She let her skirt fall. Arnold answered by stepping out of his trousers. She unsnapped her garter belt, peeled off her long nylon stockings, real good solid legs, she kicked off her shoes, so did he, all he was left with was a pair of socks with holes at the toes, and baggy shorts. If only he'd known he would sure as hell have put on fresh socks and a clean pair of shorts, but he whipped the socks away and yanked off his underpants, threw them behind him quickly so she wouldn't notice. He was beginning to understand what she'd been talking about and it almost drove him out of his skull. *She* was getting a real jolt out of this. She slipped out of her panties, he stared bug-eyed. There it was, her pubic triangle, and her eyes were fixed on his genitals just as avidly.

"It's the first circumcised cock I've ever seen."

"Is it all right for you?" Arnold asked anxiously.

"Right now even a cucumber would be all right for me," Kate said. "Only it's different. You can see the head before it gets really hard. I've only seen heads when they slipped out of foreskins, that's good too the foreskin receding, but this isn't bad and see? You've got a first-class hard on just from talking and looking."

"Yeah." Arnold's voice too was now husky. To be honest he felt a little self-conscious standing that way with an erection pointing toward the ceiling.

"Then I'll lie down on the couch and you'll *sex*plore me, every opening, you ever seen the inside of a woman's mouth?"

"No."

"You see?" She took that as another triumph. "Then you'll open the lips of my cunt and look. Really look."

The boys in the merchant marine would have loved this, and he wasn't making up any of it.

"Then I'll turn over on my belly and you look and touch, the backs of my ears, the back of my neck, you spread the cheeks of my ass apart and look at my asshole." She was so worked up she was breathing hard. "I'll bet you've never looked at a woman's asshole before."

"Or anybody's." He was so far gone it didn't even bother him that she was a little lumpy at the haunches.

"Then you turn over and I look at your asshole."

"Hey," uneasy but awed, "you get a kick out of *that*?"

"I may even stick a finger in."

"Wait, wait. I'm kind of nervous about my rear passage."

251

" 'Rear passage'? It's the asshole, and you'd be surprised how many people feel insecure with their ass exposed. Not me, I'm secure. It's an erogenous zone which means it's sexually excitable but when we get there if you tighten up, I'll stop."

"You keep this up I'm liable to come all over the joint."

Triumphantly, "Almost ready to come just from words and looking! A woman's no different, only you know what? She really loves it if you look at her with appreciation all over, and I mean all over, women are afraid they're really ugly and dirty and smelly down there, a man convinces a woman her cunt's beautiful to behold, he's really got her for good. Don't ever forget that."

Arnold nodded fervently. In the condition he was in, he had to keep reminding himself he was learning important truths.

"Then I'll turn back over." She wasn't finding it so easy to hold off as she stared at his twitching erection. She spoke faster, "I'll let you know when to slip it in and, boy, you and me we're going to fuck like nobody's business."

When it was near his breaking point, Kate moved to the couch, lay down on her back, Arnold bent over and dutifully looked at her eyes, noticed the veins in her eyelids, the line of her jet black hair. His eyes strayed down to her nose, she lifted her head slightly so he could see inside her nostrils. She opened her mouth, he looked at her tongue, her palate, the pink serrated roof, her gums, her teeth (she had two gold crowns on her molars), she made him open her ears, peer inside them. He then focused on her breasts and was surprised to find tiny bristly hairs about the nipples, let his eyes move down to her navel, then down to her pubic mound. As per promise she spread her legs as wide apart as she could. He had never seen the inside of a vagina. He was at first sorry, it looked so meaty, then she pulled back her labia so that her clitoris was clearly revealed. He'd never seen it before, either. She turned over, waited as he dutifully spread apart the cheeks of her buttocks.

He was taken aback at the color of her asshole. It was star-puckered and dark.

"You paralyzed or something?" Kate's voice came muffled because she was face down. Arnold still didn't move. "Now, what's the matter?"

"Your rear passage."

"My asshole," she said irritably.

"Why it's dark, it's kinda purplish like."

"Dark, almost purple? Well for God's sake so's yours. So's everybody's. Now get whacking. Take a last good look because I'm about to turn over."

Arnold bent his head a little lower and strained hard. He wanted the image to remain, he wanted to put it away in his sexual fantasies for future reference. She made a move and reluctantly he let go of the cheeks of her buttocks. She immediately turned over, and slipped right under him on her back.

"Now here's what comes next. You move your lips down over my boobs," which he did, "now gently, you suck each nipple." He hesitated. "Go on." His lips found the nipples and another surprise, they became erect. He sucked on them enthusiastically. "I can feel your lips wet and your tongue. It's spreading right down to my cunt." She groaned as he moved from one nipple to the other. "Now. Move your lips slowly down my belly. Slower. Let your tongue move into my belly button. Oh wow. That's great, now move your mouth down, down, more, *more*!"

Arnold lifted his head, "Hey wait a minute, wa-ait a minute. You want me to put my mouth down there?"

"Not only there, but *here*," she pulled back the pubic hair. "You are going to kiss this marvelous little thingamajig, you are going to take it between your lips." She sounded as though if he made her wait another fraction of a second she

253

would blow into bits. "Come on, it's the clitoris for Chrissake, it's the greatest thing since Campbell put soup in cans—"

"You want me to be a muff diver," Arnold was appalled. "You *want me to go down on you!*"

"Forget that street crap! You're a writer!"

"I don't know. It's kind of damp and you pee out of it."

"What do you think you do with yours? Oh for Chrissake, it's cleaner than your mouth, ask any doctor," Kate said impatiently. "You told me you were open for anything."

"Yeah but I might throw up."

It took only the slightest hint of a threat that she would leave to bring him back on her.

"There's *no* part of the human body's dirty. No part. And you won't throw up. You'll love it and so will your readers."

"I'll write about *that*?"

"Goddamn right, and you'll make it perfectly natural. All you need to sell a book is one really hot scene. Everybody will talk about that scene where Tommy kisses and sucks Diana's cunt. They'll blow their stacks."

"There isn't any scene like that in the book."

"You'll put one in. Now get shuffling."

He eyed her damp pubic area dubiously, then tentatively let his mouth stray down to her clitoris, surprised the smell was not as he'd expected, only faintly musky. His lips moved gingerly, enclosing the tiny protrusion. She responded with such unexpected violence that his head bobbed like a ship in a storm, plunging from the bottom of her vagina sweeping to the top. He was startled to find his tongue penetrating the warm humid interior with an enthusiasm of its own.

Kate writhed, groaned, caught his head, plunged his face into her, made unformed sounds, threshed about like a wild woman. She gasped, he felt the eruptions within her, amazed and awed at the ecstasy he brought to her. Although he still had a sneaking feeling it was dirty, real guys didn't do it, it gave him a sense of sexual power. He could do more than other guys. Her moaning subsided, there were two or three minor twitches he wasn't sure weren't painful, the sound by now seemed very close to groans, he had to stop himself from asking, "You okay?" She lay motionless, he could feel the beating of her pulse and the churning in her belly as he stared at her pubic hair, he'd never been that close, he was seeing an enlargement of her labia over the tip of his nose.

"Not bad for openers." Arnold looked at her incredulously but she seemed to mean it exactly that way. "Now make notes in your head what that felt like because women will get hot pants at the idea of a man liking what you just did. You liked it, don't bullshit me. Now we're going on from there. But remember everything, the way it looks, tastes, smells, feels."

His cock was raging. It had to be plunged into something, anything, even a cantaloupe. She played it slowly, pushing him down on his back. Straddling him. Maneuvering her weight she aimed her vagina unerringly on to his penis, gasped, groaned, her voice almost angry. "Look at me, look at me," she repeated. "Watch-my-face-look-you're-in-me-deep," while she lifted and lowered herself slowly, carefully, her muscles alternately relaxing, clutching. "D-eep-in-me-oh God— Remember this, each sensation, remember the sounds I'm making, the words—I'm saying—"

By that time he couldn't think or feel, there were just too many sensations. He tried concentrating on her face, was amazed almost frightened at the contortions: her head moved pendulumlike from side to side, she kept saying "no no no" when she was no longer coherent. Her vaginal muscles locked in a stranglehold over his penis, then let go, locked, unlocked, "Watch me!" she yelled. "*Watch! God-damn-son-of-a-bitch! You're looking at a woman about to come!*" She made a series of guttural sounds. "*A woman coming—*

Goddamn watch! Watch!'' At which point he hissed off in a Roman candle of his own, sperm hiccuping hysterically into her.

"And don't roll away the minute you come like you don't need me anymore." She was breathing hard as she held him clamped to her. "A woman needs a man more right after he's come than anytime. Remember that, make your hero tender, understanding."

"I'll remember," he pledged.

She was wet against him, her nipples cool and her breasts soft as she clung to him. "Ever feel anything better? Ever been fucked better in your life before?"

"Never," Arnold vowed.

"It's like anything else in life, like painting or music," Kate said drowsily. "People stand right in front of a painting and don't know what they're seeing until somebody tells them." Yeah. That was what McCabe had said about the exhibitors and the nurses. "People make their worst mistake when it comes to fucking. They think it just comes naturally. They don't know how much they're missing, the sounds, the tastes, the smells, the sights. Somebody's got to tell them and it's going to be you, only don't forget, do it for the women too. If you can do that, your book's going to be strictly nothing less than sensational."

It was.

Arnold had described it all in glowing detail. Because there was a story with *real* characters Arnold knew, for the first time people could read about smelling, sucking, writhing, looking, fucking without feeling too dirty or guilty.

Love Me Love Me Love Me (Kate had insisted on the third *Love Me*) added a new phrase to the booksellers' stock of clichés. *Runaway best-seller.* Its sales exceeded Kate's wildest expectations.

Kate tried to keep Arnold from reading the reviews.

"If you ask me they're money reviews," Kate told him. "People will read them, rush out and buy the book."

Arnold forced her to show them to him.

"*Love Me Love Me Love Me*, a novel by Arnold Elton, rises in its tumescence to a new low."

"Arnold Elton's *Love Me* etc., is a literary ejaculation."

"*Love Me Love Me Love Me* by Arnold Elton. Slurrp, gurgle, gasp."

4.

They were married a couple of months after it was established beyond any doubt that *Love Me Love Me Love Me* was going to be, as Kate put it, the biggest thing since chopped liver, just about the most widely sold book ever published. Their marriage was a natural. Everybody around them expected it so intensely it would have been wrong for them not to have married. Kate had the *Golden Touch*, almost every one of her clients turned out to be comers, and Arnold was one of the first writers to be recognized as a star.

When people approached him it was with a religious feeling. Everything had been tried to solve The Riddle. Stories were pretested in public opinion surveys. Sociologists and psychologists were pressed into service, but there seemed no sure-fire way of knowing in advance what the paying public wanted.

"They think you've been blessed," Blake told a dazed Arnold. "They think, for the moment anyway, that you're the *custodian of the mystery.* They think *you know what they want."*

Nor was Armand Harris much impressed by Arnold's success.

Armand had become a Producer—one way of not having to tear your guts out waiting for people to read what you wrote—only to discover that he had himself another problem. Now *he* had to figure out what the paying customers wanted to see.

"I don't mind giving you the end-result of some heavy analyzing," Armand told Arnold. "The trouble with most people in this business is that they *try* to make good pictures. That's where you break your heart and your balls. Statistically your chances of turning out a piece of shit are just as great if you try or don't try. So relax, begin with a piece of shit, no sweat, if it turns out great, great. I use a horoscope now. Not that I believe in astrology, but it eliminates the strain of deciding which piece of shit to produce." Armand turned his dark-tinted stare on Arnold. "As for you, Elton. You stumbled on a formula came up gold. Don't fuck around looking for glory. Stick with that formula the rest of your natural life."

This time there were interviews on the radio and for magazines. Mostly they asked questions like "Doesn't it bother you that critics are calling you a pornographer?" (He and Kate—mostly Kate—had worked out answers for that.) If he was a pornographer he was in good company: Shakespeare had written sonnets that were as explicit. Rabelais had been even more explicit. (He promised himself one day to read Rabelais.) Many of the world's greatest writers had written about sex and described it in detail, the Greeks, the Romans, the French, the British. And no, his family didn't mind. He didn't know whether they did or didn't, aside from an occasional birthday greeting to Nathan or Henrietta, he'd lost all contact with them.

And people were beginning to recognize him. Critics re-reviewed his books. Both of them. His publishers put out another edition of *Guns of Love* and it sold better than it had before. And in the morning when he awoke he felt a flood of warmth, a thrill of sheer pleasure as he said to himself, Holy Jesus Christ, I'm a writer. An honest-to-God genuine fucking writer.

Arnold waited until the very day they were to be married before he quit Publicity. He had misgivings but so much money was pouring in he would have looked like a horse's ass if he stayed on.

McCabe really did a job for Arnold. After all, one of their very own had made it; he threw him a combination going away–champagne party with the full treatment—and exactly the same kinds of canapés there'd been at the party for the five exhibitors.

They were all there. Gorham, Geisy, Blake, Harris, several starlets and a few of the prettier secretaries. The Studio head himself came, ushered in by McCabe and a cluster of photographers, posed possessively alongside Arnold and Kate.

Gorham, looking like a mortician at a rival's funeral, said solemnly, "You made it, kid."

Geisy, with an appreciative bitter grin, "No sir, I'm not buying the rights to this one, baby. All I want to tell you is that your Jake the Plumber is a great character, and baby your Cunt is one hundred percent cunt, up, down, and sidewise, and loves to fuck and says so but it'll be a long time before anybody'll do that on film."

"The movie world is still jerksville," Armand said morosely. "Even *I* can't figure out how to use your stuff."

"You?" Arnold tried to sound cheery, but the truth was it shook him badly that the movies weren't buying his book. "I wouldn't sell you this book any more than I would piss on your belly if your guts were on fire. Anybody buys this one I want guarantees they make it like the book. Or I don't sell."

They all looked at him as if he had temporarily taken off for places they didn't want to know about.

"I'm not talking about buying," Armand said. "I'm talking about stealing. Right now your book's not even worth the trouble stealing. That fucking Hays Code."

"Arnold would've made a great accountant," was Zuckerman's contribution. "But there you are. What numbers lose, words gain."

"You wouldn't believe it," Kate muttered after Arnold had been photographed with a couple of starlets who had managed subtly to edge her out of the picture. "The twats get horny the minute they look at you. If only they knew."

"Knew what?" Arnold asked with a touch of belligerence.

"Jesus Christ," Kate said, "you've even got yourself believing it."

None of it went the way he'd thought it would. Not that he'd expected a dreamy white wedding. Still.

Blake was so tensed up he almost jumped each time anyone got close.

Arnold couldn't figure that one at all. Blake had just had another big hit, which he'd written and directed. He was practically the hottest personality in Hollywood. The studios were falling all over themselves trying to get him.

Arnold said, "It's my wedding, Blake. Eat, drink, fuck one of the messenger girls. What's with you?"

"Haven't you heard?" Blake asked. "The shit is about to hit the electric fan, the House Committee on Un-American Activities—Christ you don't even know about them? They're a congressional committee set up supposedly to investigate subversive activities. They're about to move in on Hollywood."

"Well, fuck them," Arnold said heartily.

"Jesus," Blake said, "all hell's going to break loose, it's

262

going to be a shambles before they get through." He eyed Arnold with reluctant admiration. "You're a guy chasing a bare-assed nymphomaniac through a field thick with land mines," and added morosely, "what's more, you catch her."

"Fields I walk in, only explosions are pussy explosions," Arnold assumed his new sex-man aura. "And they ain't dangerous."

"I guess they're not," Blake said, then went off to get more champagne.

"Watch it, Buster, watch it," once Blake had gone, Geisy sidled up to Arnold, spoke softly so people wouldn't hear.

"Watch what?"

"Blake. Stay away from him."

"What's the matter with him?"

"Listen to him. You'll see. He talks about the Bill of Rights."

"So?"

"So?" indignantly from Geisy. "A dead giveaway. Anytime a writer mentions the Bill of Rights, it's a sure sign he's a Commie."

It was hard to tell what was wrong with their marriage or even if anything was. They'd taken a nice house on Sunset Plaza Drive right off the Strip high up on the hill. At night you could see thousands of twinkling lights punctuating the darkness as if the sky had been lowered, like a Fanchon and Marco backdrop. So they had a great view if you went for views. And sex was still by far the best Arnold had ever known. Kate would get on top of him and writhe with wild abandon. When she came, everybody on the hill must have known: Kate Sorel Elton Enjoyed It. But Arnold had a niggling suspicion that at least part of it was to keep reminding him that Women Enjoyed It.

She came home from the Agency tired and nervous and rarely had the inclination or the energy to go in for preliminaries.

"Sexploration," she finally conceded, "is more for your books than for day-to-day fucking. I already know by memory what your cock and balls look, smell and taste like—"

At that point Arnold also knew every hair on her body and had admitted, let's face it, her hips were lumpy and her ass was on the heavy side. And she was completely immersed in her career.

On their first wedding anniversary, they were in their king-sized bed about to celebrate, naturally with some strenuous sex. Arnold was surprised to hear himself blurt out, he hadn't consciously thought it out before.

"What if we had a kid?"

"You want me to get knocked up?"

"It's one of the great experiences of life."

She surprised him by not flying into the fury he'd braced himself for. "Last few months you been dropping hints all over the joint. What's with you?"

"I would just like to have a kid."

"I guess sooner or later I'll have to have a kid," she agreed morosely.

"Kate," he tried to work up a choked-up feeling. "You mean it?"

"Let's not get our balls in an uproar. Okay. I'm the only one can get knocked up, but I'm not going to spend my life taking care of a kid. I won't let it cut in on my work, we'll have a nurse."

"You've got yourself a deal." He tried to make it solemn but Kate thought about it a fast ten seconds, yanked out the diaphragm and pulled him to her as if they'd better get it done before she changed her mind. Afterward her only comment was, "Christ!" which stopped Arnold, who'd been trying to weave romantic fantasies, while their bodies were mingling, about the mystery of making a human child, the

264

wonder of your flesh and blood perpetuated. He tried to stroke her vagina with reverence. She pushed his hand away irritably, and said she had to get her sleep for Chrissake, she had a big day ahead of her, turned her naked back to him and fell into a restless sleep.

Arnold smoked almost three packs of Lucky Strikes in the Cedars of Lebanon father's waiting room. An added nervousness was the fear that he might run into Marta. He did. Marta came flying in (she was on duty in Pediatrics when the word got out that Mrs. Arnold Elton was having a baby over in Maternity), there'd been some kidding Marta confided to Arnold, everybody knew she'd been his girl friend, but, he was rapidly reassured. Marta had come only to enjoy the excitement of having known a celebrity and to congratulate him on his second book, and then hurried off. It was the last time he ever saw her.

A nurse came, mouth masked, holding a tiny wrinkled bundle.

"Mr. Elkins?"

"Elton," he corrected her with a faint trace of irritation. He was beginning to feel people should know who he was.

The nurse glanced hastily at a bracelet on the baby's wrist. "Sorry, Mr. Elton. It's a girl and here she is."

The fragile miniature human hand kept escaping from the blanket. Wet weeds of black hair were plastered over her ridged skull. Arnold had a deep sense of satisfaction. "Got a name for her yet?" the nurse asked because she suspected there was perhaps the beginning of a tear in one of his eyes and she didn't want to get into *that*.

"Jennifer."

"Jennifer has beautiful hands," the nurse smiled and hurried off before Arnold could actually form a full-fledged tear and left him wondering whether by that she meant that only Jennifer's hands were beautiful.

* * *

"Breast-feeding? You kidding?"

They'd just come home from the hospital. Arnold was holding Jennifer in his arms. Mrs. Griffith, an elderly Welsh infant nurse, was waiting to take over.

"Some of the pediatricians think it's better for the baby to be breast-fed. Dr. Spock says—"

"Screw them," Kate said. "Can you see me leaving the Agency three times a day to give titty? You just let that what's-her-face Mrs. Griffith whip up the formula."

"No sir, no stranger is going to feed any kid of mine. Or take care of any kid of mine."

"Listen, Buster. Either you grow tits, which I understand the prehistoric male had, and suckle the baby yourself, or you learn how to prepare formula, how to diaper and wipe little holes and powder them—by the way with girl babies you've got to wipe the asshole away from the slit; you learn how to burp her, get up six times a night. I've been through that with my kid sister. My mother was too beat by the delivery and we didn't have dough for a nurse." It was one of the rare references she made to her family with whom she'd broken the first chance she got. "I've produced a kid, I've pulled more than my weight." She yanked her nightgown up and insisted he take a good hard look at her shaved and bristly pubis dotted with inflamed episiotomy stitch marks. "You ought to have a real idea what it is to be a woman."

"Hey—I can't write about that. Not for my readers."

"This isn't for writing, goddamn it," she yelled. "This is for living."

It was Arnold who got up in the night, learned how to make formula, lulled Jennifer when she was fretful, hummed, badly off-key—he was completely unmusical—German lullabies vaguely remembered from Adelheid. It was he who

266

worried about Jennifer. As far as he could tell, Kate felt nothing.

Arnold had a built-in lack of faith in Mrs. Griffith. When Jennifer was three months old, there was a crucial incident.

He and Kate had been out to dinner (he now felt guilty about leaving Jennifer alone with Mrs. Griffith). Once they got home, Kate hurried to their bedroom. She'd suddenly decided she was in the mood, and when she did, she couldn't wait—Boom.

He resented that too. He was supposed to charge in any time she decided. She was so sure of him, she didn't even turn as she hurried up the stairs. This time he didn't come running. Instead, he tiptoed toward the nursery, where he'd caught a light, carefully pushed the door open.

Mrs. Griffith didn't notice. Arnold realized with shock she was trying to get three-month-old Jennifer to sit up straight over an ashtray, to pee into it.

"So what?" Kate was already in bed nude and primed.

"She's doing it just to save herself the trouble of changing a wet diaper. Look, I've been talking to Braunschweig."

"Braunschweig?"

"Dr. Braunschweig," that he and Kate had not talked about it showed how far they'd drifted apart, "is an analyst with the School for Early Years, I enrolled Jennifer there, they've got a waiting list, you have to register the kids a long time before even though they don't take them till they're two. It's a psychoanalytic nursery school, parents meet with the psychoanalyst advisers and discuss how to take care of the kids—"

"You're kidding. Psychoanalysis for a three-month-old baby?"

"That's when the complexes and neuroses start."

"Complexes and neuroses?"

"Okay, the fuck-ups, and now's when you can prevent

them. Dr. Braunschweig was talking about it the other night, one of the worst things is to toilet train babies when they're too young. There's a normal period when they play with their feces.''

"Feces?"

"Shit, okay? It's a process of development and if you stop it, you leave psychological scars.''

"Good. Tell the old bag to let Jennifer play with her shit. Now, let's fuck.''

To be truthful he really liked getting in the car and buying all the food. He especially loved rolling down to the Farmers Market, where it was all in the open air. You could get food from every part of the world, fruits, vegetables, pastries, candies, nuts, exotic Mexican, Chinese dishes, seafood, then pop over to Fairfax to stock up on Jewish salami. He was close enough to the time he'd gone hungry in Chicago in the cold and to Adelheid's garbage can man to enjoy having enough money in his pocket to buy anything he felt like.

But Kate took it all for granted, even the weekly night session he went to religiously at the School for Early Years where earnest parents listened in rapt attention as Dr. Braunschweig and occasionally other analysts explained about Oedipal and Electra complexes and infantile sexuality.

"Shopping, worrying about the baby," Kate said when he had the guts to tell her. "That'll give you another little idea what it's like to be a woman." Kate had her own logic, then added hastily, "And don't get that into your book, either. Where are this week's forty pages?" She had decided that forty pages would be his weekly quota.

She scowled as she read them, corrected the spelling and the grammar, edited out the obvious repetitions. He noticed she had a rigorous respect for what he wrote and the way he wrote it, and never touched a meaningful word. Then she'd hand him a list of suggestions, all of which made good sense.

He'd long ago suspected she never gave him a really honest opinion of his writing. "What the hell difference does it make how I feel? We're not talking about reading books, we're talking about selling books."

What communication they'd had dwindled. He wasn't much interested in any activity that could not be related to his writing, fucking, or the baby, and Kate was completely wrapped up in her work. While on the can after her morning coffee and cigarette, she sometimes handled as many as twenty calls and she had a portable miniature switchboard that she took to bed. Its presence bothered Arnold when they were fucking, especially when they were in a particularly contorted position. Arnold was sure the phone would ring when he was about to come, and it sometimes did. But because he was beginning to have a vague feeling that with Kate it was not a forever thing, he tolerated it.

From what Arnold heard of her end of the conversations, her clients tended to regard Kate as combination Mother Confessor, minister (or rabbi, depending on their persuasions), psychoanalyst, lawyer, doctor and wise but stern mother. She dealt with problems ranging from insomnia, shaky marriage, writer's block, to mistreatment by the Front Office and perennial complaints about producers; and saw nothing incongruous in discussing suicide with a well-known screenwriter while she and Arnold were in a complicated sexual position. She had become so skilled at mixing the two activities that she was able to keep pumping while describing to the suicidal screenwriter the details of his funeral, of clearing up his affairs, then the clincher—how quickly he would be forgotten. She convinced him to defer serious action until they could talk in the morning, hung up and had a tremendous orgasm.

Arnold assumed that she must have been very capable because not only did Johnny Farina give Kate several impressive raises but added her name so it became like star billing:

269

Since Arnold was the one who worked at home, it was he who took Jennifer out for airing on the Sunset Plaza hillside in her fancy English perambulator. He discovered it was quite a hill they lived on. Judy Garland and Vincente Minnelli and baby Liza lived a distance above. Movie stars were constantly whizzing up. Arnold was still enough Hollywood-struck to stop and stare.

He had a very famous fellow promenader, none other than Groucho Marx himself, who, pith-helmeted, huge cigar in his mouth, frequently strolled by with his daughter Melinda.

Groucho was as quick as he was reputed to be. Arnold found it difficult to hold his own with Groucho who had a knack of keeping you off-balance without seeming to try.

Groucho would hold improvised monologues. On a soft blue evening, when there was a particularly lavish display of meteorites, Groucho, addressing himself to God, asked if He was having some kind of premiere (all the big Hollywood galas used huge spotlights that crisscrossed the skies the way antiaircraft lights had during the war) and that if this was His idea of attracting attention, He would have done better to hire the famous Otto K. Olson Illuminating Company who *really* knew how to light up a sky. Even Cohen's, a Jewish delicatessen on Fairfax, had had a more impressive opening. Then Groucho got into a one-sided argument with God about the way the Cold War was going. Did He really know what He was doing letting Man fool around with atomic toys? This led to smaller complaints about everything from the lack of really first-class scripts for the Marx Brothers to the baby's excessive belly-aches.

Groucho explained to Arnold that he used God as kind of a therapist. "Some people pay as high as twenty-four dollars an hour to Viennese refugee shrinks for the privilege of complaining. Of course there's always the wear and tear on the couch, but most patients get about as many answers from their shrinks as I'm getting from Him.''

Groucho took particular delight in holding these monologues in the presence of a strikingly handsome man who lived a distance down the hill and who was invariably shocked at this blasphemy and disrespect to God. Eventually Groucho introduced Arnold to him.

"This hill is full of a/k/a's," Groucho began, then to Arnold, "you've been in Hollywood long enough to know that doesn't mean Alter Kackers Association."

"Oh sure," Arnold made the mistake of cutting Groucho off as the handsome stranger watched politely, "A/k/a means 'also known as' like Cary Grant a/k/a Archibald Leach—''

"Or Arnold Elton." Groucho fixed his look of mild outrage on Arnold. "A/k/a what?"

"Nothing," Arnold said apologetically. "Just plain Arnold Elton.''

Groucho thought that over.

"Like for-two-cents-plain?" he asked. "I buy that," he continued with the astonishing introduction. "Arnold Elton a/k/a For-two-cents-plain Arnold Elton, this is Misha Olinovsky a/k/a Millard Olds a/k/a Uncle Millie."

There was a quick icy grab at Arnold's gut. He'd heard rumors that a certain Uncle Millie, who had strong connections with the Mob, lived on their hill. He was much prized as a show-off piece at very "in" Hollywood parties.

Although Uncle Millie was only in his forties, his black hair was set off dramatically by a streak of gray that he was supposed to have acquired during a three-weeks' sojourn in the death house. Uncle Millie was reputed to have got his start in life as the coldest hit man in Mob history, ready to hit anybody the Mob ordered, man, woman or child, working with a short length of piano wire, pouncing suddenly and strangling his victims quickly. He spoke quietly and gently and looked like a movie star.

"A/k/a," Groucho went on, "as Millie the Olive."

"I never heard anybody call me 'Olive' to my face," Uncle Millie said. "I think it's something Groucho made up."

"From Olinovsky to Olive is a reasonable step," Groucho pointed out.

"I buy that," Uncle Millie said, then shook Arnold's hand politely. "I'm pleased to make your acquaintance." He shook Arnold's hand politely. Whatever else, Uncle Millie was a very formal man who took a serious view of life.

"For two-cents-plain Arnold Elton" Groucho continued, "writes for the *Ladies' Home Journal* under the name of Arnold Elton—"

"I've never written for the *Ladies' Home Journal*."

"You should have said so sooner," Groucho turned to Uncle Millie. "Take back that first handshake and shake the hand of Arnold Elton who doesn't write for the *Ladies' Home Journal*." He turned his suppressed outrage full on Arnold. "I hate imposters."

With that, Groucho trundled the pram off in high indignation.

"You got to know how to take him," Uncle Millie told Arnold. "He's a Funny-Man." As if such designation explained everything. "If you don't write for the *Ladies' Home Journal*, who do you write for? I got a funny feeling I know the name from somewhere."

"I'm a novelist," Arnold said.

" 'Novelist'?" with admiration. "Which ones?"

"*Guns of Love, Love Me Love Me Love Me*," Arnold enumerated nervously, then blurted, "*Instant Kill*."

"Oh yeah," Uncle Millie said a little too quietly, but invited Arnold and the baby into his fancy apartment. It was on the ground floor (Arnold wondered was it so he could escape in a hurry if he had to?). But Uncle Millie's manner was relaxed and, oddly enough, there was an immediate and strange bond between them. Later, Arnold decided it was maybe because they had both come out of nowhere.

And Uncle Millie handled Jennifer with surprising assurance. Like a born father.

"You read *Instant Kill*?" Arnold was appalled by his own temerity. The central character was a top gangster. (All the central characters Arnold wrote about were Horatio Alger types who made it to the top in whatever field they were in.)

"I read it," he said quietly as he tickled Jennifer. "I like to read. These days," it was marvelous how he could get off very mysterious lines without you realizing at the time they were mysterious, "I got plenty time to read," he indicated the full bookshelf.

Arnold took that as an excuse to look around. Everything, including the blond furniture, was expensive creamy ivory except for several ornately framed lithographs, each with a brass nameplate. These seemed all to be by French painters with names like Renoir, Dufy and Matisse. It gave the apartment a real look of class. On the other hand, there was something about the place that indicated nothing in it belonged to the present inhabitant. Except the books. *Gone With the Wind* was there. *Forever Amber*.

"One of the big regrets of my life," Uncle Millie said softly as Jennifer cooed and reached up with a chubby hand for his glasses, "I never married, I never had kids."

"You're young yet," Arnold said.

"I'll tell you what," Uncle Millie confided as he played with Jennifer, "in my profession it's better with no wife and kids." His manner changed slightly. "Now, am I right you would like my opinion of *Instant Kill*?"

"I'd like your opinion," Arnold said tightly.

"The hero of your book," Uncle Millie continued, "this 'Doc Santori'? Am I wrong you based him on a certain 'Doc' Salvatore?"

"You're right," Arnold said, scared.

"It so happens I personally know something about 'Doc' Salvatore." Uncle Millie was having fun fighting off Jennifer, who was trying to pull at his streak of gray. "First I'll tell you why the boys call him Doc. Because he's always prescribing, always telling the boys about their health, you know to lay off rich foods, take exercise, to tell you the truth I learned to respect my body from 'Doc.' I like the idea in your book how 'Doc' is deported and finds out in his home village in Sicily how his grandfather was a beloved doctor. I like the way you ask the questions without giving the answers—Who knows? if his family had not left Italy for golden America—same as mine, that his life could of been different, he might of been a beloved doctor himself, which deep down is what he really wanted. Only two things, Elton—"

Here it comes, Arnold thought, panicky, why did I ever start?

"What you wrote in that book is okay by me if we're talking about a book—" Uncle Millie said gently. "If we're talking about real life, you want my opinion? I mean books, that's your griff—" strange how this soft-spoken man was frightening. Uncle Millie proceeded into the devious crannies of life as he understood them. "From what I heard, the real Doc Salvatore first got his name 'Doc' in a different way. I heard he started out as a hit man, an ordinary soldier-hitter. He used to say when he got sent out, like when he went to do his famous job on Fingers Falucci, who was not an easy man to do a job on, Doc said, 'I'm going out to visit a sick friend and bring him some pain-killer, a sure cure even if the poor bastid don't even know yet he's sick—' Ever after he said the same thing so the boys began to call him 'the Doc with the sure-fire cure,' like Ripley says, 'Believe It or Not,' the boys got a sense of humor. Secondly—'' and Arnold would remember that ''secondly'' for years—''when we meet your Doc Santori he's already on the high pillow, the top banana. Now I'll tell you something about the top banana no matter who he is, president of a corporation or a *capodecapi*, he's got it made, he's there, he's got nothing to prove. The way you can spot the real top banana is not because *he* acts tough, he doesn't have to, it's from the people around him. *They* all act like he's the top banana. That's how you tell.''

''I got it.'' Arnold knew, as surely as the time Kate had come to him that Saturday afternoon, that he had learned an important lesson that he could apply in his writing. Uncle Millie looked at him and seemed to understand Arnold had caught on. There was a moment of emotion between the men, which they both honored with a long silence neither of them felt embarrassing.

''I hear you're fast with the pasteboards,'' Uncle Millie said. ''We got ourselves a game going here once a week, we could use another hand, poker is best with six . . .''

It had been years since Arnold had played. He was surprised at how much he'd missed it. More often than not he was alone nights. How long could a man do nothing but work nights? So Uncle Millie was maybe with the Mob but it was hard to associate him with anything like that. And even so, what harm could there be in a game of poker with him and his friends?

The first night Arnold left to play he told Kate casually he was going out for an evening of poker, not mentioning with whom. She seemed relieved. She'd been uneasy about how he spent his after-dark hours when she was away. A card game was a very good idea. Women were never involved. It was strictly an all-male activity. And there were prestigious games going all over Hollywood. Duke Wayne and his hard-drinking cronies had their game; on the other end of the political spectrum Dalton Trumbo and Ring Lardner, Jr., had theirs. There were dozens in between. It would do Arnold no harm to play in one of these games. Arnold was being accepted.

Arnold didn't understand what a signal honor Uncle Millie had conferred on him until he saw who the other four players were: Kate's Johnny Farina (did his presence confirm the rumors that he was Mob-connected?); Bo Lundberg, the producer of extravaganza musicals, who, it was said, had been the author of that statutory rape that had been the basis for Gorham's promotion; Charles Anson Thube, pronounced "tube" as if the "h" didn't exist, who not only handled every spectacular Hollywood divorce but was seen with his female star clients at all the hot spots; Langley Schurz, the health foods man who was thought to be the lover of the shy beautiful Scandinavian film star with the huge eyes and throaty laugh, who was so frightened of germs she had her doorknobs disinfected immediately after anyone touched them.

It was a faster and headier company than any Arnold had ever been near before. On that first night he was acutely aware that Uncle Millie was watching him, maybe even testing him.

When the stakes were announced, Arnold's plaster-faced expression came in handy. A dollar a chip with a twenty-dollar limit. His heart was pounding in his ears as he made swift calculations and concluded that in a game like that a man could lose five, maybe ten thousand dollars, if he got real unlucky, in one session. No matter how much money he was making, Arnold had a hard time seeing himself playing for such stakes, but finally figured, hell, he was there. He'd see this one through and gracefully decline future invitations. Also he heard faint echoes of Adelheid teaching him that real gambling was only when you played for more than you could afford to lose.

Quickly Arnold saw that with the exception of Uncle

276

Millie, the others were not much better than the boys Arnold had taken so easily in the poker and crap games in the merchant marine. These men, too, played for luck. They didn't remember what cards were out and calculate the odds. The game was some kind of superstitious testing of their fortune; they hoped the game would prove they were naturally lucky.

Uncle Millie, obviously as good a player as Arnold, played strangely, maybe thought it wasn't right for him as host to win too much.

Arnold won consistently. He was almost sorry, for he found himself losing that exciting awe with which he'd looked on famous Hollywood personalities. When you got down to it, they played like schmucks.

In a seven-card poker, Arnold bluffed Schurz, who had a straight, out of a several-hundred-dollar pot with a twenty-dollar bet. Schurz hadn't even called. Arnold thought about it carefully, then decided it was to his advantage to confuse these schmucks further by showing he'd bluffed.

Schurz fought a losing battle to preserve that calm he was constantly preaching to his clients as the cornerstone of health.

"But I had the winning hand," Schurz blurted out. He and the others, except Uncle Millie, glared at Arnold. "The sonofabitch plays to win," as if this was the ultimate crime.

"That's right," Arnold said in the ensuing silence, figuring if they didn't invite him back, that was okay with him too. "I play to win. In everything I do."

Later, when they were gorging themselves at the deli-catessen-laden table (there was so much food Arnold figured that maybe *that* was one of the reasons Millie had won the affectionate honorary designation "Uncle," the Jewish counterpart of the Italian "Don"), Uncle Millie made it a point to invite Arnold back and there wasn't the slightest opposition.

Arnold became a regular player at that game and won practically every time; he assumed they kept inviting him back in the hopes of one day slaughtering him.

"Congratulations," Groucho told him one midafternoon on a baby-wheeling promenade, but Groucho's tone gave no hint of approval. (Groucho, it seemed, never gave anything whole-hearted approval.) "I hear you're a bigger sonofabitch than I imagined, and I don't promote people to sonofabitch lightly. What's this I hear, you play *to win*? And I hear you're taking Uncle Millie's twenty-fingered friends for everything they haven't got. Keep up the good work and by the time you're thirty-five we'll both retire to Catalina Island on your ill-gotten gains. Make that Palm Springs. Only don't expect any help or sympathy from me. Remember what they say here, be nice to the people you meet on your way up, not only will you meet the same people on your way down but you'll be stuck with them while you're up. On second thought I think I'll retire alone on your ill-gotten gains. Why should I share with you, Felton? Don't look at me like that. It won't help. Just don't come whining to me for a buck when you're in need. I won't even give you one of my half-smoked cigars. Who are you to smoke my half-smoked cigars? The last half is the best, for which the first was made. The most you can expect from me is that if you're tired I may carry you a few feet. And don't turn up your nose at that. I've never carried anybody in my life, especially full-grown able-bodied males like you who play to win. I don't even carry Melinda and she wets her diapers, which is more than you do."

At about the tenth game Arnold decided he ought to lose. But when he deliberately tried to lose, they interpreted it as some new trick and played like bigger assholes. Arnold won even more heavily.

After the others had gone, Uncle Millie said, "Okay, Arnie, you're a hotshot poker player, but what about gin?"

"Oh, I hold my own," Arnold answered carefully. Uncle Millie didn't ask questions idly.

"You know those important gin games," Uncle Millie went on, "the very top guys. Let's take one, let's say like the game Darryl Zanuck, Jack Warner and Sam Goldwyn play..." Arnold nodded. Those were the legendary games. Studio heads, fabulous stakes. "Now forget I mentioned names, especially those three names. Now gimme three names—any names—"

"Hart, Schaffner and Marx," Arnold supplied.

"Fine." It didn't elicit a smile from Uncle Millie. "Now here's the situation. There's a real game going with three other Studio heads. We'll call them Hart, Schaffner and Marx. There's a fourth plays with 'Hart, Schaffner and Marx,' a young guy, heir to an oil fortune. Let's take another name, Rockefeller. The thing about this 'Rockefeller' is that he's been taking 'Hart, Schaffner and Marx' regularly."

"I've been taking our guys regularly too."

"That's because they don't *play,*" Uncle Millie said. "*You* do."

The point was that in the last few weeks "Hart, Schaffner and Marx" had become convinced young "Rockefeller" was cheating but couldn't figure out how. Certain people approached certain people who approached others until they got to Uncle Millie.

"You'd be surprised what people come to me for," Uncle Millie turned philosophical. "Life is fulla situations the law and lawyers and the whole schmear can't handle. Normally, I got a rule. I never mix business with life. But seeing it's absolute top characters, 'Hart, Schaffner and Marx' themselves. Right? So when I was asked do I know somebody could be brought into that game who could spot how is this rich young punk cheating, I figure I'll import maybe somebody from the East, or a specialist from Vegas. They got dozens who do nothing but that, but then I get me a better idea. You.''

''Me?'' Arnold blinked in shock and started to back away.

''You,'' Uncle Millie was not in the least affected by Arnold's movement of recoil. ''It would be more natural, you—and you're better than any card pro I know . . .''

''*Me*?''

''I been watching you, kid. You *play* and look.'' Uncle Millie gestured generously that after all it was up to Arnold alone to decide. ''Then I ask myself, Could it do the kid any harm to be on such a basis with men like 'Hart, Schaffner and Marx?' The answer is no harm and plenty of good.''

Although the game rotated from place to place, the first time Arnold met with them it was in a nothing place, a bungalow on the ''Marx'' lot. Not a goddamn thing had been done to brighten up the one-story functional building. Several card tables and chairs had been brought in. Apparently all the three Studio heads wanted was complete isolation where they could play undisturbed.

They treated Arnold gingerly.

''We were expecting a professional.'' ''Hart'' played nervously with the longest cigar Arnold had ever seen—or maybe it looked so big because ''Hart'' was a comparatively short man. ''We were set to make a deal with a pro, a flat price.''

''Let's not play footsie around the bush,'' ''Marx'' was famous for his malapropisms and was a very irritable man. ''What do you want?''

''Uncle Millie thought I could help you out,'' Arnold said. ''That's it.''

That stopped all further discussion.

The three agreed they would underwrite Arnold's losses. It was only fair and furthermore it would free him psychologically to turn his full attention to the business at hand; to establish as quickly as possible if this young sonofabitch heir to a fortune was taking them and if so how.

A few minutes later young "Rockefeller" came in. He accepted Arnold without question. It made no difference to him whose money he took.

Arnold wondered why a new player didn't bother the rich punk.

The players rotated too. They'd play so many hands with the same opponent, then switch.

Arnold fared no better than the others. Before the evening was over "Rockefeller" had taken him for fourteen grand and Arnold hadn't a clue as to how he was cheating.

All in all it was a pretty miserable evening. Arnold hated losing, even somebody else's money, and the food was unbelievable, a glorified vegetable plate—boiled endives, carrots and beets. "Marx" had built a special lunchroom on the lot for his ulcer. It was practically compulsory for "above-the-line people"—Stars, Directors, Writers, Producers—to lunch there, despite the daily menu of boiled vegetables, grilled lamb chops, milk and rice pudding. Not only did that help defray the cost of the lunchroom, but it was well known "Marx" was paranoiac about how his top people spent their working hours. He liked to have them where he could watch over them.

At the end of a month's play, Arnold was down twenty-three thousand dollars. The game had rotated to the Octagonal Room of the "Hart" Brentwood estate, an enormous eight-sided room where the "Schaffners" threw parties catered by Chasen's.

Even for the gin game the room was filled with cut flowers. The air was heavy with a scent that made Arnold's eyes stream and brought on a fit of sneezing, and from time to time, Alexa Brooks Schaffner came in and surveyed the group with amusement. She was a former English movie star who'd married the Studio head. Arnold couldn't keep his eyes off her porcelain complexion, fine features and fragile blond indoor beauty and delicate fuckable body to match.

"Hart" had telephoned he would be a few minutes late and to start without him. He was helping Sam Goldwyn, who was having trouble with his latest film.

"Let's start," "Schaffner" said to "Rockefeller" as the two sat down at one of the tables.

For the first time, Arnold was not playing while "Rockefeller" was. Arnold was able to give the latter his undivided attention.

"For my money," "Schaffner" was droning on with the Olympian assurance of a Studio head, "Goldwyn's in big trouble. Nothing'll help him, he's winding up this story about a baseball player. Now let no one get me wrong. I got nothing against stories about baseball players, I'm a hundred percent for our national game, even night games." (Night games were cutting into motion-picture box office take.) "The mistake Goldwyn made is it's about a *sick* baseball player." He and "Rockefeller" started to play, "People don't go to movies about sick—or dying. Nobody wants to see a movie about death. Universal almost broke its back with *Death Takes a Holiday*. Death in the title is death at the box office." "Schaffner" realized a few seconds late, as he always did, that he'd made a joke and laughed belatedly.

"Maybe Goldwyn's ahead of his time," Arnold said quietly.

"Gin!" "Rockefeller" said, laying down his cards. "Schaffner" turned pale. He'd been caught with seven face cards plus two nines. "Schaffner's" losses came to over eight hundred dollars on that one hand alone.

Arnold sneezed several times in a row.

"I guess Mr. Belton's allergic," "Schaffner" said. He was famous for not remembering names.

"The name's Elton," "Rockefeller" said as he shuffled.

"I know his name's Elton," "Schaffner" said, "his name's a household word. I always get directors' names confused."

"His name's not a household word in your household," "Rockefeller" said. "Elton's not a director. He's a writer."

"Writers are worse, we've had so many writers in and out of the Studio their names float in front of my eyes like migraine spots," "Schaffner" said. "Imagine, in this day and age doctors can't give me a pill for my migraine. They don't even know what causes it."

"Maybe it's the same heavy scent that makes Elton here sneeze," "Rockefeller" said. "In this octagonal room I feel I'm lucky if I get out with less than black-lung."

"It happens *I* know what sets off my migraine," "Schaffner" said testily. "Glints of light. Like when I'm being driven home, glints of light from the back of the car in front of us hits me. Whammo. Migraine with floating spots." He shielded his eyes. "Even glints from your ring—sharp little nasties now and then."

They all glanced at "Rockefeller's" ring, and for the first time he seemed to lose his composure. He quickly turned his large dark-stoned ring inward so that his palm covered the stone. "You should've said something sooner," he said apologetically.

"They hit me, nothing to do but suffer," "Schaffner" said. "Come on. Play."

Suddenly Arnold focused on that ring. It had been bothering him for quite awhile. It was a funny piece of jewelry for a young guy dressed casual California. The ring was a wrong note. It was too ornate, it didn't belong.

"Rockefeller" straightened the deck so he held it firmly in his left hand. Arnold waited until "Rockefeller" had turned the ring right side up, it was too awkward to deal with it in his palm, and then when he started dealing, Arnold drifted idly until he was standing in an ostensibly friendly kibitzer's pose directly behind "Rockefeller," who dealt two or three cards more, then realizing someone was behind him swung around.

"I've got a thing about people standing behind me," "Rockefeller" said sharply.

"Sorry," but Arnold didn't move.

"Rockefeller" continued dealing, then stopped and waited.

Arnold moved away. It was all over. He had caught it all, a flash of a reflection of the card "Rockefeller" was dealing to "Schaffner" in a facet of the stone of his ring.

Arnold was in a high fine excitement. He had the sonofabitch. He knew exactly what he'd been doing. And yes, there was no question of it, he *had* been doing it. This punk who came from one of the richest families in the West.

When he dealt, he kept the stone of the ring below the level of the cards as he dealt. That way he could see his opponent's cards. In gin all you had to know was *one* of your opponent's cards and you had it made, for when the game was on that high a level, that was enough of an advantage.

Arnold never did learn the details of how "Hart, Schaffner and Marx" handled the situation. He heard vaguely that arrangements had been made for the punk's family to repay large sums of money. No scandal, only a few uncertain rumors.

Three days later, a brand new white Cadillac convertible with red leather seats was left on the Elton driveway. It was "Hart, Schaffner and Marx's" gift to Arnold for services rendered.

"I'm not a convertible type myself," was Kate's only comment. "For me a car's not a car unless it's got a top."

Johnny Farina invited Arnold out to lunch and told him that there was a job waiting for him as producer with any one of the "Hart, Schaffner and Marx" studios.

"I'm a novelist," Arnold said unhesitatingly. "I'll stick to books."

Uncle Millie took special pride and almost paternal pleasure in Arnold's feat, made Arnold repeat how he'd discovered the rich punk's secret. Arnold now filled a very privileged place in Uncle Millie's life.

It took Arnold a little while to understand that Uncle Millie was lonely. He had no one to talk to, not even a steady girl friend for boffing purposes.

"A man should get hamagooched regularly," Uncle Millie counseled Arnold. "Strictly as a matter of health. So I have found that for me the cheapest is to pay for it. No complications, I never use the same girl more than two or three times, I pay good, let me tell you, kid, when it comes to hamagooching, always pay the highest. Everybody's happy, no complications."

But Uncle Millie was very nervous. He seemed to be waiting for something big to happen.

Uncle Millie always had a toy for Jennifer, one of the new educational toys. He loved watching her try to put two boxes together, and would applaud when she succeeded.

"What do you think is the Organization's biggest source of income?" Lately Uncle Millie had taken to talking more openly about the Organization. Arnold guessed dope. "Small potatoes." Gambling? "Peanuts." Girls? "Negligible—I'm talking about important money."

"I give up," Arnold said.

"Banking," was Uncle Millie's surprising answer. "The Organization makes loans no bank in the world will make. Need a loan? No collateral? Unemployed? No questions asked. Why? Because the boys don't worry. Collecting? What's the problem? Twenty percent a month interest payable every month. He doesn't pay? A broken arm here, a broken leg there for starters. He pays and keeps on paying, because he knows next thing his wife will wind up without a mouthful of teeth. Banking. Big. The Organization right now is maybe number four or five as a financial force in the U.S. of A. Way up there with General Motors and U.S. Steel. Maybe you'll write a book about it.''

"Maybe," Arnold said dubiously. He had already written a book about what he *imagined* the Mob was like. Now that he knew a little more, he wasn't sure.

"I've been working on something's so simple it's stupid." Uncle Millie was in a strange jumpy mood, a couple of times he went to the front window to look out. Arnold had seen two men parked in a car nearby and had the distinct impression they were Uncle Millie's bodyguards. "Take a movie company, any of the big ones. Take Twentieth Century-Fox, okay?" Arnold nodded. "I've had a crew of numbers men figuring out on the QT how much it would cost to buy up all the shares of Fox, okay?" Again Arnold nodded. "Then I ask them to find out what Fox is *really* worth when you sell everything off. Buildings, real estate, movies, TV rights. Everything. Okay?"

"Okay," Arnold said.

"They give me the answer," Uncle Millie said moodily. "Twentieth Century-Fox, right now, is worth five times what you'd have to pay if you bought up all the stock that's out on it."

"You won't be able to buy up all its shares. People who own big blocks won't sell."

"You don't buy all the stock," Uncle Millie said thoughtfully. "All you need is sixteen percent. That gives you control. You do what you want. Take over. And sell off. That's the name of the game. But I got me a dream. Las Vegas. The world's biggest honeypot. Take over, sell off, real estate, TV rights, then siphon the money over to Honeypot City. Build hotels in Vegas. There's a problem. You any idea what the problem is?"

"No," Arnold's head was swimming. He was beginning to believe that Uncle Millie was some kind of genius. Uncle Millie looked deeper. He dared. Someday Uncle Millie would be the biggest and some small inner voice added, "If he lives."

"The problem is, if you take over a movie company, the law is you got to keep on making movies. The Feds won't let you 'destroy an industry.' But the trouble with making movies," Millie said moodily, "you never know which will be a dog, which will be a hit. There's no guarantees. How can you do intelligent business when you don't know what your product will turn out to be? So the problem is how to take over a movie company and not make movies." Uncle Millie turned to Arnold. "But I got me a schviggy, a little solution buzzing around in the noodlebox. You got any idea what it is, kid?"

"No."

"You stop making movies gradually, kid," Uncle Millie said, "that's the schviggy. Right now Fox is making what? sixty, seventy films a year? Okay. You take over. You cut down slowly. In five years you're making maybe twenty-five films a year. In ten years you're making five films a year. In fifteen years, maybe three." Uncle Millie made a gesture with his hand extending from his eyes. "Long-range, look ahead, that's the secret. Never forget that."

"I won't," Arnold promised.

"From making three movies a year to making zero is a small step," Uncle Millie continued. "Now I been watching these big film companies. They ain't changing with the rest of the world. Remember what I'm saying. *More and more they'll mismanage*! Their stocks will go down and down. I got my eye on one certain company. Your alma mater—Associated Artists—they've got the worst management of all, and I'll know exactly when to move in." Uncle Millie walked over to the window, looked out, seemed reassured. "Right now I got to work as a loner. Once I got it going, I'll go to the boys. I'll cut with them, but my way.'' He sighed. "So we're at the dangerous time. The boys don't understand why they're not cut in from the beginning. But if I come in with something all made and say here's how we divide it, that's okay. They'll buy that. And I'd be the top banana. But right now, careful, careful. We're walking on eggs.''

Uncle Millie wasn't careful enough.

Two days later toward evening, the hillside echoed with shots, then a few minutes afterward the wail of police cars.

The next morning Arnold read in the papers that Uncle Millie had had the back of his head shot off while peacefully reading in his Sunset Plaza apartment. One of the newspapers mentioned the book he'd been reading, Arnold Elton's *Instant Kill*.

The first moment Uncle Millie was off the critical list, Arnold went to see him at Cedars of Lebanon Hospital. Two armed guards let him pass.

Most of Uncle Millie's head was hidden by enormous white bandages. Uncle Millie, lying on his side, managed a crooked smile for Arnold, motioned for him to bend close.

"The boys were less patient than I thought,'' Uncle Millie whispered.

5.

Jennifer, a year and a few weeks old, smiled and gurgled, her few strands of black hair gathered in a ridiculous topknot tied with a pink ribbon. She was a happy child, ate well, crapped on schedule. Arnold cleaned and powdered her bottom and put on fresh diapers. Kate was off to the Agency. She was one of the rare ones who worked on Saturday.

Mrs. Griffith, instead of just calling out from the living room, where she'd answered the telephone, came right into the nursery and announced solemnly, "It's the Bank calling you."

Arnold tried not to show his excitement. He wouldn't let himself believe what he was almost certain it was. He was still in awe of Banks and Bankers. A Bank was a bulwark, a fortress, an area of comfort and security. He enjoyed being in a Bank and making a deposit in person, which he could only rarely do. The Agency handled all that for him, sending his royalty checks straight on to his account. He deliberately did not keep a personal record of how much money he had in his account and for a special reason, which was about to bear fruit.

"Mr. Elton? Mr. Arnold Elton?"

"Yes."

"This is Mr. Pitchford, the managing director of your bank."

The managing director. In person. It had to be. "I have before me your written instruction to notify you when your account attains the million-dollar level?"

"That is correct."

Jennifer on the floor yanked at the cord.

"I can now give you official confirmation," Pitchford's voice was aggrieved, "your special tax account is generously provided even to cover today's excessive income tax." Pitchford was a devoted Republican who'd voted for Nixon for Congress. "Your savings account with us now stands at one million and thirty-seven thousand dollars."

Arnold sat down suddenly on the floor alongside Jennifer. One million dollars. I made it.

"Are there any particular instructions, Mr. Elton?"

"Yes, I'd like you to bring me one million dollars, in bills of various denominations, here to my home."

"Today? Saturday?" Pitchford's tone was close to panic.

"Yes, please. Now. I'll return it later today."

"It won't be easy," Pitchford said anxiously. A sudden million-dollar withdrawal from a small Beverly Hills bank could play hell with the bank's business for months. Then when Arnold didn't answer, he added gruffly, "I'll arrange it. Have a nice day, Mr. Elton."

"Jennifer, Jennifer," Arnold picked her up and rocked her in ecstasy. "You'll never lack for anything, baby. We've got a million dollars, a million dollars." Jennifer fell asleep, Arnold carefully rose and tiptoed her off to her bed.

Not more than forty-five minutes later a girl of twenty or so stood at the door holding a valise. She was honey blond, interesting-looking and unquestionably not Jewish.

"I'm Barbara Jane Pitchford."

"Oh, Pitchford. Are you?"

"I'm the Banker's Daughter." It took him a second to realize she was kidding it.

She slipped inside holding the valise so that it preceded her, he hastily shut the door behind her, as she leaned against the wall. For all her coolness, she'd been under considerable strain. After all she was lugging around one million dollars.

"There's a whole folklore about the Farmer's Daughter. I've often wondered why there are no jokes about the Banker's Daughter."

"From the way your father talked I thought he would send an armored truck."

"I'm it," she said. "And I'm much cheaper." She handed him the valise. "Well. There it is."

He tried to think of something witty, then he suddenly remembered, and told himself "With a million who needs to think of anything witty?" He simply started off.

"Oh. You're supposed to count it in my presence, then sign a receipt for it." She made a slight mocking face, "Standard Banking Practice."

"I trust you. I'll just sign the receipt," he said uneasily.

"There might not be a million dollars there."

"If your dad could take a chance, I guess I can too." He felt an almost physical need to get off by himself with the valise. He took the slip of paper she handed him, quickly signed the receipt.

"May I wait here?" she asked.

"Make yourself at home," Arnold gestured hastily. Despite the turbulence, he found himself appreciating the way she sat in the armchair, a graceful relaxed movement, shucking off her saddle shoes, stretching her liberated toes, folding her legs under her. Katharine Hepburn was the only other woman who could seat herself like that.

Inside the study, he moved on the double, actually locking himself in, then seating himself in his chair before the desk.

"Your Writer's Chair." A gift from Kate after he'd topped the best-seller list for ten unprecedented weeks. *"Custom-made to fit your ass."*

Arnold carefully placed the valise on top of the desk, opened it, sat a long moment luxuriating in the opulence of neatly stacked elastic-bound packages of bank notes. The smaller denominations were on top, the fives, tens and twenties, as if thoughtfully presented that way so there'd be a build-up to the real goodies—the fifties, the hundreds, and even a few thousand-dollar bills. He'd never seen a thousand-dollar bill before. Lovingly, tenderly, he took each package out separately, taking his time, no hurry, placed each one in an exact pile on his uncluttered desk.

Then, meticulously, he undressed each pile, removed the elastic band, the fives first, counted them very carefully, five hundred of them, then the tens, the twenties, the fifties, the hundreds, unaware he was groaning. He stopped at the thousand-dollar bills. There were a hundred of them. He held each bill separately, noted the amount on a pad.

He totaled the figures—one million dollars.

Somebody said something. He realized with surprise that it was *he*. He was saying, "Three and a quarter percent $37,629.20 a year, over $3,000 a month. Three g's every month, month in month out." He walked over to the draped window, which gave on the street, and said out loud, very formally, "Ladies and gentlemen, I, Arnold Elton say fuck you one and all! Thank you." He walked in circles, panted, made grunting sounds, then went back to the money. There'd been something he hadn't been able to stop for first time around. There it was. One hundred-dollar bill too many. He counted a third and fourth time. No doubt of it. One too many.

All he was supposed to do was return a million dollars. He pocketed the extra hundred-dollar bill, replaced the stacks of currency precisely in the valise, stood a long moment fighting it, then quickly, as if catching the valise by surprise, snapped it open. Reality. A million dollars nestled in the valise.

"Miss Pitchford?" he called out from the study doorway. The girl was still ensconced in the chair as though she were sitting before a fireplace. "Would you mind coming in here?"

The girl crossed gracefully. He shut the door behind her. The old bag Mrs. Griffith must be somewhere in the vicinity.

"The count right?"

"On the nose," he tried to keep his voice even and casual.

"Now I have to count the money here in your presence." She made a wry gesture. "There's your Sound Banking Practice again."

"You'll be comfortable in my Writer's Chair, Miss Pitchford."

She examined the chair with interest, then wriggled her ass testing it.

"It *is* comfortable."

"It was custom-made for me."

"It seems to fit me, too."

She counted quickly, her forefinger flicking through the piles deftly.

"You never count the last bill in the stack. If it's a bundle of twenty you stop counting at the nineteenth, you can see there's a twentieth. The only mistake there could be, a second bill might be stuck to the twentieth, so it would be in your favor. That's of course only if you're being paid. If you're *paying out*, that is a horse of a different color. Then you count them all."

"Isn't that kind of dishonest?"

293

She stopped, made a note of an amount on a slip of paper.

"I guess you mean that." She looked up at him. "I've read your books. I found parts of them very stimulating."

She bothered him. After all she was a banker's daughter.

"Aren't you worried about getting that money back? Isn't your father waiting for it?"

"Dad's a banker. He's used to taking chances. He's been through this before."

His gut lurched. "You mean you've done *this* before?"

"Oh sure. Other people have asked to have the money brought to them at home when their accounts hit a million. Dad always does it on a Saturday when there's nobody around and he always sends me." She sounded a little like Agnes had when she'd told him about the goose trick and the whip man.

"You know why I wanted the money delivered to me here?" Arnold asked nervously.

"Oh yes." Beejay crossed that frontier. They were definitely in Agnes-land. "You wanted to see it with your own eyes. Was there someone in here with you? I thought I heard sounds."

"Maybe I was humming, sometimes I hum to myself."

"I read somewhere that you said you actually personally did all the things you described in your books."

"You could more or less say I have. Yes."

"I think it's liberating, your second book especially."

" 'Liberating'?"

"Most people are ashamed of their bodies, at least parts of them, but I think, for example the scene between Diana and Tommy, I mean where he makes Diana feel that there's no part of her that's shameful? I think it's reassuring, it frees people."

"It's gratifying for a writer to know he's helped people."

Beejay nodded. "I'd better get this money back to Dad, but you seem to understand a lot more about women than most men.'' Her fingers twinkled through the bills. "I enjoyed talking to you.''

Arnold suddenly felt that something was there. She had looked at him oddly, speculatively. Was it possible? A girl like that? Barbara Jane Pitchford? With Arnold Elton?

"Could we talk again?'' he asked suddenly.

"Yes, of course,'' and it was hard to tell if she was more than just polite. "You can always reach me at the bank.''

"Just call the bank and ask for Barbara Jane?''

"That's all.''

Jennifer was making sounds from the nursery. Naturally Mrs. Griffith wasn't around when she was really needed. A baby crying was what the moment didn't need.

"There was one hundred-dollar bill too many,'' Arnold said suddenly. "I guess it was stuck to another one or something.''

Her eyes were soft hazel.

"It was Dad who counted the money in his office. He's always nervous in a situation like this because he does take personal responsibility for the money. Technically it's yours.''

"Your know what? Is there something crazy you like, you never let yourself indulge in?''

"Wil Wright's pecan crunch ice cream. Although if you're going to suggest I buy myself a hundred dollars' worth, I don't think I can manage that.'' She took the hundred-dollar bill he held out to her. "I'll get just about as much out of telling Dad he made the mistake and it'll be a lot less fattening, but thanks anyway.''

Kate worried him by coming home at five-thirty, which was early for her on a Saturday, her "best workday.'' Even more ominous, she didn't wait until her usual six-thirty to mix herself her vodka martini. She plopped Jennifer on her knee, and because a burning cigarette was almost continually pasted to one corner of her mouth right over the baby's head, it made him nervous.

"Who was that beautiful blond twat you had here?" She held her head back to keep the smoke out of her eyes. "I tried to call you, but Mrs. Griffith said you'd locked yourself in the study with a blond twat with a valise."

"That was no twat. That was a Jehovah Witness girl," he said. "They come around with a portable phonograph, play you a record to convert you."

"It took her an hour to convert you?"

"She didn't convert me."

"She *some*thing'd you, I can tell by the look on your face."

"What look?"

Kate got up quickly but twisted in time so the long cigarette ash missed the baby's practically bald head. "The look of a guy who got his rocks off. You got your ashes hauled this afternoon. It's written all over your face. I can smell it."

"With a Jehovah's Witness?"

"Female Jehovah's Witnesses don't have cunts?"

"You couldn't prove it by me."

"Okay," grimly Kate dipped her still-smoking cigarette in a vase of cut flowers, which always annoyed him. "Okay, Buster. You can't make it twice in the same day. So let's you and me haul ass to the bedroom and fuck."

"Do you *have* to talk that way in front of the baby?"

"What's she going to understand?" then bellowed, "Mrs. Griffith!"

"Dr. Braunschweig says babies understand a lot more than you think, especially girl babies."

"Fuck Braunschweig," said Kate as Mrs. Griffith came scampering up looking as innocent as a boiled egg, and this right after having stooled on him.

296

In their bedroom Kate slipped out of her clothes so fast it seemed like a sleight-of-hand trick.

"I don't feel like it," Arnold said, as she lay before him, her legs yawning wide.

"You never don't feel like it." She made it sound like an insult. It was irritating because it was true. "You just can't produce again."

"You're going to see a hard-on like you've never seen—"

"Any time you say, Tiger."

But she was scared. She'd never seen him so belligerent, and by the time he was out of his clothes a full-fledged erection had come blossoming out of his crotch.

"Look who's here," Kate tried to keep it light. "You sure could have fooled me."

Without a word Arnold pushed her roughly.

"Wait a minute," she protested angrily. "What is this?" He got on top of her, ripped her thighs apart brutally. "Hey! Come on! That's no way." He pressed his full weight on her. She tried to squirm and fight her way out from under him but was unpleasantly surprised. He was far stronger than she'd realized. She hadn't known it before simply because he'd never had occasion to display it. "Goddamn you! What do you think you're doing?"

"I'm fucking you, that's what I'm doing!" he shouted, jabbing his angry erection at her underbelly.

She started to yell back but he clamped a hand over her mouth. They wrestled wildly, he clearly in command. Coldly he forced her over on her belly, her face deep in a pillow, pinning her hands at her sides. It was only when he had penetrated her that he let her arms free. She thrashed about, fumed, raved, made incoherent sounds as he worked away ferociously. Months of hostility had been brewing in him, he pumped at her with majestic disregard of her complaints. He had a fleeting vision of Beejay as he spurted to an orgasm, his body slumping in dead weight over her.

Gradually he realized she was sobbing. He rolled off, tried to touch her, but she punched at his hand with her small fists.

He tried to tell himself that he'd only done what she'd done to him dozens of times when she'd decided, without even bothering to ask if he was in the mood, and had just gone at him. Of course when a woman did it to a man it was okay.

He was disgusted with himself for this niggling feeling of guilt, but the more he tried to talk himself out of it the guiltier he felt.

They never discussed it openly but from then on it was always there between them. Nor was he able to make up for it by lavishing on her the elaborate foreplay she'd taught him before they went into a sexual scramble; when she did have an orgasm she made it sound as though it had been torn from her.

In retribution Kate made a variety of demands. She forced him to buy a huge several-acre property in the heart of Beverly Hills, which neither one of them particularly wanted. He'd told himself a thousand times, each time remembering Adelheid, that if he ever made it he'd never squander his money living high the way most Hollywood jerks did. He was going to live modestly and comfortably, and the next thing you knew there he was buying the enormous house.

And it took every penny he'd gotten for the film rights to *Love Me Love Me Love Me*. Kate also forced him to spend a shitpot of money having a French art director who was hot at one of the studios redecorate the house in red, white and gold—Empire they called it—with red *N*'s and gilt laurel branches all over the place.

The bathroom was resplendent in red and gold, a big red *N* on the toilet bowl but there were no towel racks. The master bedroom had two rickety but authentic Empire bed tables, a sumptuous custom-built king-sized bed and nothing else. The total furnishings in the immense living room consisted of three armchairs, which, like giant overstuffed children's toy animals, clustered wistfully about the TV set waiting hopefully for someone to pet them. Kate had been among the first to acquire a TV set. Television, she pronounced, was going to be the biggest thing since hot buttered popcorn, but Arnold had taken one look at the small glowing screen—the programs were almost entirely tap dancers or vaudevillians— TV won't amount to shit, Arnold judged and refused to give it a second glance.

Drapes tightly drawn, the study door locked, Arnold attacked his fourth novel. All he needed was his Writer's chair, table, his typewriter, and one bright lamp zeroing in with such intensity "like he was giving his typewriter the third degree," Kate would tell their infrequent guests.

His work schedule was sacred and never violated. It was a shock one day when Kate barged in.

"Work or no work, this you got to see," Kate said grimly.

She half dragged him into the living room where the lonely TV set was glowing balefully.

The House Committee on Un-American Activities was having televised hearings in the Federal Courthouse District of Southern California, Los Angeles. As Blake had predicted, they were investigating Communist infiltration into the motion-picture industry.

"Jeezus," Arnold wailed, "you didn't drag me away from my *work* for that?"

He started back to his workroom.

"Don't go away, Bubby, *this* you're going to want to see."

The tiny screen was suddenly aglow with a huge close-up of Gorham. Dressed immaculately, fatter, Gorham carried a heavy impassive authority.

Arnold made three grunting sounds, the first when he realized it was Gorham, the second after the Committee counsel asked what the witness's occupation was, and Gorham replied with a quiet modesty, "Banker."

The third grunt came after one of the Committee members

explained with an indulgent smile, "Actually Mr. Gorham is the head of one of the largest savings and loan associations in all Southern California. And I might add, its founder."

"They're kidding," Arnold said with passionate indignation.

"A congressional committee kidding?"

Gorham had even grown banker's jowls. And he was wearing a vest with piping. Nobody in Southern California wore vests, let alone with piping.

"When did this happen?"

"Shit has it," Kate took a perverse pleasure in Arnold's discomfiture, "that he's been working on a bank license for years. Came up like a bat outa hell about six months ago—"

"Yes, sir, I did go to two of their study gatherings, the first one was devoted to something they called male chauvinism," Gorham's voice came from the TV as he permitted a rueful smile to flit over his large face, "in a Beverly Hills mansion. You may wonder, sir, why I went to the second—" Gorham had developed an unsuspected gift for comedy, his timing was great— "couldn't get myself to believe the first."

The Committee counsel, the chairman, the Committee, the Federal Courthouse audience laughed very heartily on cue.

"Gorham a *banker*? A *banker*, for shit's sake? And big? *Gorham*?" Arnold demanded.

"Biggest thing since Seven-Up," Kate assured him.

Counsel now asked Gorham if in his opinion these so-called study groups were not in fact Communist Front organizations. And Gorham hazarded the opinion, as a very responsible member of the community who knew the importance of his words, "Yes, sir, they were most certainly Communist Front organizations."

"Gorham," Kate explained, "is what is known as a friendly witness. He's going to sing, to name all his friends, tell all on everybody. So the Committee treats him like the sun rises and sets in his ass."

300

Arnold hadn't heard her.

"What I want to know is," Arnold asked frantically, "how a nothing like Gorham gets to be the head of one of the biggest banking outfits in the state, practically while I'm not looking? Somebody please tell me. Somebody explain that to me."

Now Kate wasn't listening to him. She was fascinated, for Gorham had just been asked by the Committee counsel if he could and would name others he'd recognized at the study groups and who he thought might be Communist.

"Here it comes," Kate said warningly, "the naming of names."

"If a schmo like Gorham can make it in banking," Arnold prounounced with deep passion, "something's wrong with banking."

Gorham consulted a list on a snappy gold-trimmed crocodile notebook and droned off names. Arnold suddenly stiffened.

"Blake," Gorham enunciated each letter clearly, "Lawrence Edwin Blake."

"I'm calling from a phone booth," Blake's voice carried condensed panic. "Can you meet me at the Schwabadero?" Schwab's Drugstore had become filmdom's favorite meeting place.

After a few uncertain moments of cogitation, after all, Blake had done him a real service, *I Owe Him A Favor,* Arnold went to Schwab's.

Blake was pale and kept looking behind his shoulder nervously. "I'm being tailed but nobody will attach any particular significance to *you* meeting me here."

They stood in front of the newspaper and magazine section, Blake pretended to look through *Variety* and didn't talk directly to Arnold.

A mid-level male star came in, began a reflex greeting to Blake but turned away quickly, without greeting him.

"I thought you and he were friends," Arnold said.

"Before Gorham's appearance at the hearings we were," Blake's manner became urgent. "You know the routine?" As Arnold looked blank, "A federal marshal comes to your house with a subpoena. He asks if you're you, and if you lie, it's a federal offense you can go to jail for a year for that. So you say you are you. The marshal then slips you a subpoena ordering you to appear before the Committee. If you don't appear, that's a federal offense too, also worth a year in the slammer. So you present yourself. Next thing you know you're an unpaid star on their TV Un-American Activities Committee hearings. Once you've appeared you can't work at any studio and you're fucked every which way."

"I know all that."

"My only hope is to take off—just like that—for New York. They won't notice me as much there. I might be able to work. That means I have to leave everything in my Beachwood Drive house. I can't get the stuff moved out because it would be immediately noticed and reported. That's where you come in."

"Me? *Me*?"

"All I want you to do," Blake said (Arnold noticed the "all"—Blake was making it sound like nothing much,) "is drop in on my place from time to time just to see if everything's okay. Take the junk mail out of the mailbox before it gets cluttered and people realize the place is empty. And water the plants."

Actually Arnold was slightly relieved. He'd expected Blake to ask him something bigger and more dangerous. But even this made him a little uncomfortable.

"There's nobody else you can ask?"

"You're the only guy I've been close to who's been completely uninvolved politically. Oh hell, Arnold, you could do it, no sweat. If a federal marshal comes to the door while you're there, he'll say, 'Are you Lawrence Edwin Blake?'

And see, that's the weenie. You can say in perfect truth, 'No. I am not.' Then you send me a cable to an address I'll give you in New York.''

"Christ, Larry, they'll trace that telegram."

"I'll give you a name and address that will never be traced. You're safe and I'll know they're really after me and make some permanent arrangement for myself and my things. You could even work there during the day every now and then. Hey. Don't you need a place to take a babe once in a while? It's a perfect setup. You'll be alone. Nobody'll bother you."

"I'm not into that yet. With Kate there's barely enough for the house."

But it was at this point that minuscule wheels whirred in Arnold's head. He took the keys to Blake's Beachwood house.

"I want to do a book about banking," Arnold said to Pitchford, a tall, tanned, trim man in his late forties, whose office was as lean and unadorned as he; two chairs, a desk on which sat a telephone, a bristling cluster of highly sharpened pencils in a small black leather cylinder and two silver-framed photographs, one of the late Mrs. Pitchford, the other of Beejay, looking slim, collegiate and demure.

On the wall behind Pitchford, an official portrait of the Executive Team obliged whoever was facing the desk, as Arnold now was, to gaze at President Eisenhower and California's own Vice-President Nixon.

'I think I've found another hell of a combination,'' Arnold had tossed it casually to Kate, "fucking and banking.''

"Fucking and anything is a hell of a combination," Kate replied. "Even fucking and raw herring. But you're on to something, Bubby. Fucking and money. The chemistry is right."

303

"May I first tell you how much I liked your Andy Hardy series?" Pitchford said with a paternal indulgence that puzzled Arnold. "I may be antediluvian," there was no way of stopping him, "but I really appreciated the Hardy boy saying Sir to his father. We've neglected our good old-fashioned family values. I've always wanted to congratulate you for the Andy Hardy films—you *are* the writer of the Andy Hardy series?"

"No, Mr. Pitchford," Arnold said apologetically, "I'm Arnold Elton, the novelist."

Looking down his chin, Pitchford stealthily consulted a card in a box, gave a slight start. "Oh. You're the writer of *those* books."

"I thought maybe we could just talk," Arnold half rose. "But I see you're a busy man. Maybe some other time."

"I'm never too busy for a client," Pitchford made it sound like something framed and hung in all executive offices. "But I'm afraid I don't understand what you want."

"There's some, I guess 'secret' is the word, to every profession," Arnold sat down tentatively.

"Secret of banking?" Pitchford managed to rip the stitches out of his lips and free a puckered smile. "I wish someone would tell it to me."

"Maybe that's the secret," Arnold wondered what he meant by that while he was saying it, but they were both saved by the telephone buzzer. Pitchford stared at it with a studied sense of injustice as though someone had let a loud fart.

"Yes? Oh, Barbara Jane—" Startled, he looked dubiously at Arnold. "I'll ask him," to Arnold. "My daughter seems to have seen you as you came in and wonders if she might say hello."

"That would be very nice, Mr. Pitchford." Arnold couldn't help himself, he was deliberately trying to act like Andy

Hardy. A "sir" had almost escaped him, and his guts were churning like a Waring Blender. He'd been thinking of the girl constantly, of showing her off to Geisy and to Harris and the boys. He fantasized making an entrance with her at Chasen's or Romanoff's, all heads turning to wonder who was the interesting-looking wasp girl Arnold Elton was escorting (Kate certainly didn't look Wasp).

"Hi, Mr. Elton," Beejay swung breezily into the office. Even in a Kakhi shirt and blouse it was amazing how good it was just to look at her. Not that she was really beautiful but for the first time he was not looking at tits and ass, although that was there too.

"I was just telling your father," no, his voice sounded okay, "I'm researching banking for my next book."

"You think you can make banging exciting?" she corrected herself so quickly that you wondered whether it was really a slip of the tongue. "Sorry. Banking." Her father shot her a black look, which she disregarded. "The trouble with banking is. Well, it's run by bankers."

"Now, Beejay, I happen to consider banking a very exciting profession." There were obvious points of conflict between father and daughter. And she had a plaster mask of her own, a smiling, bland innocent mocking college girl expression that was hard to pierce. "I believe anyone who attacks banking attacks the very heart of just about the best system there is."

"Mr. Elton still hasn't had a chance to tell us what his book is about," Beejay said.

"It's about an outsider." As frequently happened, Arnold made it up as he went along, "who breaks into banking. I was thinking of having the central character based more or less," he felt his way cautiously, "on the rise of a man like August Gorham."

"I think it's a peachy idea." The more Beejay thought

about it, the more her enthusiasm grew. "From the whispers I've heard here and there I'm sure you'll find scads and scads of rich material for your kind of book."

"I hope Mr. Elton will not give the impression to his readers that we're all like that man," Pitchford said tartly.

"Oh no," Arnold Andy-Hardy again. "You can be sure of that. Only it's becoming clear to me I'll have to approach this subject with care. I was just wondering," he was able to get that out by reminding himself he still had hundreds of thousands of dollars in the bank in a savings account, "with your permission," again he barely managed not to say "sir," "maybe Miss Pitchford could steer me in certain directions—"

"Gee willikins!" Was she deliberately trying to sound like Andy Hardy's girl friend? "Helping on one of Mr. Elton's books. That would be superduper."

"You've read *those* books?" Pitchford, despite himself, looked aghast.

"After all, Mr. Elton's a major depositor here." Pitchford was forced to bow to that one. "I've read all three of them." She turned quickly to Arnold. "What you're after is a general feeling, a peek under the bedsheets of banking?"

"Well, yes," Arnold didn't dare look at Pitchford, "more of a general feeling, I'd say."

"Anytime," Beejay said lightheartedly. "For example now?"

"Now would be fine," Arnold glanced at Pitchford.

"We're having the Plymptons for dinner. I was counting on you."

"Thanks for warning me, Dad."

"I thought you liked them."

"The Plymptons? Why, Dad, ever since they gave that party the day Roosevelt died . . ."

"You've always had a vivid imagination, Barbara Jane," Pitchford snapped at her. "They gave no party the day Roosevelt died."

"Why, Dad," Beejay said quietly. "You yourself took me to it. Coming, Mr. Elton?"

"Shall we go somewhere we can talk?" Arnold asked.

"Yes," Beejay said. "Why not?"

They drove silently down Sunset. Neither one spoke until they hit Beachwood Drive.

"You keep looking in your rear-vision mirror. Do you think someone's following us?"

"I always look in my rear mirror."

"You didn't on Sunset."

"I didn't?"

Arnold remembered just as they turned into Beachwood that Kate had mentioned that it was being called Red Star Drive. Apparently several unfriendly witnesses mentioned in the House Un-American Activities Committee hearings happened to live on it. Each time the Committee ran into an unfriendly witness, Committee counsel would make sure to mention his address clearly, repeating it several times. Even the most obtuse neighbors would register the address. The Committee had managed to make it clear it was the solemn duty of every American to report the comings and goings of such dubious neighbors to the FBI. And people were reporting in droves, Kate had said; evidently people loved telling on their neighbors.

As they approached Blake's house, Arnold's apprehension grew. It had been a week since Blake disappeared.

He should have taken Beejay to a motel.

But despite the way his last two books sounded, he'd never been to a motel with a girl. He wasn't sure what the procedure was. Did they ask you for a marriage license? Hollywood was more Puritan than people believed.

He put the car lights on dim and crawled along until he recognized Blake's house, swerved into the driveway abruptly and almost crashed into an enormous cactus. Blake had cut a chunk out of the driveway to give the spiked plant living space.

Arnold got out of the car, stalked the distance to the front lawn. Keeping himself as hidden as possible, he peered down the street to see if there was a parked car with two men in it. Conceivably the FBI could have the house under surveillance.

There were no parked cars with men in them

She asked no questions as he fumbled with the keys to the back door. It should have been apparent to her that Arnold had never opened that door before. She was close behind him as he groped his way into the kitchen and found the lights.

Crisp white curtains, a mini herb garden on one windowsill, copper pots hanging on whatever wall space was not covered by prints of garden vegetables, giant onions, carrots, celery, a huge oil of a single red succulent apple, made Beejay exclaim, "Now there's a man who loves kitchens. I could spend time in a kitchen. Not cooking," she added hastily, "making little tasty indigestible things."

In the living room Arnold switched on a floor lamp.

"Oh," Beejay said in awe, "your friend has great taste." She moved about slowly. "That's a Siqueiros, those two are Tamayos, that's a Rivera—" she turned, stopped before an adjoining wall, "Toulouse-Lautrec drawings."

She walked around and around the room, sipping excitedly at a tumbler full of straight Scotch Arnold had handed her. She looked down at the drink. "I won't need that much. Pour half of it back. I hate waste."

Arnold noted that she'd said "need."

She meant it. A Banker's Daughter. Actually she didn't touch the rest of the whiskey until he'd poured a good part of it back into the crystal decanter.

He watched her go from one painting to another, then stood so close to her they touched. She didn't pull away, instead took a long thoughtful sip of the whiskey.

"Whose house is this? Or is it a mystery?"

"It's Lawrence Blake's house."

"Lawrence *Blake*? Lawrence Blake the poet?"

"I didn't know he wrote poetry," Arnold said.

"His plays. The way he understands people and loves them. And, oh, the words he uses."

"Poetry, like that," Arnold said as if he'd known that all along.

"We put on a play of his at Radcliffe. I fell in love with his lines the way a woman falls in love with a man." Beejay turned away from the Tamayo. "But you must be close if he lets you borrow his place."

The friendship with Larry gave him a big advantage with her.

"Larry worked on my first book," he said.

"Lawrence Blake *worked* on your first book? *Lawrence Blake*?"

"Well, hell. I helped him on his first film," he said, hurt.

"Sorry—it's only that what he writes seems so remote from what you do."

"I am what I am."

"Oh, are you?" The whiskey was taking effect. She looked at him over the rim of her glass. " 'The delicate cheer and good wine soon banished all reserve,' " Arnold had no idea what she was quoting from, only that it seemed to excite her, " 'but these professors of pleasure knew too well to evaporate the imagination before time of action.' That's from *Fanny Hill, Memoirs of a Woman of Pleasure*."

"But that's a pornographic book," Arnold said in shock.

She burst into giddy laughter. "You don't think it's funny, *you* saying that?"

"You memorize stuff like that?" he asked. The laugh lines faded from her face. "I've never heard anybody memorizing prose before."

Her look held unwaveringly on him. "At Miss Adams's Finishing School I memorized pages of it. 'But he threw

309

himself instantly over his charming antagonist who without flinching, like a heroine, received his plenipotentiary instrument into her.' How about that, Elton? 'Plenipotentiary instrument.' " She shut her eyes as she continued the quote, " 'She closed her eyes in sweet death the instant of which she was embalmed by an effusion which drowned her nether parts.' "

He took her in his arms and put his mouth to hers. It was not happening the way he'd fantasized. Crystal chandeliers, a gleaming white table, shining silver, flowers, perfume in the air and soft dreamy music—

Still.

It was happening. She was actually in his arms, alive, warm, the eager body brimming with hunger, this girl he didn't dare dream he'd ever get close enough to talk to. She held herself in an attitude of expectant waiting as his lips brushed her eyes, her throat, his fingers worked at her blouse, unsnapped her brassiere. His mouth grazed her breasts. For the first time she flinched. She watched him distantly as he undid her skirt, worked clumsily at her panties. She was nude, her body slim, her pubic hair golden. He picked her up, she was surprisingly light considering her height, and carried her to a couch, laid her down on it, his fingers busy. She lay there, her arms spread wide, passive and unresponsive. Arnold, bewildered, remembered the stirring when his lips touched her nipples, brought his mouth again to her breasts, moved his lips down. She murmured in response as his mouth glided down to her navel, gasped as his lips found those nether parts she'd spoken of, writhed, tossed frantically, but he persisted until her body was arched and taut with expectancy, then pulled his lips away, drew himself up over her. She made an unconscious movement of protest, but he held her in place as his penis, poking blindly like a nocturnal animal bewildered by sudden daylight, hit alternately abrasive pubic hair and frustrating thigh. When he was ready to give up, miraculously he found the opening. She made small sounds of fear, her muscles rejecting.

"Let go, let go," the whispered words came easily because he was quoting from his own *Love Me Love Me Love Me*. Would she recognize them? "There's nothing wrong with you enjoying it. Why shouldn't women enjoy it?" And those he'd stolen directly from Kate.

She still seemed bewildered, tight and cold but he kept on murmuring the quotes. "Open up, relax, throw it all in, all of you, let it all go." He remembered suddenly what Beejay'd said the first day they'd met, and he quoted from another part of the book. "You're not ugly there, I put my mouth to you there, it's beautiful because it's part of you."

Little by little she began to respond, it grew in intensity until her belly hit at his frantically. He had to hold her, she seemed to be trying to escape, then suddenly he felt her spasm, they were both seized together, she moaned in deep release, his body spread-eagled over hers.

"Was that good for you?" he asked uneasily.

"You can bet your boots that was good for me," she said when she stopped panting. He felt a thrill of triumph. He'd done it for her. He, Arnold Elton. She, Beejay Pitchford, Banker's Daughter. He felt exaltation, confidence, pride. He felt almost as good as when Geisy had told him he would pay him twenty thousand dollars. He wanted to tell people, "*I* did it for her." *I* did it.

"Was it good for *you*?" Beejay asked.

"The greatest," Arnold said softly.

"Then would you mind rolling off me? I can hardly breathe." He withdrew hastily and rolled off.

"I must leave. I guess we all do what we're expected to if people expect it hard enough. Dad's so sure I'm daughter-hostess, he's convinced me," she said.

"Will I see you again?"

"Well." She pronounced it like a speech. "I enjoyed the

311

sex with you and I think I want to see you again. Is that all right or are you a man who needs his life laid out neatly?"

"I've played most of my life by ear."

"Fair enough." She touched up her makeup as she looked at herself in an antique mirror. "Such an untidy experience, isn't it? But it doesn't seem to show."

Apparently it didn't show on him either.

Kate was home when he got there. Out of habit she gave him a quick scrutiny and the standard, "Where the hell you been?" then went back to watch a replay of that day's televised Un-American Activities hearings.

But as he looked at her it hit him hard. Her ass was lumpy. She was not bad-looking, okay, but nothing you would sprain your left ball for. He knew suddenly that he no longer needed her. There was nothing more that he could learn from her or that she could do for him.

He thought of Beejay more than he'd expected. So much it interfered with his writing.

He tried sealing himself off totally in his study but each time he sat, the typewriter seemed to roll over on its back, its four paws in the air, stone dead. He paced, scratched his ass, clipped his nails.

Then Beejay would call suddenly and he'd rush to pick her up, telling himself he was in love for the first time in his life. At Blake's Beejay would zip out of her clothes before they reached the couch. They would strain, tug, groan, sweat copiously and fight each other to a noisy but satisfying culmination.

Afterward, they wouldn't talk much. She would quote *Finnegans Wake* or García Lorca in Spanish and he would pump her about banking and its secrets.

"It's no more mysterious than the art of warfare," Beejay told him. "Like George Bernard Shaw said, it's the art of the stronger killing the weaker. Its basic secret is simple—you

312

take money from people and pay them less interest than you get when you loan it out.''

"Yeah—but there's a risk," Arnold said.

"Not the way the Pitchfords do it. We're covered upward, downward, backward and sideways." She was enjoying telling him. "And of course, there are a thousand little tricks—you have transfers of money, you work out ways of not transferring as long as you can. It draws interest for you and you don't pay out any interest at all. Even if it's only for a few days, it all mounts up."

They'd talk maybe a polite half hour, then she'd get dressed and ask him to drop her off near her car.

She'd call him three days in a row, then not call him for a week or two days or ten days. There was no pattern. Maybe she wanted it that way. But when she didn't call, it was impossible for him to work. Then she'd call, bright, breezy, casual as if it hadn't been two days or seven days or ten days.

Kate was preoccupied with her career. She was in trouble. Another two clients she'd had particularly high hopes for had gone through the ritual of being unfriendly witnesses before the McCarthy committee. Now most of Kate's comers were blacklisted or graylisted. When Kate did make sexual demands, it would be at odd times as though she were doing a spot check.

"You've been with a broad," she flung at him when in fact he'd spent the afternoon in exhilarating negotiations.

He'd pound dutifully at her until she had an orgasm, after which she'd say, "So I was wrong. Call me *pisher.*"

Early one evening when Arnold and Beejay had settled down to some serious sexual threshing on Blake's couch, the doorbell shrilled. Beejay's fingernails sunk into his back; in the two months they'd been using Blake's house, no one had rung the doorbell while they were there.

313

"We'll just disregard it," Arnold whispered, "he'll go away."

But Arnold's car was in the driveway, if there was someone looking for him, he'd get the license number.

Arnold rolled off her angrily, slipped on a pair of pants and a shirt, then, barefoot, whipped to the door, peered out.

Some young jerk in a dirty sweatshirt with matching dirty trousers was leaning on the bell. Furious, Arnold opened the door.

"My name is Harley Davidson, believe it or not," the young man said before Arnold could yell at him.

"Your parents pulled a dirty trick on you," Arnold said.

"Happens I'm a United States Federal Marshal." He flashed identification, "Mr. Blake?"

"No. I am not Mr. Blake," Arnold said tensely.

"I have a subpoena to serve on you, Mr. Lawrence Edwin Blake, issued by the Congressional Committee on Un-American Activities. You will hereby appear—"

"Then hear this, Davidson Harley, I am not, repeat, not, Lawrence Blake, Edwin or otherwise," Arnold cut him off.

"Mr. Blake, if you refuse a subpoena legally served on you it's my duty to warn you that's a federal offense right there."

Harley gave Arnold a thorough and professional once-over. Color of hair; black. Color of eyes: gray. height: tall build: scrawny. Distinguishing marks: scar on forehead, twisted left hand. Wearing no socks when subpoena refused. Pants unzipped.

"That your car I saw you drive up with?" Harley asked. Arnold felt an icy grab at his guts. "You've been coming here regularly with a woman. If you're not Lawrence Blake, what are you doing in his house?"

"Look, I'm not Blake."

"You got any idea where L. E. Blake is?"

"Not the slightest," Arnold answered promptly.

"Aren't you ashamed of yourself, Mr. Harley Davidson?"

Beejay, wearing Arnold's jacket, stood directly behind Arnold. "Hounding men like Blake?"

"No, ma'am," Harley said. "Beg your pardon, but I didn't quite catch your name?"

"And you won't," Beejay snapped. "Sneaking around that way," her anger grew as she went along, "why aren't you out catching thieves or something?"

"You know Lawrence Blake?" Harley asked. "You any idea where he went to? You Mrs. Blake?"

"I don't know Lawrence Blake," Beejay said coldly. "And if I did, I certainly wouldn't tell you." Harley was doing it to her now. Color of hair: blond. Eyes: gray. Five feet seven in bare feet. Wearing man's jacket.

"Seems logical to me you're using a man's house you got to know where he is," Harley had a look of bland satisfaction. Like a man, Arnold thought, who had just taken a good healthy shit. "You getting excited seems to me you got obvious connections with a well-known Communist."

"Now you leave the premises at once," Beejay snapped. "Go on! Git! You're trespassing!"

Harley took another deep fix on her then as she made what might have been a menacing gesture, disappeared with surprising speed, loping off, his sneakers whispering on the flagstones.

"They've poisoned the whole atmosphere," Beejay, nude, paced angrily. Arnold watched her and worried whether Harley's visit would make trouble for him, then began to wonder how he could get her back to their interrupted fucking. "Goddamn them. Dad's slowly getting rid of everybody at the bank he suspects of having voted Democrat. We've got this lovely young black woman as a housekeeper." Beejay came close enough so he could reach out and snag her and hold her in place with one hand firmly on each buttock. "Dad's going to fire her too."

"We're looking for a new nurse-housekeeper," his eyes

were level with her crotch, his lips skimmed her pubic hair, he blew gently on her clitoris.

"She'd be perfect for that," she said, squirming. "This is serious," as his tongue flitted over the tiny protrusion, she tried to pull away. "Our basic rights are being threatened."

"Here's where our basic rights are," Arnold said softly.

"No—no—no," she had a hard time speaking. "I don't think. This is serious." She twisted hard, trying to break away but he held her tenaciously, for he suddenly sensed this was a fateful moment. If she pulled away now he'd lose her forever. Slowly she yielded, her body softened as his mouth moved over her. She made a last feeble protest but her voice trailed off and a series of ecstatic sounds lazily escaped from her. She gasped then wilted, her belly draped over him.

"Tomorrow morning," Arnold whispered, "I'll cable Blake."

She seemed pleased.

"That's the club those girls hold over our heads," Kate fumed to Arnold. "Always threatening to walk out."

"For Chrissake," Arnold got excited, "Jennifer's getting really attached to her, and the house is working like a dream."

Mrs. Griffith's successor was Margaret Heatherington, the black girl who'd worked last for the Pitchfords and whom Arnold had insisted on hiring. Kate had complained she was too goddamn attractive.

"And Dr. Braunschweig says it's important we try to keep the same nurse," Arnold went on heatedly.

"He says even a young child works up like an anxiety neurosis, she gets attached to a woman like Margaret, and worries all the time she can lose her."

"*Okay*! Okay!" Kate yelled.

"Hey now, what did you say to her that made her threaten to quit? You must of said something, goddamn it."

316

"Stop yelling! Where the hell you been all afternoon? And every afternoon last week and the week before that?"

"When I can't work, I get in the car and drive."

"You going to ask me to believe you've been out just driving?"

Beejay hadn't called for over a week. He couldn't reach her at home or at the bank. She was never in. Something was up. He left his name at least three times without any response.

He couldn't think or talk straight, work, eat, sleep and could barely fuck when Kate demanded it.

"Yeah. I'm going to ask you to believe that," Arnold said. He was close to not giving a good goddamn what Kate thought.

It was two weeks before Beejay telephoned and it was in the middle of the afternoon.

"I've got to see you," but there was nothing playful, mocking or expectant in her tone. In fact she sounded exactly like Blake when Blake had called from a phone booth. Scared.

At Blake's she came in looking pale and tired.

"Were you followed?" she asked.

"Me? Why would they follow me?"

"They've been tailing *me*," Beejay said wearily.

"Who?"

"The FBI, I guess," she said tightly, "who else could it be?"

"Going to all the trouble of putting a man on you? Why?"

"I've been trying to think." Frightened. "Maybe because at Radcliffe I belonged to the American Student Union."

"What's that?"

She shot him a hard look. "A student organization that's now on the Attorney General's list as subversive."

"You belonged to a Communist Front organization? *You*?"

"Oh, come on, 'Communist Front,'" Beejay bristled. "And what do you mean by *you*?"

"Your father head of a bank and all," Arnold said.

"That's probably why they're after me," Beejay said. *"Daughter of Bank President.* Small headlines for them for one more day. I've been tailed ever since that Harley Davidson popped up at Blake's house. But that's not the weenie."

"What is the weenie?" Arnold braced himself.

"I'm pregnant. I haven't been able to have the test because those tails follow me so closely. They'd check on the lab. But I don't need a lab. I know." She took a swallow of the warm whiskey for courage. "And I can't have an abortion. Just turn your writer's imagination loose on that one, 'House Un-American Activities Committee uncovers Abortion Ring. Subversive Daughter of Bank President Kills Unborn Illegitimate Child.' I tried to convince Dad to let me take a trip abroad. I might've had it done in some private clinic in Europe somewhere. But all that did was get him suspicious. He's never let me have money of my own. He says one way to learn the value of money is by not having any. He's right on there. Or I could have tried to slip into Mexico, where it would be filthy and more dangerous and besides they might check me at the border."

Arnold took her hand. She didn't withdraw it.

"You had to keep all that to yourself. Why didn't you come to me?"

"Here I am. You know any friendly neighborhood abortionists?"

"Have the baby. I'll get a divorce. It's not much of a relationship now, anyway. We'll get married."

"That's a hell of a reason to get married."

"I keep thinking of you so much I can't write. I couldn't have kept it up much longer with Kate, anyway."

She turned away, then forced herself to look at him again, getting more and more frightened as she went from the first quick out-of-hand rejection, then watched it slowly grow from the unthinkable to the possible, then to the probable.

She needed a moment to absorb it; then, astonished, found herself relieved.

Midmorning of a smoggy summer day they met in the offices of Werner, Blatt and Tigar, in downtown Los Angeles, to discuss the divorce settlement with Kate. Arnold's lawyer, Blatt, was a big slow-spoken man recognized as the best divorce lawyer in Southern California.

Seated opposite them was Oscar Brenner, a strange flabby man with huge round glasses. Any man who looked like that had to have a great deal going for him.

"Strictly speaking I am not here representing Mrs. Elton as her lawyer." Oscar made a joke: "For the simple reason I'm not a lawyer."

The joke didn't go over very well with Blatt. "Then what are you representing her as?" he asked icily.

"What I am—financial counselor, tax adviser and long-standing family friend. You see, Kate—Mrs. Elton is a classmate of my wife Estelle."

"Mrs. Elton should have a lawyer." Blatt, offended by Oscar's mere physical presence, was now offended professionally.

"Mrs. Elton wishes it to be strictly friendly." Oscar was not a man who ruffled easily. "I think all parties concerned will only profit by being friendly, so I have some friendly proposals to make."

Blatt listened with sour skepticism then in incredulity as Oscar unfolded his "friendly" proposals.

First—Arnold would hand over two thirds of everything he had earned since his marriage to Kate. Plus a 25 percent interest in all returns from his future work but merely for the next twenty years and not for the rest of his life as some women might have asked. In addition she was to be included in his will—for a 25 percent share of his estate.

"My will?" Arnold asked incredulously. "She's almost six

319

months older than I, what's she got in mind to kill me or something?"

"And naturally custody of the minor child Jennifer."

"You call that friendly?" Blatt asked with bitter admiration.

"The baby." Arnold had had hopes. "Kate considers Jennifer an obstacle to her career. She's a lousy mother. Are you sure?"

"I do not make proposals lightly," Oscar said quietly.

"I"—Blatt radiated icy scorn—"have never been confronted by more outrageous demands. This woman is vindictive."

"Reason I say it's friendly"—Oscar's imperturbability was invincible—"is that Mrs. Elton is prepared to leave the entire Beverly Hills house, all its goods and furnishings, to Mr. Elton. Inventory not even requested."

"Since this is a friendly meeting, just call me Arnold," Arnold said.

"Sure, Arnold," Oscar agreed immediately.

"Just refer to me as Mr. Blatt," Blatt said.

But Blatt, who had shattered the most distinguished lawyers and prosecutors in Southern California, was not able to make a dent in Oscar. By the time Oscar left, Blatt was in a rage.

"We'll go to court with this." Blatt studied Arnold intently. "Whatever you do," his words were like spikes, "have no contact with Oscar Brenner. Don't go near him."

"I won't," Arnold promised; the first thing he did on leaving Blatt's office was call the modest hotel where Oscar was staying and make a date for drinks.

"A Cutty Sark on the rocks," Oscar ordered.

The Polo Room of the Beverly Hills Hotel was studded with important people from the industry—agents, stars, writers. But there was more tension and nervous animation than usual, and strangest of all, no table-hopping. The smog from the Un-American Activities Committee had penetrated even that bastion of boozy excitement.

Arnold felt a peculiar satisfaction. He hadn't been chump enough to get caught up in anything remotely political.

Oscar took a long sip of his Cutty Sark.

"I'll tell you, Arnold, the way I work I handle only a few clients. We become more like a family. I devote all my time to them. Now I know you think of Kate—how? 'Don't worry about her she knows how to take care of herself, she's a tough little cookie?' A tough little cookie?"

"What would *you* think after the demands she's made on me?"

Oscar shook his large head gravely. "It can't be too easy for you, either. Father of the child. I understand for you too. But Kate comes to me tells me about the broken marriage. She cries like a kid."

"Cried? Kate cried?"

"Cried. For a broken home."

"Jesus, she was almost never home."

"Maybe cries for herself, too. No. Kate is not a tough little cookie. So I estimate she's entitled to compensation. I have a personal code. I believe that a deal which is not fair to both sides, sooner or later, trouble. So okay, Arnold. Maybe two-thirds is too much. But she should have something more than the fifty-fifty community property split California law allows for a wife who's done nothing to enhance their joint wealth. Kate has made large contributions. Fifty-eight percent of present property. Is that fair, Arnold?"

"Okay," Arnold acquiesced. "But twenty-five percent of everything I make for the next twenty years?"

"Listen—that's a very small amount for the support of the kid so you can look on that twenty-five percent as pretty much for Jennifer while she's growing up—fair, Arnold?"

321

"Yeah, I suppose," Arnold didn't want a court fight. Besides he liked this man sitting opposite him.

And Oscar did yield on three weekday and Sunday visits with Jennifer. Probably, Arnold thought, because Kate wanted her Sundays clear for work.

For a long moment Arnold permitted himself to mourn life without Jennifer. Not to sing her to sleep at night. Arnold loved to sing and Jennifer was the only human being who was willing to listen to his uncertain off-key half-octave singing. Not to have her come toddling in to be lifted into his bed in the morning, to cuddle next to him, both to fall asleep, Arnold to be wakened by a cold puddle in the bed.

"You're lucky you're a writer, Arnold, your time is your own, you can take the kid out any time suits you. A divorce situation like this, the man leaves the wife for another woman, four visitations a week, including Sunday, that's more than most normal undivorced fathers see their kids."

"Have another Scotch," Arnold had noticed how much Oscar enjoyed his drink.

"Only one more. That's my limit. I know myself."

"I liked the way you handled this situation," Arnold said when Oscar was on his third. "Frankly, Oscar I've been looking around for somebody like you, somebody who could concentrate on me. Listen, all my money's in a savings account, uninvested."

"Absolutely wrong for you and also on behalf of Kate— money in a bank is lazy money. Unhealthy. Money should work. There's a thousand possibilities. Think about it. You should have a corporation. Arnel Enterprises, for example. It sounds important."

"My thoughts exactly." Arnold was to discover that Oscar had a gift for formulating ideas which seemed obvious only after he formulated them.

"Go into many areas. Diversify." It was the first time Arnold had heard "diversify." "Horizontal."

"We're on the same wavelength." By now Arnold knew that Oscar had to be a part of his life. "Will you handle me?"

"I'd have to discuss that with Kate first."

"I accept that. But in the final analysis anything that betters my situation betters Kate's."

"Absolutely sound thinking. Now Estelle and me, we read your books. Pure entertainment. Straight pleasure from one end to another. They never upset you, they hold you, you will ask Estelle when you meet her. I think you have a big future."

"I have a good feeling about you, Oscar. I'm now looking ahead, I would want you to be a top executive in Arnel Enterprises, devote yourself to Arnel exclusively. I know you have ideas."

"I have one idea I want to leave with you. Just one."

"What idea is that, Oscar?"

"Paperback," Oscar said. "Think about it. Let it cook."

"Paperback."

Arnel Enterprises should have its own paperback. You know what paperback is going to be?"

"You know what I get out of paperback rights now?" Arnold asked bitterly. "*Bubkes.*" Oscar apparently didn't know what that meant. "Peanuts. Shit."

"I know," Oscar gave deep sympathy. "I know. Arnold, I wouldn't even want you to hazard a guess what your own paperback will bring. I have exceeded my drink limit and you will attribute it to that. Only one thing I will suggest to you, Arnold. Exercise care when you sign the paperback rights on your books from now on. You're big enough. They'll yield. And I'll keep my eye open for a paperback house of our own we can acquire."

It was like a crazy unexpected love affair.

They would place money everywhere. Like he said. Horizontal. Real estate. Both on the East Coast and in California. Even a couple of good restaurants here and there. Eventually film production and distribution.

"Only one condition I would make," Oscar said. Arnold was ready to agree to anything. "My home life."

"Your home life?"

"It's sacred to me. I live my life."

"You won't find anybody in the whole world understands home life more than me, Oscar. I got this gut feeling. This is right. And I promise you. You'll have your home life."

Arnold had never felt this great before.

Arnel Enterprises.

The punk kid who'd left home with twenty-three dollars in his shoe at the age of fourteen, with his own publishing house.

Money working everywhere.

A corporation.

It would take his mind off not having Jennifer all the time. Even there, too, Arnold knew some day Kate would get tired of the responsibility of the child and give her back to him.

And Beejay, his wife. Wherever you went people turned to look at Beejay. Class. It shone from her. A baby by her.

Life can be goddamn good, Arnold said to himself.

Kate got a Las Vegas divorce. She lost three workdays and five thousand dollars at the crap table, which last bit of information Armand Harris passed on to Arnold at the wedding (it had come to Armand via Uncle Millie) and it brought Arnold a twinge of pleasure. He'd always known Kate was a lousy gambler and fundamentally a loser—which convinced him he was right in divorcing her.

6.

It was not only a quiet wedding—"Nothing ostentatious" Pitchford had suggested nervously—but everything was done to make it look as though it was not happening at all.

It took place at the home of a justice of the peace, a friend of the Plymptons, in Calabassas, deep in the horsey area of the San Fernando Valley. Pitchford proposed that only the Plymptons, his oldest friends, need be there but Arnold insisted on inviting Bernie Zuckerman, Harris and Geisy, now vice-president in charge of production at the Studio.

They all made effortful bright conversation, little bursts of jokes and anecdotes that flared then faded into the prevailing disbelief that this marriage was taking place at all.

Beejay, her cheeks flushed hyper-bright, in a simple beige dress made no effort to look bridelike but no matter what she wore she was stunning.

"Feel like a patient smiling-through," she whispered to

Arnold as she clung to him in a parody of the shy bride, "about to go to surgery."

"What kind of surgery?" he asked, imitating her manner.

"Hemorrhoids," Beejay replied.

"Well that's about the classiest way I know of saying pain-in-the-ass."

"If you'll excuse a mixed metaphor," Beejay whispered sweetly, "if the shoe fits—"

"I thought maybe you might want to redecorate the house," Arnold said to Beejay. "Isn't there anything you want changed?"

"That *N* framed in golden laurels, right on the john itself. Doesn't it constipate you?"

"We could have it taken off."

"Oh no. I'll think of Josephine de Beauharnais or something. It might actually help."

"We could at least redecorate the kitchen. You seemed big for Blake's kitchen. We could make it kind of more kitcheny."

"Let's just leave it Empirey. Besides, Margaret seems happy with this kitchen."

They inherited Margaret Heatherington. Arnold felt uneasy about that. It might have been better for Jennifer to have Margaret.

"Oh no," Kate had said, that last time they saw each other, "I want to be my own woman. You take the schvartze."

Robbie, not for Robin or Robert, Robbie for Robbie (Beejay insisted) was born one lovely Monday morning in January easily and painlessly with natural childbirth. Beejay refused the anaesthetic in spite of Dr. Melinkoff's assurances that she might not like the last few minutes when the head crowned. She wanted Arnold to be present, "How can you not want to see it?"

Arnold hoped the Doctor would oppose it, but no, Arnold

was outfitted with a white cap and surgical gown, Beejay was helped onto the delivery table.

It seemed only a moment later that Beejay held the small glistening body close to her, looked at it in awe, murmuring, "Why he's beautiful, he's so beautiful," looking over at the nurses, the doctors, at Arnold, repeating, "he's so beautiful." For a moment Arnold felt a fleeting irritation at her insistence, as if part of her surprise was that something so lovely could have come partially out of him.

When Robbie was three weeks old, Arnold, on one of his regular visitation privilege days, brought Jennifer to meet her baby brother. It was also her first meeting with Beejay.

"I don't want her around that blond banker's daughter broad," Kate laid down the law. "Only reason I agreed you could see Jen so often was you wouldn't be taking her in your house."

"Where the hell you think I'll be taking her?" Arnold demanded.

"Take her to the ponies on La Cienega. Or the zoo at Griffith Park. This fucking town is busting with places for kids. Basically it's a kid's town. Thing it wasn't made for is adults. Well, I see the Un-Americn Activities Committee finally got your pal—"

"Which pal?"

"Lawrence Blake."

"Gee, I'm sorry." She waited for him to say something more but he didn't.

After Robbie's birth, Arnold insisted on bringing Jennifer home.

"How you doin'?" Beejay got down on her knees so as to be level with Jennifer.

"I'm fine," Jennifer was a very articulate child. She stared at Beejay with suspicion and curiosity, poked an exploratory finger in Beejay's eye, then another at Robbie. "He make pee-pee?" Jennifer asked. "Mommy gave me a doll, he wets."

"He not only makes pee-pee," Beejay said. "He also makes poo-poo. He's better than your doll. And he's your brother."

Later on when Robbie did indeed make poo-poo, Beejay showed it proudly to Jennifer and let her help clean him up.

"He *is* better than my doll," Jennifer conceded.

Sundays had now become an unrelieved pain in the ass. There were no games Arnold played and at twenty-seven he considered himself too old to begin. He felt a tolerant contempt for those who needed hobbies to keep occupied, or games to rid themselves of excess energy. What hobby could be more engrossing than his work?

As for exercise, how could golf or tennis compete with fucking? Except there was no fucking going on. The obligatory six weeks' abstention after childbirth had passed four days before but Beejay gave absolutely no indication she was ready.

Despite the openness with which the characters in his books discussed such situations, in fact dwelled on them with great relish, Arnold could not broach fucking to Beejay.

The night before he'd sidled up to her in bed, but she'd remained curled like a spoon.

"Beejay?" he whispered, she didn't respond. "I wanted to keep it as a surprise but what the hell." He wheezed slightly. "Oscar's negotiating for the sale of *Again and Again* and he won't tell me the exact figures, I'm not asking, but all I'll say is I think it's going to be astronomical." The rhythm of her breathing had remained so unaffected, he asked anxiously, "You asleep?"

"No."

"I've never seen Oscar so worked up," Arnold's agitation grew. "It's going to be a breakthrough if it happens."

She lay there absolutely motionless as his fingers searched for her clitoris.

"You don't read," she said.

"You mean, like books?"

"I mean, like books."

"It affects my style," he had a full erection as he busily sought her clitoris but she kept her thighs closed, or more to the point, didn't open them.

"Your style," it was impossible to figure how she meant that. "You don't even read a newspaper."

"There's always too much going. Like now. The negotiations." His penis was hot and throbbing. He pushed it tentatively against her thigh. "Beejay. One thing I know. There's going to be an escalating clause, the more the book sells, the higher the price. It's pioneering. Paperback sales will count too." He began to position his erection carefully. "If the paperback sells the way we know it will, it'll be outa sight."

"Lawrence Blake's been cited for contempt of Congress," Beejay said. "It could mean a year in prison."

"I wish I could help him," Arnold said as he maneuvered his penis into position, "but he's the only person who can help himself."

Just as his erection found the opening, she pulled away.

Arnold lay there with aching balls. The doctor had warned him to expect strange and moody behavior. It was well known that after giving birth women were depressed and sometimes cried for no reason. He patted her shoulder to assure her that he understood and would be patient. Tomorrow was Sunday. Margaret would be off. They would be alone. They'd fuck, possibly in the open air around the pool. The idea appealed to him tremendously. Beejay would like it. In nature. In sunlight. Roll on the lawn.

"I'm taking off for the Club," Beejay announced first

thing Sunday morning. There was no question of it. She was, as Henrietta used to say, a regular bundle of nerves. "Dr. Melinkoff says there's nothing better for the old belly muscles than tennis. And Margaret swears she doesn't mind giving up this Sunday so you won't be alone with the baby. I've persuaded her to have a swim. I was so busy being pregnant I didn't realize she'd never been in the pool. I was a little surprised you hadn't suggested it to her before." There must have been something about the way he looked that made her feel guilty. "Maybe you ought to think about taking tennis lessons," she said nervously. "I know I sound like Dad, but it would be good for you."

"I guess I naturally prefer things that are bad for me," Arnold said hopefully. She looked so slim, fresh, cool in her tennis things, her breasts full. Maybe she would still send Margaret away. Maybe they would still roll on the lawn.

"You ought to give tennis a thought," she said uneasily.

Arnold shrugged in irritation. He couldn't see himself being instructed like a child how to hold a racket, how to hit a ball. Friends of Beejay would see him, they all played tennis so well, he'd look a jerk.

"I've got other thoughts right now," Arnold said.

Beejay mulled that over, nodded and slipped away.

Arnold moved over to a beach chair and dutifully turned his face sunward for a tan. You sat in the sun so you could get uncomfortable enough to slide into the pool to cool off and you paddled around in a lot of chemical-smelling water so you could sit in the sun again. This time sitting in the sun was more than a pain in the ass. The tighter he shut his eyelids the clearer the images became—at first Beejay's breasts and buttocks—then it got to be anybody's—he hadn't been laid for over two months. Christ, he was getting images of Kate belly down ass up on that first sexploration.

A sound of a door opening made him sit up.

Margaret, in a white bathing suit, was just leaving her

330

ground-floor room. She glanced around tentatively as if to make sure no one was watching her. Arnold was surprised. He'd never really seen her in anything other than the ivory dress, which was like a uniform. Her skin was a deep brown, she had firm breasts and swelling hips and she walked with a shy grace he'd never appreciated before.

Halfway across the lawn she became aware that Arnold was watching, stopped in embarrassment, fluttered an uncertain hand in greeting. Then with the haste of a woman who'd suddenly been discovered nude, plunged into the pool. Surprisingly, she swam with a powerful easy stroke. When she emerged, she spread the bath towel, and panting and exhilarated, lay facing the sun.

Arnold sat down alongside her, watching the rise and fall of her breasts. There was a long silence.

"My brother's only fifteen's in jail," she said. "They tryin' to slap a felony on him, claim he was stealin' hub caps. My ma's got this cough, doctor won't say, we don't need no doctor, we know. They call my pa almost sixty shoeshine boy."

"Yah? Well I guess everybody has troubles."

"Difference is ours is live or die."

They stayed that way for several more silent moments, she with her eyes closed so he was able to look at her steadily, until they heard a car in the driveway. Margaret rose quickly and hurried away.

Pitchford came in wearing a short-sleeved La Coste shirt and tennis shorts. He looked surprisingly young.

"Ran into Beejay at the tennis court." Pitchford was able to affect the same offhand casualness Beejay was so good at, especially when it was serious. "Margaret use your pool?"

"All the time." Arnold enjoyed the pained look, pulled up another beach chair, Pitchford sank into it.

"It always surprises me how people let these servant situations get sloppy." Pitchford had felt their taking Margaret after he'd fired her as an affront. "I've found the best policy is to draw a very sharp line so there's no question about who's what and where their place is. I manage it simply. I never look at them. That does it."

"I guess it's different when you have a nurse for your baby. Can I get you a drink?" Arnold asked. The unexpected visit had to have some important purpose, "You must be thirsty after your tennis."

"Didn't play."

Pitchford's Sundays were holy. He spent them religiously at the tennis club. For him not only to cut short his Sunday tennis but to drop in without telephoning first was ominous.

"I thought I'd take advantage of this opportunity to visit the grandson and to talk to you alone."

"Do you have to do that now?" Pitchford could barely hide his distaste as Arnold undid Robbie's dirty diapers.

"He'll be uncomfortable unless I change him," Arnold folded the diaper expertly so that the baby shit was well wrapped, lifted Robbie's legs high so he could wipe his bottom clean.

"I have a question to ask you," Pitchford tried not to watch as Arnold worked vigorously cleaning between the baby's buttocks. "And I want you to give me a full and honest answer." There was another speck of shit near the baby's testicles, which Arnold wiped away meticulously. "I know people get nervous when money matters are discussed, but look here. Have you not been giving my daughter money?" Arnold let Robbie's leg drop. "What have you done to the child's penis?" Pitchford asked querulously.

"Why he's circumcised."

"I've never seen one before," Pitchford stared at the baby's middle in distaste. "What did you do? Have some bearded rabbi do it?"

"It was done by a doctor at the hospital. Beejay wanted it. What do you mean—I don't give her money?"

332

"Well, she came to me," Pitchford said thoroughly annoyed, "and asked me to authorize a five-thousand-dollar advance from the trust fund her mother left her. Why would she need five thousand dollars?"

"I don't know. Besides, she can have all the money she wants. All she has to do is ask."

"I must say *I* always knew when the late Mrs. Pitchford needed money and why," Pitchford said reprovingly. "You don't know why Beejay would need five thousand dollars?"

"No."

Pitchford was even more irritated, "I had the feeling it was some sort of emergency. I'm afraid I'll have to allow her two thousand," then glanced down at his watch, decided he could squeeze in a set of tennis before sundown and left abruptly.

Beejay came back late in the afternoon, flopped on the shaded outdoor swing near the pool, the only piece of furniture she'd bought.

"Bushed," she said. Her white tennis blouse showed sweat stains. She lifted her arm, sniffed her armpit absently, enjoying it, which bothered Arnold. "A good healthy smell. Imagine people using chemicals to get rid of it. Did the Chairman drop in on you?"

"Well, yes—he did."

"The Chairman would never give up half a Sunday's tennis lightly."

"He said you came to him for money. I don't understand why you had to go to him," Arnold said. "You've got charge accounts everywhere, you need something all you have to do is ask me."

"Of course you don't understand, but I don't want to have to ask." Beejay lifted the baby off her breast. "This is liable to poison my milk." Robbie made only the slightest of complaints. "It's really my money, Mother left it to me."

"We could open an account for you if you feel that way."

"No!" Beejay said bitterly. "Oh, goddamn. Goddamn."

333

"What's the matter?" Arnold asked anxiously. "Is something wrong? What are you upset about?" She sat there, mute, not looking at him. "Can't you tell me?"

Robbie had fallen asleep, his head snuggled between her breasts. It was a long moment before she answered.

"That crackerjack psychoanalyst you're always talking about?" she asked with effort.

"Dr. Braunschweig," Arnold said eagerly.

"Perhaps I'd better see him," Beejay said morosely.

At breakfast a few days later, she said carefully, "I saw your Dr. Braunschweig. I'll say this for him. He's got a powerful personality and he sure as hell can make you unloosen the old tongue."

"But?" Arnold asked.

"So far what I've come away with is that my difficulty is I have no penis. I don't see clearly what I can do about that."

"You giving him up?"

"Dr. Braunschweig went to the toilet for eleven minutes during the session," Beejay said. "So I suppose it's not reasonable to expect a clear answer to what's troubling me in thirty-nine minutes, I'll give it one more fling."

Normally Arnold slept like a log but he hadn't closed an eye because of the big three-way telephone conference set for the morning in New York. Oscar on one extension, McCabe of Associated on another—McCabe had leaped out of Publicity to a vice-presidency in charge of production—and Arnold in Hollywood. They were in a crucial phase of the negotiations for the rights to Arnold's latest, *Crestview 5* which had outsold all his others. Associated must have been prepared to pay big, because it was McCabe himself who was doing the bargaining. And Arnold had used Geisy's ultimatum technique. Associated knew they would either buy in the morning, or were out of it.

Oscar gasped when Arnold told him what he was going to ask. No literary property had commanded such figures and conditions in the whole previous history of motion pictures. "They'll never go for it. No company will. The big companies will close ranks. They're already grumbling about the prices they've been paying—"

Arnold cut him off. "We hang tough," he said icily.

"Okay, Arnold, but one last word. When we make demands like these and lose—we got nowhere to go. We're stuck."

"We hang tough." Arnold, shaken, tried to sound calm.

But it was true. No one, but no one had commanded conditions like that before. Arnold knew McCabe—tough as a callus. The morning three-way conference wasn't going to be a picnic.

So for the first time in years Arnold slept badly. It was a contagious restlessness—Robbie, for the first time, fretted most of the night. Arnold sensed Beejay going to him several times. It must have been four o'clock when she finally dropped off. It wasn't just Robbie, Arnold was sure. Something else was bothering her.

Arnold stopped himself from worrying about that. His mind had to be clear, sharp. He had to react fast and know the implications of each decision.

The phone rang at seven in the morning. Arnold jumped for it frantically. He'd forgotten to unplug the telephone in their bedroom so Beejay wouldn't be disturbed, another indication he wasn't running on all cylinders. He did manage to get the receiver on the second ring but Beejay was already sitting up.

It was Oscar and McCabe.

Arnold took one look at Beejay, who strangely had a copy of the *Los Angeles Times* in her hands. She looked distraught and the newspaper fell loosely in her lap.

"Hang on a second, gentlemen," Arnold half-whispered.

"I'm taking the other phone—this is the bedroom—Beejay had a tough night—"

"Let's get on with it," McCabe said tersely. "I've got three of our top lawyers here at my side. It's ten o'clock New York time."

"Don't move," Beejay said strangely. "I'd like to see you in operation."

Arnold hesitated a moment.

McCabe's voice came sharply, "Arnold—are you with us?"

"I'm here," Arnold said, trying hard to keep the quiver out of his voice.

"We've got an amplifier here," McCabe said, "so everybody's in on it. Let's not fuck around. What do you want for your book? How much?"

"It's just money," Arnold began warningly.

"We know that," McCabe answered grimly. "We're prepared to each give a pint of blood—"

"Not enough," Arnold fell into their black humor. "I'll need a couple of gallons—"

"Now, how does that translate into gold of the realm?" McCabe asked sarcastically.

"One million dollars," Arnold said quietly.

"We make entire pictures for that price," McCabe said.

"And nobody goes to see them," Arnold said. "Plus five percent—"

"Of what?" McCabe's voice was sardonic.

So, okay. They wouldn't make the deal. So, he overplayed. Arnold looked over and saw Beejay watching.

"Five percent of the box office gross," Arnold said evenly.

Oscar gasped, goddamn him, he'd lost his cool. He wasn't helping.

"Did you say five percent of the *gross?*" McCabe asked. "You're kidding."

"You know how many people have bought my book?" Arnold demanded. "They're waiting for the film. McCabe, either we make a deal this morning or you're out. Think it over."

Unbelievably, McCabe didn't go away. "I want to talk with the boys," McCabe said. "I'll get right back to you."

Arnold could imagine the scene.

Oscar scared shitless in that luxurious office, McCabe huddling with the lawyers.

McCabe was back in twenty seconds.

"The legal beagles want to make sure if we say yes you don't throw something else at us."

"Only the right to a monthly accounting," Arnold said. "Access to your books at all times. My approval of the major stars—"

A silence.

"That it?" McCabe asked.

"That's it," Arnold said.

There was a long silence.

Beejay moved out of the room, in pajama tops, bare-bottomed.

"Okay, sonny-boy," McCabe said. "Hang on tight. We're prepared to meet those conditions—"

Arnold swayed a little.

"We're flying out today. We'll bring the contract later. Where will you be?"

"Right here," Arnold said numbly. "I'm not going anywhere."

"Because we're going to publicize this deal," McCabe said. "*Variety* will headline it. So will the *Reporter. New York Times* has promised to run it as a news story—" That was McCabe the ex-publicity man speaking.

But Jesus. They'd known before they would go that distance. Maybe he could have squeezed them more.

337

He caught himself. He realized McCabe had said something.

"They're gone," Oscar's voice came over the phone choked with a grave jubilation. "Do you realize what happened? We pioneered. We blazed a new trail—Unprecedented. And all hell is breaking loose with the paperback people. I won't even tell you what the paperback guarantees will be. It's a dirty shame we haven't got our own paperback house but it's too soon. For the paperback rights, I'm a conservative man, I'll give you a conservative estimate. Another half million."

Arnold mumbled incoherently. Oscar mumbled back, then had to attend to some reporters who'd just come in. Arnold hung up, staggered blindly over to an armchair, fell into it, covering his face with his hands. He was dimly aware of a presence.

"Something awful happened?" Beejay hazarded, frightened by his manner. "Your half-brother? On, no. Not little Jennifer." Arnold shook his head numbly. Beejay was exasperated. "Well? Tell me! What happened!"

Arnold was able to bring his stunned face up to hers.

"Over two million dollars," he was finally able to say.

"Lost? In some venture?"

"I made the deal of the century," he clutched her hand. "After taxes, after percentages, after everything." He was wheezing, barely able to breathe. "I'll come out with two million clear. Paperback and movie rights." Beejay stood over him utterly motionless, uncomprehending. "Don't you understand? I'm going to make two million dollars clear, out of my book. It's an all-time record. It's history-making." Vaguely he realized she was looking at him oddly; as though he was someone she had never seen before and when he reached out blindly for her hand, she whipped it away. He remembered later being puzzled, and thinking, if you could call what his mind was doing in all that turbulence thinking, that she was looking at him with aversion. But she moved away rapidly and he turned back to visions of two million dollars and the tax problems they would cause.

He'd have to work out some tax shelters. Foolproof shelters. There'd be so much publicity given to the fantastic sale, they wouldn't be able to hide much, if anything, from the Internal Revenue people. They'd have to look into that gag Arnold had heard about, where you bought a big plane and then leased it to the commercial airliners. You were allowed a huge depreciation; at the end of a year you wound up with a big chunk of your money tax-free.

Arnold tripped down the stairs and into his study, worked with pencil and paper furiously, then floated out.

Margaret, who was setting the breakfast table, stopped and watched as he sank into a chair, sat hunched over, trying to get himself calm. She disappeared, came right back with a silver percolator full of bubbling coffee.

"You'll feel better after you have yourself some coffee," Margaret said soothingly. "I know how you feel, Mister Elton."

Beejay, in a robe, her hair mussed, appeared in the doorway.

"You know how he feels?" Beejay asked.

Margaret offered Beejay a copy of the *Los Angeles Times*. "I know Mister Blake was a friend of yours but I didn't expect you all would take it so hard."

"What about Blake?" Arnold asked.

"They threw the maximum at him," Beejay said. "A whole year in jail. Imagine. Lawrence Blake—"

"But we expected that," Arnold said impatiently. That fucking Blake. Getting himself a year in jail just when Arnold had made the biggest sale of all time. Spoiling it for him.

"Yes. We expected that," Beejay said, then stared at Arnold, Margaret, the room, hurried out.

Arnold started after her, bumped into the table, sat down and lost himself in tax shelters.

"Mister Elton," Margaret shook him gently. "Mrs. Elton's gone, baby Robbie with her." Arnold didn't understand. "She took off in her car—"

"What are you talking about?" Arnold asked. "She was here two seconds ago."

"You been sittin' like that for longer'n you think," Margaret said nervously.

Arnold ran wildly up the stairs.

The bedroom was in total disorder. Arnold tried to calm himself. She couldn't have gone far, she didn't take much, but even as he was thinking that, another part of himself spat at him, Face it, Buster. She left you. Your Barbara Jane Pitchford has gone and she's taken the kid with her. Gone, split.

"I seen her dressin' in a hurry," Margaret said, frightened. "She always been strange like she gets moments, but when she come down with the baby and she had *him* all dressed up I got worried so I run outside and I see she's got this valise and just got into her car and went streakin' off before I could stop her without sayin' good-bye or nothin'..."

Arnold ran outside, stumbled over the step.

Her car was not in the garage. There was no sign of her.

A large man in his early thirties with a crewcut appeared at the Beverly Hills house. Arnold would have sworn he was FBI except he was too heavyset.

"My name's Don Wacszinski," the man was surprisingly soft-spoken. It made you want to confide in him. "Sounds like a sneeze but that's my name. I've done some private investigation for your father-in-law. He's asked me to see what I could do about your wife and child."

"I appreciate that. It's five days now and the police haven't gotten anywhere."

"I know how you feel," Wacszinski said. "The minute I came home from Iwo Jima—you know what the war was—I

340

read your book. I was dreaming of my wife waiting for me. Well, sir, she met this civilian. I got a 'Dear Don' letter.''

"I feel lost. I want my kid back.''

"I hope you don't mind but I've already done a little simple tracing. Mrs. Elton had a personal bank account, not much but she had the account transferred to San Francisco, I don't think it'll be too hard to locate her, Mr. Elton.''

"Oh Christ, Don, call me Arnold.''

"Okay, Arnold. Now I have some tough news and I hate to be the one who has to tell you but your father-in-law and I are convinced you didn't know. Your wife's been making contributions to Red causes in the last year or so.''

"You're kidding.''

"I wish I was, Arnold. Also, she belonged to Red groups when she was in college.'' (Arnold thought he ought to react in shock on that one too.) "Your wife is in a very vulnerable position. I don't think we'll have any trouble getting her to come around, it's a matter of making her use a little common horse sense.''

Wacszinski located Beejay quickly in San Francisco, but she wouldn't listen to horse sense, "Once they get bitten by that Red bug, it gets into their bloodstream,'' Don explained.

Against all advice, including her own lawyer's, she filed for divorce, asking only for custody of Robbie and not a penny of alimony.

Beejay, thin and tired-looking, sat on one side of Domestic Relations Court, Arnold on the other, as their attorneys droned on.

"All I want is the kid,'' Arnold had told Blatt. "Fuck her.''

"For God's sakes don't take that line,'' Blatt had snapped at him. "This Judge Donovan is big on families. You're supposed to want to rebuild your family, understand?''

The judge listened unsmilingly as both lawyers had their say, then proposed that Beejay and Arnold meet with him in chambers without counsel.

Beejay refused to look at Arnold.

"I have a considerable report on you, Mrs. Elton," the judge consulted a file. "Why were you seeking psychiatric help?"

"Not psychiatric, psychoanalytic," Beejay corrected him, shooting Arnold a look of weary revulsion. Only *he* could have told the judge.

"Did you know, Mr. Elton, that your wife had sought such help?" Judge Donovan didn't bother with whether it was psychiatry or psychoanalysis.

"Yes. But practically everybody in Hollywood's been under analysis," Arnold felt it was smart to sound magnanimous.

"Mr. Elton," Donovan said sharply, "you understand your wife is asking for complete and sole custody of your child? And that she has been contributing to subversive causes?"

"Your Honor," Arnold was surprised at how sincere he was able to sound. "All that matters is that I love my wife and son and want them to come back to me."

"Are you willing to return to your home and husband, Mrs. Elton?"

"I can't, Your Honor," Beejay said. "I just can't."

"Why did you ask for psychiatric help, Mrs. Elton?" he demanded.

"I was hoping I could be helped to accept my marriage."

"Was your husband cruel to you?"

"No," Beejay answered.

"Did you love your husband?"

Beejay sat mute.

"I see here," Donovan glanced at the file before him, "that Mr. Elton filed for divorce from his first wife, according to the records of those proceedings, very suddenly and that the two of you were married almost immediately after and that your child was born seven months after the wedding.

342

You obviously had sexual relations with him while he had a wife and child and, by your own admission, without loving him. Why did you marry him?''

"It was a mistake, Your Honor. It should never have happened.''

Arnold felt that as a physical blow.

"Have you been drinking, Mrs. Elton? One of the court investigators reports you've been buying quantities of liquor.''

"I don't drink normally, but this has been a difficult period for me.''

"Mrs. Elton,'' Judge Donovan made a mighty effort, "would you agree never again to engage in subversive activities?''

"I don't believe they're subversive,'' she said quietly.

"It's a solemn matter to deprive a child of its mother,'' Judge Donovan pronounced in court moments later. Beejay looked hopeful. "Especially a child of such tender age. And the Court is aware it is equally grave to deprive a mother of her child, but I have no choice.''

"Oh, Your Honor, please!'' Beejay lost control. "I love the baby so much. He's the only thing I've ever loved.''

"The woman is of obvious emotional and psychological instability and has a drinking problem,'' Judge Donovan continued. "Therefore I am awarding sole custody of the child to his father.''

The casual, mocking, disrespectful *Fanny Hill*-quoting Barbara Jane Pitchford whimpered like a wounded animal. But Arnold wouldn't let it bother him, he figured "Fuck her, she's the one who said the marriage was a mistake, it shouldn't have happened.'' He looked at Beejay huddled, whimpering, broken, the tragic face with no makeup, dark circles under the eyes, and realized that all that about The Big Love was a crock of shit.

* * *

Dr. Braunschweig had the gentle look of a man who has seen and heard too much. That day, he maintained a friendly Olympian distance like a benign deity. Although it was summer he huddled in his shaded sun room with a shawl thrown over his shoulders and this last, too, gave him a curious mantle of authority.

"The asthma which you are now experiencing," Braunschweig's Viennese accent came soft and musical, his *th*'s were sibilant, as *zat* for that, his *w*'s were *v*'s and they all rode easily on Arnold's wheezing, "comes just as you have broken with your wife." He held up a cautioning finger. "But it is not because of that."

Arnold was having an acute attack and Dr. Braunschweig had agreed because of the emergency to see Arnold.

"You are recapitulating a childhood experience," Braunschweig went on, "when you discovered your mother had abandoned you. You are now doing the weeping you did not do as a child. What is asthma but internal weeping? Instead of your tear glands, you cry with the bronchia of your lungs. So. Again you have been abandoned. This is the great fear you will carry your whole life and it will make you afraid to give love. To give love is to risk being rejected." Braunschweig made a forceful pushing away motion with both hands. "You will try to buy love. You will be attracted to women you can pay. With money you will feel sure you have them. For you, money *is* love. It is the security and warmth you never had—"

"The judge asked her three times," Arnold was wheezing harder, "would she come back to me—she refused, the dirty bitch."

"Ah. Now we come to your wife. She was working out a neurosis of her own. Since the death of her mother, she has great guilt because of unconscious attractions for her father.

344

So she set out to hurt him, thus proving her innocence to her dead mother.''

"Also because he's a shit," Arnold gasped.

Braunschweig disregarded him. "She becomes pregnant by you thus forcing herself to marry you, knowing you would be a most unsatisfactory choice of son-in-law, that he would be hurt—"

"Why did she leave me?" Arnold was almost choking. "Sex was great with me. I made her have orgasms all over the joint, listen, she admitted to me she had never had it so good."

"Of course," Braunschweig said softly. "Your wife was like the obsessive gambler who must constantly challenge the father figure by taking foolish chances, risking everything. Now what is it that happens when the obsessive gambler wins?" By now Arnold didn't have enough breath to speak, could only shrug that he gave up. "Your wife won when she acquired a rich and hitherto unknown sex life with you. Both she and the winning gambler have successfully destroyed the father figure. That is unendurable. The money he has won burns in his pocket. The winning gambler is compelled to play again and again until he has lost, just as your wife had to create a situation in which she would lose you."

The wheezing abated somewhat.

"You mean if I hadn't made her come so much, if it hadn't been so good, she wouldn't have left me?"

"*Grosso modo*, yes. And now—what must Arnold Elton do? The first step is to understand that his wife was not his mother, who *is* irreplaceable. His wife is replaceable. The answer for the loss of one woman is to acquire another."

Arnold's wheezing abated entirely as Braunschweig had promised.

That night Arnold sat at the dinner table but didn't touch his food, shooting glances at Margaret.

345

"If it's Robbie you worried about, Mr. Elton," Margaret was deeply troubled, "I just want you to know I'll give him all the nursing and loving that baby goin' to need."

It had been well over two months since he'd fucked. He left the table abruptly, rushed upstairs, and sat on his bed making loud wheezing sounds until Margaret came in, hovered over him anxiously.

"Maybe I better call a doctor?" she asked but Arnold reached for her hand imploringly, wheezed harder as he shook his head. She let him take her hand. He held it close to him, pulling her slightly so she sat on the bed next to him. He lowered his head against her breast. She stroked his forehead and made comforting sounds. Gradually he toned down the wheezing, began to caress her as though not really aware of what he was doing. At first she moved away, but he wheezed again. She watched him uneasily as his caressing movements evolved very gradually into taking her clothes off. She surprised him by quickly ridding herself of the rest of her clothes and sliding into bed. There was no longer any need for wheezing. He pulled her to him hungrily. They made frantic love as if both were blotting out nightmares, he the image of Beejay pushing him away violently; Margaret hungry for warmth and the feel of a man's body, trying to writhe out of the color of her skin. After he came she leaned her face on his bare chest and he felt her cheeks were wet. He thought with vague satisfaction that it was like the last scene in *Guns of Love*. Arnold thought how wrong the Oklahoma asshole had been about black body odors, for Margaret smelled crisp and clean. And not only was fucking and anything a great combination, but fucking was good for you. It was healing, Braunschweig would have said *therapeutic*, which in Braunschweig's mind was a blanket blessing, justifying practically anything you did.

Although Arnold felt secure and protected and knew he could go on to other things, that he couldn't bring Margaret to orgasm rankled. He tried harder and knew she knew he was trying harder and threw herself even more fervently into their lovemaking, but fooled neither one of them.

One night he came home with many packages, one of which was a beautiful raw silk evening gown, another a pair of slippers of a matching color. That evening she dressed in great excitement, saw herself in the evening gown, knew that for once she looked as beautiful as she ever could. She entered the dining room; the table was softly lit with candle-light, Arnold looked very elegant in a dinner jacket and black tie. A bottle of champagne nestled in an ice bucket and romantic music floated in the air. He popped the champagne, poured two glasses full. They clicked glasses, looked at each other long and soulfully, looks they both remembered from a dozen movies. He took her in his arms and they danced clinging to each other. She was light and responsive as they dipped and whirled until she was giddy. They stood motion-less, barely swaying to the music, the silk of her skirt clinging to her thighs.

He undressed her slowly, letting the gown fall about her ankles, sweeping her up in his arms and carrying her to a couch, where he made gentle and tender love to her, murmuring to her until she came. It was a great letting go, as though the years of deprivation were rewarded in this one strange moment and she kissed him with deep gratitude.

Twenty minutes later he was in his old bathrobe sitting at the dining room table and she was serving him barbecued spareribs, which was one of his favorite dishes.

Margaret never took a designated day off like the other black housekeepers, for example Thursday. She prepared dinner for him in advance, then at the last moment asked for the day off. He invariably agreed. So, unlike the other maids, she was free on any day of the week, sometimes even a Saturday night.

She seldom bought herself clothes but when she did it was

347

the very best, a dress from Saks, a coat from I. Magnin's. When she did visit her relatives in East Los Angeles (it was not too often, for she went weeks without a day off), she went to them by cab. Practically no one in Los Angeles took cabs, so her visits were mysterious momentous occasions. She and Arnold never went out together and were never seen together.

It was perfect for him. On top of everything else there was the supremely comforting thought that with her there could be no conceivable possibility of complications such as alimony or breach of promise. No court in the land would have agreed seriously to hear such a case if she tried to make one, and it couldn't have been farther from her thoughts. Every now and then when he returned from a trip, he'd bring her a new evening dress. Over the years he added accessories like earrings, a tiara, a golden comb. They'd have champagne and caviar and then dance and fuck lovingly.

7.

Jennifer, at twelve, suddenly decided she wanted to live with Arnold and Robbie in Beverly Hills. Did the fact that she started menstruating, Arnold wondered uneasily, have anything to do with it? He made a note to ask Braunschweig.

"New York's too tough." Jennifer had her mother's capacity for directness. "Kate and me, we get on fine, when she has time for me, which isn't often and I think she's kind of glad to be rid of me right now. The only motherly advice she gave me was that the drug scene out in California is pretty heavy. She said, 'A little pot here and there, okay, but stay away from the hard stuff. And when you start thinking about fucking and that jazz, only one thing I have to say. Do it only when you're goddamn sure you want to. No other reason. And any time you want, you can come back. Okay?' "

Arnold listened uncomfortably. The idea of a preteen daughter who used the word "fuck," disturbed him. Still, he was pleased. Now he had both children completely for himself.

Jennifer and Robbie weren't the easiest kids in the world, let's face it, but then all kids that age were like that, and she and Robbie got along fine. There were no complications with a troubled wife. Arnel Enterprises was booming. Wacszinski, whom he had hired immediately after the divorce, was always available with a variety of skills, a hell of a negotiator, a prudent advisor and a fine manager. Besides, he knew a variety of top people in the DA's office, important members on the L.A. Vice Squad. Wacszinski had never remarried and was on tap, as he kept assuring Arnold, twenty-six hours a day.

Jennifer managed to convey a faint general disapproval of Arnold, disturbingly reminiscent of her mother.

"You never have any chicks around," Jennifer said at Sunday breakfast. "You abnormal or something?"

"Me? Hell. I'm normal," Arnold said cautiously.

"What do you do?" Jennifer asked. "Sneak out to one of those motels in the Valley?"

"Yep." Both Jennifer and Robbie eyed him suspiciously. He didn't want them to know about the arrangement with Margaret. The only problem was to make sure the kids never caught Margaret going up to Arnold's room, nor tiptoeing out in the middle of the night back to her room on the floor below.

"Don't want no more man-complications," Margaret once said in bed. Nor did she want any gift, birthday or otherwise. She was satisfied with things the way they were. And happily she never did tell him what man complications had marred her early years, so he didn't even have the strain of having to sympathize with her for that.

"Which motel you use?" Jennifer asked. "The girls at Beverly High say a lot of movie people use Top Hat Motel."

"Well, I don't use Top Hat."

"Reason I mentioned it is that the girls in school say that Top Hat has a motion-picture camera synchronized with the

350

air conditioning," Jennifer went on. "They take pictures, then blackmail you."

Arnold remembered vaguely that there *had* been a scandal of that kind, years before.

"It doesn't work that way with me." Arnold wondered whether Jennifer ought to see Braunschweig. He'd sent Robbie for a few sessions when Robbie had asked why he'd never seen his mother. "Sometimes the lucky lady has an apartment of her own. You know? We meet there."

"What time a day you do it?" Jennifer asked. "Before lunch? Nooners? I hear they're the greatest."

Robbie nodded approvingly, apparently he'd heard that too.

"Hey, Dad, what's cunnilingus?" Jennifer asked.

"Where'd you get that?"

"From your last book," Jennifer said.

"You want to know something? You're too young to be reading my books."

"Am I going to have to look it up in the dictionary?" Jennifer threatened.

"It's a form of sex activity," Arnold said.

"You mean a way of fucking?"

"Hey, listen, Jen, you shouldn't throw that word around like that," Arnold said.

"It's all over your books," Robbie said.

"*You* been reading my books too?"

"Oh sure," Robbie said. "They're interesting. I enjoy reading about those captains of industry and all that. The way they have their own jet planes and all."

"There's a lot in them you won't understand," Arnold said.

"Oh, I don't know," Robbie said.

Jennifer got up, disappeared into her wing. Arnold waited uneasily.

"The dictionary says," she explained when she returned, "cunnilingus, it's when the boy sucks the girl's pudding."

"Sucks?" Robbie asked in astonishment. "With his mouth?"

"You know anything else you can suck with?" Jennifer asked disdainfully.

"Why?" Robbie asked.

Arnold waited uneasily, not saying a word.

"It must feel good," Jennifer said.

"Ecch," Robbie said.

"You know what fellatio is?" Jennifer asked Robbie. She even pronounced it correctly. Robbie shook his head. But he was willing to learn. "Well, it's when the girl sucks the boy's thingy."

"The girl takes my thingy in her mouth?" Robbie asked. "You mean it?"

Jennifer nodded vigorously. Arnold was silent.

"Why?"

"It must feel good too," Jennifer said.

"Ecch," Robbie said. Arnold had stopped eating. "You never told me those things, Dad."

"I explained about sex to you," Arnold said.

"You just explained how the man puts his penis in the woman's vagina and plants a seed with his semen, so then a baby grows," Robbie said.

"That's only for baby making," Jennifer said. "The other part's fucking."

"We ought to talk about this some other time," Arnold said. "When we can just sit down and have a nice talk."

"Kate says there's nothing we can't talk about," Jennifer said. "She told me when my pudding got hot and itchy, I could rub it with my finger until I felt good. Say, Robbie. Your thingy ever get hard?"

"Yep. Sometimes when I climb a pole in gym. Kind of hard."

"Isn't he supposed to rub it when it gets hard?" Jennifer asked of Arnold.

"Listen, you guys," Arnold tried to make it bright and cheery, "you're still kids—"

"Yeah, but my pudding gets kind of tingly and Robbie's thingy gets hard."

"Robbie'll know when he's supposed to rub it," Arnold decided he should send them both to Braunschweig right away.

"Aren't you going to show him how?" Jennifer asked. "If you're too uptight to show, maybe tell him."

"When the time comes, we'll talk about it," Arnold said.

"Kate's not tightass, I never would have thought you'd be tightass," Jennifer said.

"They're going to find out one way or another," Margaret said that night when they were in bed, "no big reason to worry. They ask again, you just tell 'em."

But they never asked again. Even so his relief was partial. Over the next three years they didn't seem to talk much to him at all. Or maybe it was part of the process of going into adolescence.

Arnold would surprise the children in the kitchen with Margaret. The three would always fall silent, then the kids would drift away.

"Just talk," Margaret replied evasively after Arnold asked.

"About what?"

"They're curious what it's like to be black."

"What have you been telling them?"

"That it ain't easy."

"You think they ought to worry about problems like that?"

"Kids ask, you got to tell 'em."

"I should be the one telling them."

"You ain't black."

"They're not *black*, either. Only black kids need to know about being black."

"Black kids know without being told," Margaret said.

353

"Somebody's got to talk to those kids. Jennifer's fifteen now. Robbie's thirteen and a half."

Arnold had gotten so he could tell when Margaret had something on her mind, but there were just too many pulls on him, his new book, the screenplay they'd done of his last novel was lousy, he had to get into that because he had a percentage of the profits.

"Okay, Margaret," he said resignedly, "what's wrong?"

"Pusher's been at Robbie at Beverly High, almost got him hooked on horse."

"Horse?" Jesus. Robbie on heroin...

"Robbie tried, like out of curiosity, pusher gives it to the kids free at first. I think I talked him out of it. I ain't sure but maybe I'm not a good influence, maybe it would be better all around if I left and went to my family in Watts."

"Oh, no," Arnold said in panic. "They're crazy about you, Margaret. All I meant is they're not average kids. They're children of a celebrity. Their lives are different. We've got to be sure they're not too mixed up."

"Most Beverly Hills kids are mixed up one way or another." Margaret amended that. "Most kids today are mixed up. Right now I don't know any way of unmixing."

But she stayed on.

After that Arnold decided he should get close to the youngsters, and took them to dinner at Scandia; Robbie and Jennifer enjoyed luxury restaurants. It was the one certain way he knew to put them in a good mood and Arnold took great pleasure in the way the three of them were looked at and in knowing that people whispered, "Look, Arnold Elton and his two kids—"

"How you making out in the romance department?" Arnold asked Jennifer cheerfully.

"Lousy," Jennifer said belligerently as if it were his fault. "Guys just never call me."

"The phone never stops ringing," Arnold looked at her in disbelief, "and it's almost always for you."

"Dumdums," Jennifer said with distaste. "And they don't call me. They call Arnold Elton's daughter."

"Well, you are Arnold Elton's daughter."

Jennifer made a moaning sound at Arnold's obtuseness. Robbie nodded in sympathy with her.

"Jesus Christ on a toilet seat!" Jennifer said in exasperation. "That just gives these dumdums weird ideas. They think I do the things you got in your books."

"They can't all think that," Arnold said.

"Every now and then a straight dumdum calls," Jennifer admitted. "I went out with a couple of straighties; unbelievable. If I wanted to make out with them, I'd have to talk to them the way you talked to Robbie when he was eleven. The ones who turn me on don't call me."

"Then you call them. That's no big deal these days," Arnold said.

"Oh, shit, can you imagine what some dumdum would think if Arnold Elton's daughter called him? What he'd expect me to do? No thanks."

"You're exaggerating," Arnold said testily. The evening was not turning out as he'd expected. "Listen. You're a pretty kid, and you're bright..."

"Average," Jennifer cut in. "I know my I.Q." She took a quick slug of Arnold's aquavit while the waiter and Maître d' weren't looking. "Let's get serious," it sounded exactly like Kate's *toches* on the *tish*. "Would it bug you if Robbie and I took your sixteen-millimeter Bell and Howell—"

"Can I ask why?"

"We want to make a film, that's why," Jennifer said.

"We want to be filmmakers," Robbie added.

"Like we want to do a documentary on Forest Lawn. You know like the world's fanciest cemetery? Robbie knows how to handle the camera, he's been studying up."

355

"You've got to get permission to shoot at Forest Lawn."

"Only assholes go that way," Robbie said with a hint of contempt. "You can't get permission. Basically they don't want *anybody* shooting there. But we figured out a way."

"We're moving in at night with portable lights," Jennifer said. "We know exactly what we want to shoot. By the time their guards get to us it'll be over."

"Why does it have to be Forest Lawn?" Arnold asked irritably.

"Because nobody's done it," Jennifer flung at him. "Because we figure we can sell the footage."

Footage. Filmmakers. The new title for those who made films no one ever saw, or more often than not, who never even managed to make a film. It was the first inkling he'd had of motion-picture ambitions.

"Okay." Arnold was a great believer in kids learning the hard way. "Take the Bell and Howell and go shoot Forest Lawn."

When they did go late at night, Arnold couldn't sleep, but they came back very early in the morning, triumphant. They'd gotten their footage.

Except that when they talked to Wacszinski about selling the film, they discovered that if they did try to use it commercially, Forest Lawn could sue them blind, and since they were minors, in the end, no matter what phony companies they set up, it would be Arnold who would have to pay.

"Why the hell didn't you tell us before we went out?" Arnold had never seen Jennifer so furious. "Here we got this fantastic footage and that crew-cut creep Wacszinski tells us we can't use it."

"You didn't do your homework," Robbie hurled at Arnold.

"*I* didn't do my homework?" Arnold in turn exploded. "Now listen you, I'm setting up a film production company, a distribution chain, I'm about to acquire a paperback publishing house, I'm up to my ass. This was your baby. And goddamn it I told you you couldn't get permission, and if you can't get permission you can't use the stuff commercially—"

"We're going to look into that," Jennifer said grimly. "It's a public institution. We'll take it to court."

"It's a goddamn cemetery," Arnold yelled at her. "I told you before, no court will find for you."

"*Now* he tells us," Robbie said with disgust.

"Don't worry, Robbie," Jennifer said darkly, "next time *we* do the homework."

Oscar's East Fortieth Street office was getting bigger and more luxurious all the time; Estelle kept adding oil paintings she carefully picked up at art auctions. She had a shrewd eye. "Will somebody puleeze tell me why shouldn't an office have beautiful things?"

Arnold and Oscar sat and looked at each other.

"You know what?"

"Tell me what," Arnold said.

"We did it."

"Oscar Brenner says we did it," Arnold imitated Oscar's tone. That also was part of the game they played after every big one they pulled off and this one was the biggest yet.

"Now I'll give you my opinion," Oscar said.

"Now he'll give me his opinion," Arnold was terrific at getting the exact breathy croaking of Oscar's tones.

"My opinion is this calls for a celebration."

They'd been holding themselves in, refusing to yield like small boys who had to pee and were waiting to see who would give in first. Another man would have let out a shriek of triumph or danced a jig or grabbed Arnold and hugged him. A peculiar coughing laughter escaped from Oscar. Arnold immediately mimicked it, which set Oscar off into a series of barking coughs, which Arnold again imitated, which brought Oscar practically to a convulsion of barking so that he had to hold up a pleading hand. Arnold stopped. Oscar's breathing subsided, they both leaned back in the huge leather armchairs, heavy with the inertia of success.

For years they'd been waiting. Oscar had finally signaled. He'd found it. Laurel Publishing, a paperback house dying on its feet when the growth rate of all other paperback houses was (Arnold's words this time) "far-out-man, not-to-be-believed."

They'd circled about Laurel lazily, taking their time, watching it like a hawk (as Oscar said), knowing that any one of a dozen schmo publishing outfits who'd been in the game for years should have pounced, even when Oscar began to lose his guts a couple of times and said, "Oooh-Oooh—we'll lose it—somebody else has got to notice!" Arnold kept saying "Not yet, not yet, a little longer, let em get in deeper!" Then Arnold—who knew where this incredible sense of the right moment came from?—said, "Oscar, Now! Now!" and had flown in from the Coast.

They met with the wildly distracted Laurel lawyers, who were trying frantically to salvage what they could. The young jerk heir, huge family wealth behind him, had thought publishing would be fun. He'd seduced the family and some of its wealth with the magic words Publishing, and, Paperback. How could you lose? But young jerk heir had promptly proceeded to fuck it up, using paperback for Chrissake for girlfriends', boyfriends', just friends' avant-garde works-in-progress. It was even better than Oscar and Arnold had dreamed. Over seven hundred thousand in the red, losses cascading like a drainage sewer in floodtime.

And now Arnel had its own paperback as Oscar had planned years before. They would bring out Arnold's last two best-sellers themselves. It would go "like a house afire" (Oscar this time) and with a little manipulation, Laurel would be made to show close to a million-dollar paper loss. With that as a tax write-off, in the immediate future, Arnel stood to come off with a fortune.

"Estelle has anticipated," Oscar said when he was able to talk, "she has fixed us a celebration with a cuckovan" (only years later when Arnold and Krystina were dining at the gastronomic three-star Moulin de Mougins in the south of France would Arnold realize that what Oscar had meant then was a *coq au vin*) but all Arnold knew was that Estelle was given to making gourmet dishes that took hours to prepare and never quite came off. "Estelle will be heartbroken if you refuse."

"You keep pushing yourself," Estelle sounded aggrieved as she chastised Arnold on the telephone. "This once-in-a-lifetime occasion, you don't give yourself a chance to enjoy. You know, Arnold, it won't be a celebration without you."

"Estelle," Arnold said with deep sincerity, "if there's any two people in the whole world I would like to celebrate with, it's you and Oscar."

"Is it the kids?" Estelle wouldn't let go. "Believe me, Robbie and Jennifer with that black jewel Margaret you've got there, believe me she takes such good care of them they couldn't be in better hands you could stay over another day nobody would know the difference it wouldn't be a catastrophe."

It was then, listening to Estelle, it became clear to him. Just as, when he started, the deeply personal meaning of his success had been for Adelheid, the way he'd imagined her eyes filling with tears of pride, he'd done it all for her, now it was Robbie and Jennifer. They were the ones with whom he'd share his triumph, the only ones who would give him that soul-warming satisfaction, even though they wouldn't have the slightest idea of what having a paperback publishing house meant nor why it was such a giant step forward.

Of course Margaret had to be in on it, too. Without her it would be incomplete, he could hear her whispering, "I'm real happy for you," and see her eyes glowing with pride, but she never seemed surprised. Her manner was, of course

Arnold would be a huge success. What else did you expect?

By the time Arnold landed at Los Angeles Airport he had it all planned. A champagne party. The first real champagne party the kids had ever had. Robbie would have not much more than a couple of gulps, Jennifer maybe one glass. There'd be smoked sturgeon, which Robbie was crazy about with slices of Bermuda onion, caviar which Jennifer loved, yes and even some soul food for Margaret, who was always longing for black-eyed peas and chitlins. This time he'd persuade Margaret to join them at the table. It would seem natural. Although never a peep out of them, the kids probably thought him a shit for not having included Margaret in other family celebrations but it had always been Margaret who had refused.

"Just right the way it is," she'd always say when he'd suggest she join them. "Things goin' right I say don't fool with them."

As he got out of the plane the August heat came down heavily on him. He was able to breathe only when he managed to make it into the air-conditioned Lincoln Continental waiting for him at the airport.

The timing was perfect. He'd be home by four and Margaret would have plenty of time for leisurely shopping.

As he pulled up the driveway he honked jubilantly but no one came out to meet him. Okay, it was a letdown but what the hell, Jennifer and Robbie could be out somewhere with their friends. But Margaret. That was strange. Never missed. Invariably after he'd been away, she'd come to meet him as he drove up honking. It was possible she was somewhere deep inside the house—vacuuming, and couldn't hear.

For the first time he could remember, the house was empty. He should've called from New York and warned them he was coming. Surprises were a lot of crap. Jennifer's and Robbie's rooms were untidy, their beds unmade. Margaret always straightened their rooms, made their beds first thing in the morning. Even stranger, Margaret's bed was unmade. It was the first time in years he'd been in her room. He was startled to see his old Dr. Elliot's five-foot shelf of books over her bed. A complete high school education, she'd embarked on a program of self-education. It made him uneasy. What was she thinking of? What did she hope that would do for her?

He waited twenty minutes or so until he was half out of his skin with impatience and then decided he'd do the shopping himself. Even though the beach was only partially integrated, the kids might have talked Margaret into going with them. Margaret would sit on the sand, dressed, content to watch them frolic in the surf.

Nate 'n Al's Delicatessen in Beverly Hills was one of the loves of Arnold's life, fragrant with spicy smoky mouthwatering smells. The countermen were great standup comedians. They kept a running patter of cracks as they cut, weighed, wrapped, calculated. There was always an atmosphere of banter, bustle and movement. You could almost feel the salivary glands secreting as impatient customers waited goodnaturedly to be served.

Jewish penicillin! (Nate 'n Al's homemade chicken soup).

Two heartburn specials! (pastrami, corned beef, stuffed derma).

"The works," Arnold said when his turn came to be served. It was five o'clock California time and there were surprisingly few customers. "A big tin of beluga. A pound of smoked sturgeon, a pound of smoked salmon, a couple of salamis."

"Okay," the counterman said. No gags, nobody was joking.

"Family celebration," Arnold offered.

"What I figured." The counterman worked swiftly, slicing the sturgeon like an artist.

"Know any take-out soul food joints?" Arnold made another try.

The counterman nodded with wry understanding. "Like in Watts, for example?"

"Anywhere. Watts, I'm not particular," Arnold said.

The counterman stopped slicing. "You kidding, Mr. Elton?"

"Excuse me, I forgot there was a law against asking for soul food in Nate 'n Al's—"

No smiles. The counterman looked at him as though he were a freak.

"Where you been these last few days, Mr. Elton?"

Cautiously, "New York."

"You haven't looked at TV? You haven't read a newspaper?" the counterman asked in stupefaction.

"Naw, nothing," Arnold said. "I was up to my neck in heavy negotiations." Arnold loved telling the countermen about his deals. "Hey, what's going on, anyway?" Arnold looked around uneasily. It was eerie. Now that he took a good look he saw the place was practically deserted.

"Watts?" the counterman tried it for effect.

"Watts what?"

"Charcoal Boulevard," the counterman still wasn't sure if Arnold was playing. "Hot summer nights?" Then, when Arnold didn't react. "The worst riot in L.A. history. Half Watts burned down. Thirty dead minimum, maybe more, who knows? Mostly blacks, some cops too. They won't even let fire trucks in. Snipe at the firemen coming in to save their buildings, how you like that? Soul food, Mr. Elton, is kind of out right now."

"Okay," Arnold said, "I didn't know. I guess these things happen." He was already saying to himself, "No skin off my ass," then wondered if that was true.

He rushed home and was not really surprised to hear the telephone ringing while he was parking the car in the garage. He ran like a bastard but he needn't have. It kept ringing through his fumbling with the kitchen door key until he was in and grabbed the receiver.

362

"We're at the Watts police station," Margaret had to shout. Arnold had never heard her frightened before. In the background, sounds of sirens, something that could be screams, people shouting. "They're holding Jennifer and Robbie. They aren't hurt but they won't let them go." Despite the panic, he found himself noting how much Margaret's speech had improved. It had been so gradual he'd never noticed. "You've got to find some way of getting through to us."

Less than twenty minutes later Wacszinski and Arnold were in a Beverly Hills police car driven by two cops whipping through Los Angeles at eighty miles an hour.

Watts was a smoldering war zone, some of it in flames. A couple of times there were sharp swift metallic sounds against the car.

"Snipers," said one of the cops, adding professionally, "potshots—not really aimed, hitting low."

In Watts the police car careened to a halt, the four doors flew open simultaneously. The two cops elbowed a path for them through the crowd huddled around the police station. They were mostly women and kids and they'd apparently come for news of those close to them who'd either been hurt or were being held or had disappeared.

Inside, like a vast highway wreck, black bodies were scattered on the floor, some unconscious and still bleeding, cops were pushing and tugging at blacks of both sexes and all ages. Guns were everywhere, there was a trigger-finger tension, a confusion of uniforms, teenagers cowering against the walls, gun butts being used as prods, groans, shouts, obscenities.

Wacszinski found them on the far side, Margaret standing over Robbie and Jennifer, who were seated legs straight out on the floor, Margaret stubbornly clinging to Robbie's hand. There was a ring of caked blood about his mouth. A cop hovered over them with a drawn gun.

"Looting," the Watts officer shouted. "Caught them with

the nigger, red-handed with a movie camera, brand-new, little cunt tried to get me in the balls.''

"Sonofabitch was hitting Robbie," Jennifer yelled.

"Those are my kids!" Arnold shouted. "That's my camera, there's some mistake!"

"Just stay where you are, mister." the Watts cop waved his gun.

"Pig bastard!" Jennifer screamed. "Make the sonofabitch give back our footage!"

"Cool it!" Wacszinski barked at her, intervening his bulk and flashing a badge. He was an honorary member of the Beverly Hills force.

"Get the film back!" Robbie yelled.

"I said, Cool it!" Wacszinski whirled on Robbie, then led the Watts cop off to a comparatively quiet corner where they spoke earnestly. Arnold wasn't sure. A few bills slipped from Wacszinski to the Watts cop.

Wacszinski hurried back. "Move it! All of you, fast."

"You folks just go on without me," Margaret said. "I can't leave here. My pa's hurt. Lord knows where they got him or what they're going to do with him."

"Come on, Heatherington," Wacszinski snapped. "They ain't going to do nothin' to your pa." If Wacszinski was parodying her, he was out of date. "You stick around another few minutes and I can't guarantee anything. I'll look for your old man. Now git!"

"Hey!" Jennifer wailed. "What about our film?"

"Get out of here!" Wacszinski shouted at her.

The Beverly Hills cops led them back to their car quickly. Arnold, Margaret, Jennifer and Robbie got in the backseat. One of the cops told Margaret to sit on the floor so she wouldn't be seen, otherwise it might look like police pulling in a black—a similar incident had set off the whole Watts insurrection in the first place.

Roaming bands of young blacks were running wild and four square blocks were still in flames. Sporadic gunfire, could be heard from all directions.

Beverly Hills was serene and peaceful in the summer evening.

Small lean Japanese gardeners were moving with swift efficiency, cleaning up the wide crew-cut lawns before darkness fell.

"I don't know how to thank you," Arnold said to the two cops as they pulled up before the house.

Margaret, Jennifer, Robbie watched blankly. They didn't seem as grateful as Arnold.

"All in a day's work, Mr. Elton," one of the cops said. He turned to Robbie and Jennifer. "What *were* you kids doing out at Watts?"

"We were making a documentary news film, okay?" Jennifer answered sullenly.

"There's a train, all empty, makes one run a day right through the center of Beverly Hills," the first cop said to Jennifer, after all he was from Beverly Hills, he understood about films, "now there's a nice interesting subject for a documentary. Beverly Hills Phantom Train. How about that?" Jennifer and Robbie greeted that with elaborately blank faces, an almost transparent layer below was disgust and anger. The cop's voice got hard as gunmetal. "Stay away from places like Watts. You got lucky once. You might not a second time."

"Okay," Arnold said once they were inside, "what happened?"

Was it by chance that the three were together facing him?

"What do you want to know?" Margaret asked wearily.

"I want to know how come they went to Watts."

"Goddamn it," Jennifer flared at him, "if you're trying to

365

make out like it was Margaret's idea, it wasn't. She got a panic phone call her dad was hurt in Watts she had to leave in a hurry, we told her we'd be all right, she went off.''

"Oh, I knew it was mean out there but I thought I'd be back in a couple of hours," Margaret said. "I figured it would be safe leaving them. The kids phoned a couple times at my folks' place, asking me how it was. I kept telling them I didn't know, last thing I expected was for them to come."

"Then we went out with the camera," Robbie said.

"Into Watts, for Chrissake, with a camera?" Arnold demanded.

"You know something better to shoot film with?" Jennifer demanded. "Watts is real."

"You want to be a real filmmaker," Robbie said, "you got to film real life."

"Hey, now," Arnold asked, "what's all this about?"

"Nothing," Robbie said hastily. "Nothing."

"Oh, shit, why don't you tell him?" Jennifer said disdainfully.

Weariness and fear had taken Margaret beyond ordinary restraints. "If you don't, Robbie, I will." Robbie was jumpy with fright and shock. "He's been writing to his mother in Frisco. I been mailing his letters. She's been sending her answers to Watts."

"Okay," Robbie replied with elaborate casualness. "I saw *her* a couple of times."

"*We* saw her," Jennifer said defiantly.

"Saw her? In person?" Arnold asked.

"Last time was a couple weeks ago. I wanted to know how come you busted up." Robbie, ordinarily so retiring, took on some of Jennifer's belligerence. "She's my mother, right? Basically I wanted to know what she's like, that's no crime, right?" Then, added with disappointment, "I didn't expect her to be driving an old beat-up Mercury, her dad being a banker and all."

366

"Okay, did your mother say anything about me and why we broke up?"

"No, all she said was basically she kinda hopes we have a good relationship and stuff like that," Robbie said.

"You and *Jen* talked to her," Arnold pointed out.

"What is this, the third degree?" Jennifer asked.

"I don't mind," Robbie said. "She asked us were we interested in anything special we told her it was still filmmaking, she said the only way was to film *real* life, basically that's what we talked about so when Margaret phones and tells us about what's happening and Orrin and all—"

"Orrin?" Arnold demanded. "Who's Orrin?"

"You don't even know the name of Margaret's dad?" Jennifer looked at him.

"So Jen and I figured that was pretty real out there."

"I'm sure your mother didn't mean for you to go out alone to anything like Watts. You should have talked it over with me. I know about films."

"You? You always got so many things going," Jennifer flung at him. "Besides, you were off in New York making some crappy deal while they were beating up Orrin."

"Jesus Christ," Arnold exploded. "What was I supposed to do? Go into Watts single-handed and stop them? Let's get this straight. Don't you think I'm sorry this is happening and that Margaret's father got hurt?"

"Watts is a real Happening," Jennifer said. "You didn't even try to get our film back to us. You know what footage we had?"

"You had shots of looting and burning," Arnold said angrily. "Every goddamn newsreel and TV station has it."

"Oh no, oh no," Robbie stuttered in excitement, "we got something none of them got. We got a killing, that's what we had on film, a real killing. We filmed them killing a couple of guys."

"You just show us some TV newsreel guys got that," Jennifer stormed.

"There's these young guys, black guys, leaning against the wall, with two cops standin' over them with guns," Robbie rattled on, "arms over their heads, two guys, then pow pow they just shot them next thing you knew these black guys just fell over," Robbie imitated them, he just let go and fell to the floor, "dead."

"And you could have been killed too," Arnold shouted at them.

"Naw," Robbie said, "they were only killing black guys."

"We shot it in close-ups, that's why they whacked Robbie if you want to know, they didn't want us to have that footage."

"Boy," Robbie said admiringly, "you should have seen Jen let fly and kick that pig cop in the balls. But you know what? It's like on TV. They shoot and the guys are dead. Basically that's it, they fall over dead, I can see them, bang bang and both black guys dead, deader than a doornail."

"Fantastic footage," Jennifer said. Margaret turned suddenly and started to run off but Arnold grabbed her and held her.

"Wait a minute! Wait a minute!" Arnold shouted. "You've got nothing to worry about, Margaret. Wacszinski'll find your father! Now! Stay here!" Margaret wouldn't look at any of them. Arnold turned to the young people. "You guys have convinced me. You're serious about making movies. I'll tell you what I'll do. I'll get the camera fixed. I'll supply all the stock you need, even color. Only one condition." Jennifer eyed him suspiciously. "That you stay away from things like Watts."

"I knew it! I just knew he'd say something like that!" Jennifer cried in bitter triumph to Robbie.

"Jesus Christ!" Arnold exploded. "With the whole world to pick from, why do you have to pick Watts?"

"What do you want us to do?" Robbie demanded. "Go to Vietnam? Basically that's the only other place I know they're killing guys."

"Listen to me, goddamnit!" Arnold yelled. "Make up your mind. You want to make it big as filmmakers? The way I know you can? Well, Watts is not where it's at, understand? Hey, Robbie? What's the matter, Robbie?"

"I keep seeing them with my eyes open," Robbie said, "the two guys. They keep falling."

"Come on, Robbie!" But even Jennifer was frightened.

"Pow, pow, two dead guys."

"Now stop that, understand, stop it!" Arnold spoke rapidly. "We're going to do what we used to do when I was a kid and we saw things we wanted to forget."

"What things?" Jennifer demanded suspiciously.

"People covered with blood after an accident," Arnold said. "An old lady I saw stabbed. A dead rat. An old guy looking in a garbage can. Now just shut your eyes, you guys. You, too, Margaret." Margaret glanced at him incredulously, but Jennifer and Robbie finally shut their eyes. "Now think of all the horrible stuff you saw in Watts. Got that? Now think of pow, pow, and the two guys falling— don't try to hide it, see the blood, everything. Just keep thinking about that, then say after me, Not for my breakfast then you spit like this hard," Arnold spat hard, there was a moment's hesitation, then Robbie repeated the words, then spat, "Not for my lunch," spit, "not for my dinner," spit.

"Not for my breakfast," this time Jennifer chorused in, they both spat hard, "not for my lunch," and spat again, "not for my dinner," they spat vehemently.

"You'll never think of those things ever again," Arnold said. "They're gone."

There was a dead silence.

"Anybody ask me," Margaret said. "You'll never make

things like Watts go away by shutting your eyes and spitting.''

"They can clean it out of their systems," Arnold said tersely. Then to the children, "Now imagine a Spitfire."

Robbie opened his eyes in excitement. "A Triumph Spitfire?" He was big into cars. "A TR4?"

"A Triumph Spitfire TR4," Arnold said, "only shut your eyes." Robbie did. "The white Triumph Spitfire. You see it? Both of you see it?" They both nodded. "With red leather seats?" They nodded again. "It's yours, Jennifer, the minute you've passed your driver's license, I've ordered it for you."

"Oh wow," Robbie said.

PART III

*"No matter how long you've lived,
death comes as an unpleasant surprise."*

PART III

1

A vague sound, frightening because every sound was frightening, jarred Arnold back to now, to Mougins, to the Villa Lou Soleillou, to the viscous puddle of fear spreading in his gut like warm blood from a body wound.

Yet Michel and Germaine were close at hand puttering in the kitchen within quick and easy calling distance and it could not have been all that long that he had been sitting there in the lightless gloom of their living room, for the fragrance of Krystina still lingered. An amorphous form glided toward him and before it could shrink away he saw it was Sri Lanka, standing alongside him protectively. The one-man dog was being a one-man dog. Arnold caressed the puppy tenderly.

Germaine materialized and asked if Monsieur wished the lights on now. Arnold said no. She was not surprised. When the Writer sat that way it was because he was creating and was not to be disturbed. Germaine knew a great deal about the Writer's *petites manies*, his little quirks. One was never to touch his desk; the Writer had fantastic visual memory, could immediately sense the most minute change in the scrambled pattern of the myriad objects on his desk.

Germaine learned to empty the huge specially woven wicker wastebasket only in the Writer's presence. Arnold would spend long minutes checking and rechecking its contents before he reluctantly let her empty it. He was unable to let go of even an old envelope until he'd examined it for a last time. He saved everything that was on paper—bills, theater tickets, programs, invitations, *Their Serene Highnesses the Prince Rainier and the Princess Grace request your presence at a Gala supper for the benefit of the Monégasque Red Cross.* He told everyone that these memorabilia acted as mnemonic devices: from them he could reconstitute whole scenes. But the truth was, he was a saver. He couldn't bear to throw anything away. Telly, his Australian secretary, and Sarita, his Mexican secretary, spent much of their time trying to figure out under what classification they could file such items as an old betting stub from the Cannes nighttime horse races, an invitation to a preview of a cut-rate men's clothing sale, or five used tickets for the boat to the islands off Cannes.

Arnold tried again to focus on the business of who could possibly want to kill him; concluded dismally that he'd gone over his life as well as he'd been able and had come up with nothing particularly helpful.

All he knew was out there somewhere some sonofabitch didn't give one shit about what Arnold Elton meant to Krystina to Jennifer or Robbie or to Arnel Enterprises (which would surely collapse once he was dead); nor about the baby that was coming, the books he would write, or the marvelously worked out take-over he was about to pull and which would make him a real force in the movie world. And that self-same murderous sonofabitch couldn't care less about the wheeling-dealing, fucking, eating or plain everyday living that Arnold Elton had yet to do. The no-good bastard was perfectly willing to convert Arnold Elton into the equivalent of a rock or a lump of shit, which could be flushed away with a rumpled piece of tissue thrown after it by way of remembrance.

Sri Lanka shivered. Arnold petted him reassuringly.

"You scared?" Arnold crooned. "So am I."

Sri Lanka was apparently reacting to sounds that he seemed to hear long before Arnold did, for a moment later Arnold heard a sound at the entrance. He half rose and crouched in fright as he peered at the black doorway.

"You need the darkness for any special reason?" Scott said. as he and Telly burst in. They were both breathing hard, for they must have run up the steep driveway. "Like, are you naked or in transcendental meditation?"

They were so festive, animated, young. He was annoyed. How could anyone be so untouched by his trouble? And a mere six weeks ago when he'd left, Telly, his beautiful, cultured secretary whom he kept almost as a showpiece, had been so reserved.

But Telly swept over to him carrying with her a turbulence of suddenly vivid femininity. As she bent over him, Arnold understood. She tingled with the excitement and mercurial assurance of one who's in love and knows she's loved.

"We can tarry but a brief moment," Scott had absorbed some of Telly's British mannerisms. "We have a cab waiting below."

Everything they did and said had the hurried tentative quality of those who have a cab waiting.

"Welcome home," Telly's lips brushed Arnold's cheeks, as if wanting to share with him some of her newfound happiness. "Krystina asked me to pick up a few things for the party."

"And most important of all, here is a gift for Arnold Elton," Scott brandished a long cylindrical object wrapped in what seemed to be gift paper left over from Christmas. A baseball bat? Scott was perfectly capable of making some

375

crappy inappropriate joke like, "One baseball bat, apply forcefully to skull three times daily thus beating your alleged brains out for the way you kept me dangling here all these weeks when you could at least have left a message." Anything was possible with Scott. Arnold remembered Scott's first gift to him.

In May, shortly before beginning the in-depth interview, Scott had appeared one morning with two small packages. "A gift for you," Scott said to Arnold, "a vial of earth from the Holy Land." (Scott had covered the peace parleys in Jerusalem and Cairo.) He opened a tiny package marked Holy Earth. "A flacon of holy water from the River Jordan," and he opened a tiny glass bottle, labeled Holy Water. Arnold was pleased; he was superstitious and he liked the idea of holy earth and holy water, but before he could reach for them, Scott said, "Just mix the two, like this," spilling the water from the vial over the earth, "and what do we get?—Holy Mud." Arnold had felt a burst of anger as though he'd been betrayed.

"You both look great," Arnold said, "six weeks of the good life seems to agree with you."

"Only four at your expense." For a moment it looked as if Scott would not even bother to unwrap the gift.

Arnold looked the two of them over carefully, tried to sound casual. "When did this happen? You two?"

The atmosphere got crisp. Scott took Telly's hand with elaborate tenderness. "Why, it was when we exposed our bookshelves to each other," Scott said, "and we realized we had in common Oscar Lewis's *The Children of Sanchez*, Bertrand Russell's *Autobiography*, Sean O'Casey's *Pictures in the Hallway*—"

"Jean-Paul Sartre's *The Words*," Telly went on apprehensively, "and what about *The World According to Garp*?"

"Yah," Arnold said. "But you'll never marry each other."

"Oh, Arnold!" Telly said. "Did you *have* to do that?"

"A little bullshit goes a long way with me," Arnold said. "What's the gift?"

"Well," Scott had to make an effort to get himself back into the spirit of it. "I heard the terrible news about how our man Oscar fouled up on our shipment of New York delicatessen and knowing you are a displaced person if you're more than ten minutes from a kosher salami—are you ready, Arnold?"

Scott whipped off the last paper wrapping, revealed a long shiny salami, held it close to Arnold's nose.

"Touch it. Smell it." Scott urged. "And after we've gone, taste it. It's the real thing. One hundred percent kosher salami."

It was the real thing, pungent with pepper, garlic and spices. With the smell came a surge of nostalgia.

Nathan combing eight-year-old Arnold's hair, Nathan taking him to Loew's Orpheum, Fanchon and Marco girls, Nathan buying him a salami sandwich.

"Where the hell did you find a Jewish salami in this area?" Arnold tried to sound gruff. Actually he was touched.

"We were combing picturesque side streets in old Cannes, Telly and I," Scott said, "which is a fine way to comb picturesque side streets, when all at once, there before us was Boucherie Sam, Cacher—French for Sam's Kosher Meat Market. Do you appreciate the full implications of that? I found it for you, Arnold. A salami connection."

"Telly," Arnold said suddenly, "I've got to talk to Scott alone."

"Oh. Well," Telly said, "you do look a bit odd. But I thought it was the journey."

"Tell Michel to pay the cab off."

Telly hesitated. That was a change too. She was not the social secretary (that was how Krystina introduced her) who a month and a half ago would have shot off the split-second Arnold suggested the slightest chore.

"We bust a gut getting a cab," Scott protested. "Sarita tooted off with Telly's car. It's the Fourteenth of July eve and it'll be practically impossible to dream up another cab."

"And we must get to the yacht quickly," Telly added. "Krystina was so anxious that I find out exactly how the Princess is to be addressed—"

"The Princess?" Arnold demanded. "The Princess who?"

"Why, the Princess Alexa," Telly let drop on him. "There wasn't much I could find out in this short time. I'm not certain how she's to be addressed."

"Oh, hell," Scott said, "I know her. A modest 'Princess' will hold her—"

"She's here?" Arnold asked in consternation.

"Indeed. And coming to the party. At least someone called on her behalf," Telly was disturbed by Arnold's reaction. "I felt it was someone's butler."

"Oh, shit," Arnold said with sincere, deeply felt dismay.

"I just assumed you'd invited her." Telly was upset. "And you and Krystina do invite so many people at the last moment and forget to tell me so I can include them on the guest list."

Princess Alexa's presence on board could lead to a first-class calamity. She might let slip around Wade Vernon that it was her proxies that were the bulk of the voting weight Elton carried. And if for some crazy reason Dennis ever took it into his addled head to come to the party, too, he would need only one glimpse of the Princess, one of the most powerful Associated stockholders, to put it all together—that Arnold was behind this whole operation.

"She didn't by any chance leave a number where she could be reached?" Arnold asked hopefully.

"No," Telly was distressed. "And I don't have a clue as to where she's being put up. It simply never occurred to me that you could possibly have any objections to her coming."

"Objections?" Scott asked lazily. "Krystina did nip-ups." (An article had appeared in a London magazine, making

378

snide comments about how no Elton party was complete without a faded bouquet of spurious titles.)

"I had the distinct impression that the Princess was simply accepting an invitation," Telly said. "From you."

"Oh, no, not from me," Arnold said. "Look, Telly, while I'm talking to Scott maybe you could inquire around and see if somebody knows where she could be reached."

Telly cast a worried look at Scott, then at Arnold. "I'll try," and hurried off.

"Christ," Arnold said shakily, "it's creeping up on me from all sides. Scott, how well do you know this Alexa?"

"She's on several of those international children's relief funds," Scott said. "We've run into each other in a couple of those miserable African wars where the children always seem to be the main victims. I was never quite sure whether she meant it or was there for kicks. To answer your question, you tend to get either very close or very far from people you've been with in that kind of a situation. I would say we're quite close."

"She's the kind of stubborn old broad," Arnold said, "who once she suspected I wanted to get rid of her would deliberately stick around."

"She rarely appears at affairs like this," Scott said. "Getting her off would depend on why she came."

"If she does come, you've got to help me get her the hell off. Like immediately."

"I'll see what I can do, but that can't be why you wanted to talk to me? You seem as uncool as I've ever seen you." When Arnold didn't answer immediately, Scott went on, "Is it about Telly? The legend has it you get nasty when one of, well, let's say your ex-girl friends leaves you, or is taken away from you. But from what you told me about her I thought you'd be relieved to have her off your hands."

"I don't remember talking to you about Telly." Arnold tried to recall if he had and couldn't. He didn't want an antagonistic Scott right now. He needed a friend. Someone he could talk it out to, all of it, and who would listen.

"In the first two days we were together," Scott said, and it seemed without any apparent malice, "you went into great detail about twenty-eight—I kept track—twenty-eight women you fucked. Now, guys have talked to me about their women when we first met, but you set a record. You were very colorful about Telly. Quote. 'She's like one of those beautiful English mansions, the kind you can't sell or rent, they look great on the outside but are a pain in the ass to maintain.' Unquote."

"Okay," Arnold said, meaning he had deserved and taken his lumps.

"Two mysteries," Scott wouldn't let him off that easily. "One. How you, a man who writes books, could be so far off, and Two, whatever attracted her to you. For the last all I can think of is that she was in a very vulnerable state when she first met you."

"So I missed something," Arnold said. "I mean, okay. Now I've got a problem and it's urgent."

"I can see it's urgent. Squeeze a little harder and you'll bleed that salami."

Arnold loosened his grip on the huge sausage.

"The goddamnedest thing has just happened to me, at the goddamnedest moment. Here I am in the middle of a complicated deal that involves millions and millions of dollars."

"Wait a minute," Scott stopped him. "You don't have to go any farther. I'm not your man. My mind boggles over anything more than two dollars and thirty-nine cents."

"You wait a minute, Scott. There's something heavy weighing on me. I need somebody I can talk to."

Again there was the unmistakable sound of a car grinding up the driveway, stopping. There were electronic voices at the gate, buzzing and clicking as the gate was opened.

"My life's been threatened," Arnold said hastily.

Scott, who had been about to leave, came to an abrupt halt.

"Christ," Scott stared at Arnold. "Yeah. You look like a man whose life's been threatened." For the first time since he met Scott there was no banter in his tones. "Is it for real?"

"It's for real."

"Then call the cops."

"That's their car you hear," Arnold spoke rapidly. "I need more than cops. I need somebody I can talk this out with."

"You need an expert in life-and-death threats."

"No, goddamn it," Arnold said intensely. "I'm in trouble, Scott. Look, you felt close enough to me to charge a four-week luxury hotel bill to me."

"Maybe it would be simpler all around if you let me pay you back. It may take me awhile, but I could do it..."

"Oh, no!" Arnold said in something close to anguish. "Fuck it! Fuck the money! I didn't mean it that way, I only meant you aren't a guy who can take hospitality without having some feeling for the people you took it from. Jesus, Scott, I'm slightly hysterical." Arnold took a deep breath. There were the muffled sounds of voices speaking French. "I've told you already there's this huge deal I'm about to close, money'll be coming out of my ears, there'll be money for everybody's near me."

"Are you that scared?" Scott said in wonder. "Christ."

"I'm scared shitless. They're out for me and I don't even know who." Arnold looked around with quick fearful glances. "Or where. Or why."

"I don't know what good I'd be," a touch of sympathy in Scott's tones, "but whatever I can do, Arnold, sure."

"Thanks," Arnold felt a great warm wave of reassurance even though at the same time he couldn't suppress a fleeting suspicion that the change in Scott had come when money had been mentioned. But no, he told himself hastily, that was not right. Scott really was one of those elusive schmos who did things out of the goodness of his heart. Ordinarily Arnold kept away from that kind. They were too fucking complicated and how could you be one hundred percent sure of them? But the guy you could buy—him you had nailed. He had to be there where you wanted him.

Arnold yanked himself up. What the moment needed was exactly a schmo like Scott: even better, if you ever got a guy like that in your pay you could not only swear by him, but he would anticipate. And, besides, it would have grated on Arnold to feel there was a type like Scott who couldn't be bought. In the final analysis anybody could be bought. That was the basis of every one of Arnold's operations, and in a more subtle way, his life-style.

Still, Arnold breathed much easier. There was someone close at hand he could rely on all the way.

"Now don't forget," Arnold said, "if I'm not on board when the old bimbo gets there, whisk her below and keep her out of sight until I get to you. As few people as possible must know she's aboard."

"You just don't know Alexa," Scott said. "Once she's on board everybody'll know it. That's the very essence of her being. Is she related to that threat?"

"I don't know. I doubt it."

Telly, her arms loaded with cartons of silver and china, came tottering in. "It's the police," she announced.

"We'll talk more on the *Delphi*," Arnold said. His tones were so laden with significance that Telly swerved her head to study them both.

Scott took a carton from her.

"Now starts the phoning for a cab," Scott said.

"No, no," Arnold said and, as if to seal the new relationship, offered, "take the Monte."

"You'd trust Scott with the Monteverdi?" Telly was shocked.

Arnold managed a tight smile. "According to him he's handled everything from a Maserati to a Honda. He won't

382

have trouble with the Monte. And I'd like you over on the *Delphi* as quickly as possible.''

Scott hesitated a moment as he and Telly exchanged glances, then Scott took the keys and they hurried out.

Where else but in France would a cop kiss you on both cheeks and look at you with shining eyes that asked, What can I do for you?

A top cop. An Inspector.

And what a name.

Inspector Orfeo Bellarosa. Orpheus Beautiful Rose. Like so many on the French Riviera if you stepped back a distance, Bellarosa was French of Italian extraction. Up closer Bellarosa was Corsican.

He'd been a frequent guest of the Eltons at their numerous cocktail parties. And Arnold had named a character in one of his books Orfeo Bellarosa. After that, the Inspector was his for life.

''Then to resume, a warning was telephoned about an hour ago. In what language?'' The Inspector's manner was that of a doctor who knows his patient has a terminal disease.

''English,'' Arnold said carefully.

''Which accent? American? French? English English?''

Arnold thought carefully. He had to say enough so Bellarosa would come to the right conclusion himself and realize that it couldn't look as if the information had come from Arnold. ''Sort of Italian,'' Arnold said after a moment.

''Arnold,'' Bellarosa said with a hint of sharpness, ''I have an unpleasant feeling you are not taking this as seriously as you should.''

''I'm taking it very seriously. After all, I've never had my life threatened before.''

''You are not behaving at all like a man who may be killed any moment,'' Bellarosa was a little annoyed. ''Now repeat

383

to me exactly what the person who telephoned said—''

" 'I am your friend. Somebody is trying to kill you,' "
Arnold enunciated slowly. " 'You are an intelligent man. You
will know what to do.' "

"A strange friend. You did not take it as a threat?"

"Well, the way it came," Arnold said thoughtfully. "I felt
it as a—warning . . ."

"Explain to me the way it came."

"The sound of the voice . . ."

Bellarosa grunted. "Not even a hint of money demanded?"

"Nothing."

"If it is the work of professionals, it is difficult to understand why there was not at least a suggestion of le pay-off.
But of course what was meant by 'intelligent' was that you
will pay off."

Outside, the Monteverdi in low gear growled its way down
the steep driveway. Arnold hunched his shoulders, bracing for
stripping of gears but Scott handled the car beautifully.

"Let us consider another eventuality," Bellarosa mused.
"A hired killer has been engaged. Someone friendly hears
about it and warns you, but is frightened to be involved
further. Can you think of anyone who would want to have
you killed?"

"Not really."

"Let me help your thinking. In most murders, the killer
and his victim know each other well." Bellarosa waited to see
if that would bring something from Arnold. Arnold shrugged
helplessly. "An indiscreet question. How did you part with
your former wives? Your mistresses? Were they friendly,
civilized ruptures?"

"My mistresses," Arnold made a helpless gesture. That
would take too long. "My former wives?" That Arnold had
to suppose was possible. But Arnold tried mightily to fantasize
Kate and Beejay holding smoking revolvers or blood-wet
daggers. All he got was Kate pointing a pistol at him, pulling

384

the trigger, which spurted a viscous liquid that looked suspiciously like sperm. As for Beejay, he could only imagine her dropping a weapon in revulsion. "It seems impossible."

"Every murder is impossible before it happens. So few people understand death and know it the way we in the police do." Orfeo Bellarosa was quite a philosopher for a cop. "And since they have no real conception of death, few understand what murder really is; they have a very incomplete idea of what they're doing when they commit murder. Did you part with your wives badly? With bitterness?"

"Yes," Arnold finally admitted. He felt an unpleasant twinge as he thought of Margaret. Although he was not a man given to feelings of guilt or remorse, Margaret, not by anything she did, but just by the very fact of their relationship, was the cause of occasional spasms of guilt.

"Let us put aside the question of women for the moment," Bellarosa went on. "Has there been any unusual event in your recent life? Forget about how or why."

"Yes," Arnold said. "A very unusual event. An unusual business deal."

"Unusual? How?"

It was like talking to your shrink. There was no point in hiding anything.

"Unusual," Arnold said carefully, "because it involves a huge amount of money, and because it involves taking power away from one group and switching it to ourselves." He shook his head emphatically, rejecting it. "These are Americans."

"American businessmen?" Bellarosa raised an eyebrow at that.

"Film people," Arnold replied. Bellarosa raised his eyebrow even higher. "But Americans have no tradition of settling their business by murder."

"And what about the two Kennedys and Martin Luther King?" Bellarosa said gently. "And even if they are film people, they cannot take kindly to having power removed from them. Can you not conceive of them hiring paid assassins?''

Arnold thought of Armand. He had known Armand longer than anyone else in Hollywood, but how much would that count for with Armand? He was a vindictive bastard. He must have found out about that clause in the contract by now. Armand could kill. But because he had a motive, it would be stupid of Armand to set Arnold up. Armand was not stupid.

"All right, it could be film people, but actually hiring somebody to kill me. No. I can't believe it.''

"We were merely examining the possibilities. It may help us to determine a direction in which to look. Aside from your ex-wives, has there been an unusual woman, under unusual circumstances, recently in your life?''

Clover. And she was curiously and indirectly related to the unusual deal, for after all it had come about indirectly through her.

"Well, yes, there was an unusual woman," Arnold said carefully, "and as you say, under peculiar circumstances. But there would be no reason for her to kill me. Her mind runs more to gas stations.''

Bellarosa decided to let that pass. "Let us go back then. You mentioned Italian accents. Have you seen your friend the Baron lately? There are rumors. We have some reason to believe he has connections with the Mafia," Bellarosa hesitated. "Do you have any relationship with the Mafia?''

Bellarosa was watching him carefully.

"Not a business relationship," Arnold was thinking of Uncle Millie. "But it's a good relationship. I could go to him for help.''

"If it's the Mafia, no one goes to them for help. That is a myth.''

"This man is like an uncle to me. It's impossible. As for

Alfredo, he's among our closest friends. His wife *is* Krystina's closest friend." Arnold wasn't making it too convincing, which is what he wanted anyway because he hoped Bellarosa would then keep the Baron in mind. "I would have recognized his voice, if that's what you're thinking."

"I wasn't thinking anything yet. Well. You, dear Arnold, have chosen the most awkward day of the year, from a police point of view, to have your life threatened, besides which you are giving a party on your yacht. Perhaps you should seriously consider calling this party off."

"Oh no," Arnold was appalled. "Krystina would be destroyed."

"Far less unpleasant than being a widow."

"The party is already under way. It would be impossible."

"Nothing is as impossible as being killed," the Inspector said. "I strongly urge you to cancel this evening."

"No, I can't."

"Then you must stay here," Bellarosa said, "until we can arrange to protect you."

"This is Krystina's night. I'd have to tell her."

"This *is* the worst possible night of the year." The Inspector stopped suddenly, for there was the piercing sound of screaming brakes and tires in the distance. They both held their breath, for it was the kind of sound that must end in a crash, which came a moment later; and almost simultaneously the sound of shattering glass and screams, then a silence disturbed only by an idling motor.

In the garden Michel's face was white in the gloom as he pointed below. Arnold and Bellarosa broke into a run.

The Monteverdi's right fender was badly crumpled but the motor was still running and in its lights Scott and Telly, his arms about her, were silhouetted as people in a night accident always seem to be. It had happened not more than a hundred meters down the road from the Villa.

"We were taking this curve, suddenly this lunatic shot out," Scott stuttered in disbelief.

"Utterly mad, a huge white car coming at us from nowhere," Telly said softly.

"Swung deliberately toward us on the crest of the curve," Scott went on. "Deliberately tried to force us over the hillside. Flashed a bright light on us, then at the last second veered away but I couldn't avoid hitting this tree."

"He passed you on the outside, on your left," Bellarosa was puzzled, "then flashed a bright light on you?"

"So powerful that he practically blinded me," Scott said. "He must have wanted me to lose control."

"Or possibly he wished to see who was in the car," Bellarosa suggested.

"Strange. It's what I felt," Telly said eagerly.

"You said it was a white car," Arnold said. "Could it have been a white Peugeot 604, or didn't you have a chance to see?"

"Only that it was white," Scott looked at Arnold suspiciously.

"Why do you suggest a white Peugeot 604?" Bellarosa asked.

"Coming home from the airport on the superhighway," Arnold avoided their eyes and tried not to make it sound too serious, "there was an incident. A white 604 swerved at me and forced me off the road, then veered off. But I hear there's been an epidemic of nut drivers in white 604's."

"Will you forgive me?" Telly asked politely. "Granny taught us when we'd been frightened, as after a thunderstorm, we children were to spend a penny. Pee," she explained. "It seems to help."

She disappeared into the brush.

"You had that happen to you on the highway?" Scott asked Arnold the moment she was gone. "You had your life threatened, and yet you let Telly and me take off in your tomato red Monteverdi?"

Arnold could only see a fragment of Scott's face, white and angry, in the peripheral light from the car's headlights.

"Come on, Scott," Arnold chided. "Do you think for a moment that I'd have let you and Telly go out in the Monte if I thought there was the slightest possibility it could have been a target?"

"Talk me out of it," Scott said.

"You exaggerate, Monsieur Goldman," Bellarosa intervened quickly with a hint of offense, "Monsieur Elton is your friend."

There was a rustle in the brush and Telly emerged from the side of the road brushing leaves from her hair and dress.

"Much better thank you," she said, as if in answer to a question they surely would have asked. "Very odd but it does help, you know."

Bellarosa drew Arnold aside. "I believe we must consider this to be the work of those who threatened your life."

"It doesn't make much sense," Arnold said. "If they are threatening me because they hope to get me to pay off, why then was the attempt made on the autoroute before the threat was delivered? And before I could have paid off?"

"Perhaps it is not for a payoff," Bellarosa said. "I'm beginning to feel that this homicide has for its motive, let us say, personal reasons, such as revenge. Perhaps it's not well organized."

"Then why didn't he knock me off on the highway coming from the airport?" Arnold asked. "He could have easily. And why didn't he force Scott and Telly off the road right now? He must have thought *I* was in the car. Why did he move away after he flashed the light?"

"Because he saw they were not the victims he wishes to make," Bellarosa said. "It is possible that whenever he sees the Monteverdi he must get close enough to make sure whoever is in the car is the one or the ones he is after. What I am thinking is that if the car is not too accidented, one of our

389

men, in civilian clothes, will take it now. Mademoiselle and Monsieur Goldman can accompany me in my car; we will be directly behind the Monteverdi. If we do draw him out again, we shall be able to intercept him, and of course interrogate him. And if it is as I suspect, he will throw much light on this threat, enough so we will know you're safe and you may go to your party lightheartedly.''

Telly and Scott had come close enough to hear the last.

"I don't think he'll come out," Arnold said, "but it's certainly worth the chance."

"If that is agreeable to Monsieur Goldman and Mademoiselle," Bellarosa asked, "we will conduct you to the *Delphi*."

"Of course," Scott said quickly. "It'll be much safer transportation than the Cannes taxi drivers, especially on a night like tonight."

"Good." Bellarosa turned to Arnold, "You still insist on holding this party?"

"I can't call it off."

"We'll try to make the risks as small as possible," Bellarosa said. "You will take every precaution, Arnold. You will remain at the Villa, where you will keep all the lights on. You will react to the slightest suspicious sound or movement, you will call me if you have the least doubt, and you will not make the voyage to the yacht until I have provided police escort for you. Also I shall have two armed men stationed below the Villa standing guard."

"But I must get to the yacht," Arnold protested.

"Not until I consider it secure. I'll be as rapid as I can."

"I know you will," Arnold said hesitantly. He was thinking about Alexa on the yacht. And Dennis.

"Don't worry," Bellarosa misinterpreted his hesitation. "We will take good care of you. What would the Riviera be without you?" Bellarosa had a large sentimental streak. He put an arm around him. "You may smile at this but I am a

Corsican and I consider you, Arnold Elton, not only my friend, but an honorary Corsican.''

"For those who understand such matters," Scott said dryly, "that's the ultimate compliment.''

Arnold halted before the living room, which was now in complete darkness. To move into the lightless familiar room required an effort; he heard himself thinking "There's nothing threatening in that room. A few feet and on the left there's a switch for the dimmers. The room will glow with light.'' He took a step, stopped, flipped the switch, the lights came up slowly. Sri Lanka moved to him, put his cold moist nose in Arnold's palm.

As Arnold bent over and touched the dog lovingly Michel and Germaine materialized from the kitchen and stood frozen in the doorway.

"*Ça alors*!'' Michel said irritably and Arnold followed Michel's gaze and saw the source of his irritation.

The beautiful protective animal had peed in three different places on the antique Oriental rug. Arnold deliberately ruffled Sri Lanka's copper mane affectionately, thus proclaiming the puppy's sovereign right to pee anywhere, even on the expensive rug. Arnold thought, "How strange. Here I am a target for murder and I'm watching the two older people trying hard to suppress their anger.'' They wouldn't move. They were dueling with each other for position and it was Michel who finally broke and went off to attend to the rug stains.

Germaine, having just established for all time that the puppy was Michel's responsibility, softened.

"Oh, but Monsieur hasn't eaten,'' she said with maternal concern. "Surely Monsieur must be greatly hungry.''

She was referring to the fact that Arnold was invariably famished after bedroom sessions with Krystina, especially the first one after a long absence.

"I must save myself for the *Delphi*.'' Arnold couldn't stand

391

the idea of Germaine and Michel fussing over some elaborate dish he had no stomach for. Besides, he needed desperately to be alone. There were urgent phone calls he'd been too panicked to make. "Madame must have ordered too much food as usual," Arnold heard himself say testily. "There will be a great deal left over. I wish this time you would make a real attempt to see that it is used."

He was irritated again with Krystina. She ordered like a goddamn fool. The caterers took advantage of them and just piled the dishes on. And between Captain Dougherty and Michel and Germaine the vast quantities of leftovers mysteriously disappeared, sometimes in a matter of hours. Then Krystina's persistent protest, "But, darling, it's all deductible." He could never make her understand that deductible was not the same as free. It still cost them something.

Germaine shook her head in grave disapproval as she and Michel, he straightening himself with considerable audible effort, disappeared into the kitchen.

The moment they were out of sight, Arnold jumped on the phone and called the Colombe d'Or. "I wish to speak to a Monsieur Hume."

"What with the Fourteenth of July," the voice replied, "it is difficult to note the comings and goings of guests, but *tiens,* one of the waiters has just informed me that Monsieur Hume left in a limousine ten minutes ago."

"Now, tell me," Arnold asked grimly, "how long will it take a limousine to descend from St.-Paul to Cannes?"

"With the Fourteenth traffic," the voice replied, "it could take anywhere from one to three hours."

Arnold would have pursued the conversation but he was speaking to a dead line. He called the *Delphi,* but that line was busy—a telephone on board ship was enough of a curiosity for some of their guests just to use it for the fun of it—Arnold then called Reilly in New York. It was now two in the afternoon there.

392

Reilly came on the phone breathing hard. Arnold was not surprised. A good ninety percent of the time when Arnold called Reilly he got him when he was fucking.

"Get rid of whoever it is you're on top of," Arnold said. "We've got important talking to do."

"Why sure thing, Ar," and Reilly lowered his tone, which took on that sly confidential timbre he used for fuck talk. "The chick's a sociology major at NYU but she's got a physiology major's ass and boobs, she has no afternoon classes."

Arnold was again unpleasantly reminded of Reilly's fantastic talent for the inappropriate. "This is heavy," Arnold stopped him short.

"What's up, Ar?" Reilly began with weighty concern, which lightened as he went on, "in case you're worried everything is copacetic here. The stocks have just hit the magic number, Getz, Littrell and Shelley have just bought up over a million dollars worth of AA in the East—just that little leak and down it went like you predicted, Ar—their western group has earmarked practically all the liquid Arnel cash to buy there. This is it, we're in business, I saw the old bimbo like you said, everything is just fine there."

"What do you mean 'just fine'? Did she give you the proxies as we agreed?"

"Now just keep your shirt on," Reilly said, and Arnold went ten degrees colder. "She said . . ." Something suddenly seeped through to Reilly. "Hey, Ar. Didn't she bring you the proxies?"

"Bring me?" Arnold howled. "Jesus Christ Almighty, she was supposed to give them to you. Reilly, goddamn it if something went wrong there—"

"Wait a minute," Reilly said soberly. "She told me she was taking the Concorde to Paris and then going on to the south of France, where she'd deliver them to you in person.

393

She said she didn't want the transaction to take place on American soil."

"On American soil?" Arnold was almost speechless, his chest heaving, his breath a straight whistle, "what kind of shit is that? Why didn't you call me immediately?"

"She must be there now. I'm sure she'll get in touch with you any minute, I impressed on her that time was of the essence . . ."

"Why the hell didn't you call me?" Arnold shouted at him. His life-long cool had deserted him. "Don't you realize what a fuck-up it would be if Hume sees the bimbo with me? Couldn't you figure that the one place in the world she shouldn't be is where he is?"

"I don't know what we could have done about it. I couldn't have stopped her."

Well. That couldn't possibly be why the Princess was coming to the party; nobody in his right mind could believe she would have displaced herself just to give Arnold proxies on French soil. What was amazing about Reilly was that he was exactly as stupid as you thought he was.

"Now listen to me," Arnold was again almost in control. "It's not what I'm calling you about. I'll know soon enough about *that*."

"I'm listening, Ar."

Arnold chose his words carefully. Transatlantic calls were monitored, Arnold's especially, at least by the Internal Revenue people. "Now I'm going to ask you an important question. Seen your *classmate* lately?"

Naturally, Reilly didn't get it. "My classmate?"

"Your fucking classmate," Arnold yelled.

Lightning finally hit. "Oh, *him*."

"Him. That's right. Him."

"Oh, now and then." Playing it casual now to fool the monitors.

"There's a complication in my life," Arnold said slowly. "I want you to go to your classmate."

"I'm with you, Ar."

"And I want you to ask your fucking classmate if any of his friends have a legal document out for me. You understand?"

"A legal document out for you?" Reilly asked. "Oh." He gasped. "Jesus, Ar. You don't mean like a contract out on you?"

For the umpteenth time Reilly had proven himself to be not only stupid but also a first-class putz. "I have reason to believe there's one out on me. I've got to know if it's so and if it is, where it comes from and why. I've *got to* know. Understand, Reilly? *Got to*."

"Sure, Ar," Reilly was dripping sympathy. "Right away, Ar. Mike's only a few blocks from here. He'll know, or find out for us. I know how you must feel. I'll get right to it. But I don't believe it." As Arnold didn't even bother to protest, he asked, "Got anything to go on that would be helpful?"

"My grandmother Adelheid used to tell a joke," Arnold said, but his tone was not of a joke teller. "Lady writes to Sears Roebuck asks for their special five-cents-a-roll toilet paper. Sears answers advising her to look on page one thousand two hundred and ninety-three of their catalog, where she'd see the toilet paper was six cents a roll, not five. Lady writes back, Dear Sears Roebuck, if I had a catalog with one thousand two hundred ninety-three pages, do you think I'd be ordering your toilet paper?"

And hung up.

Arnold decided that Alfredo was with the Mob. Alfredo was acting on orders from them. The Mob, probably because they had smelled out the coming take-over of AA, smelled money. Lately, the Mob had been alert for that kind of

395

wheeling and dealing. That was why they'd nailed him the moment he got to France.

Okay. If he had to pay off, he would.

It was only money.

The contract would be withdrawn.

Arnold would not be killed.

Not to be dead, not to leave it all. The proxy situation would work itself out. He'd handle the Princess if she showed up. No reason to panic. He called Wacszinski's house in California. Instead of Don he got Don's fucking answering machine.

"Sorry," Don's voice came over the machine. "Mr. Wacszinski's been called away suddenly. Leave your name and number. You'll be called back. Time: zero eight seventeen Pacific time."

Normally Don checked his machine at least every hour. To have gone three hours without checking, at a critical moment like this, was unthinkable with twenty-six-hour-a-day Wacszinski. And not to leave a number. Everyone on the executive level in Arnel, bar none, always left a number where he or she could be reached at all times. With a minimum of smart calculating you could then tell from the number they left exactly what was going on, who was doing what, whether it was a noonday roll in the hay or lunch at the Bistro. Arnold felt more comfortable when he knew whom his executives were fucking.

Something had happened. Something was radically wrong. Arnold immediately called Dorothy, at home. Like Don, she was another Arnel jewel. Her life, too, was all Arnel, and true to the old Studio tradition, because she was an Executive Secretary she was not bangworthy. Bangable secretaries never lasted long enough in the Arnel setup to prove they were executive secretary material. Arnold caught her as she was about to leave for the office. The fact that Don had not left a number where he could be reached upset her, but because she was big into Christian Science nothing upset her long.

"Where are you?" she asked.

"I'm at the Villa."

"What?" Dorothy's indignation made it across a continent and an ocean. Dorothy of course knew what time it was at Mougins. "And you're leaving poor Krystina to handle that party all alone?"

"Something's wrong," Arnold said resolutely. "I've got to wait here until I get Don."

"Don't do that," Dorothy wheedled, "go enjoy your party. We'll take care of everything at this end. I know how worried you are but do me a favor. Relax. Enjoy. I promise you Don will check in any minute. I'll be on top of it. I'll get to you on the yacht. Now promise me you'll go to your party."

But Arnold had decided to punish them on the West Coast for Don's unforgivable lapse.

"I'll be sitting up here at the Villa," he said. Dorothy groaned. "Until we hear from Don."

"I can't stand the idea of you alone, and Krystina will be destroyed," Dorothy said.

"I'm waiting up here," Arnold was adamant.

Dorothy sighed, accepted it.

"I'll find him. But I'm sure Don's got a good reason. He always leaves a number."

Which didn't reassure Arnold at all.

Hidden in the shadows of the street below, Michel reported to Arnold there was a police car with two cops armed with machine guns. Bellarosa was true to his word. How many people, especially Americans, could say they rated a police guard on the Fourteenth of July?

Arnold paced. He kept punching his Pulsar. The blue figures showed it was almost two and a half hours since Alfredo had dropped it on him.

397

There was something Arnold was trying to recall and didn't know what it was.

Finally it hit him.

Scott's salami. That's what he'd been aching for. That would bring him solace. He pounced on the salami, searched frantically for a knife. Now the craving was overpowering. He couldn't go into the kitchen. Germaine and Michel would gloat.

Monsieur was hungry after all.

There'd be no stopping them. They'd whip up some fancy dish with Provençal herbs when what he craved, hungered for, was kosher salami. Even if Krystina would mumble under her breath the moment he came on board, "Arnold, you didn't! I can smell it from here!"

It was okay if you reeked of garlic from snails, that was acceptable, that was French Haute Cuisine. But kosher salami. No way.

Frantically he prowled about the living room. It was ironic that there were no cutting instruments in the living room. He would settle for anything that could cut salami. All he found was a dull bronze letter opener, but at least that had an edge and a point. Clutching the salami with one hand, he jabbed it with the letter opener, stabbing and hacking, but couldn't penetrate the skin, or maybe it wasn't skin anymore but some plastic crap. He growled as he fought the sausage savagely, at last pierced the covering, sawed away furiously, but the goddamn letter opener wouldn't saw. He tried everything. Cut-slice-chop, stab, who cared as long as he was able to claw off a part of the casing and expose the naked succulent salami flesh. He chopped at it with chin-high strokes. The casing gave way, releasing a powerful odor of garlic and spice.

Sri Lanka stirred. A car came roaring up the driveway and there was the buzzer, shouts of boisterous young voices. He chopped desperately, but before he could get even a chunk of salami small enough to pop in his mouth, Germaine was at the doorway. He dropped the bronze letter opener and the salami guiltily. Germaine pretended not to see or smell the offending salami.

"Mademoiselle Jennifer is here with several friends," Germaine's voice had the quality of a death in the family. She and Michel knew who Bellarosa was. In the background Michel held an excited Sri Lanka by his collar. With a deep sigh of regret Arnold relinquished the salami. He couldn't face Jennifer with salami breath.

A Coca-Cola ad was waiting for him on the back terrace. Jennifer, Robbie and the Plaything stood in the white overhead garden light, behind them the Jolly, a jeep with a tasseled canvas top Arnold had bought for Jennifer some three years before, for her to use on the Riviera. She seldom drove it and most of the year it was kept in the Villa garage. Arnold had hoped it would be an inducement for Jennifer to visit them more often in the south of France but she came only when there was no way of avoiding it.

The Jolly was crammed with young people.

"Jesus Christ, Krystina's busting a gut worrying why the hell you haven't come down." It was a new record even for Jennifer. She'd put him on the defensive within ten seconds of their seeing each other. "What have you been doing up here anyway?"

"I had to make a few calls."

"So that's why nobody could get through—you couldn't have made the calls from the *Delphi*?" Jennifer asked. "That boat of yours is like a spy ship, it's wired for any spot in the world. You've left your wife with a horde of hungry, thirsty freeloaders."

"Hey," Arnold managed to say. "Like we haven't seen each other for months. Aren't you going to kiss your old man?"

Jennifer submitted to the paternal kiss. "Come on, pile in,

let's haul ass out of here," she said. Arnold looked at the Jolly. "Friends of Robbie's and mine. We invited them to the party, we've got to have some kind of life for ourselves while we're here."

"I didn't say anything," Arnold defended himself.

"Don't tell me you're going to hang around here some more? You've got to come, like this second." There was no refusing Jennifer. She would have made a hell of a drill sergeant. He eyed the Jolly in dismay. There were at least nine and it was hard to tell what sex they were. "Work yourself in. I'm not even going to try introductions. Most of them nobody'll ever see again anyway and they all know who you are. Come on! Come on! We haven't got all night. Jeezuz. Michel and Germaine will switch calls to the boat." She swiveled her full attention to her father. "What the hell's with you? Staying up here like some kind of a nut?"

Germaine and Michel were in the doorway. Michel held Sri Lanka by the collar. Jennifer finally noticed them.

"So that's the dog," Jennifer said. The young in the Jolly had fallen silent as they stared at the puppy.

"Afghan," Arnold said. Then, unnecessarily to Michel and Germaine, "Be sure the gate is locked. We'll never find him if he gets away."

"Da-ad—" Jennifer was down to her last shred of patience.

Arnold shot a wistful glance at the Villa and yielded. Besides, going with all those young was probably as safe a way as any to make it from the Villa to the *Delphi*.

There was a silent slithering and twisting of young bodies. The Plaything lifted her ass, inviting Arnold to slide under her, then wriggled the practically bare buttocks to a comfortable position for her on him, threw one arm around him so that one breast blinded him. He had a moment of near panic as he tried to move his head so he could see but wound up with a nipple practically in his mouth, realized as he settled in that he had an immediate incipient erection to contend with. The Plaything pretended to be unaware of it. She must have known that simply being young steaming female inert weight was more than enough. Arnold tried mightily to straighten when they shot down the driveway. As they pulled away, he remembered Inspector Bellarosa's two armed cops and made a desperate attempt to get out from under and tell them he'd left. It was important to let Bellarosa know where he'd be. He should have called down.

The two armed cops would never in a million years consider the possibility that the man whose security they were responsible for, a fifty-year-old American, was buried in the squirming mass of teen and post-teen flesh. When he finally surfaced and fought his way for a backward glance, the street below the Villa was no longer visible. Nor was there any car behind them, dashing the faint hope that the cops had caught on and were following. Bellarosa's men had stayed put. They'd probably stay put all night if nobody told them differently.

Arnold sank back and thought dismally that if he bought it here in the Jolly smothered by the Plaything's tits, the cocktail obituaries would be How appropriate a way for Arnold Elton to go.

And Jennifer drove like a nut.

"You know what this holiday really celebrates?" Robbie yelled. The young were caught in a crazy excitement. "The taking of the Bastille by the rabble!" Each time Jennifer passed a car, Robbie leaned way out of the Jolly and shouted, "In the name of the King!" in French, stunning the driver into momentary paralysis. It was hardly a slogan to shout on a day celebrating the French Revolution.

The Boulevard de la République, a three-lane road, was bumper to bumper in two southbound lanes for what must have been at least a kilometer.

Without hesitation Jennifer swung out into the third lane,

which had been left open for northbound and emergency traffic.

"In the name of the King!" Robbie kept yelling like a wild man at traffic-jammed cars that had been basting for long minutes practically immobile in the heavy heat and suffocating car fumes.

In the Jolly there was a shrill tension, for Jennifer was betting that there would not be even one car coming from the opposite direction. If she was wrong, it would mean a head-on collision.

Arnold made wincing sounds and writhed involuntarily each time Jennifer swerved. The Plaything must have interpreted those sounds in her own way, for every now and then she turned and flashed him an enigmatic smile.

As they penetrated deep into the outside lane, the entire traffic jam sensed a car had jumped the lane. But Jennifer coolly out-aggressed them all and they made it to the critical overpass where she would have to try to force a left turn eastward. After that they'd be home free on open highway. A car heading toward them loaded with adults and what must have been six children was forced to slam to a frantic stop. The infuriated driver thrust his head out of the window, screamed a string of epithets in French, "You type of cunt! You cheap sausage! Bitch!"

Jennifer smiled demurely. "Up your asshole." She called it out so sweetly that it took the driver and the dozen spectators a second to realize what she'd said. His rage skyrocketed.

The Plaything, keeping Arnold pinned, his erection firmly in place between her ample thighs, leaned over, her face a few inches from the raging driver's, "Fuck you," she said politely.

"I understand English!" the driver screamed back. The children and the other passengers listened in subdued fascination.

"That's nice." Jennifer leaned way out from the Jolly and

without raising her voice, added in English, "Up your wife's asshole, too."

The other young whooped in appreciation as Jennifer whipped the Jolly in reverse and got a flying start. The opposing driver, incredulous at first, realized his car would be hit by the Jolly, chickened out and swerved, letting her pass.

There was a wild shout of triumph from the Jolly as Jennifer made it to the traffic-free eastbound overpass.

The Plaything bounced up and down in lunatic childlike exultation as Arnold, now fighting a full-fledged erection, tried desperately to hold her down.

The Jolly swung off the highway and into the New Port's private road. The young took this too as a triumph over the rabble, for they yelled in chorus, "Long Live the King!" For the Plaything it was an excuse to lift her buttocks a good two feet up, then come whomping down. At the last split-second Arnold managed to maneuver his rigid penis to a safe haven between her thighs.

In the spirit of the evening, the Port guards waved the Jolly on, Jennifer gunned it to an insane hundred kilometers an hour in what was normally a strictly enforced twenty-kilometers-an-hour zone before she came to a stop on the quay alongside the *Delphi*. The young unscrambled and tumbled out.

"That was quite a ride," the Plaything's breath ran like a mouse over his eyes and cheeks. "Wasn't it, Mr. Elton?"

"Call me Arnold," he said once he was able to get his mouth free of her breast.

"I wouldn't think of it, Mr. Elton." The Plaything did not relax her thigh grip on his penis. "A world-famous writer like you?"

"Break it up you guys, for Chrissake," Jennifer called out.

"We're here." Robbie as always followed Jennifer, picking up her note of irritation.

The Plaything, with the smallest of regretful sighs, lifted her sticky flesh off Arnold and got out.

"You all right?" Jennifer barked as Arnold sat unmoving. For one thing there was his erection, which refused to subside. And for another there was the heavily shadowed quay, the unprotected area between them and the *Delphi*— And of course who knew what was on the *Delphi*? "What's the matter with you, anyway? You going to sit there all night?"

Arnold had to stoop so his erection wouldn't be too apparent, and like a man with a strange handicap, let himself slowly out of the car.

The whole harbor crawled with parties and every yacht was crammed and noisy with music. The music from the *Delphi* was by far the loudest, the lights the dimmest, the deck the most crowded, the chatter the most strident. It was exactly the kind of confused agitation in which a man could slip a knife into another man's gut or fire a gun pointblank and walk away.

But there was Bellarosa's car, hidden in the shadows of the quay and when you looked harder, two other police cars side by side. Three cops, two in uniform with machine guns at the ready, kept the yacht under surveillance. Bellarosa wasn't fooling around. Arnold blew in relief. Any sensible assassin would know he could never get away in one piece.

"They weren't there before," Jennifer said. "You expecting a commando attack from the PLO?"

"Those police cars?" Arnold asked innocently. "Why— didn't you know, we're expecting royalty." Maybe because he was bent over with the still-persistent erection he wasn't too convincing. "The Princess Alexa."

"Princess Alexa?" Jennifer was tasting the words as if they were sour. "You can't mean that old second-rate English star who married a studio and a broken-down prince among others? Cops to protect *her*?"

"She wasn't a second-rate star." Arnold was hoping his erection would wilt. "She was big in her time. . . . You sure can whip a car around," he said admiringly, still not able to straighten. "I never noticed before."

"You've never been in a car driven by me before." He was startled by the charge of hostility which emanated from her. "Nobody else ever takes the wheel when the great Arnold's in the car." Irritably, she went on: "What's the matter with you? You got back trouble or something? For Chrissake stand up straight. You're like an old hunchback."

Arnold's erection wilted. "No," he said clearly. "There's nothing wrong with my back."

He straightened and was now able in the fading light of sunset to get a full view of the *Delphi*'s soft golden flowing lines. Ordinarily, each time he saw the yacht, his heart would do a quick-time step of small ecstasy. There it was—undeniable proof you'd made it. How many people had oceangoing yachts? The *Delphi* drew a magic circle around him, keeping out all fear.

Only now she seemed cold and frightening. Maybe death walked her high polished hardwood decks. The flowers scattered about with such colorful abandon suddenly seemed like wreaths.

2

"Hey, what are we standing here for like a couple of dum-dums?" Jennifer asked irritably. "I'm no more anxious than you to go to this crappy party of yours— Now come on—"

Arnold waited another moment before he slunk on behind Jennifer.

They made it well onto the deck without one head turning. Though perhaps they couldn't have turned even if they'd wanted to. The guests were packed in like subway passengers in a Tokyo rush hour, an animated mass of Pucci, Gucci, and De Blausse, milling against a background of flame gladioli and Baccarat roses.

"*Anybody* could come aboard," Arnold grumbled to Jennifer before the crowd ground them away from each other.

"Like all your parties," Jennifer snapped. "Half the people you invite you met yesterday. The other half are Krystina's hairdressers."

She suddenly dipped off. Scott, a little high on champagne, bobbed up in her place.

"Telly and Bellarosa checked discreetly. So far only two guests can't be accounted for." Scott gestured with his head. "Over there somewhere, you can't see them from here."

"Dennis Hume," Arnold asked tensely, "do you know what he looks like?"

"I've seen photographs. Are you expecting him?"

"I heard he was in this area. It's just possible he may drop in."

"He certainly hasn't appeared yet," said Scott. "A hot item like Hume couldn't have escaped notice even here. If Alexa's coming you'll have two star attractions. Your party'll be made."

"If she does come," Arnold said, "don't forget."

"I know," Scott said with mild doubt. "Down below."

"Before she can bat one of her two-ton eyelids, I'll join you."

Arnold moved away before Scott could protest.

Jennifer was right. In that seething mass of faces, only now and then did one he knew swirl past him.

Wade Vernon and Joyce had found chairs and were sipping champagne. Joyce, slightly high, waved with mock gaiety at Arnold as if to say Texan multimillionaires, once they took their pants off, were exactly like other men. Evidently Joyce had not had all that much experience with multimillionaires. Arnold, over a sea of heads, tried to nod to Vernon, but the latter made no response. It was possible he didn't recognize Arnold in that crowd.

"The music's so goddamn loud!" Arnold shouted when he sighted Krystina.

"Robbie!" Krystina called back. Automatically, the moment Robbie entered a room he whammed on whatever amplifying equipment there was to its full skull-shattering volume. "If I've asked Captain Dougherty once I've asked him a dozen times to keep the sound down. The minute he does, Robbie sneaks back, turns it all the way up.''

Shortly after the Watts episode, Robbie had announced he wanted to learn to play an instrument and Arnold bought him an expensive trumpet. It was the only gift Robbie ever asked for.

Robbie was brought in by the Beverly Hills cops about six o'clock one Sunday morning.

Three Sundays in a row, the cops explained, Robbie got himself up at five in the morning, positioned himself directly under some lavish bedroom and blasted away on his trumpet something which seemed to be ''When the Saints Go Marching In,'' shattering the dominical peace of dozens of the most luxurious Beverly Hills homes.

To get himself up at five in the morning. Robbie, a boy you couldn't get up out of bed with a crowbar.

Robbie couldn't offer much of an explanation.

''I don't know why I did it,'' he said shyly when pressed by the cops. ''Basically, I just felt like it, I guess.''

''But Robbie hasn't been here for the last hour. He came with Jen to pick me up at the Villa.''

''Well, I thought he was here all the time,'' Krystina called out. ''And where's this Princess Alexa of yours?''

Postcoital party hostess Krystina was far different from the soft and clinging wife who had greeted him at the Villa. He was irritated that she did not even sense the fear he carried within him.

''I didn't invite her,'' Arnold shouted. ''Maybe she just thought she'd pop in because she's in the vicinity.'' He decided he ought to try to placate Krystina. ''I heard she's a friend of Grace and Rainier.''

Krystina turned to take a good look at him. ''There's something bothering you,'' she shouted. ''You've got that something-wrong look! What is it?''

"It's only the tension of the deal."

"Is that it?" Krystina called. "Well, I've got everybody hopped up waiting for the Princess. She better get here before the fireworks or she'll never make it with the traffic."

"Krys," Arnold called, "if you should see Dennis Hume, grab him and bring him to me . . ."

Krystina jumped. "I hope you didn't invite *him*? I mean there are people here who wouldn't like to be at the same party with a man with criminal connections."

"What criminal connections?" Arnold said irritably.

"What?" Krystina shouted.

"I said Dennis has no criminal connections," Arnold shouted. "He's a friend in trouble. This goddamn music!"

"Robbie does put the captain in a funny position, after all a captain's supposed to have some authority." Krystina added, "Oh, and I think the captain wants you."

Up above in the glass-enclosed pilot's cabin, Captain Dougherty was trying to catch Arnold's eye, miming there was a phone call for him.

Still breathing hard, Arnold fought his way through a shoulder-high wall of warm flesh. Twice earlier, before the Baron, and when Arnold could still worry about such things (it seemed so long ago), while they were dressing, Krystina had let escape a primal fear she had about their parties, "What if *nobody comes*?"

Well, the party was a runaway hit. Standing Room Only.

Normally Arnold was able to block out all party chatter but as he fought his way to the pilot's cabin, he was unwillingly alert and caught muddled fragments:

Madame de la Porte's voice piercing the hysterical hubbub, "Sweden England Italy France . . . Communist . . . no place left to run to." Two real estate promoters' wives and the Elton gynecologist's wife (had Arnold really fucked them all or had he just told everybody he had?) something about, "the English pound . . . very favorable . . . no real chic in En-

410

gland . . . one can pay the cost of the voyage with cashmere.''

In the pilot's cabin Arnold paused. He was wheezing hard.

"It's from overseas," Captain Dougherty said. As Arnold leaned over the captain's desk to take the phone, he caught a glimpse of the important papers the captain had been working on. You would have thought meteorological charts, plotted courses, but no it was next week's menu for the *Delphi* and an accompanying shopping list. Arnold managed to catch "twenty kilos of tomatoes" and wondered resentfully if it was possible that they'd eat over forty pounds of tomatoes in the next few days. In Arnold's order of things, a captain should be above pocketing a percentage of the food money.

The call was from Reilly and his voice was a mixture of excitement and smartass but, to be fair, there was also a tinge of fear. "Your information is sound, Ar." Arnold groped around for a chair. His breath whistled in his chest. Dougherty immediately slid a canvas chair under him, saw enough on Arnold's face to make him leave.

"It's for real, all right," Reilly's voice came over the phone cautiously. "It was almost like Mike was waiting for my call. He got the data so fast you wouldn't believe. That's some organization they got there, Ar. Well. Somebody's got a whatchamacallit out on you, all right. Yeah."

"Oh," Arnold wheezed. "Well. That means they know who took it out and why."

"Yeah," Reilly said, "they know."

"Who is it?"

There was a lot of transatlantic static before Reilly answered. "It's not going to work like that, Ar. They're going to want a fee for releasing the data, you know what I mean, Ar?"

"Okay," Arnold said. "How much of a fee?"

"We're negotiating. All Mike would say so far is that you know who you're dealing with. We've got to brace ourselves for big."

"How big?"

"He wouldn't say, Ar. But I figure he's on our side, Mike, that is. See it just happened Clover dropped in while he was here."

"Clover?" Arnold's voice got shrill. "What was *she* doing at your place?"

Arnel personnel were not supposed to fuck around with Arnold's ex-girl friends. Once Arnold was through with them they were outsville. *Verboten*. Do not touch. Reilly had breached Arnel sexual protocol.

"Clover's been dropping in on me from time to time," Reilly said. "You know it was me who brought her to you. Just drops in and jabbers. Not that I encourage it but a good thing she came. Michael took one look and fell like a ton of bricks. You know Michael's wife was killed in an accident when Mike was driving, never been able to make it with a chick since then. I've got this feeling he'll make it with her, and if he does Michael would be disposed in our favor."

"How do I know they're not using the fact I sent you to him to rip me off? How do I know it's not a setup?"

"It's no setup, Ar. And they're going to tell us who it is. If we know that, we'll know why."

"Listen, for Chrissakes, didn't he give you any idea how big is big?"

"Well, like I said, he didn't give me a number, Ar. But I had the feeling it's going to be around at least a One."

"One?" Arnold wheezed. " 'One' what?"

"A Big One," Reilly said. "Now that's just my idea, I wouldn't want to be quoted but Mike mentioned a similar situation that was quoted at One. I'll get precise information soon. But, Ar, we got to be set for at least that. But I'm just guessing."

"One," Arnold choked. He had a vision of Oscar mumbling to him, "One million dollars that we can't deduct? Arnold. Do you have any idea how much tax-free capital we have to generate to meet that sum?" And Oscar would

412

shudder like he was having a self-induced orgasm, and say, "I hate even to think of it."

"But I've got an idea, Ar. What's the security like your end for you, Krystina and the kids? Can you get yourself protected for, let's say, twenty-four hours? Follow my thinking, Ar, if we can stall on the payment for twenty-four hours, I've got a stinking hunch, now it may turn out full of shit."

"Reilly. You know something, you better goddamn well tell me now."

"Take something for your asthma, Ar," Reilly said gently. "If my hunch turns out right, follow my thinking, Ar, we then drop it on them. Oh, let's not kid ourselves, we'd still have to pay off but for information that won't be hot we'd get away with a more reasonable number. I'll run my ass off, Ar, I might not even need twenty-four hours, but you've got to decide your end, question of security, twenty-four hours."

Robbie slipped in, walked over to the hi-fi system and, right there in front of Arnold, turned the volume all the way up, but slowly, so that the guests on deck wouldn't jump out of their assholes.

"Turn that fucking thing down!" Arnold, who'd never in his life raised his voice to the boy, shouted. Robbie grinned an accomplice grin, mouthed some words that Arnold couldn't hear, made a shy gesture, and with the hi-fi left on at full boom, slipped out. Arnold dropped the receiver, rushed to the amplifier, turned it down gradually. Through the glass he could see Robbie on deck with the Plaything and other young. Arnold gestured furiously. Robbie leaned forward, held his hand playfully to his ear, questioningly, as if he couldn't imagine why Arnold was angry. The Plaything and the others observed it all with great interest. Arnold whipped back to the phone.

Reilly was jabbering away, he hadn't even been aware that Arnold had left the phone. "So it's your decision, Ar. Twenty-four hours, I think I can find who's behind this."

"If you know, tell me."

"I can't," Reilly said.

"Why can't you?"

"Because you'd think I was fulla shit."

"Take a chance."

"No, Ar. You've got to trust me. If it is who I think it is, you're in no danger. Not for twenty-four hours, anyway."

"Exactly what in the hell are you asking me to do, goddamn it?"

"They want to be paid like right now," Reilly said, agitated, "right away."

"How the hell would they expect anybody to raise that kind of bread right now?"

"They'll trust you," Reilly said. "All they'd want is a commitment to pay." (Yes, of course. And if I didn't pay, the hit would be arranged to take place right away. Or probably on Krystina first. Or maybe the kids. No. They didn't worry about a guy like me not coughing up.) "What I want is your permission to ask for a twenty-four-hour delay."

Arnold looked around for help, saw Dougherty looking Australian and solemn; on the swarming deck Krystina bustling, a feverishly solicitous hostess; caught a glimpse of the kids; saw that Armand Harris, looking black and grim, had just come aboard.

"Okay, Reilly, stall them for twenty-four hours." He hung up, turned to the captain. "Captain, could we put out for a cruise right after the party tonight?" Arnold asked. Dougherty looked very captainy and dubious. "Only for twenty-four hours, anywhere on the high seas?"

"Not before noon tomorrow, Mr. Elton," the captain replied. "The pumps closed down early today because of the holiday and we didn't fuel up."

Arnold exploded internally, the stupid kangaroo sonofabitch, I pay for a fucking yacht and crew to stand by and he didn't fuel up? What if there was some emergency and we had to

414

take off in a hurry? What if, Hell, this *was* an emergency.

"We could fuel up in Italy," Arnold said.

"I'm afraid we can't make it to Italy, sir," Captain Dougherty said solemnly. "Not on what we have."

"Very good, Captain," Arnold had to say something. Dougherty was eyeing him doubtfully. "Just try to keep the volume of the music down."

"I'll do what I can, Mr. Elton," Captain Dougherty wouldn't even promise anything there. Arnold stifled a groan. Killers around and a captain who didn't even have enough authority over the kids to keep the sound down.

"All in all, a really super party," Krystina had picked up a few speech mannerisms from Telly. But she was worried. You couldn't hide much from her. "Anything bad? Your call?"

"No, nothing," Arnold said dismally. It began to seep through. He was going to have to pay the boys a huge number of dollars. For nothing. Rage rattled his spine.

"There is something. I can always tell."

"Sure," Arnold was able to say. "Jet lag. Fucking. That takes something out of a man. Not that a man doesn't enjoy having it taken out of him."

At least that quieted Krystina.

He could now distinguish other knots of guests.

Armand Harris listening with that frightening intensity of his to Dr. Jean-Louis, their prudent gynecologist. Alfredo and Gina also very attentive, everybody was attentive when a doctor talked. At Harris's side very close, Sarita, who had once dismissed Harris as a wall-eyed low-crotch asshole.

Each time one of the white-coated waiters supplied by Ernest's Catering Service (the ones who overloaded and overcharged like bastards) came within grabbing distance carrying the standard tray of twenty hors d'oeuvres, only four of which were smoked salmon, only three real caviar, the rest bits of ham, sliced egg, anchovy, sausage or paté, Harris held the waiter in place with one hand, speared the caviar

415

with the other, made a hypocritical show of offering the caviar tidbit around, then gobbled it quickly. Sarita, unbelievably, there was no doubt now she was *with* Harris, took the second caviar, as Harris snagged the third and last. After that he gobbled a couple of smoked salmon. The sonofabitch had taken all the goodies.

Sarita whispered, her lips practically in Harris's ear. Armand turned and glanced in Arnold's direction. Even in that half-shadowed part of the deck and despite all the clamorous distractions, Harris's hatred made it in one piece, glittering, naked, open. The de la Portes, who had joined the cluster, saw Arnold and loosed a laser death smile of their own. The place was jumping with people who would pop open a bottle of champagne, at least, if Arnold were to kick off.

Armand, with the electronic directness of one of those smart bombs, no weaving in and out for him, crashed through, pushing people out of his way. He yanked Arnold away and over to a comparatively quiet spot, backed him against the railing so that Arnold had the Mediterranean behind him, Harris facing him.

"You shafted me good," Harris spoke with the exaltation of the utterly desperate. "You knew all along there was this shit clause in the contract, you just sat back and let me go ahead."

At last someone Arnold could vent it all on. "You're the guy wanted to be a hero with the Studio, you went to them with the brilliant idea you could make a second picture from my book without paying an additional buck—And aren't you the guy told me way back when, 'Read the contract, you'd be surprised how many of those Front Office hotshot pricks don't read the contract'? Didn't you read the contract, Armand?"

"It was a *writer's* contract, who reads past the money clause in a writer's contract? How was I to know you had this shitass clause in it about how any second picture made from your fucking book has to be paid for exactly like for the first

416

picture?'' The very idea sent Armand Harris almost beside himself. "Show me the writer ever had a condition like that, one million dollars plus ten percent of the gross for a second picture, I'll kiss his ass.''

"This writer. Kiss my ass.''

"Listen to me,'' Harris was practically croaking. "You let me get in up to my neck. I've signed director, stars, pay or play. I've got a crew and cast eating their fucking heads off right here on the Riviera, I've committed myself to studio space at Victorine Studios in Nice.''

"Pay or play,'' Arnold said approvingly. "You can't walk away even if you want to.'' A waiter came by and out of force of habit, Harris grabbed him, gobbled all three caviar canapés. Arnold's anger spiraled. "I don't think you read the whole contract yet, baby. There's a clause gives me script approval. When and if you get this one off the ground, show it to me first, baby. Because you can't make the picture unless I like your screenplay.''

"You've got to be kidding,'' Harris choked. He *still* hadn't read the rest of the contract.

"One million bucks plus ten percent of the gross and you think I'm kidding?''

"There's more riding for me on this than the picture,'' Harris said. "Nobody's going to stop me.'' That was said nicely, quietly, the way a man who had faced up to the possibility of extreme measures would talk. "Now how about it? Let's fuck-off this party of yours, that music's blown my fuses, I've got something to say to you.'' From what he saw on Arnold's face, he added quickly, "Something you can't afford not to listen to, Elton.''

"*All* my life I've been waiting for exactly the right occasion to say this,'' Arnold said, "and now at last I've found it. Armand Harris—consider this formal notification. I, Arnold Elton, tell you to go fuck yourself.''

He heaved a huge sigh of pleasure. He *had* been waiting all his life and now that he'd said it, he was beginning to wonder if the small satisfaction it brought him was worth the total hatred that burned in Harris's eyes.

But still there were few pleasures that could get through to a man who might be knocked off any minute, and this had been one of them.

There was a subtle commotion on the quay-side of the *Delphi*, then almost the entire party surged in that direction. Excitement rippled out. Arnold abandoned Harris and fought his way through the pushing crowd.

What they were all looking at was Princess Alexa. She had just gotten out of a creamy Rolls-Royce. Two well-dressed attractive young men, subtly exuding that aroma of professional suspicion that marks the bodyguard, preceded her toward the yacht. Heads swiveled as at a tennis match following her as she undulated up the gangplank. Slim and sensuous in a sarilike dress with a spangled wisp of silk framing her face, she looked twenty years younger than her biological age. There was a communal sigh of appreciation as she stepped aboard. And if Arnold had cherished some small hope that her presence there could be made to seem purely a casual social event, Alexa squelched it immediately by heading with unwavering instinct straight for him, the crowd making way for her.

"Ah, there you are," Alexa said with a trace of annoyance as though he should have been somewhere they had agreed upon before. "I trust you will not mind dispensing some champagne to my two charming escorts." She turned to the two bodyguards. "I think we can consider ourselves fairly safe under Mr. Elton's protection." The two men first cased the joint carefully, then drifted off. Alexa moved close enough to Arnold so bystanders could not easily overhear. "I shall go below in a very few minutes. You will join me, in a cabin. You and I have matters to discuss," this last with a touch of grimness that immediately gave way to a big smile of delight. "But isn't that Scott Goldman?" She turned to Scott, offered him both hands, which he took as she examined him. "What are *you* doing here? Is there a war on I don't know about?" She turned to Arnold and the others, Krystina had just bubbled her way over. "Scott is the only valid male in active service with whom I've had a protracted nonsexual friendship."

"I don't know how to take that," Scott said as Alexa offered him the plastic smoothness of surgically unwrinkled cheeks and he kissed her chastely but with appropriate pleasure. "Alexa claims she never sees me anywhere where there isn't or won't soon be violence."

"How sweet," Alexa said, "he's given me an opening to use a bon mot that I invented. I call Scott 'the bar-fly of chaos.'" She looked around. "Or is that sort of bon mot wasted here?"

"Not wasted," Scott said, "but not very useful in describing me. I'm neither a drinking man nor a chronicler of violence."

Krystina kept nudging Arnold: her face was almost obliterated by an adoring smile as shiny-eyed she gazed expectantly at Arnold and their glittering guest.

"Princess Alexa," Arnold positioned Krystina more favorably, wondering all the while how the hell he was going to get Alexa off the deck as quickly as possible, "May I present my wife?"

"So you are Mrs. Elton?" Alexa said, as if it were an answer to some puzzling question. Krystina nodded and looked as though she might curtsy. "Well. Yes. How do you do." The Princess did not offer her hand to Krystina, instead took Scott's arm. "We must talk old times and new times. Do forgive us."

"Of course, Your Highness," Krystina said. At that, Arnold

had to suppress an impulse to kick Krystina in the ass.

The music came up thunderously as Alexa swept off with Scott.

"Imagine," Krystina shouted as Arnold was trying to think what to do, "she came with two bodyguards. We've never had a guest important enough to have two bodyguards."

She was interrupted by Bellarosa, who seemed pissed off and worried. "Do you have some connection with this Princess Alexa? And you seem apprehensive about something on the quay." Krystina glanced at Arnold with a frown.

"Oh, no," Arnold said with elaborate off-handedness. He turned to Krystina. "Why don't you do something about the goddamn music?"

Krystina, still excited by Alexa's presence, nodded nervously and took off.

"You can stop looking toward the quay," Bellarosa said. "My instinct tells me if there's danger, it's here—on board the *Delphi*."

"You know something?" Arnold asked eagerly.

"No, nothing more than when we first talked," Bellarosa said coldly. "Only I must tell you officially I can no longer be responsible for your safety. You left the Villa without notifying me."

"I couldn't help it," Arnold said grimly. "I *had* to be here."

"Will you and Madame be returning to the Villa or will you sleep here?"

"We'll go back up."

"Make sure you keep me informed," Bellarosa said curtly. "I'm not sure how long I can keep these men immobilized here. It is, after all, the Fourteenth of July."

"I'll keep you informed," Arnold vowed.

"There are two Americans among your guests who appear to be totally uninvited. At least Mademoiselle Telafora informed me they were not on the guest list. No one seems to know who they are. When you can, without making it too obvious, glance behind me and tell me if you know anything about them." Bellarosa turned slowly and indicated two men with a small movement of his chin.

Arnold looked but couldn't see them clearly. One seemed to be in his fifties, the other much younger; nor did they appear to be particularly together.

"I don't know who they are." Arnold strained for a second look. At that moment the younger man turned. Arnold caught a brief glimpse of his face. "Wait. One of them looks vaguely familiar."

"I'll speak to those two," Bellarosa said severely. He hadn't forgiven Arnold for taking the protection he was offered so lightly.

Krystina hurried to Arnold. "Oscar wants you for something urgent."

Arnold headed in the general direction Krystina indicated. It brought him directly behind Wade Vernon and Joyce. It was strange when you thought about it, how these big-time executives, from whom you couldn't get a confidential word normally (their attitude was even small talk could be used against them in some eventual deal), talked their goddamn heads off to their girl friends.

"What the public doesn't understand," Wade was telling Joyce, his voice had marvelous carrying quality, its distinctive nasal twang triumphed over the music, "is that the government has kept the price of gasoline actually at its 1952 level. For the oil companies, that is. Now think about that, you're actually paying today the same price per gallon for gasoline that you paid in 1952 in real money value."

Joyce had seen Arnold, flashed him a knowing smile of complicity.

Wade saw the smile but missed the nuance.

"Lovely party, Elton," he called heartily. Arnold managed to squeeze out something close to a smile, when Oscar suddenly oozed into view.

Oscar was so full of liquid it seemed to cause his body to sway, his horizon shifting as on a heaving deck.

"The English writer," Oscar tilted. "Scott Shmott—"

"American," Arnold shouted, vaguely annoyed.

"Whatever. And the beautiful bimbo."

"That's Alexa," Arnold boomed, his lips two inches from Oscar's ear. Normal people would have had ruptured eardrums.

"Princess schmincess. Whatever. Downstairs. In a cabin together. I don't think it's for anything sexual. But the bimbo, I judge we must be watchful of her in the current situation." Arnold had to lean so close he could smell the sour whiskey vapors billowing out from Oscar. "I am referring to the take-over. Hundreds of millions of dollars involved. Dollars. American. Millions and millions." Oscar was both euphoric and dire.

"Any special reason we should be watchful? Oscar! Goddamnit—"

"No, thank you." A judicious palm raised in refusal. "Not a drop more. My quota."

Oscar tilted dangerously.

In the corridor below deck it was a mere flicker of the eyelid and Arnold was yanked into a cabin by Alexa, who shut the door quickly behind her. Scott was already there.

"I've been trying to persuade Scott to do a piece about a Hollywood-style take-over," Alexa chilled Arnold's blood by announcing gaily. "I think I could persuade the chairman of the about-to-be-outgoing, if I'm not mistaken, board of a major-minor studio to bribe Scott with a solid advance if Scott would do an exposé of the I believe you Americans call it hanky-panky now going on, the nasty little maneuvers that I suspect involve the district Attorney's high office, the

422

ruining of a man's reputation, and of course, inevitable in all latter-day American business deals of any magnitude, considerable payoffs, some of it in transfers to numbered accounts in Switzerland."

Arnold stared at her unblinkingly. The only payoffs he knew about were to the Princess herself, which made no apparent sense and it was well known that most of what the Princess did, when the smoke cleared away, made very good sense for her.

"I've always admired your capacity for not listening," Scott said to Alexa, "I've just told you that I'm not interested in scandal, especially involving high finance. I consider most of high finance a rip-off from the start."

"Scotty is not really for or of this world, are you?" Alexa said sweetly. Scott shrugged apologetically. Alexa's manner didn't really change but Arnold had a sudden image of her with a long bare cold steel blade in her hands. "Is this stateroom bugged? I've heard you record your guests' sexual grunts for kicks, as it were."

Arnold was baffled. Why was she doing this? She herself stood to be one of the major losers. No one had ever mentioned anything self-destructive about the Princess before.

"Believe only ninety-five percent of the shit they spread about me, Princess," Arnold said.

"One never knows with you Americans. You seem to have a compulsion to put everything on tape, as witness the utterly baffling behavior of Mr. Nixon. One of the reasons I agreed to turn over my proxies to you," Alexa said in one of her characteristic sudden shifts, "especially in view of the board's reluctance to take a stand on the embarrassing rumors about Hume, was the speed with which you acted on the occasion of our first meeting."

"And I was impressed by the speed with which you made up your mind," Arnold said. It was still vital to get her the hell off the *Delphi* as quickly as possible. "I hear the stock is now below the level I told you it would fall to. In forty-eight hours if we hang in there . . . we'll all be a shitpot richer."

"Your breathing apparatus seems badly in need of attention," Alexa said dryly. Arnold was whistling like a kettle at full boil. "So does your transfer apparatus. The money you promised me would be available in Zurich never made its promised appearance."

Arnold gasped in shock. "Are you sure?" Death, taxes, and transfers to numbered Swiss bank accounts were the few verities of modern life you could absolutely count on. "That's impossible. It was made the same day the moment I left you. It should have been there the next day; and the next day only because they're six hours later than New York." Any slip-up must have came at the American end—at the Arnel source. "There must have been some crazy unheard-of misunderstanding."

"In matters of this kind misunderstandings are unthinkable," Alexa said primly.

She was right. There must never be slip-ups. Any slip-up could only have been caused by Reilly or Oscar.

"And furthermore, Mr. Elton, if you thought you could work the proxies out of me without making the transfer to me, you sir, are an utter asshole."

"And that's why you didn't give Reilly the proxies?" Arnold asked. "I just want to get it clear."

"Isn't that reason enough?" Alexa demanded tartly. "I'm a woman of my word, but you shan't have proxies until I have ironclad confirmation that the money is there."

Arnold groaned, controlled himself. "I need those proxies tonight, Princess Alexa."

"Oh, you could have them tonight." She held up a little jeweled handbag. See how providential I am?"

"I don't know what happened," Arnold promised fervently, "but I'll straighten it out first thing in the morning..."

"Then you'll have the proxies first thing in the morning."

"I need them tonight."

"Then you have a problem."

"We both have a problem," Arnold said. "I've planned a certain key operation that will bring Associated stock up..."

"Then what you counted on isn't, is it?" Arnold suddenly realized that she was raging with anger. "You thought you could frighten me with the threat of my stock going down in value and that I'd fork over the proxies. Well. Rather than get taken that way, I'm prepared to make a real scandal. I'm afraid, Mr. Elton, I rather have you by the balls." She made a malicious snipping gesture. "And I shall not hesitate to snip them off."

"If you do, you'll be cutting your own throat..."

"What an absolutely first-rate mixed metaphor," Alexa cried in apparent delight, turning to Scott for approval. Scott nodded quickly that he understood and there was no reason for her to belabor the point.

The phone rang. Arnold pounced on the first ring. It was Krystina at the other end.

"Your friend, that awful Dennis Hume," Krystina said indignantly, "has just driven up and he's on the quay now. My God, Arnold, you didn't invite that horrible man here. I mean we can't have him here. Did you invite him?"

"I'll be right up," Arnold cut her off and hung up quickly. Alexa had been trying to eavesdrop in her subtle and elegant way. Arnold turned to her. "I'll tell you what, Princess Alexa," Arnold said carefully. "I'll be back in seven or eight minutes at the outside. Just don't move from here, because I'm coming back with title of ownership to the *Delphi*." Alexa now looked interested. "Meantime, you draw up two memos, one from me to you stipulating that if the transfer of

425

two hundred and fifty thousand dollars to you is not confirmed to your satisfaction by noon tomorrow, this yacht is yours . . ."

"How nice!" Alexa exclaimed in delight. "I find the idea of an ocean-going yacht enticing . . ."

"You'll prepare a second document giving me the proxies," Arnold said.

"Oh, I already have that," Alexa said gaily. "You are serious about the yacht?"

"You'll find pen and paper in that desk," Arnold said grimly. "Scott will witness it."

"Oh, lovely lovely lovely," Alexa clapped her hands and then again made a playful snipping motion with two fingers, toward his middle this time.

"I don't mind in the least having my balls held by you, Princess," Arnold said on his way out.

"*Chacun à son goût,*" Alexa said sweetly as Arnold hurried off.

Krystina was waiting for him on deck, her manner conspiratorial. Apparently someone had managed to convince Robbie that his music could be listened to at one-third the volume he had inflicted on the gathering. The guests, suddenly released from the oppression of the sound, were speaking to each other with the animation of people who hadn't seen each other for years.

With Krystina at his side, Arnold wove his way across the deck, eluding Dr. Jean-Louis, the de la Portes, Gina, who was tipsy and who aimed a kiss at him but scored a near miss on his chin, smearing lipstick all over. Armand, however, grabbed Arnold by the arm and held him physically.

"I'll get back to you in exactly four minutes," Arnold broke out of his grip and it was as though the go-fuck-yourself had never happened. "I don't want to leave it as it was—"

Arnold scooted toward the gangplank, reached Krystina in

426

time to hear her utter a cry of pure delight. Hume, looking drawn and tearful, had met Krystina halfway up. His emotion was so great he hugged her fervently.

"What a wonderful surprise!" Krystina squealed in delight. "Dennis is here! Look, Arnold—Lovely Dennis."

They were near enough the bottom of the gangplank so that Arnold could encourage them back down to the quay.

Dennis stopped flat-footed and gazed at Arnold with eyes dangerously close to moist.

"I don't know whether you know what a wonderful guy you're married to," Dennis said huskily to Krystina. "He's . . ." For a brief moment Dennis's voice was too cluttered with phlegm and emotion to speak. "He's just a . . . beautiful human being."

Arnold tried to make a modest disclaimer, but Dennis gathered him in his arms and hugged him hard. Arnold looked around furtively. So far only Robbie and the Plaything were peering over the ship's railing.

"It wasn't anything," Arnold said. "You would have done the same for me."

"It wasn't anything?" Dennis asked with deeply felt indignation. "In that shit—excuse me, Krystina—town that is Hollywood, where no hand is without a knife." He paused to check his emotions, "After what they did to me. Arnold. Believe me. I'll never forget how you came out of the blue—What you've done for me—What you're doing—"

"We heard," Krystina murmured with deep sympathy.

"You can't imagine how it hurt me," Dennis said to Krystina. "Do you know what happened? Some dirty sonofabitch leaked terrible rumors about me, that's all they needed. I'm no fool. I know it's got to be some sort of stock manipulation—but to use a human being that way, to play with a career, a life . . ." He broke down.

"It's over," Arnold said paternally as he put his arm on Dennis's shoulder. "Forget it, put it behind you."

"Never," Dennis vowed, "and I want to tell you, Arnold. All the lousy, rotten things they said about you," Dennis's voice was dangerously wavering between a sob and outright incoherence as he enumerated, "that you are a heartless shit, a selfish bastard, a shark of the worst kind, a killer," Arnold tried to stop him but Dennis would not be stopped, "an arrogant, conceited bastard; anything bad mouths can spit out." Here Dennis literally hung his head: this, Arnold was thinking, is a man who caused Associated stock to rise twelve points and who made four blockbusters in a row. "And I believed them, Arnold. I have to tell you, yes, I did. Can you forgive me? I mean after that leak, that goddamn Associated board of directors, as vindictive a bunch of puritanical bastards as ever lived, were ready to destroy me, playing right into the hands of whoever is pulling this." Dennis shivered. "I've been through hell. Arnold, your man Wacszinski is a veritable prince, a prince among men the way he took care of me in the worst moment, the worst of a hard life ... And so are you, Arnold, so are you, it makes a man want to live again ..."

"Past is past," Arnold said, frantic to get them both out of sight. "Listen, Krys, why don't you get yourself back on deck?" Krystina hesitated. He turned to Dennis and lowered his tone. "Listen. There are some shits on board, you know we figured you should keep a low profile for a while, it's just as well they don't see you, Dennis, like Armand Harris, for example."

Dennis groaned. "Armand Harris! I thought he was my friend."

"Never in a million years," Arnold said softly. "You should have heard him sound off about you."

"Oh, God," Dennis said with exquisite bitterness, "you never know, but boy, one day I'll get them, the bastards who leaked those rumors about me, I'll get them. And, Arnold, how can I ever repay you?"

"Let's just worry about that later." Arnold said hurriedly to Krystina, who seemed glued fast to that small area she was standing on, "now come on, Krys, get your lovely little ass back up on deck. You're supposed to be the hostess. Now get in there and start hostessing before we have a crowd at the railing." Armand Harris and Sarita had joined the others at the railing. "We don't want Dennis the center of any attention right now. He took a hell of a chance just coming here."

"I know your guy Wacszinski wanted me to lay low," Dennis said, "but I just had to come. I was thinking about it and it occurred to me, why the hell should I lay low? Let the bastards see me."

Arnold was drenched. Any second Princess Alexa might saunter to the railing and call cheerily, "Oh, there you are."

"Come on now, lay off with the gratitude," Arnold said with good-natured gruffness. He was simultaneously trying to utz Dennis toward the limousine.

"Oh, Arnold is like that," Krystina confided, "he does things for people and hates it when they try to thank him."

"For Chrissake, Krys," Arnold said.

"I'm going, I'm going," Krystina planted a soothing sympathetic kiss on Dennis's forehead and fled.

By now Arnold had managed to edge Dennis into the safe shadows near the limousine. The driver, who knew Arnold well, saluted with military precision.

"Now if I were you," Arnold said paternally, unsticking his sweat-stained shirt from his steaming armpits, "I'd just get myself back to the Colombe d'Or. You comfortable there? Everything all right? Great, and I'd play a little Scrabble with Yves Montand and Simone. Avoid the paparazzi, but I don't think they'll bother you, the Colombe d'Or people are experienced in handling situations like that."

"I don't feel like being with strangers," Dennis said uneasily. "I'm all keyed up. Listen, Arnold, your party looks kind of interesting. I seemed to notice some elegant-looking dames. I need something to keep my mind off my troubles—''

"My party? Don't believe it." Arnold half shoved him into the limousine. "They're a pain in the ass and lousy lays besides. I know. I fucked over sixty percent of them. Believe me, this party's to please Krystina. . . ."

"You can be frank with me, Arnold," Dennis said nervously, "if you'd rather not be seen with me."

"What are you talking about? Not be seen with you? Never in a million years—"

"I don't feel like going to the Colombe d'Or just yet. Nothing but Frenchmen up there, mostly film people, I need something. A little company—"

Dennis started to step out of the limousine. Arnold pushed him back quickly, got in after him.

"Okay," Dennis said. "There are people in your party maybe shouldn't see me, but listen. I know Harold Robbins has a yacht around here and I think Irwin Shaw has one nearby. And there's always Sam Spiegel's. Maybe I could crash in on them."

"No, don't do that. They're bound to have Hollywood people there. I've got a better idea. You need to loosen up?"

"Yeah, I'm all wound up tight."

"You know what?" Arnold said quickly. "Here," he pulled out a bundle of five-hundred-franc notes. "Have yourself a ball. The Casino is two seconds from here, roulette, chemin de fer."

"The Casino?" Dennis was stunned. "You know I shouldn't go near the wheel. You know it's killing me but I'm breaking myself of the habit. That's the last place I should go." He pushed the money away.

Arnold gently pushed it back. "You're not really cured until you can handle it in moderation, Dennis baby. Take the loot, Dennis, you *are* all keyed up, have yourself a ball, take

430

your mind off the troubles. So you lose a few francs—it's on me. What's the difference?''

"Arnold, please don't encourage me," Dennis was trembling. "It's like poison for me. I'm trying to get it out of my blood. An hour or two at your party—"

"Go ahead, go ahead have yourself a time," Arnold insisted. "What is this shit? What harm will a few turns at the wheel do?"

"Arnold, please, I know myself."

"I have faith in you," Arnold said. "It'll be good for you. You'll see, a little action'll fix you up—go on. Enjoy."

From the yacht's deck Arnold had the distinct impression of Alexa's pitched melodic voice . . .

"Maybe you're right," Dennis said uncertainly, then looked full into Arnold's eyes. "Arnold, what can I say," Dennis was trembling with gratitude as he took the money, "more than from the bottom of my heart, thank you. Thanks, Arnold." Dennis leaned back. "You've given me confidence. I appreciate your trust in me."

"Just mention to the guy at the door there that you're a friend of mine. Play a little, then get yourself back to the Colombe d'Or, stay put, you'll hear from me."

"God love you," Dennis murmured.

And finally the limousine took off.

Arnold hurried up the gangplank. He was met by Sarita, who was dragging Armand toward him.

"Hey, Arnold," Sarita called imperatively.

"Get this broad off my back," Armand growled as Arnold approached. "She's been bugging me about a part in the picture. I've been trying to tell her there may not be any picture at all—who was that you were talking to out there? He looked familiar."

Fortunately, Armand was practically blind.

"Hey now, Arnold," Sarita wheedled, "like tell your

431

friend here, hey there's a juicy part for me in the picture, you kind of promised it to me when you were writing the book, hey."

"You mean the belly dancer?" Arnold asked. "I remember. I did." To Armand, "That's the one who goes down on that whole orchestra right before she does her dance?"

"I'm trying to explain to her," Armand said, "we're not doing *Deep Throat*. None of our writers could figure ways of getting that scene into the script."

"Why not do the scene as written in the book?" Arnold put his arm around Sarita and gently turned her around. "I'll arrange a test for you tomorrow. You'll suck Mr. Harris's dong, and if you pass that test I'll put in a good word." He gave her a not-too-gentle push. Sarita stumbled and glared at him. "Get lost," he said quietly. "I have to talk to this man."

For a moment she seemed to be considering kicking Arnold in the balls, Sarita's standard reaction to being pushed around, then slouched off.

"I've been thinking, what the hell, Armand, you and I we go back to the year one. Right?"

Arnold tried putting his arm around Armand who was having none of that.

"Now what are you setting me up for?" Armand demanded. "Say, wasn't that Dennis Hume I saw you talking to just now? What are you two cooking up?"

"Dennis Hume? Who? Where? You must be seeing things. You had your eyes checked lately, Armand? Look. I want to make it possible for you to shoot this film, right?"

"How do I know, right?" Armand, whose natural look was chronic suspicion, hunched himself over like a boxer expecting a severe body blow.

"I'll make a quick deal with you," Arnold said calmly. "I'll make you a proposition you answer with one word, yes, no, go fuck yourself. Okay?"

432

"What's your proposition?"

"You've got a heavy numbered account in Switzerland," Arnold said, as Armand visibly braced himself. "All I want you to do is transfer two hundred and fifty thousand dollars American by tomorrow noon to a numbered account, I'll give you the number..." There was such visible relief mingled with doubt on Armand's face that Arnold changed the terms he'd been prepared to offer, "and I'll let you begin the film."

"Two hundred and fifty thousand in Switzerland? You'll settle for that?"

"Well, no," said Arnold quickly. "You'll pay the other seven-fifty off over the years. Like three years. Two-fifty a year for three years."

"It'll come out of my blood," Armand howled. "I won't even be able to charge it to the film."

"Fuck it," Arnold forced his unwilling limbs to start carrying him off. Armand didn't stop him. Arnold turned. "Tell 'em at the studio you didn't read the contract. Tell 'em you were a schmuck like the others."

"Make that over a period of six years," Armand croaked. "And it's a deal."

"Okay," Arnold breathed again. "Six years. And you pay only twelve percent interest per annum on the unpaid balance..."

"How much?" Armand howled...

"Only fifteen," Arnold said.

"You just said twelve," Armand half strangled.

"Only sixteen, just to teach you not to fuck around with friends."

"Twelve," Armand forced himself to say, "you'll have yourself tax-free dollars in Switzerland." Then added quickly, "You'll forget about the percentage, huh, Arnold?"

Arnold thought he saw the Princess Alexa.

"Yeah," he said quickly, "forget the percentage. What the hell, we're friends. You've got ten seconds of my generosity

433

left. And I'll want confirmation by eleven o'clock tomorrow. I'll have my people in Zurich check and call me. Take it or leave it."

"What's the number?" Armand said.

"Account number 4594. Credit Swiss, Zurich," Arnold said, and half ran off up to the pilot's cabin, where Dougherty was laboriously making out the week after next's menus.

"In the ship's safe," Arnold said quickly, "is the title of ownership of the *Delphi,* also articles of registration. Bring them to me right away. I'm in a hurry, Captain."

"Aye, aye, sir," Dougherty's face was strained as he hurried off to the ship's safe.

Bellarosa sidled in. "Those two suspicious Americans," he said coldly, "are very suspicious. Your presence will be helpful."

"No scandal," Arnold cautioned.

"Your sudden assassination on the decks of this yacht," Bellarosa said dryly, "would make more of a scandal than anything I could stir up," and hurried out.

Dougherty, holding a large manila envelope and several smaller ones, came rushing back in.

"It's all there," Dougherty said gravely, "everything pertaining to the *Delphi.* Mr. Wacszinski's been calling for you from Beverly Hills. He'd like you to telephone him at the office in all urgency."

Well, at least Don was alive and kicking.

Arnold skipped out down to the deck, past the milling guests. Oscar was still slumped in the canvas-backed chair. Arnold passed him, then turned back, touched him. No. Oscar was warm and breathing. Arnold was getting jumpy.

In the stateroom below, Alexa was seated as if lost in meditation. She *was* in fact lost in meditation. Emerging took her thirty seconds.

"Thank heavens for TM," Alexa said. "I was ready to walk out on you. You also say thank heaven for TM."

"I thank heaven for TM," Arnold said and handed her the manila envelope. She opened it fastidiously, like a cat toying with a freshly killed bird, studied the contents carefully for a few moments, then handed him an envelope and a note that she had written on *Delphi* stationery.

Arnold read the note carefully. It was simply written. It attested to the fact that Arnold Elton had clear title to the yacht *Delphi*, and that unless two hundred and fifty thousand dollars was deposited to account number 4594 Credit Suisse, Zurich, by noon of 15th of July, Princess Alexa was to have full ownership of the yacht. It was dated Cannes, July 14.

Arnold signed it immediately, handed it back to her. She then handed him a document giving him the right to vote her block of Associated shares in proxy for the period of one year. It was a notarized power of attorney.

"Well," Arnold said, "it's what we agreed upon."

"And now let's see the notorious Elton wheeling and dealing in action," Alexa said dryly.

There'd been a subtle change in their relationship. Arnold was in the driver's seat again.

"I'd appreciate it," he said, "and we'll all be better for it if you avoid the environs of Cannes for the next few days. That is if you still plan to remain on the coast?" The last hopefully.

"I understand why you don't want my name linked with yours," Alexa said sweetly. "Until you've done your fiddle with the AA stock, but I do plan to stay awhile. I'm enjoying myself immensely. And of course if there's another misunderstanding between here and Zurich, I shall be very busy. I shall want the yacht completely refurbished and I shall want a new color scheme—it's so obvious—and I shall want her prepared for a leisurely cruise of the Greek Islands—which I've promised myself for years." She leaned forward and touched his arm reassuringly. "Your yacht will be in

435

loving hands. You couldn't have found a better home for her."

"I'm relieved," Arnold said, "but the transfer will be made by tomorrow noon."

Alexa flashed him a smile that could have been used to cut diamonds on, and slipped out.

The moment she was gone Arnold grabbed the telephone, and called the West Coast office. Wacszinski answered.

Arnold launched into, "Where the hell have you been?" From up above came the sudden whomp of the loudspeakers. Robbie was once again in charge.

"Gimme a chance, Arnold." Don's voice was steady. "There's a hell of a good reason why I've been out of contact, but listen. I've got good news and bad news. I'll give you the good news first. It's all set. The stock has been bought. If you've got the proxies and Vernon has bought his share, we're in control of Associated."

"I've got the proxies. Now what's the bad news?"

The line seemed to go dead.

"Don . . ." Arnold prodded.

"There are two kinds of bad news. One I can handle, the other—I don't know."

"Just give it to me Don."

"You know Tatum—"

"Don't tell me he's found a tie-up between Dennis and the guys."

"No, Arnold. He hasn't. But he's wondering about a tie-up between us and the stock manipulation."

Now Arnold needed ten seconds. Then: "You assured him, didn't you Don? You're buddies . . ."

"Arnold," Don said quietly, "Tatum's my friend—"

"Christ, Don, if we don't work this we're blown. Arnel Enterprises, everything. If we do work it, we're on top, we're major."

"I lied to him," Wacszinski said. "This is the first time."

"Don," Arnold said. He hadn't anticipated anything like this. Don Wacszinski and Dorothy were the two rocks of Arnel, the toughest most unflappable. Don was getting old. He sounded ready to crack. "Listen to me. I'm going to low-profile our participation in this for at least two years. There won't be any sign of me. Once we're there nobody'll want to bad-mouth us. We'll be the power behind—way behind. Okay?"

"Okay," Don said finally, his voice eneven. Old Don Wacszinski wanted a little love, just a word that Arnold knew what he'd gone through.

I played it right, Arnold thought. "Couldn't be better," he said. "Now what's the bad news?"

"There's been a robbery at the Bel Air house. Break-in-and-enter except there was no break-in. They just walked in. We're still at the inventory stage but so far everything in the wall safe's gone. Nothing much else has been touched, that we can find."

"Shiiiiit," Arnold groaned. "Krystina's jewels. When did that happen?"

"We don't know for sure," Don said cautiously.

"What do you mean, you don't know for sure? Margaret must know." There was no response to that. "Don . . . ?"

"I'm here."

"Margaret's been living in," Don must have known that. What was going on? "She had to be there, for Chrissakes. She doesn't leave the premises. She was sitting the house and taking care of Joker." Joker was their Bel Air poodle. "She had to be there all the time to feed Joker and to walk him."

"Well, all right, Arnold, I know how you feel about Heatherington but it's a classic inside job. There's no sign of anything forced. My thought is Heatherington turned the alarm off, left the house, somebody else working with her slips in while she's out, does the job."

"That's just plain fucking dumb, and Margaret isn't dumb."

"Her explanation is almost as dumb. She claims she went shopping a few times and since it always was broad daylight, she didn't bother to set the burglar alarm. She says she only just noticed when she was cleaning up that the picture that hangs over the wall safe wasn't exactly in place. Then she took a look and saw the safe was open. *She* know the combination of that safe?"

"A lot of people do."

"I plan to sweat her a little more because in my book she's it."

"Don, I don't want Margaret sweated, understand? And don't call the cops. Or have you already?"

Now Don was really hurt. The essence of his job was to keep the cops away from anything affecting Arnel. "No, Arnold. I haven't called the cops. But we've got ourselves a problem. We've got to notify the police for the insurance on the jewels."

"We don't have any insurance. Insurance on jewels these days comes to like sixteen percent of their value a year. Six years and you've paid off the total cost."

"No insurance?" Don was rocked. "You're ready to write it off as a total loss?"

"Just don't worry about it. Anything else?"

Another pause. Was it possible there was more?

"There's something else you should know about. While you were in New York. Did you read the papers? Maybe the obit didn't make the New York papers?"

"Obit? Obit? Who, for Christ sake?"

"Your ex-father-in-law, old man Pitchford. About ten days ago. After a long illness. Must've been cancer. You didn't know?"

"I didn't know."

"I can't give you a definitive opinion but from what I've

picked up, he didn't leave a cent to your ex. According to my information she wasn't even at the funeral. And of course if he'd left anything to Robbie, we'd've been notified.''

Arnold bowed his head. The old sonofabitch. Even though they practically never saw each other. Still. Robbie was his only grandchild.

"Which is a shame because my information is that there was heavy money there. Your ex's been coming down from San Francisco to see Heatherington. She was here last week.''

"What are you getting at?''

"We've got to be tough. Your ex knew the combination of the safe?''

"Okay. She knew it too.''

"My thought is this, Arnold. Your ex counted on the old man leaving her something. When she found he didn't, since she knew the combination of the safe, she and Heatherington got together.''

"Forget it.''

"But Arn, the timing is so right. It fits.''

"Forget it, I said!'' Arnold's voice ran away from him. 'Sorry, Don.''

"I know, Arnold, I know.''

"Maybe it *is* an inside caper,'' Arnold spoke crisply. "But Kate knows the combination. Oscar and Estelle know it. That safe was a joke . . . Tell Margaret I want to see her here. I've been promising her a vacation in Europe for years. Try to put it on that basis. Get her over here.'' He'd never brought Margaret over because Krystina felt Margaret was still part of Beejay, who was the only one Krystina was really jealous of. 'Get her on the first plane over, make sure she talks to nobody. But nobody. Whatever you do, don't let her feel we suspect her. I've got to talk to her first.''

Don couldn't let go of the cop in him. "I know a little something about when people are guilty and lying, Arn. I've got a high percentage of accuracy on my judgment there. Heatherington's into this, and there's only one way with her kind."

Arnold never had to pull that kind of rank before but deep-rooted prejudices were being touched. "Let me handle this, Don—my way," he said quietly. "I want her here."

"Okay, chief," good-soldier Wacszinski replied. "Your way. Will do."

On deck, Inspector Bellarosa, flanked by a couple of his men, had surrounded the two Americans, whose backs were against the rail. Oscar, wobbly upright, was scrutinizing one of the men with a curious intensity. The de la Portes, Gina and Alfredo, were fascinated spectators; Harris, Arnold noted with irritation, was still very much around. So was the Princess. She had been about to leave when she noticed the commotion, and headed for it. Alexa was naturally nosy.

Arnold pushed his way over to the trouble spot.

"What with so many distinguished guests assembled here," Bellarosa explained, "I was simply making a routine verification of identities."

The older of the two men who were the focus of attention wore glasses, had frizzy graying hair, a slight paunch, a vague air of small-time authority. He was sweating copiously.

The second, a large man much younger, in his late thirties, with a curiously disjointed stance, wore a fake Hawaiian-style multicolored shirt. The nimbus of loser hovered over him and he looked vaguely familiar. In Arnold's book he was an undoubted wrongo.

"What are you doing at this party?" Oscar peered at Frizzy Hair and spoke with long-suffering indignation. "Who invited you? You know who this man is? He's Chittick, a busybody from the Internal Revenue Service of the United States Department of the Treasury. That's who he is. And he has the gall to come on board ship."

"Let's forget it," Arnold said hurriedly. The de la Portes, Gina and Alfredo, and a few others, were utterly fascinated. "Maybe the best idea is for him just to leave."

"No. I want to know what he's doing here," Oscar said. There was no stopping Oscar. "What are you doing here, Chittick? You're disturbing the party. Now are you or are you not going to explain why a busybody from the IRS had to come aboard a private yacht?"

"Oscar," Arnold said warningly.

By now the Princess's two bodyguards, both with their right hands in jacket gun-pockets, looked at Chittick coldly.

"I can explain why I came aboard," Chittick said hastily. Arnold could easily have strangled Oscar on the spot. "I'm here on a tour which spends two days on the Riviera," Chittick said. "So I thought I would look around on my own. I remembered about the Elton yacht so I came to look." To the others he felt obliged to explain, especially to Alexa's two obviously armed bodyguards. "Elton has what he calls a Golden Book. He makes all his guests sign it, which they do thinking they're signing because they're celebrities, but no, he then submits it to the IRS as proof that he's had movie people aboard and claims these parties were for business reasons." To make matters worse someone had turned the music off completely and each word Chittick uttered could be heard clearly, "He then makes these parties tax deductible."

"But how divinely astute!" Madame de la Porte asked sweetly of Chittick, "and Monsieur Elton, as you Americans say, will not get away with it?"

"Why doesn't somebody turn on the music?" Arnold asked cheerfully. He glanced down at the quay, and his heart sank. Hume's limousine was pulling up. "How about getting the waiters to freshen up your champagne?" Nobody moved. There was an animallike quality in the way they all stood and gawked.

441

"You'll never be able to use that in tax court," Oscar said triumphantly. "You will not be able to present any of this as evidence, since your entrance here is illegal."

"I know that but I don't mind telling you, Brenner," Chittick said, "that I found names in that so-called Golden Book who aren't here tonight."

"How do you know they weren't here and left?" Oscar asked.

"I sat on the jetty for hours, and I saw no Robert Redford or Clint Eastwood come on this yacht," Chittick said.

"How very assiduous of you," Alexa murmured approvingly.

"I'm telling you this as a friendly gesture. If you try to claim," Chittick made a broad gesture, "any of this, you'll be chopped."

"Leave the yacht," Arnold cut in coldly to Chittick, "before I press charges of trespassing."

Chittick scurried with surprising speed toward the gangplank and off the ship.

Arnold sidled up to Scott, spoke to him in intense whispers.

"For Chrissake," Arnold said, "don't let the Princess leave until I can get rid of that limousine on the quay. Do anything. Take her below. Fuck her. Anything."

Scott shot Arnold a sardonic look, then nodded and moved alongside Alexa, and whispered something to her. She laughed her famous trilling laugh. Someone had once said she laughed Mozart.

Bellarosa turned to the younger of the two unknown quantities.

"I'm just a garden-variety gate-crasher," the Wrongo proclaimed with touching modesty as he made a wide gesture with both arms. "My name's Orville-Billie Hutchins."

By now all the other *Delphi* guests, even the young, had torn themselves away from the free food, champagne and arrangements to get laid, which was the normal business of

442

Elton party guests, drifted over and were crystallized in a fascinated half circle about Arnold and the others.

"I've seen you before somewhere," Scott said suddenly to Orville-Billie.

"Why everybody gits that feeling," Orville-Billie's face opened with the kind of ingenuous smile very young children draw, round eyes, round nose, lips turned up so far they seem to touch his ears. "Happens I'm a stunt ma-an from Hollywood, been hangin' aroun' here, I heard Mister Harris there," Orville-Billie picked out Armand Harris unerringly, Harris listened with deep interest, "is shootin' a picture in the vicinity." Was it possible Harris and the Wrongo knew each other or had some common bond? "I been hopin' there might be some kinda part for me, was jist moseyin' round all these yachts all them purty ladies and all—kinda well—just walked on," he added shyly, "gate-crasher."

"I've seen that face of his in a lot of films," Jennifer made a valiant effort to end it.

"So have I," Robbie said.

"I've even had me a role in one of them spaghetti Westerns," Orville-Billie added with modest pride, "only a featured part."

"I've never seen a spaghetti Western," Scott said, "but I've seen you."

"Been in over forty films," Orville-Billie enjoyed the attention. "I've cumulated me eighteen bone fractures, two concussions," he glanced at Arnold and realized his patience was running out, added quickly, "I've worked with Yakima Canutt's boys, got me my Guild card," he fumbled in his pants pocket and flashed a card. "Full member in good standin'."

Oddly, it was one of the Princess's bodyguards who took it and examined it with the intense scrutiny a bureaucrat gives any official document, handed it on to the other bodyguard who studied it, passed it on to Bellarosa, who studied the card, then handed it on to Arnold.

"It's a Screen Actors Guild card," Arnold pronounced. The onlookers had been prepared for blood of some kind: disappointed, they drifted away.

Arnold shot a quick look at the quay. Horrified, he saw Dennis's limousine maneuvering into position in the now overcrowded narrow parking area.

Oscar staggered away and landed safely in a comfortable chair.

Orville-Billie carefully replaced the card in a battered cowhide wallet, braced for something unpleasant. But Bellarosa was no longer interested in a chunk of American flotsam that had been washed ashore on the Riviera. Orville-Billie scampered off leaving the distinct impression he felt he had gotten away with something.

"I swear I've seen that face before," Scott said as Telly came up. Orville-Billie paused for a moment at the gangplank and took a last look behind.

"Why, he's—" Telly began. They all turned to her. Orville-Billie vanished. "I don't know."

She glanced over at Scott, who seemed to be holding Alexa in place almost by physical force.

Arnold scurried over to Oscar.

"The transfer," Arnold whispered to Oscar, shaking him, pinching his cheeks, slapping him gently, "the transfer! To the Swiss bank." Oscar looked up at him, saw it was Arnold and smiled affectionately. The more violently Arnold shook him the more affectionate the smile became. Arnold straightened and looked around for Estelle. She was, as usual, in the galley helping with the food.

Dr. Jean-Louis's wife and a woman Arnold wasn't sure he'd fucked or not, drifted by, stopped, watched with mild curiosity as he slapped the smiling Oscar. Arnold left Oscar,

444

slid away from the others down to the quay, loped over to the limousine. Dennis, looking bewildered and completely helpless, stood uncertainly before the huge car. He had the look of a man who had lost his sense of direction. He kept turning in all directions, as if trying to pick up some spoor.

"They won't let me in." Dennis's voice could have been used to announce the end of the universe.

"Where?" Arnold asked sympathetically.

"The Casino. The Casino. Jesus. Arnold. I'm barred from the Casino." That sonofabitch Nadelman was really vindictive. He must've pulled a tangle of strings to've convinced a casino way down in the south of France that Dennis was a bad risk."

"Take it easy," Arnold said soothingly as he eased him back toward the limousine. "We'll fix that."

"They wouldn't let me past the main lobby." Dennis was badly shaken. "Jesus Christ, Arnold, they've got a worldwide network, I'm barred from every casino in the world!"

Arnold tried to push Dennis back into the limousine. "Believe me, we'll fix this. You won't be barred, our connections."

Dennis refused to be consoled. "They pushed me, just like you're pushing me now."

"Have confidence, it'll be no problem." Arnold glanced back nervously. Alexa was right there on deck, very close. "Do yourself a favor, Denny, and get back to the Colombe d'Or. And, listen, feel free to call me if things get too tough."

Dennis looked up at the deck of the *Delphi*. "A few minutes at your party may be just what the doctor ordered. Just a few minutes."

"Now come on, Dennis. Go home. We'll get you reinstated at the casino. You watch. Straighten up and fuck off."

Dennis took another long wistful look at the *Delphi*. You had to admit that, from that angle, it looked very glamorous, but Dennis finally got back into the limousine.

Arnold made an imperative gesture with his right arm to the chauffeur to whip that gigantic limousine the hell out of there as fast as possible.

He ran back up the gangplank and hurried over to Wade Vernon.

"Can I see you alone?" Arnold asked.

"You can speak here," Wade smiled at Joyce. "I trust Miss Humboldt completely and I don't believe in being secretive."

"Okay," Arnold announced with fitting solemnity. "Arnel Incorporated now controls nine percent of our stock."

"Congratulations," Wade said, "my brokers have an option on seven percent. I'll telephone them tonight to finalize the purchase. By three o'clock Texas time it'll be done."

"Together we'll have a block of sixteen percent," Arnold said.

"We'll be well in control," Wade said calmly.

Arnold took a moment to digest it. Christ. They were in control of Associated Artists. Was Vernon as cool as he seemed to be?

"Can we meet sometime tomorrow to discuss AA's future?" Arnold asked. "We've never had a chance to talk."

"I have complete confidence in you. You do whatever you think is necessary. We'll meet of course, but on other matters, I hope." Wade's voice was grave. Then he turned and looked at Joyce. His features softened. He became playful. "Miss Humboldt has been asking me to recommend a safe conservative investment and I was trying to explain to her that they don't exist anymore. In fact we've been thinking of making certain placements of our capital in rubles." He laughed heartily. "But I think, Joyce, now there is some advice I can give you." He leaned close to her. "You might very well put whatever money you have in Associated Artists. It's not only a safe investment but an exciting one."

446

"Providing you buy tomorrow," Arnold said. "And don't let it get around."

"I won't," Joyce said quietly.

Over Joyce's shoulder Arnold caught the two bodyguards shaking hands with Bellarosa. They were apparently leaving.

As Arnold excused himself from Joyce and Wade Vernon, Alexa surreptitiously held up her jeweled handbag and smiled a conspiratorial smile. Only she and Arnold knew it held clear title to the *Delphi*. She brought the bag almost to her lips and made a fond kissing gesture.

"Imagine," Krystina said with hurt reproof, "the Princess can't even stay for the fireworks."

"I've been invited to watch them from the Palace at Monaco," Alexa said, "if we hurry we can make it. It would be ungracious of me not to make an appearance."

Krystina held her creamy arm out at full length, the way she'd seen the titled people in the movies do. "It was so lovely you could come even for so short a time," Krystina murmured.

"I'm delighted I did," Alexa said, holding up the jeweled bag again. "I've had such a splendid, and quite possibly, rewarding time."

"You'll be relieved to know," Arnold said to Alexa, "that everything is hunky-dory."

"On the contrary," Alexa smiled sweetly, "I would be sorry to hear that."

She took hold of several of Krystina's fingertips, crushed them together, gave the hand one shake, and turned away to Telly and Scott.

"Telly, for Telafora, is it? A Spanish name. From an ancestor washed ashore on some Channel port after the defeat of the Armada?" Telly seemed astonished. The Princess had hit it. "It's possible I may be cruising the Greek Islands in my own yacht. If I do, you and Scott must join me."

447

She leaned over, kissed Scott quickly on both cheeks, shook hands warmly with Telly, perfunctorily with Arnold, then disappeared with her bodyguards.

"Did she say she was sorry to hear everything was hunky-dory?" Krystina asked.

"Who knows what she said?" Arnold muttered.

The fireworks erupted without warning. A gasp of awe rose from the thousands of spectators on the beach and on the Croisette.

The pyrotechnics strutted across the sky like a peacock. It was as if it had all reversed itself, the sea turning itself upside down, displaying its exotic underwater population in all their changing opalescent colors. In the glow of reds, golds and greens the Princess could be seen stepping swiftly into her white Rolls, the two guards at her side. Then she was whirled away into the darkness.

Krystina was very upset.

"How can anyone leave just as the fireworks begin?" she asked. "It's practically—rude. And her a princess."

"Split," Arnold told Orville-Billie disagreeably, surprised the bum hadn't left yet.

"I could sure use a drink," Orville-Billie suggested wistfully, dropping his drawl for the moment. "I'm a genuine movie man, no two ways about that and I could sign your Golden Book and make it look real good for you."

Several of the young had come up and were interested.

"We'll struggle along without you," Arnold said. "Get lost."

"That's a real shame," Orville-Billie was philosophical, licked his lips at the sight of the Plaything. "I took me a real shine to you. I like you so much, Mister Elton, you was to invite me to your place, I swear I wouldn' pee in yoh pool."

A series of hiccuping giggles erupted from the Plaything as he left.

448

"What he said," she gasped and tried to imitate his Beverly Hillbilly at the same time, "I wouldn' pee in yoh pool."

Jennifer looked at the Plaything with open disapproval, then turned to her father. "You should've thrown him in the drink. He's a bummer."

"I wonder how he knew you had a pool," Scott mused.

"Stands to reason," Jennifer said with a hint of contempt, "any man has a yacht has a pool."

At the word "pool" the Plaything screeched off into uncontrolled laughter, which became convulsions, stopped suddenly, made a telltale gesture covering her shorts, then rushed off in embarrassment.

"Jesus," Robbie said.

"You sure pick 'em, kid," Jennifer said dryly and drifted away.

"I know what you are feeling," Dr. Jean-Louis said to Robbie with champagne-steeped commiseration. "You have pointed your camera at them so often and I, I have seen them with their legs spread wide in the stirrups, even the most beautiful ones, I no longer see their faces. I see the horizontal mustache and vertical beard which is between their thighs."

"Maybe you're getting stale," Robbie said. "Jennifer and I are taking a vacation. Maybe Sweden, Scandinavia, hitching."

"What about your film?" Arnold asked shocked. "Nobody drops a project in the middle—"

"We're not dropping anything," Robbie was irritably defensive. "Basically we've already got the ball rolling. We're tired, Jennifer and me, besides we're only thinking of taking off."

Another two seconds, Arnold thought, and I'll say things to Robbie I might regret.

A few feet up ahead he bumped into the Plaything, who, apparently dry now, was on her way back to civilized society. "Hi, Mr. Elton," she said shyly.

For a fleeting moment Arnold saw Dr. Jean-Louis' horizontal pubic mustache and a vertical beard on her face. Was this going to be permanent? Had Dr. Jean-Louis done it to him? Had the doctor spoiled cunt for him? Arnold pushed past the bewildered girl, stood alone at the railing, but that goddamn image persisted.

He shut his eyes, but it didn't go away. He was out of control.

He could hear Braunschweig's soft voice, "Perhaps you really fear female pubic hair, possibly because of your unfortunate first sexual encounter with that prostitute, you spoke of her having a bushy growth. You may consider it something from the wilderness, an animal. It is a common child's fear."

Arnold got panicky. In spite of himself now even Krystina's image rose in his inner eye. Krystina. No eyes, no nose, no mouth. A copper pubic triangle instead of a face. Wildly he thought if the worse came to worst, he could ask her to shave it off. But the pity of it.

If Dr. Jean-Louis really had succeeded in spoiling sex for him, he was near the end. Without sex Arnold Elton had little reason for living.

Arnold shut his eyes hard and conjured up the vertical mustache and beard on the Plaything.

"Not for my breakfast," Arnold muttered fervently and spat, "not for my lunch," Arnold spat again, "not for my dinner," and spat with passionate vehemence.

"You been vomiting?" Scott asked with polite concern. "Gyppy tummy?"

"Something lousy I ate. But I'm okay."

"Well, we got the Princess off, but Bellarosa, he and all his men left suddenly too."

"You're kidding. He couldn't have gone. He wouldn't have left us unprotected."

In the pilot's cabin Arnold dialed the Cannes Police.

The police officer on telephone duty replied politely. "Inspector Bellarosa? We have an emergency contact for the Inspector tonight. But it's your yacht number. Where are you calling from?''

''From my yacht,'' Arnold replied.

''Oh, I see,'' the officer's voice was suddenly cagey. ''The Inspector may very well have been called away suddenly.''

''But he would have informed you where he was going.''

''Not necessarily,'' the officer replied carefully. ''But I will ask him to contact you the moment he can.''

From the deck Arnold surveyed the jetty anxiously. A thin line of cars trickled out of the Port parking area. The fireworks were almost over. Old-hand fireworks-watchers wanted to beat the impending traffic jams. There was not the slightest sign of Bellarosa or his men.

The grand finale came quickly, tearing the sky in a wild pattern of color and explosion. Orange flares signaled the end, turned red, then with a dazzling brightness lighted up the entire kilometer or so of the Croisette, the sixteenth-century Abbey high on the *Suquet,* the hill on the far side of the bay. A vast communal sigh of surprise and regret rose from the thousands of spectators.

Why the surprise? They had known at the beginning exactly when it would end. Like dying—Like dying. No matter how long you lived, when you faced death it always came as a surprise. But it was Scott who had said that.

He jumped as he heard Vernon's voice. Vernon and Joyce came up suddenly. ''Arnold—'' Vernon made a slight gesture toward Joyce, ''we must leave. I used your telephone. We've acquired the stock.'' The emotion of sixteen percent of Associated stock, of the take-over, of control, flowed through Vernon's voice and surged through his arm, out his fingers as he clasped Arnold's hand. And he'd called Arnold by his first name for the first time.

The fireworks may have ended too suddenly but the party did not. The *Delphi* seemed to attract a particularly hardy breed of lingerers. Even battered by hours of booming music and an unending intake of champagne and indigestible hors d'oeuvres, they seemed fresh and ready for anything.

Then for no understandable reason there was a sudden lull in the night's rhythm and an equally mysterious acknowledgment the party was over. They'd probably eaten and drunk as much as they could. The less affluent had finally resigned themselves to the dreary reality that none of the spectacular wealth about them would ever spill over on them.

Estelle must surely have been dead on her feet with all the useless fussing she'd done in the galley, and keeping Oscar from falling on his face. She made heroic efforts to slip away unnoticed but Oscar was now practically deadweight. Robbie spotted her dilemma, hooked one of Oscar's limp arms over his shoulder, and the three stumbled off.

"Poor guy," Estelle called out, realizing that they were the center of fascinated attention. "Dead tired. Not as young as he used to be."

There was a moment of lurching fear as Oscar staggered and almost slid under the ropes and into the debris-filled water below. But Estelle and Robbie made a spectacular save, and Oscar finally made it to the quay, he with the decorous stiff-legged dignity of the utterly drunk.

The moment of leave-taking came for even the hard-core hangers-on.

"I spoke a great deal of nonsense," Dr. Jean-Louis mumbled contritely. "Say you forgive me."

"I wasn't around to hear much of what you said," Arnold replied stonily, unforgiving.

"He doesn't forgive me," Dr. Jean-Louis lamented. "Doctors are never supposed to say anything stupid."

He tried to kiss Arnold, who subtly avoided him. Instead he kissed Krystina fervently and she kissed back as fervently.

Did he linger too long on Krystina's lips? Arnold recalled

452

whispers about Jean-Louis and some of his more attractive patients. Was the pubic beard talk just a ploy?

"We're taking off," Jennifer said, as always especially belligerent when Krystina was around. "We're making the rounds of street dancing."

"Street dancing?" Arnold looked around uneasily. There was still no sign of Bellarosa or his men.

"I thought we'd all drive up to the Villa, and get a good night's sleep—"

"Oh, but we plan to be up all night," the Plaything sounded like a little girl making exciting plans for a doll tea party, "then we're all going to my place, I've got the Bridal Suite at the Hotel Provençal at Jewan Less Pans," it took Arnold a moment to realize she was saying Juan-les-Pins, "it's real neat and there's more than enough room for everybody."

It was probably safer, or about as safe as anything, Arnold told himself uneasily.

"Okay, but don't come back too late, you guys." They looked at Arnold peculiarly. "Krystina has to rest," he explained as he put his arm around her protectively, "Sri Lanka makes a hell of a racket when anyone comes near him in the night."

Jennifer said, "Nobody's coming near the Villa."

"Okay, but take it easy, you guys," Arnold said.

"Take it easy on what?" Jennifer's irritation mounted.

"What the hell. Just in general," Arnold said.

There were quick ritual kisses.

Robbie took Arnold aside. "I need a couple of hundred bucks."

"A couple of hundred? Right now? What for?" Arnold asked.

"Jesus, Dad," Robbie said in angry frustration. "I've got to pick up the check for all of them."

"Why do you have to be the big honcho?" Arnold demanded. "Some of them are from richer families than us."

"Oh, shit," Robbie said. "They're our guests, for Chrissake. I can't let them think we're cheap. Oh. Fuck it."

He started off.

"Wait!" Arnold quickly handed him the bills. Robbie hesitated, then took the money as he always did. Arnold told himself he must not make it hard for Robbie to ask for money.

The moment they got away from the adults, they dashed off like young animals released for their first spring gambol. On the gangplank Robbie goosed the Plaything vigorously. She jumped high in the air and almost toppled over but Robbie caught her *in extremis* as she shrieked with laughter.

Harris materialized like a prehistoric creature fighting his way out of the tar pits. "I'll call you in the morning," he said.

"Before eleven," Arnold said, "and if I'm asleep, leave a message. Just say it's done."

Harris growled an inarticulate reply, leaving a vague cloud of menace behind him.

"Don't forget," Sarita told Arnold, through clenched teeth, "you promised to put in a good word with shitface. I want that part, goddamnit."

"Give him a good blow job," Arnold said reassuringly. "I'll do the rest."

"*Cara,*" the Baronessa embraced Krystina with the conspiratorial togetherness of one woman for another who is pregnant, "as always the Elton parties, *molto molto simpatico.*" Then kissed Arnold lightly. "*Tanta cosa.* And always surprises."

The Baron lingered. The Baronessa, indulgent, long suffering, came back for him, "That Alfredo, he would stay with his Eltons forever. Alfredo! *Vieni vieni subito! Su su. Su.*" *Su-su-su* was the sound Italians made when calling their dog.

454

"*Si si si si,*" Alfredo cupped Arnold's hand fervently in his two hands. "*Ciao, Arnoldo.*" With an almost mournful intensity, he turned away, took Krystina's hand and brought it to the prescribed one centimeter away from his lips and with the same mournfulness, said "*Ciao, Bella,*" as if parting forever.

"*Ciao, Alfredo,*" but Krystina was touched. "*Fino a domani* . . . Well," she said with a heartfelt sigh, "the party's over, I guess."

Krystina settled herself comfortably alongside Arnold in the station wagon. From up ahead came the sound of Scott starting Telly's car, then their headlights came on.

"Love you," Krystina said, snuggling up to him.

"Love you."

Even in the misty light of the dashboard, her hair was radiant, a rich copper glow. Arnold whipped the car out and the powerful lights probed the darkness as they drove effortlessly past the parked cars, the silent yachts dark now except for dim work lights.

At the Port's gates, their headlights picked up Scott and Telly outside their car, the motor idling.

Arnold jammed to a halt, ripped the handbrake on, gestured to Krystina to sit where she was and jumped out.

"A white 604 Peugeot," Scott spoke excitedly but low so Krystina wouldn't hear, "laying over on the other side of the Croisette. It shot out just as you drove up, then turned right at the first intersection. We couldn't get his license number, he was driving without lights."

"I'll take out after him. I'll nail the sonofabitch. I'll crush the cocksucker," Arnold raged.

"You've got Krystina with you. Get back to the yacht," Scott said sharply. "We'll go on. He's waiting around the corner for you but he won't make trouble for us in Telly's car. At least we'll get his license number."

Arnold hesitated, then yielded.

"The car's lights are out of focus," Arnold explained to Krystina. "Scott noticed it. We'll sleep over on the *Delphi*. The two of us in our specially built bunk doesn't turn you on? I must be slipping."

"Trouble is," Krystina, reassured, snuggled up to him some more as he whirled the car around, "I get turned on too much. What's that you say? 'Once a Mason always a Mason but once a Knight is plenty?'"

"Not only beautiful," Arnold said as they pulled up before the *Delphi*, "but a memory like an elephant. That joke must be older than God."

3

Arnold woke suddenly cold with fear. He'd been dreaming nails were being pounded into his skull. Gradually he understood someone was knocking on the cabin door.

"Mr. Elton," Dougherty's voice came muffled, urgent.

Arnold slid out of the bunk. Krystina sat up in sudden fright as Arnold opened the cabin door cautiously.

"Michel just called," Dougherty spoke in whispers. "Someone's broken into the Villa. He and Germaine heard them moving around in your bedroom upstairs. They haven't been able to get the police. They think the intruders may still be there but they're sticking to their room, they're afraid to investigate. I've tried the police also but all I get is a vague promise from them."

"I just knew there was something wrong," Krystina trembled. "I felt it all day."

"There isn't a villa on the Riviera that hasn't been broken into," Arnold said. "What time is it, Captain?"

"A little after three-thirty."

"Why we barely fell alseep," Kristina said.

"Call Scott for me," Arnold said to Dougherty. "Tell him
I'll pick him up in ten minutes. And call the Commissariat
again. Insist they contact Inspector Bellarosa."

"Oh, darling," Krystina clutched at him. "They may still
be up there, maybe they have guns or something. Why won't
the police come?"

"They don't say they won't come," Dougherty said. "They
don't say much of anything."

"Maybe Captain Dougherty should go with you," suggested
Krystina, "the Captain has a gun and knows how to use it."

"I'd sooner have the Captain and his gun here with you,"
Arnold said.

"Bellarosa had a couple of his men sitting in a police car
on the road right below the Villa," Arnold told Scott as they
drove along in the station wagon. "I wonder why they didn't
see the burglars."

"Bellarosa's men are not there," Scott said shortly.

"He would've warned me."

"I don't function at top form at four o'clock in the
morning," Scott mumbled, "but I'm sure he couldn't keep
his men immobilized. The Fourteenth of July has one of the
highest crime rates of the French year."

Arnold kept glancing nervously at the rear-view mirror.
The Cannes streets were still animated. Every now and then
they passed a street celebration, red, blue and white lights
strung overhead and small orchestras with plenty of accordi-
ons, hammering away. The "girls" were out in full force on
rue d'Antibes, Cannes' principal street. Several of them
waved in holiday spirit as Arnold and Scott drove by. "Krys
and I were on our way up to the Villa. If you hadn't stopped
us, we would have surprised the intruders."

"Or to put it another way," Scott said, "they would have
surprised you and Krys."

"Burglaries in two of my houses. What is that?"

They passed more outdoor dancing. It was only when they hit the country road leading past what had been Picasso's house that there was silence and darkness. A lone car zoomed toward them but it was only a battered Renault carrying two young couples singing boisterously.

The hillside road to the Villa was dark and narrow. A car coming downhill could smash them.

"I ever tell you about Agnes? A little hooker I met in Cleveland when I was a kid on the lam. Cute little blond . . ."

"Please. Not at this hour. Not another story about a girl you laid even if she had six tits and two cunts. I'd sooner listen to the nightingales and concentrate on being numb shit-scared."

"I didn't lay her. She's the only girl I had a friendship with and never fucked."

"You never had a friendship with any of the women you laid?"

"Friendship and fucking don't mix."

"Why, Arnold, fucking is the friendliest activity a man and a woman can engage in. Or I suppose a man and a man or a woman and a woman. But especially a man and a woman."

"I'm talking about real fucking," Arnold said.

Arnold switched the lights off, and pulled up a distance from the Villa. They listened but heard only the faint strains of accordion music from the nearby Mougins village square. They both got out, shut the doors of the station wagon noiselessly.

The street was without sound or movement. There was no police car. Bellarosa's men were definitely not there.

Above, the Villa Lou Soleillou waited for them with brooding patience.

They climbed the steep driveway silently, carefully.

"The gate," Arnold whispered.

"Maybe Michel left it open for you."

"I don't hear Sri Lanka, and they weren't supposed to keep him tied."

"Maybe they took the dog inside the house with them."

"Michel and Germaine? No way." Arnold's forehead glistened. Angrily, "The puppy's taken off."

"He's hardly a dog that will pass unnoticed."

They slipped past the open gate, up the rest of the black driveway.

At the terrace above, Arnold suddenly stopped.

A vague figure was sprawled on the ground near the kitchen door.

"In a war zone I would have said a corpse," Scott said.

But they both knew before Scott snapped on his cigarette lighter and held it high. Sri Lanka's magnificent burnished copper mane was a mass of blood. His body lay in the utter relaxation of death.

"He kept on battering long after he was dead," Scott said as he let the light die. "You see a lot of that in war, a frenzy when they start killing."

"A crazy killer."

"I think all killers are crazy."

At the kitchen door Arnold, with Scott directly behind him, threw it open with a sudden movement, switched the light on.

The kitchen was untouched.

They moved cautiously into the corridor. A blade of light sliced out from under the door of Michel and Germaine's room.

"It's me," Arnold called out.

The old couple emerged, Michel with his bathrobe inside out, the seams making lumpy ridges.

"We think he's gone," Michel spoke with the choked voice of a man in shock. "We heard him upstairs for at least five minutes. Then footsteps coming down the stairs, then a car rolling away."

Arnold and Scott inched cautiously up the stairs and into the master bedroom.

There was no one there. The built-in closets, tall enough to hide a man, had not been disturbed. The bathroom was empty.

Arnold pulled out a drawer, rummaged through stacks of his varicolored shorts, which ranged from fireman red to robin's egg blue. He came up with a fistful of five-hundred-franc notes and some jewels. It was Krystina's secret cash hiding place. Nothing seemed to have been touched.

"A good old-fashioned burglary would have been reassuring," Scott said wistfully.

Below, Michel and Germaine were seated on a couch, Michel's robe still inside out. He looked old, moth-eaten, beat.

"Such a beautiful animal," Germaine didn't sound real, "and his color so like Madame's. If we had known we would have done something."

"You were wise not to," Scott said. "Poor Michel," he added after the old couple had gone back to their room and he and Arnold were in the living room with all the lights blazing. "He's already had his one nightly barbiturate suppository. He's like your Oscar. He limits himself to one, if that doesn't do it, he spends a sleepless night. Could this be connected with somebody at the *Delphi* party who knew when you were coming and waited for you?"

"Can you even imagine anybody on the *Delphi* tonight doing what was done to Sri Lanka?" Arnold asked.

"What about hiring somebody to do it?" Scott said. "That's different. It's abstract, like the generals sitting around at the Pentagon planning a raid, they don't see the blood and shit."

"Now *I* can't. Not at this hour. Spare me the ideology. I'll make you a deal. Every time I talk fuck, you have a right to equal time for ideology. Speaking of deals. You made twenty-one thousand dollars last year.''

''You go over my tax files with Mr. Chittick?''

''I want you to join Arnel. I hinted at it before.'' Scott listened attentively. ''I want you to sign up for a minimum of three years and I'll pay you enough so that at the end of that time you wouldn't have to worry the rest of your life.''

''I'm not worrying now.''

''You could be wherever you want to be, and the work will be the kind you can do without interfering with your writing. I know how much you enjoyed living it up at the Port Club. I'd pay you a hundred and fifty thousand dollars a year.''

It was a few seconds before Scott could reply.

''Why?''

''I want you as Executive Head of the Arnel Story Department.''

''Is this one of those night-things? Shock? The threat to your life, the killing of the Afghan puppy?''

''I don't make offers of this kind lightly.'' Arnold found an odd bit of paper, tore off a clear portion, wrote rapidly, handed it to Scott. ''That's a contract with my signature.''

Scott read it in amazement. ''So it is,'' he said finally.

''Roll that up and keep it in your pocket the way you do those sudden notes you write to yourself. All it needs is your signature. An offer like this will never come your way ever again. You don't know what it's like to be able to tell everybody to go fuck themselves.''

''That's not been one of my unfulfilled desires.''

''Don't be stupid,'' Arnold said curtly. ''You know what I mean.''

Scott stared at the jagged piece of paper.

''I'm staying here tonight,'' Arnold said. ''I'd like you to stay.''

''I'd hate to meet whoever did in Sri Lanka, in a dark alley or an isolated villa in the south of France where the cops are unaccountably too busy to come. So just leave the lights on, Arnold. I'll rest in this armchair."

Scott didn't say in so many words he'd accept the offer nor did he throw the bit of paper away.

There's a price on everybody and everything, Arnold told himself and found it sufficiently reassuring to drop off into sleep in a nearby armchair.

Arnold awoke slowly and uncomfortably. It took him a few seconds to understand he'd slept for hours on the white couch in the living room. Nearby, Scott pushed his body out of the shape the armchair had given it during sleep. Although the drapes were drawn, there was a feeling of heavy sunlight outside.

"Monsieur Reilly is here," Germaine came into focus, carefully groomed and controlled; it was hard to remember the terror-stricken elderly woman of a few hours earlier.

Reilly hovered over Arnold as though he were an invalid.

"Hi, Ar," Reilly was dressed New York, smelled of jet lag, bull-shot, Mennen's aftershave lotion (none of that French cologne crap for him), toothpaste, and was seething with excitement.

"Michel disposed of the dog," Germaine enumerated. "The police never came, there were many phone calls for you, I have written them down on the tablet for you, one very urgent message for you from a Monsieur Harris. His words were—'It's arranged.' He said to be sure to tell you he called at ten-thirty-five this morning."

"Thanks," Arnold felt only a small relief. At least the *Delphi* was no longer in danger.

"Oui, monsieur," Germaine said and left.

"What time is it?" Arnold asked.

Reilly glanced at his wristwatch. "It's nine o'clock in the morning."

"It can't be. Germaine said Harris called at ten-thirty."

"You're right," Reilly said, "I'm still on New York time." Hastily he reset his watch. "I've got plenty to tell you, Ar. Can we talk?"

"Scott Goldman," Arnold waved an introduction. "He's a new addition to Arnel. We can talk."

"Hi," Reilly barely acknowledged Scott. "This is inner-inner, Ar."

"So's Scott," Arnold said tersely.

"Hi," Scott returned Reilly's nod, and rummaged in his pocket, found the tattered bit of paper, held it high over his head, and reread it carefully.

Reilly paced nervously. "I've been running like a bastard. I checked on Kate. She's got big money raised for a top Broadway production so we can forget her, I don't know about your second ex, but I think we can eliminate her too. I spent several hours at Oscar's office, going over the books. It was the only chance I've had for years to go over the books without either him or Estelle over me."

"Why were you going over Oscar's books?" Arnold asked.

"I'll come to that in a minute," Reilly said. Arnold smoldered. He hated build-ups and Reilly was big on them. "But first there's other pressing items on our agenda."

Germaine entered with a tray of freshly squeezed grapefruit juice and coffee.

"You're on," Arnold said the moment Germaine left.

Reilly glanced irritably at Scott. "My classmate's here."

Arnold sat up. "Saintsbury? Here? On the French Riviera?"

"With Clover," Reilly said carefully.

"Clover? What the hell is he doing with Clover?" Reilly really was a stupid bastard. On top of everything else now Arnold had to worry about what would happen if Dennis met Clover. Boy. It would blow everything. "Where are they?"

"At Eden Roc," Reilly said. "He's killing two birds with one stone."

"How long are they staying?" Arnold demanded.

"I'm not sure. This is a kind of honeymoon."

"So what's the second bird Saintsbury's going to kill?"

"You." Reilly then added hastily, "He's expecting to see you sometime today. Mike's the bagman. He'll pick up the payoff. Our twenty-four hours are up, Ar. That's why I've been running around like a nut. I been to Switzerland, I broke my ass getting back here. Ar—I know who took the contract out on you."

Scott sat up. Even the birds seemed to have stopped singing.

"You know who's been threatening Arnold's life?" Scott asked.

"All right, Reilly," Arnold said. "Just tell me without any horseshit buildup. Lay it out. Fast."

"You been to Oscar's office lately?" Reilly queried.

"As a matter of fact I have," Arnold said icily. "With Wade Vernon not so long ago."

"Yeah," Reilly said. "Only you were thinking of other things so you didn't notice the oil paintings Estelle's been buying over the years. She kept saying, 'for investment.' Well, they're gone. Reproductions are up in their place. That's what started wheels going in my head."

"In two seconds," Arnold said, "I'm going to start wheels going across your gut. Who took the fucking contract out on me?"

"Take it easy, Ar," Reilly said. "Maybe you better sit down, Ar."

Arnold sat down.

"It was Oscar who took the contract out on you."

"Oscar?" Arnold demanded. "You've got to be kidding."

"No," Reilly said quietly. "And I know why."

Scott and Arnold lay on rattan chaise lounges on the back terrace. Reilly was somewhere in the Villa resting. To have made it in those few hours from New York to Zurich then to Nice was no mean feat. Arnold, curled up in fetal position, emitted intermittent groans. "Oscar. Estelle. Oscar. Twenty years."

Germaine appeared, carrying a telephone with the receiver off the cradle. "A Monsieur Saintsbury. I told him you did not wish to be disturbed—but he says it is of a great urgency."

"Mr. Elton," Saintsbury's voice was crisp and business-like, "are you free for a late lunch? Around two?"

"How is Clover?" Arnold asked.

Saintsbury's voice softened for a moment, "Gorgeous," then got crisp, "and looking forward to seeing you."

"Not this afternoon," Arnold said. "How about dinner?"

"I think you might want to give this matter priority." Although Saintsbury's voice was friendly, it had an easy authority that came from holding life-and-death power. "Clover and I are here only for a few hours."

"I'm sorry, I really can't break this one," Arnold said.

"Hang on. Hey, Clover!" He didn't bother to cover the mouthpiece of the telephone with his hand. "That friend you wanted to see tonight—think you can see him this afternoon so we can see Mr. Elton tonight?" Arnold had a flutter of panic. Could that friend be Dennis? But then it seemed too farfetched. Clover would never see an ex-boyfriend when she was with somebody like Mike Saintsbury. Still. Who knew with a hunk of stuff like Clover? And the power of the curved schlong? By the time Clover's voice reached the telephone, it was almost straight Shrimpsville and unintelligible. "Okay," Saintsbury said into the telephone, "Clover believes she can rearrange her program. My place. Seven?"

"Eight-thirty just as good for you?" Arnold wasn't sure why he'd said that, perhaps to keep the dirty businesslike bastard off-balance.

No more concessions from Saintsbury. "We're flying to

Palermo early tomorrow morning. I want to show off Clover to the Sicilian part of my family. Seven.''

There was a sound of a car on the driveway below, then a crazy exuberant shout. Arnold sat up creakily.

"Oh, shit," Arnold groaned. "Wouldn't you just know."

The Jolly was hanging on the steep driveway before the gate; Jennifer at the wheel, Robbie and the Plaything unnecessarily on his lap up front; Oscar and Estelle, absurd, misplaced, misshapen in the backseat. They tried vainly to get into the spirit of things by leaning out and waving; the sudden movement of the car, as Jennifer ripped its gears, and ground up the rest of the steep incline, almost hurled them out. Estelle clutched desperately at Oscar.

"*Salut*, Scott!" Robbie called out cheerfully. "Hi, Mr. Elton!" the Plaything called in a specially intimate tone.

"Who the hell's goddamn idea was it for Jennifer and Robbie to bring Oscar and Estelle here?" Arnold mumbled to no one.

The Jolly shuddered and rattled to a halt. The Plaything ripped herself off Robbie's lap. Jennifer looking tan, windblown and purposeful, bounced out. Estelle laboriously lifted her ass off the plastic seat. The back of her dress looked as though it had just come out of a washing machine.

The Plaything went through a series of ingenious contortions, airing her armpits, pulling the thong out of her crotch. "Hot," she explained to the world.

"With all that excess frontal baggage," Jennifer dabbed her forehead with the upper part of her sleeve, "no wonder."

As she got older, Jennifer looked more and more like her mother, her body taking on that same businesslike proportion and, with it, the same misleading manner of complete assurance.

Oscar oozed uncertainly out of the car. Estelle was obliged to support him with one arm, and with her other hand tried to smooth the seat of her dress.

"You sure got a lot of sunlight here in California," Oscar said.

"It's not California," Robbie said. "It's the south of France."

"Same thing," Oscar was ready to agree with anybody.

"Move him out of the sun," Arnold said.

Robbie and Estelle steered Oscar toward the house, and as they approached, Estelle shot Arnold her perennial look of gratitude. She could never repay him for everything he'd done for them.

"He's pretty," the Plaything judged Scott. "Where you been hiding him?"

"He's not up for grabs," Jennifer said with an edge of annoyance. "If he was, don't you think I would have been in there?"

"Nobody's been hiding him," Robbie was mildly impatient, "you met him on the boat."

"Not boat," Jennifer corrected him, "schmuck—yacht."

"So I'm a schmuck," Robbie said, as Reilly, having just awakened and looking it, emerged.

"He's cute too," the Plaything said, "with a tan he'd be sexy."

"Don't let that turn your head," Jennifer said to Reilly. "She thinks anything has balls is sexy, including Santa Claus."

"The liberated generation," Estelle's laugh came off a laugh track.

"How long you staying?" Jennifer asked Reilly.

Reilly shot a glance at Arnold. "Probably eat and run."

"Maybe I can get to the boss," Jennifer said, "I've got a thing for Reilly only Reilly's too dumb to recognize it."

Reilly smiled his pickle smile, nose and lips approaching each other, as he went over to Jennifer and kissed her. He was another one who didn't know about the French protocol of not kissing on the lips. It annoyed Arnold.

468

"Rule of the house," Arnold's smile was waxen, "anybody works for Arnel can't marry into the family."

"Nobody around here is allowed to get married," Jennifer said bitingly. She never allowed Arnold to forget that he had broken up her affair with the bearded asshole who wouldn't accept a student deferment from the Vietnam war. Still, he was probably a lousy lay and if she had really wanted the guy, she could have put up a fight for him, which, thank God, she hadn't.

"We're staying for a swim," Jennifer announced.

"We are?" the Plaything asked, confused. "I didn't bring a suit."

"Who needs a suit?" Jennifer asked tartly.

"Listen, you guys," Arnold said, "you know the neighbors can see you skinny-dipping."

Arnold had planned the layout of the gardens and the pool himself, so it was his fault. The pool was high enough above the street level so it couldn't be seen from below but he'd completely overlooked the neighbors perched over them, who had a perfect unobstructed view. Jennifer and Robbie had taken to skinny-dipping together. Half-brother and sister cavorting about nude together was enough to make Arnold uneasy and the idea of the neighbors having a ball watching them was unbearable.

"She won't skinny-dip, anyway," Robbie, aware of his father's discomfort, shifted to the Plaything. "On account of her boobs, they collapse without mechanical support."

"It's not because of my boobs at all," the Plaything said hotly. "It's because I'm basically shy."

"Basically shy. Wow!" Robbie said.

"Hey now, why don't you guys get yourselves back to the *Delphi?*" Arnold suggested. "I'll call Captain Dougherty and tell him to take her out far enough so you can get a real unpolluted Mediterranean swim. How's that?"

"We're here now, and we're sweaty and sticky," Jennifer

said crossly. "You guys coming?" To Scott, "You want to join us? To see her," she pointed to the Plaything, "is alone worth the price of admission."

"Scott is in on this too," Arnold said.

Estelle, who had been watching with a growing uneasiness, shot a troubled look at Scott.

"You part of Arnel?" Jennifer asked Scott. "That's new."

"Jen, we've got important talk," Arnold said impatiently.

"Okay, okay," Jennifer said placatingly. "And don't worry, Mr. Elton, we-all promise not to pee in your pool."

The Plaything again let loose with that explosive giggle but Robbie yanked her on fiercely. The three went flying down the incline.

"Kids," Estelle tried to muster a maternal indulgence but it didn't quite come off. She was obviously uneasy about their leaving. "I'll go talk to Michel and Germaine. Krystina asked me to discuss tonight's dinner with them."

"I won't be here for dinner," Arnold said.

"I'll tell Germaine," Estelle said.

After a moment Oscar saw Estelle had left and was upset.

"Okay, Corporal," Arnold said to Reilly, anxious to get it over quickly, "let's get these men out of the hot sun."

Reilly, like the warden in death row, touched Oscar's arm.

"It's time," Reilly's manner seemed to say.

The four men swung wide, avoiding the kitchen, where Estelle could be heard explaining the night's meal as Michel and Germaine listened to her battered French with that patience it had taken several generations to acquire.

It was inconceivable. Estelle, shapeless, sweat-stained, middle-aged sweet-old-fashioned mother face, could she have discussed with Oscar all the details of contacting the boys, having Arnold destroyed? These days Oscar never made a move on his own, Arnold knew; he and Estelle planned everything out to the last detail, even to rehearsing lines—"If he says that Oscar, you say this."

In the living room, Reilly sat Oscar down in the white armchair, unconsciously, or maybe consciously, choosing the dead center of the room, shut the door leading to the connecting corridor with the kitchen, seated himself, still like a warden or a guard would, alongside the condemned man. Scott flopped in a chair to one side, Arnold stood directly facing Reilly and Oscar.

"It's been a hot thirst-making day." Oscar made sucking movements with his lips much like a nursing infant. He was bewildered, Arnold was the most hospitable of men, Oscar never had had to suggest a drink before, and he avoided Arnold's eyes.

"You're not drinking right now, Oscar," Arnold said.

"Just a small one," Oscar wheedled. "What with the heat."

"Show it to him," Arnold ordered Reilly.

Reilly held up a slim attaché case.

Scott slid so far down on the chair his ass hung over its edge.

"Gucci?" Oscar peered at Reilly's attaché case.

"Hermès," Reilly answered, "a gift from Krystina."

Oscar said, "I didn't know Hermès makes briefcases."

Reilly pulled out a folder, riffled through its contents quickly, singled out a document, handed it to Oscar, who arched his head way back. He wore trifocals and had to read down the length of his nose.

"It's a power of attorney," Oscar announced as he read. "The one you gave me June 22nd, 1959."

"It's not the one I gave you." It was unbearable for Arnold, he wanted the destruction over with quickly. "See? There, the third page, it gives you complete power of attorney for everything. You faked that page."

"I did what?" Oscar leaned forward politely.

"You faked it," Arnold repeated, "you faked it. You added it to the rest. You slipped it in."

"Why, Arnold," Oscar asked gently, "how can you say such a thing. I am your financial advisor. That would be a breach of trust."

"Cut the shit," Arnold's tone was like a scalpel. "That's a photocopy of a photocopy you gave Wade Vernon, and we have a copy of the personal contract you made with Vernon."

"Vernon?" Oscar stuttered.

"We know the whole setup," Arnold lost control, his voice became shrill. "We've got it all. Now I know why the Swiss bank didn't pay the Princess. You used all our Swiss account money."

From outside came the sound of splashing and the shrieks of delight of the young people in the pool.

"We've got it all," Reilly reaffirmed gravely. "I was in Switzerland. They confirmed to me that you used everything from our account."

Estelle had opened the corridor door and come in. It needed only a look at her face to know she was in on it.

"On account of you we almost fucked up the whole deal! And almost lost the yacht. Alexa wasn't paid! I trusted you," Arnold shouted. "I picked you up when you were nothing."

"Lie!" Estelle shrieked. "He was a tax accountant with a future, people respected him."

"He screwed me out of three hundred and fifteen thousand dollars, Reilly found the Swiss account missing three hundred fifteen thousand!" Arnold yelled at her.

"Lie!" Estelle shrieked.

"Three hundred and *fifty* dollars," Reilly corrected Arnold gravely, then had to correct himself hastily. "Three hundred and *fifty thousand* dollars."

"And don't try to bullshit your way out," Arnold bellowed. "We've got it all, all, all, the faked page, copies of your drafts on our Zurich account—"

Oscar was cornered.

"You sucked him dry!" Estelle was a real screamer. "Like

472

ou suck them all dry! You sucked the manhood out of him!
You're a vampire man!''

Scott slid down in the chair, his ass touched the floor.

"You're not denying it?" Arnold screamed in shock.
'You're trying to justify? Not even denying?"

"You made a drunkard out of him," Estelle could sob with
rightening volume.

"You admit?" Arnold asked shrilly. "You *admit?* Do I
ear right?"

Oscar held up a pudgy lumpy hand, calm, judicial, some of
is old training as a negotiator had stuck to him.

"I admit," Oscar said, as Estelle sank to the floor, an
nendurable spectacle, the mother figure turned into a blob of
lubber and sweat. "No problem," Oscar continued judiciously.

"No problem?" For once Arnold's writer curiosity took
recedence as he looked at Oscar with outraged incomprehen-
ion. Even Scott now pulled himself up a little as audiences in
he theater do when their interest has been suddenly reawakened.
Reilly regarded Oscar with open distaste. "No problem?"

"I'll merely kill myself," Oscar said. "I have procured
hese fast-acting pills." They all watched, stupefied. Oscar's
oice lowered. "The doctor, your doctor, Arnold, told me I
got nothing in the way of time left. The liver's shot, whoever
gives a thought to the liver? You? Me? Then all of a sudden
here's the liver you never thought about."

Estelle's sobbing was total, it was impossible to be aware
of anything else. "Drove him to it," her words raucous, thick
with mucus and tears.

"So when the doctor tells me I have practically no time
eft," Oscar's face was yellow green with blue circles under
he eyes, and in the light of what he was saying, he spoke
with a strange dignity, "I play the international money market, lire, D-marks, pounds, Swiss francs, drachmas, I lose,
wiped out. I leave this vale of tears and my Estelle, oh my
eloved Estelle, and my two children, sixteen and fourteen,

473

with nothing. I can't do that, Arnold. You understand. So I take a chance, a flier, with Arnel funds. Gold. Everybody says gold's sure, it will skyrocket. Gold skyrockets. I'm doing good, I'm almost there but then it falls. Gold is heavy.'' Oscar meant that as an intentional joke? ''Gold fluctuates. It's not me alone, just ask around you'll see there's hundreds caught on gold, people we know. Turkell? You know my good friend Mo Turkell?''

''Fuck Turkell,'' Arnold croaked.

''Mo Turkell loses Two,'' Oscar mumbled on, blind words in a lightless tunnel, who the hell was Mo Turkell? ''A Big Two, everything goes, New York town house inclusive, all Impressionist paintings.'' This time Arnold made a gargling sound the meaning of which was apparent even to Oscar, who came to the point. ''Power of attorney. All right. I faked page three, that is one hundred percent true.'' Estelle's sobbing had hit a steady pitch. ''But the deal with Vernon, finder's fee, bringing you together, will bring me a little something, not much but something which I will throw in to cover what I took from Arnel. All I can do but it gives me honor even if it leaves Estelle and the kids naked in the world.''

''What was going on in that jughead of yours? The empty account in Zurich. That couldn't be hidden. What were you thinking of there?'' Arnold asked incredulously.

''By that time I figure you are in a controlling position on the Associated board and making a fortune on the take-over,'' Oscar continued, ''and I would be dead. I figured you wouldn't find out before I was dead and then the deal goes through and—'' A complete blank. ''Where was I?''

''The deal went through and you were dead,'' Reilly said helpfully.

''I leave a letter to my old friend Arnold Elton,'' Oscar continued. ''I point out that the tough money, the Wade Vernon money, came through me. I point out a widow an two children—''

"You took three hundred and fifty thousand dollars out of Arnel," Reilly's words were like icicles. "And *you* point out?"

"No argument, I agree," Oscar sounded peculiarly reasonable. "I betrayed my sacred trust." He looked around blindly, stumbled across the room as they watched.

At the open garden window he made a huge effort to lift one leg over the sill. Nobody understood exactly what he had in mind. Despite Oscar's mightiest effort, he could lift the flabby leg barely halfway up to the sill.

Estelle shrieked, and almost fell on her face in her frantic effort to get to him. "No, Oscar! No!"

The other three didn't move, Oscar lost his balance and fell heavily on Estelle, who made a grunting sound as they both hit the floor.

"There's only a few inches fall from the window," Arnold said, "it's soft lawn, he couldn't hurt himself."

"Never mind," Oscar puffed as he and Estelle managed to sit up, then to Estelle, "did I hurcha? It's okay. No problem. The pills." His thick fingers tried to reach his pocket, got entwined in Estelle's dress. "The pills work even faster." Oscar actually found some pills, Estelle clawed out as his hand tried to bring the pills to his mouth. Arnold was on him, slapped Oscar's hand savagely, the pills were flying everywhere. Oscar got down on all fours and groped aimlessly.

"Stop it, goddamn it, stop it!" Arnold yelled.

Oscar had flopped over on his back and lay there as Estelle—her skirt hiked up high above her waist, she was wearing a bikini panty over which folds of her belly bulged—tried desperately to pull Oscar to an upright position.

"I'm orright," Oscar gurgled, "no problem. Other pills."

"Mary Sweet Mother of God!" Reilly murmured prayerfully. "The man keeps saying 'no problem.'"

Oscar's glasses dangled at a crazy angle, one earpiece broken. Without the cover of the lenses and thick black frame, Oscar's eyes were startlingly tiny and almost blotted out by the heavy pouches that bubbled up from his cheeks.

"No pills!" Arnold screamed at Oscar. "Pills are out!"

"A matter of strict Arnel policy," Scott murmured, "there will be exemplary discipline for all Arnel personnel taking cyanide pills."

"What were you thinking of?" Arnold yelled at Oscar.

"Who can think?" Oscar mumbled, still on his back, Estelle was valiantly trying to get him upright.

"You're dying. I think Estelle and the kids..."

Scott went over and managed Oscar to a sitting position, but had to support Oscar's back, or he'd have toppled over.

"Now I'll tell you what you're going to do, Oscar," Arnold even though hoarse, continued to yell, but avoided Reilly, who was now eyeing him suspiciously. "You're going to work for me." Reilly looked baffled. Arnold yelled even louder. "And I'll tell you something else you stupid sonofabitch!" For a moment there was a glimmer of hope in Reilly's eyes. "You're going to live long enough to pay me back!"

"How's he going to do that?" Reilly asked querulously.

"How? I'll tell you how!" Arnold shouted menacingly at Reilly. "We can still fuck up the books to take a tax loss," a stab of pain as he realized what he was saying, "of three fifty, we'll say the currency speculation was some other Arnel operation, a small picture, anything."

"Arnold!" As Arnold's meaning seeped through, Estelle let out a scream like forked lightning. Everybody in the neighborhood, including the kids in the pool, must have heard that. "Arnold! Arnold!" Now it must have sounded like a massacre.

"I'm off you!" Arnold bellowed at Estelle. Germaine and Michel were in the doorway. "How could you have thought," to Oscar, "I'd let Estelle and the kids go hungry if anything

476

happened to you?'' He turned fiercely back to Estelle. "And what were you thinking of?''

"Oh, Arnold. Forgive! Forgive! I told Oscar to go to you! But he says no. He can't face you. How can I blame him, you, our best friend.'' Estelle began sobbing again.

Jennifer, Robbie and the Plaything, their wet bodies barely covered by towels edged Michel and Germaine out of the doorway and stood dripping, fascinated. The Plaything looked as though she were wrestling with an imaginary opponent as she fought a losing battle to keep the towel around her ass and formidable breasts at the same time. Jennifer's breasts, hard and firm, were practically bare. Estelle, still on her knees, grabbed Arnold's hand, kissed it, covering it with tears and wet lips, moaning, "God bless you, Arnold Elton. How can you forgive us?''

Arnold disengaged himself from her only to be caught by Oscar, who, finally realizing what Arnold had said, his thick-lensed horn-rimmed glasses again dangling diagonally across his face, tried to grab Arnold's other hand, and kiss it. Arnold recoiled, Oscar reached out blindly and hooked on to Arnold's belt and pulled desperately, Arnold's pants slid down about his knees. Arnold, fighting madly not to fall, stumbled as Reilly grabbed him as he was now trying frantically to yank his pants up over his Lincoln green shorts but Oscar held on so fiercely, and what with Oscar's not inconsiderable weight, Arnold's pants ripped open at the crotch.

"That Reilly,'' Arnold was hunched over in a chair in the garden, Scott was on the grass nearby. A sure sign Scott had it made was that Arnold was openly deprecating a trusted member of Arnel Enterprises in his presence. "Even letting himself think for a minute it could've been Oscar and Estelle taking out a contract. What bugs me,'' morosely, "is that I went for it. I'm ready to believe anything now about anybody. I'm getting, shit, what am I getting, paranoiac?''

"Id," Scott offered, "Par-a-no*id*."

"Paranoid. Can you picture Oscar going to the boys and setting up a hit on me?"

"Don't even bother to unpack," Arnold had told Reilly, "you're tired, kid, just hop the next plane back to New York, somebody's got to watch the store there."

And Jennifer had driven Reilly to the airport.

"That no-good bastard," Arnold sat up straight, "that ungrateful sonofabitch."

Jolted out of his half doze, Scott sat up.

"Who? What? Did I miss something?" Scott asked.

"I know the sonofabitch didn't take the plane. He's shacked up with Jennifer at Juan-les-Pins in the Plaything's place. I could smell it, the way they were looking at each other."

"I forgot to tell you," Scott said, "Telly had a message for you. From Reilly. He telephoned from Paris between planes. He said to tell you Associated's beginning to go up. They released a rumor Hume is coming back."

"Oh. Then he did leave." Arnold added moodily, "I guess this has clouded my judgment a little."

"You write characters for all the people who are close to you," Scott said, "then you're surprised they don't behave the way you've written them. Aren't you pleased the stock's going up?"

"Yeah," Arnold muttered. "But I knew it would. It's the way I planned it."

Scott stretched. They could see the Cannes harbor clearly. A luxury liner was in port and customs' cutters shuttled busily back and forth. Passengers were being ferried from Cannes. Their twenty-four-hour cruise layover was ended. Perhaps Chittick was on one of the cutters.

"A Monsieur Dennis Hume," Germaine announced, as if she were presenting an engraved visiting card.

"Who?" Arnold got up in irritation.

"Monsieur Hume," Germaine said. It was as far as she got. Dennis made an operatic entrance.

"You look like the wrath of God," Arnold said. "Scott is my executive confidante."

Dennis had dark circles under his eyes. "You and I must talk. This is confidential."

"That's why they call him a confidante," Arnold said.

"You want him to hear what I have to say," Dennis was sometimes given to archaic language, "so be it."

"Get Monsieur Hume a comfortable chair," Arnold said.

Scott brought Dennis a chair, but Dennis didn't sit, he continued to keep his eyes fastened on Arnold in a burning stare.

"Drink?" Arnold asked.

"No," Dennis said, then to Scott, "perhaps Perrier, cool but not cold. I never drink anything cold."

Scott reflected on this a moment, crossed the garden and disappeared into the house.

"I don't know this confidante of yours, Elton," Dennis said, "but what I have to say to you is going to be tough shit."

"Confidantes get to share tough shit with their chiefs. He's going to be an important element in my new set-up."

"He hasn't got it," Dennis said. "He's a messenger boy."

Scott arrived with a long glass of cool but not cold Perrier with a slice of lemon. "I don't take lemon with my Perrier," Dennis said.

"You have an option, Mr. Hume," Scott said very politely. "You can either deposit that slice of lemon on the ashtray right next to your dish or you may, if you so choose, shove it up your ass."

"What is this?" Dennis demanded with great indignation. "I didn't come here to be insulted."

"I know that," Arnold said. "You came here to insult me."

"How can anybody insult you?" Dennis asked with fine scorn. "You have to begin with something worth insulting. I found out who was behind this—this—Pearl Harbor."

"Pearl Harbor?" Arnold asked.

"Stab in the back," Dennis said tightly. "Two diplomatic emissaries discussing peace while the American Navy has the shit kicked out of it . . ."

"Before you tell me what I am or you think I am let me tell you—it's all been squared. The District Attorney's office has already made a statement clearing you of all charges of tie-ups with the Mob."

"When did this happen?" Dennis asked coldly.

Arnold looked at his watch.

"Today, this morning."

"It hasn't happened yet," Dennis said icily. "I was just on the phone to Beverly Hills."

"It will happen," Arnold said calmly. "In the next few hours."

"So it was you, the sonofabitch who set up this whole mess," Dennis said. "You spread the shit about my so-called tie-up. You made me go through the agony of the last few weeks. It was all a goddamn stock manipulation—and I thought— You are about the coldest—"

"You've got this wrong, Dennis," Arnold cut him off. "I'm the guy who saved your life. You were marked for a blow-away. They would never have found your body—maybe a skeleton in Death Valley."

There was a long silence.

"Jesus," Dennis said in awe. "You're the one with connections."

"There's only one thing you have to remember," Arnold said. There was a dramatic change in the relationship between the two men. Suddenly Dennis was subtly subservient. Arnold was directing things. "I'm your friend, Dennis," (shades of

Alfredo). "You were being stupid. Don't do that again. Stay away from Clover because now she's doubly dangerous."

"Where is she?" Dennis asked.

"You don't want to know," Arnold said.

"I want to see her once more," Dennis said. "I just—"

"Dennis," Arnold said. "Go near that lady again and nobody'll be able to help you. Nobody, understand?"

"Tell me where she is," Dennis groaned.

"She's here," Arnold said. "You'll never see her again. It's simple. If you ever get within gun-shot range of her, you won't live long enough to get to her. Now you're getting on the next plane out of here. By the time you arrive, your troubles will be over. You'll be immediately reinstalled as Executive Vice-President at a higher salary. You'll have complete freedom of action, you'll get more points profit on every production. Now, what was it you wanted to tell me besides that I'm the biggest bastard you know?"

"What time is that plane?" Dennis asked.

"Poor Dennis," Arnold said as he and Scott sat in the complete peace of the Riviera summer evening. "He was looking forward to wiping up the floor and walls with me. It's never a hundred percent as you imagine it. Maybe I should have given him more of a chance to let it out on me. It's liable to interfere with his functioning as a top executive. Maybe I should have worked it so he could call me a coldhearted sonofabitch."

"He did," Scott said, then looked at Arnold quizzically. "You let him think you were one of the Mob."

"He's learned his lesson," Arnold said. "He won't tell anybody. But I think I should have played it more like I was broken up by his accusations. I should have given him more satisfaction."

"There'll be plenty of other opportunities," Scott said.

Telly suddenly appeared.

"How pleasant it is to look at you," Scott said. "There's another world after all. Books, music, flowers, people talking to each other passionately about what's wrong with the world."

Telly smiled softly. Her smile enveloped Scott, covered him with affection. Arnold was uncomfortable. He was not used to men and women speaking to each other that way. He felt there should be some basic hostility between men and women, provided you wanted good fucking.

"Inspector Bellarosa called," Telly said. "He apologized for having to pull his men off, but they were on the trail of a suspect. Now they've given up, but he wants you to keep him informed so he can do whatever is needed."

"Thank him," Arnold said. "But it should be solved in the next four or five hours. What else?"

"There's a telegram which was phoned in for you," Telly said.

"Read it to me."

"You've asked me not to read personal communications in the presence of outsiders," Telly said.

"There are no outsiders here," Arnold said.

Telly shot a frightened look at Scott, who tried to muster a reassuring smile.

" 'Arriving noon,' " Telly read, " 'have reservations Cannes Résidence. Urgent we see you this afternoon.' It's signed 'Beejay-Margaret.' "

Arnold got up so suddenly his chair fell over.

"Get yourself back to the *Delphi*," he ordered Telly. "Tell Krystina I'm tied up until late tonight. Don't frighten her but make goddamn sure she doesn't leave the yacht no matter what." Telly had started to scribble it down in the notebook she carried with her constantly, but at that, she stopped scribbling. "Dougherty mustn't leave the yacht. Nobody, except Robbie and Jennifer, are to come aboard. You'd better stay on the yacht, too. Scott is going to be tied up for the rest of the day. And night.''

"We're having dinner at that lovely little place in old Cannes," Telly said to Scott. "They're holding a table for us."

"What lovely little place?" Arnold demanded.

"A tiny place I know," Telly confronted Arnold full face.

One of Arnold's biggest pleasures was collecting lovely tiny restaurants that no one else knew and which then became his. "Fabulous little place I found," Arnold would toss off to American guests, "not much to look at but it has real ambiance. And a great chef. It won't last long," ruefully, "it's too good. Once the American tourists discover it..." And there was an important unspoken Arnel house rule. No one working for Arnel was to go to those fabulous places once they became "his." Reserved exclusively for Arnold Elton.

"I've been saving it for Scott and me," Telly said. "It's the sort of place once *you* go, they'll post Monsieur Elton's photo with glowing quotes from him after which their prices will triple, their cuisines diminish, their charm vanish."

Telly of course must have known that was tantamount to handing in her notice. When any Arnel personnel upped and quit, Arnold had a shattering sense of loss. He felt his world challenged. Nobody quit Arnel. They got thrown out.

"Haven't you shown Telly that contract?" Arnold asked Scott.

Scott's hand sneaked down into his jeans pocket, pulled out the now badly crumpled bit of paper, smoothed it out, handed it to her. She read it carefully, looked up.

"That's quite a sum, isn't it?" Telly said, disturbed.

"I promise you, tomorrow, this will be over by tomorrow," Arnold said, "he'll take you to the Moulin de Mougins or any other three-star restaurant you may want, as guest of Arnel of course."

"That little place in old Cannes is more Scott and me," Telly said. And to Scott, "You're the one who made *me* see what it really is for me here."

"Do you understand what it means to make your living from free-lance writing?" Arnold demanded of Telly. "It was Scott himself who told me about the best of them, George Bernard Shaw, Sean O'Casey, Yeats, James Joyce. Not one of them had five pounds sterling they could call their own at any one time before the age of forty."

"The pound," Scott said, "was stronger then than it is now."

But Arnold would not be denied. "This will give Scott a security he's never had."

"Security," Telly bounced that back to Scott too, "you once called that notion the quicksand of this society. You said the harder one struggles, the deeper one sinks."

"You see how quotable I am?" Scott said. "The contract says I could opt out anytime I want."

"No one opts out of three-star restaurants and luxury living," Telly said. "I'm now quoting Arnold Elton."

"Arnold Elton's life is in danger, see, love?"

"I rather think when it's all over," Telly said, "we may find it's *our* lives that have been in danger."

Arnold turned to Scott. "I'll pick you up at seven-thirty at the Café du Festival."

Cannes Résidence had to be the most inexpensive acceptable hotel in Cannes, a sort of self-service hostelry stripped of everything not functional. There was no night clerk, only a wall board with dangling keys, a slot for the name of the occupant. After six, there was no house telephone so there was no way of calling to say you were downstairs.

Arnold scanned the board three times before he found the suite of Ms. Pitchford, Ms. Heatherington.

Ms.

Room 42.

That could be any floor. In these little French hotels, the room number didn't give the slightest hint of the floor. He stared at the card and wondered what his life would have been with Beejay, what Beejay looked like now.

The elevator shuddered upward creaking and groaning, lurched to a halt. Arnold barely had time to step out before it moved down.

The hallway was dingy and badly lit. He momentarily forgot the room number. It was on the third floor.

Arnold stood before 42 for a long time. There were sounds from within, the music of American voices. Women's voices, speaking so softly they couldn't be heard or understood.

Margaret answered the door.

"Come in," she said. He tried to remember who it was who had once said to him—Had it been Blake?—"You've surrounded yourself with beautiful women."

Beejay sat out on a small terrace overlooking the nearby railroad tracks, the back of an apartment house, a straggly palm tree. The Mediterranean was now a deep blue, full of brooding dark promise.

The new easy-flowing style in women's clothes was made for Beejay. She stood alongside Margaret. The two would hold any eye. Beejay in her middle forties was stunning.

"I've got something to say," Margaret started it off even before they'd asked him to be seated or offered him a drink.

"There was no reason to bring Beejay into this," Arnold said to Margaret. "Whatever it is we could've handled it. You know I've always been fair with you—"

"Fair," Margaret said bitterly. "Last four years you've been keeping me at the Bel Air house alone, a full-grown woman, I'm a dog-sitter, taking care of a poodle dog named Joker, you telephone only to make sure I'm there waiting and walking that French poodle—"

"I paid you," Arnold said, shocked, "you had the whole

485

house and pool, there wasn't much work, it was practically a vacation."

"Vacation? Rattling around in that big old house all by myself, seeing nobody, my life slipping away," Margaret said. "I only began to understand these last few weeks when Beejay came down."

"You and Beejay been seeing each other the last few weeks?" Arnold asked.

"Your faithful bloodhound Wacszinski didn't tell you?" Beejay demanded. "I was sure he had us tailed. I don't want you to bother Margaret anymore," Beejay added. "I want you to call Wacszinski off. He's been making her life miserable."

"I don't know why you came. I've got too much going to try to guess. I'm perfectly willing to refund your ticket and expenses—"

Beejay asked incredulously, "Why on earth would you want to do that?"

"Because I know you've had a rough time," Arnold said dryly. "I know your father left you nothing."

"Your intelligence setup is functioning badly," Beejay said. "Several weeks before Dad died he called to tell me he had terminal cancer and asked me to come. I did. I've been with him to the end."

"You were with him in Beverly Hills?" Arnold asked, stunned. Wacszinski had been so positive.

"After all he was my father," Beejay said. "But he didn't call me solely because he was dying. I don't know whether this will be of interest to you, but the Chairman, in his own way, was an honorable man, he'd been a true believer. The Nixon-Agnew business got to him. He understood political opportunism—politicians have to compromise and squirm. But not venal dishonesty. He really wanted me with him to make amends. He bent over several decades backward. He even told me I'd been right to belong to the Student Union and to vote for Helen Gahagan Douglas."

"The rumors were he didn't leave you anything," Arnold was annoyed. "We figured if he had, there might have been something for Robbie."

"He left me éverything," Beejay said dryly. "I suspect I have more money at my disposal than you do. As for Robbie, Dad asked me to give him whatever I thought was right, despite the fact you made no real attempt to have Robbie know him."

"Jesus," Arnold was furious at the thought that Beejay probably did have more money than he, "he never once gave the slightest sign he even knew we were alive."

Beejay's manner changed abruptly, "Robbie and Jennifer wanted so badly to do a film," she said. "Robbie asked me for money. Unfortunately I didn't have it then. I had only what I made as a social worker in San Francisco. I don't understand why you didn't give them the money."

"Because that's not the way it is," Arnold said sharply. He'd permit no sentiment to intrude on him there. It was the core of his life. "You want to break into the film world, you've got to hustle."

"Why?"

"Because that's the way it is," Arnold said.

"I'm going to offer Robbie and Jennifer the money," Beejay said quietly.

"I think it's wrong," Arnold said.

"It never ever even once in your whole life," Beejay told Arnold, "occurred to you that maybe you were wrong, or could be."

"Why, that's it," Margaret said to Beejay with a sudden understanding, "he acts like he's so right all the time, a person just didn't have a chance to stop and think maybe her life was wrong, why I'm only now beginning to see the way I was in that big house, I was pretending I *lived* there, I was playing I was white, I was the lady of the house, he took advantage of that."

"I never took advantage of anybody. I paid you well. You could have left anytime."

"And left all those years behind me," Margaret said. "Only we came here to talk about those stolen jewels, that's the reason you wanted me here."

"There's no need for that," Beejay said hastily. "I came because I want to pay you the full value of what was stolen from you."

"Now why on earth would you want to do that?" Arnold mimicked Beejay.

"I don't want Wacszinski or any of your crew-cut goons bludgeoning anyone," Beejay said tersely. "I want it dropped completely."

"You wasted your time," Arnold said stiffly. Margaret avoided his eyes.

"Wacszinski's been at her like a bull," Beejay said.

"I've called him off," Arnold snapped at her.

"Since we're here, I'd like to talk to Robbie and Jennifer," Beejay said.

"So would I," Margaret said.

When Arnold hesitated, Beejay said, "I *am* his mother."

Arnold shrugged. "By all means see him."

"Good," said Beejay grimly.

Scott waited for Arnold at an outdoor table of the Festival Café. The sidewalk was crowded. There was a sprinkling of elegance as dinner-jacketed evening-dressed English couples hurried on their way to before-dinner drinks, dinner and roulette at the Palm Beach Casino.

"How'd it go?" Scott asked.

"I don't want to talk about it," Arnold said.

"I took the Monteverdi and cruised around. I hoped to pick up a white 604. I did. Maybe *the* 604. I parked at the first

488

side street there, rue du Canada.'' Scott gestured up ahead. "I think I saw him cruise past and enter rue du Canada and stop there. Visibility is not all that good because of the crowds on the sidewalk.''

"Yeah," Arnold grunted, "we could've taken out in the Monte and maybe trapped the sonofabitch in the 604 and maybe the sonofabitch could've told us who it was hired him and who took a contract out on us, and I wouldn't have had to pay the boys an arm and a leg and if I ate enough I could shit too so let's you and me go and deliver to this high-class Harvard-trained bagman my arm and my leg.''

"No ideas who it might be?" Scott asked.

"Blank," Arnold said.

"Well, it's your arm and your leg," Scott said philosophically as they left.

"Hey—will you slow down?" There was a difference in Scott's manner. His irritation was intimate. "Rolls or no Rolls" (they were in Krystina's car), "you're doing over a hundred on this lousy ocean road.''

Although the French never swim at night, because of the heat there were still bathers on the Juan-les-Pins beach.

Every now and then a car darted out wildly from where it was parked with two wheels on the sidewalk. There were several near misses.

"Death-wish Elton," Scott muttered. "Was it that bad with your ex-wife and housekeeper?"

"They ganged up on me. And Margaret must have had a man all these years. She must've teamed up with him, they pulled the robbery together—" Arnold said.

"Jewels out of a safe she's house-sitting? She would have known she'd be caught.''

"She knew I wouldn't prosecute. She was right. And my ex-wife came to make sure I didn't prosecute.''

"How's your Harvard-trained Mafioso going to take me?"

"If he doesn't like you, you split."

They were almost forty-five minutes late.

"We play it cool," Arnold said as they entered the sub-dued elegance of Eden Roc Restaurant, and despite his churning gut, Arnold deliberately moved slowly. Across the dining room, at a table with a view of the sea, Saintsbury and Clover were waiting.

The restaurant was bursting with people Arnold knew, Hollywood agents on vacation, aging stars, rock musicians.

And Geisy, white-haired, pink-cheeked and mellow. With gaiters he'd look like the Archbishop of Canterbury. His companion was a gerontological sexpot with a see-through blouse. Geisy was in television, which was one reason he and Arnold hadn't crossed each other over the years.

"Celebrating," Geisy announced. "My series just went over the two-year boiling point."

"Scott doesn't appreciate what 'going over the two-year boiling point' in a TV series means," Arnold said. "He's an outsider."

"It means more or less several million dollars for me," Geisy explained benevolently.

He introduced them to his companion.

"Arnold Elton. One of my achievements I'm proud of. I gave Arnold Elton his first job." Geisy beamed.

"Let's face it," Arnold said. "He made me." So far there'd been at least ten other people Arnold knew about, including Kate, who'd claimed publicly they'd made Arnold Elton. "What's the name of your series?"

Geisy purred. "You're going to like this. It's called *Jake the Plumber.*"

"Do a sequel," Arnold said. "Jake the Plumber and the Cunt. It's a natural."

Neither he nor his girl friend laughed. "American television is not ready for that yet," Geisy said stiffly.

"Still checking out the obits on New Year's Day?" Arnold asked.

"They've been coming too fast lately. I guess it's that time of my life," Geisy said. "I can't keep up with them. I've given it up."

"Some boobs for a sixty-two-year-old," Arnold said as they went on.

"Although why a sixty-two-year-old woman shouldn't have beautiful boobs I don't know," observed Scott. "Don't tell me the gorgeous dark girl is the table we're headed for?"

"And don't forget the guy with her is from the gorgeous Mafia."

"I've never spoken to a Mafioso in person before," Scott remarked. "They saw us when we first came in."

"So we kept the bastard waiting. For my arm and leg I'm entitled—Clover!"

She got up tall, beautiful, spectacularly curvesome, kissed Arnold on the lips affectionately. In that same burst of nostalgic affection, she seemed about to kiss Scott, but changed her mind after a look from Saintsbury.

"Scott Goldman, my right-hand man. This is Clover."

"The future Mrs. Saintsbury," Michael amended. "We're getting married in Sicily. I don't believe in long engagements." He shook hands with Scott, accepting him without hesitation.

Arnold handed Clover a book.

"That's my latest paperback."

Clover was touched. "What a pretty title. *Love's Labor Won*." She looked inside, and read, " 'To Clover, Nothing more beautiful the world over, With love, Arnold Elton.' " She looked up, almost in tears. "Now that's what I call sweet as sugar pie—wouldn't you, Michael?"

"I guess so," Michael was not enthusiastic.

"I'm sorry we took so long getting across the restaurant,"

Arnold said. "This place is full of people from my past, some from my present but none from my future."

"Oh, I wouldn't say none from your future," Michael said dryly, but changed the mood quickly with a quick glance around. "There are beautiful people here, I'll give them that." He took Clover's hand tenderly. "I have my own most beautiful people."

"You sure have," Arnold said as he moaned to himself, Oh Christ. Why did I start this bullshit stalling? When will he tell me? Who wants to kill me?

Fear covered him like cool spray. We are about to exchange an enormous chunk of money and he is about to hand over to me a dreadful secret.

Arnold, perhaps from looking at Saintsbury, was convinced it would be dreadful. Bizarre. Saintsbury. A pleasant-looking young man, well-dressed, not quite accustomed to casual Riviera attire, looking with open pride at the impressively beautiful empty woman with him. Michael said courteously, "Would you boys like a drink first or are you ready to order?"

"I guess we could stand a drink," Arnold would play the game to the end.

Clover surprised them by taking over graciously.

"Monsieur," she pointed to Arnold, "will have a clamato tequila," then to Scott, "will you join us in our pre-wedding champagne?"

"I wouldn't think of drinking anything else."

The way Scott said it made Michael notice him. Clover smiled approval, her teeth super dazzling white.

"We have tequila," the waiter apologized to Clover, "but I have never heard of clamato."

"It's just the juice of tomato with clam broth," Clover drawled.

"I regret," the waiter was destroyed, "the broth of clams with the juice of tomatoes is completely unknown in France."

"Never mind," Arnold fought off an urge to bellow in rage and frustration, "I'll have a bull-shot."

Clover gestured for Arnold to hold it. "You-all have clams in cans?" She spoke with a new authority. The waiter nodded hesitantly. "Now you just take the juice out of those cans, mix it with equal parts of the juice of tomato then add tequila, all of it nicely chilled." Clover smiled in satisfaction at Arnold. Michael looked on proudly. "And Mister Elton will have a nice thick steak ra-are but not cold."

"Is that what you'd like?" Michael asked Arnold irritably.

"That's it." It was the first minuscule satisfaction Arnold had had since they'd arrived at Eden Roc. With what he was about to pay, at least the sonofabitch should know he and Clover had been intimate enough for her to know what he'd order.

"I'll have a *tournedos* rare, too," Scott told the waiter. "And don't keep the food waiting for the drinks. We are pressed for time."

"No, no," Michael held Clover's hand, he couldn't seem to get enough of her. "I never hurry when it comes to food." He kissed her fingers as though he were kissing the Pope's ring. "And I never talk business when my blood sugar's low."

"Never negotiate when your blood sugar's low," Scott said. "That's the sort of thing they should teach in places like Harvard Business School!" Arnold wondered whether Scott was very brave or very foolish. After all he was talking to a Mafioso.

"They do teach it at Harvard Business School," Michael said coolly. "I'm a graduate."

"So I heard," Scott said. "We're alumni." Arnold gave up.

"Can we start talking?" Arnold pleaded. He couldn't keep it up. "*My* blood sugar's low."

"Have some bread and butter while we're waiting," Michael

493

said to Arnold, then turned to Clover. "Or do you think they might have some Jewish salami for our friend?"

This sonofabitch, this Salvatore-Saintsbury-Harvard-Business-School monster is shafting me. Jewish salami at a place like Eden Roc. The boys knew a lot about you.

"But you do look kinda white around the gills." Clover hastily buttered some bread. "You havin' trouble? That deal you-all were worried about, is it workin'?" Solicitously she handed Arnold the buttered bread.

Arnold forced what he thought was a smile but which surfaced as a silent belch. "Yeah, it worked out," Arnold said. Saintsbury had been watching intensely.

"French bread," Scott said, "and Normandy butter. The bread is not only baked daily but baked three to four different times. The Parisians prefer what they call the third oven-baking. It's supposed to be the best."

"I've heard that French bread is so good," Michael continued, "because of the oil in the skin of the baker's hands. They've never been able to duplicate that in machine-made bread. I think I'll begin with their *omelette aux fine herbes* for openers. Uncle Millie says it's worth the trip for that alone. I suggest you gentlemen try it."

"No thanks," Arnold said, "I've got to watch the cholesterol. Uncle Millie was here?"

"Is here," Michael said.

Arnold felt a chill, shivered despite himself. "How is he?"

"You'll see for yourself," Michael said. "He's waiting for us at the cottage."

The chill covered his whole body.

"Uncle Millie's at the cottage?" Arnold wheezed. "Waiting for us?"

Michael looked at him carefully. "Of course he's waiting for us. You okay?"

"I'm okay," Arnold said.

494

"Uncle Millie seldom dines in public," Michael explained. "Especially in places like Eden Roc."

"Sure," Arnold said.

Fortunately the waiter came with the drinks.

"To the future newlyweds," Scott proposed the toast with a glass of champagne. They all drank.

Arnold's clamato and tequila was ghastly. He nodded emphatically to the waiter who stood by, his whole body twisted into Is it what Monsieur wanted? Arnold gave him a hearty thumbs up. Everyone relaxed.

While waiting for the food, Michael and Scott reminisced about Cambridge, Mass.

Arnold listened distantly.

How much longer, he moaned internally.

Finally the food came. The waiter had made a mistake, he brought an *omelette aux fines herbes* for Arnold also. They went through the whole ritual of a four-course Cordon Bleu dinner.

Now I am dying inside, dying, Arnold moaned to himself, and I mustn't let Michael see that it's killing me. Michael was playing it all deliberately, with Harvard Business School cool. Only he didn't need Harvard for that; he came by it naturally. You know who wants me killed, Arnold murmured to himself, and look, you pretend to flip out for the pastry wagon.

They spent minutes deciding between the chocolate *Pet de Nonne* (Nun's Fart) and the wild strawberry tart, even Scott who might have said something to hurry it up. But maybe Scott was right to play it as deliberate as Michael did.

"He never takes anything sweet," Clover indicated Arnold to the waiter. "Then that will be three coffees for the rest of us." With a tolerant smile toward Arnold, "He doesn't take coffee, either."

"Not even a false coffee?" the waiter urged Arnold politely, "without the caffeine?"

"No." Arnold was barely able to speak.

They lingered over their coffee. Everyone else in the restaurant had gone. Geisy waved good-bye to Arnold, and his see-through sixty-two-year-old chick with the gorgeous boobs clasped her hands over her head in what? Congratulations? Keep it up? You're the champ?

Finally the check came and Michael insisted on paying. Arnold fought him bitterly. It was his show. Michael added it up carefully, "You'd be surprised how they make mistakes even in high-class joints like this. And, of course, always in their favor."

"The prices are so astronomical here they don't have to cheat on the check," Scott said dryly.

Arnold made a mental note. Scott must be told that Arnel personnel never remarked about the price of a restaurant. Things like that they understood instinctively, but intellectuals like Scott had to learn.

They sauntered out of the restaurant. The air was heavy with night-blooming scents. The Mediterranean sighed sleepily as its wavelets let themselves down gently over the sandy shore.

Michael had managed to get an Eden Roc bungalow for the night.

"How'd you work it? I hear these bungalows are reserved years in advance." Another thing Scott shouldn't have done, it implied Arnel couldn't have arranged it.

"We're very friendly with the owner management," Michael said casually.

Once inside, Clover turned on the lights. Arnold froze. In the next room was Uncle Millie.

"It's the most luxurious hotel accommodation I've ever seen. And the most beautifully done." I must tell Scott about that too, Arnold thought dimly. He's got to learn to take it in his stride, not let them impress you. "Imagine," Scott went on, "signed Miró lithos, in a hotel."

"They *are* pretty, aren't they?" Clover's manner became indulgent. "Why I swear, Arnold, you look real peak-ed. You sure you-all are all right?"

"I've had a rough day, is all."

"You-all still smoke too much," Clover scolded him gently. "Now if you-all will excuse me—"

"You'll be okay?" Michael asked her in concern.

"I have me an interestin' book." Clover held up *Love's Labor Won*, smiled teasingly to Arnold, "and I do hear it's quite a scandalous thing."

"Isn't she something?" Michael asked softly after Clover had gone.

"She certainly is," Scott said admiringly.

"Maybe you better take notes when we talk to Uncle Millie," Michael said to Scott; he pointed to Arnold. "Our friend here doesn't seem to be functioning too well."

"That won't be necessary." Arnold added too quickly, "But I don't think we better keep Uncle Millie waiting any longer. I know he hates to wait."

"You may be right," Michael conceded.

He gestured toward a short corridor. Arnold and Scott followed him silently.

The large room—which was really the living room of the bungalow—was unlit, but there was the silhouette of a man's figure against the window. Michael turned a soft light on.

Uncle Millie, silver-handsome, unsmiling, looked over, his eyes avoiding Arnold.

"Uncle Millie," Michael introduced, "this is Scott Goldman—"

"How do you do?" Uncle Millie shook Scott's hand warmly. "I've read a couple of your books. You're a fine writer. Of course I'm no expert."

"Uncle Millie runs a hotel in Las Vegas," Michael explained to Scott.

"I've heard of Uncle Millie," Scott said cooly. "Thanks for your good opinion of me."

Uncle Millie nodded. He still hadn't acknowledged Arnold's presence. "I liked the one with the Algerian war as a background," Millie said to Scott. "But what are you doing here?"

"He's my executive assistant," Arnold said quickly. "Of course if you'd rather not have him here—"

"That's up to you," Uncle Millie said to Arnold coldly.

"Then he'll stay." Arnold moved to Uncle Millie with an extended hand which Uncle Millie didn't take.

"What's wrong, Uncle Millie?" Arnold asked.

"It's even worse if you don't know," Uncle Millie said quietly.

Arnold had a flash image of Uncle Millie with a length of piano wire. "You double-crossed me."

"How?" Arnold backed away in panic. Were they going to kill him there? Throw his body in the Mediterranean? "How did I cross you, Uncle Millie?" Arnold asked plaintively. Then got hold of himself. No. They couldn't kill him there. Not with Scott a witness and Clover in the next room.

"Oh, I'll tell you how," Uncle Millie said dryly. "I'm not bashful. Number One. You used confidential information I gave you about an important film personality without once thinking of cutting me in on my fair share."

"But I thought you were returning a favor," Arnold protested in panic. "You told me yourself. You owed me a favor."

"That was personal," Millie said. "For use in your personal life. You should of told me it was for business. For business it's a different story."

Arnold started to protest again, looked at Uncle Millie's face, then at Saintsbury's, changed his mind, waited in silence.

"Number Two," Uncle Millie went on sternly. "Who first

gave you the idea for a studio-takeover? Who first talked to you how the studio was worth five times the value of its stock—or have you forgotten that conversation too?''

"But this is a totally different kind of deal," Arnold argued. "We don't plan to break up the studio—"

"I'm not interested in your plans," Uncle Millie said.

Arnold looked around, without realizing it moved to a corner. They would kill him anyway. They had ways of handling details such as witnesses, getting rid of the body.

"It was you, Uncle Millie?" Arnold asked, his voice pitched high with near hysteria.

"I what?" Uncle Millie asked icily.

"Ordered a hit on me." Arnold was barely able to say it.

Uncle Millie looked at him outraged. "Are you meshuga? I'm your friend." He looked at Arnold in disgust. "And you're thirty years behind the times. I'm the man who is saving your life."

"I don't follow," Arnold whispered.

"I'll show you the way," Uncle Millie said. "I'm willing to forget the past. I'm thinking of the future." Arnold felt life return, heart beating, lungs pulling oxygen. He was going to live. "I'm a businessman now and I behave like one," Uncle Millie said.

"Yes," Arnold said.

"I came here to turn over some information to you," Uncle Millie said. "For a fair return which you should have offered in the first place."

"All right." Well. Here it was. Now we'll know. "How much, Uncle Millie?"

"No, no, not money," Uncle Millie said patiently.

"Not money?" Arnold was shaking.

"Maybe you'd better take notes," Uncle Millie said. "I don't want to keep repeating myself. This is a complicated deal."

"Okay," Arnold managed to say. He accepted a pad and pen Michael handed him.

"You now hold a controlling interest in Associated," Uncle Millie declared as if for the record. "You will sign over the controlling interest to me. Write that down."

Arnold started to write, his hands unsteady, stopped. "I can only sign what I own," Arnold said numbly, "which is four percent. I have power of attorney for five percent. A Texas group owns seven percent. Sixteen in all."

"Just sign over your four percent," Uncle Millie said. "We'll make our own arrangement for the rest when the time comes. And you'll be on the Board. We'll arrange it. Each time before you vote on any important issue you'll consult with us."

" 'Consult'?" Arnold knew he sounded stupid. "Who's 'us'?"

"Me. Others," Uncle Millie said tersely. "We'll meet you in Vegas whenever necessary. You'll carry out our recommendations. But don't worry. We'll pay you the market price for your stock as of date of sale. You follow?"

"I follow," Arnold said. "You're taking control away from me. I'll be your boy on the board."

"How do you want to do this?" Uncle Millie asked. "Pleasant?"

There was a long wait. Scott was an interested spectator.

"Pleasant." Arnold whispered finally.

"I'm glad," Uncle Millie said. "It could be not pleasant."

"I know," Arnold said.

"You played it wise-ass. If there's one thing I despise it's wise-ass." Uncle Millie glanced down at some notes he had. "You'll be paid well for your activities on the board in our behalf."

Arnold was drenched with sweat. "I'll cooperate to the best of my ability."

Uncle Millie made a note of that in a cheap notebook he had. Nothing fancy. A fifty-cent pad. "A. agrees to all conditions," Uncle Millie said out loud as he wrote. "Now," Uncle Millie's tone stayed businesslike. "Here's the information you wanted—" He read. "On Monday June sixteenth of this year certain professionals were approached in Los Angeles with a view to arranging a hit on you and your wife."

"So it was Krystina and me," Arnold's head felt like a heavy inanimate object but he managed to move enough to make a semblance of a nod of agreement.

"Considering who you are, and your relationship with me," Uncle Millie went on, "the matter was taken up with me—lucky for you. Even though you hardly ever come to see me, I had certain feelings for you. I didn't like the idea of a hit on you and your wife—you follow?"

"I follow. I was lucky it came to you," Arnold said. "But who was out to get me? Please tell me, Uncle Millie."

Uncle Millie behaved strangely. He cut Arnold off with an odd urgency.

"*That* you will not hear from me," Uncle Millie said. "There is a certain amount of emotion for me. Michael will tell you. Mr. Goldman, good-bye."

Uncle Millie nodded to Scott and Michael and left hurriedly.

"What's that about?" Arnold turned to Michael. "What does he mean—certain amount of emotion for him? How is that possible?"

"You'll see," Michael said softly. It was evident that he would not be hurried. "I've never felt there's any mystic relationship between blood relatives. If you study East Indian history, the Mogul period especially, you'll find no reigning Mogul monarch ever permitted any male relative even as far as a fourth cousin to live to become an adult."

"Oh Christ," Arnold broke down. The price had been

fixed and it was far more than he'd dreamed. He was forever at their mercy. "Tell me." There was no longer any reason to play it cool. It was over. Now he was begging.

"I'm not enjoying this," Michael said coldly. "This is a transaction I'm carrying out because Uncle Millie asked me. I think you should know exactly what happened and how." Arnold nodded submissively. "The clients who contacted our people for the hit, couldn't come through with the down payment. It was too big, and that's why Uncle Millie heard about it in the first place. So it was decided to keep an eye on them, get in touch with you and work out this arrangement with you. It was felt that was a better solution all around. As Uncle Millie said, nobody particularly liked the idea of you and your wife being hit. So some go-between over here, a friend of yours I believe, was told to drop enough on you so you'd figure you would be better off coming to us."

"Alfredo," Arnold mumbled.

"I don't want to know who it was," Michael stopped him.

"It was so roundabout I almost didn't figure it out."

"You would have been gotten to," Michael reassured him grimly. "I mention this only because it's got to be clear the go-between is completely neutral. He doesn't benefit. Only from our friendship."

"Oh, Michael, Jesus Christ," Arnold pleaded. "Tell me." Wildly. "Who, goddamn it, who wanted Krys and me killed?"

"If you were thinking cooly you should have figured it out by now," Michael said.

"The clients who tried to take a contract out on you were your daughter Jennifer and your son Robbie. The price asked for the double hit, by the professionals, was a percentage of the inheritance which would be coming to them from you. Your children refused that."

"Where's the can?" Arnold asked.

Michael escorted Arnold swiftly to the toilet. Arnold barely made it in time to lift the toilet seat before he vomited, the convulsions tearing at his guts.

He could hear the murmur of Scott and Michael.

"He didn't suspect them?" Michael asked.

"Who would?"

"Bad thinking. Elton had arranged trust funds for his kids with principal they couldn't touch until they were forty. It was obvious he didn't trust them. And Uncle Millie knew them as little kids and loved them. He was shocked. He thought Elton was stupid with his kids—an insulting will which gave them nothing in the hand, and there was a pregnant stepmother threatening the inheritance."

Arnold lurched back in as Clover, irresistible in white pajamas, appeared at the door. Michael gestured reassurance and although slightly disturbed, she withdrew.

"There's more," Michael said tersely. "We kept a close eye on the kids, who shopped around for a cheaper hit, as we knew they would. They finally glommed on to some stumble-bum who's been on the stock-car circuit, punch-drunk from too many wrecks, works with cars, been busted a couple of times for small stuff. The reason Uncle Millie and I came over so fast was to pass that on to you, because this guy is nuts and dangerous and he might have hit the two of you before we could make our proposition to you."

"He almost succeeded," Scott said.

"Uncle Millie expects you to handle the whole mess without scandal," Michael said. "We need you on the board. In other words he wants you not to do anything which would make it impossible to elect you to the board."

Arnold nodded abjectly.

They took the same road they'd come on, twisting along the brooding shoreline. Suddenly Arnold pulled over to the oceanside, stopped, staggered out, scrambled over some rocks. Scott waited just outside the car.

Arnold peered at the gloomy blackness of the Mediterranean, stood precariously on a boulder, then let fly with a sound that must have come from prehistoric times. It welled out of him, towered above the subdued seething whisper of the small tide, a scream, a roar, despair, death, anguish, "Arrhhharrhhhhh——"

A young couple who had been fucking peacefully a few feet away in the security of darkness scurried out in panic, holding their clothes, the girl whimpering in fear as they ran.

Lights popped up everywhere with surprising speed. There was a crazy blind agitation, like an ant heap suddenly disturbed.

Arnold sat on the rock, hunched over. Scott came over.

"I don't want to talk about this either," Arnold said. "I don't want to wonder whose fault it was."

"Okay," Scott said.

"We've got to stop them."

"Right."

"Once the cops are in, it would be too late."

"For what?"

"For my kids, goddamn it, for my fucking kids."

Arnold coughed, made sounds that came from somewhere low.

4

The Croisette was bubbling with life, crowded with the summer people who'd worked all year for this month on the Riviera. It was past midnight but cool and there was a delicious breeze.

The Iles Lérins across the bay were lit up, the Abbey glowed. Cannons boomed in the distance as the nightly tourist attraction, a sound and light reenactment of the storming of the island fortress, wound up. Ice cream vendors dished out the creamy Italian ice cream to patient queues. Children were out bursting with the exaggerated energy that came from staying up much beyond their normal bedtimes.

Arnold and Scott walked away from the crowd to the darkened rue du Canada.

The white 604 was there several cars behind the Monteverdi. Arnold and Scott froze. There was a small movement in the 604 as a hulking shadow of a head and shoulders looked behind and, it seemed, directly at them, slid back to his place behind the wheel, patient as death.

"Go to the cops, Arnold," Scott whispered. "Tell them we've got the crazy white 604. They'll keep it quiet."

"No. This I want to do my way. The cops can't handle it."

"They can hold him overnight on suspicion, just long enough so you can immobilize the kids."

"He's liable to spill his guts to the cops." Arnold's eyes were wild. "Can you imagine what the media would do to a story like this? Me, they've been waiting for years to crucify me, my own kids, I know how to shut the fucker up if he comes out of this alive."

"That fucker of yours is a stunt man. He knows how to handle collision and sideswiping. He's got the advantage. You're the one who might not come out alive."

"I know cars, too. I'll have the advantage. He'll think he's after me, what he won't know is that I'm after him. And I'll do this with you or without you."

"Listen. This is my last crack at talking you out of it. understand why the sonofabitch flashed that bright light on Telly and me after we left the Villa. He had to make sure it was you and Krystina. Because unless he gets you and Krystina together it doesn't work. Just you knocked off Krystina and the new baby would inherit everything." He stopped, puzzled. "But why did he take after you on the superhighway when you came in from the airport yesterday? You were alone."

"Sri Lanka was sitting in the front seat alongside of me and he, too, mistook Sri Lanka for her. The parking attendant at the airport made the same mistake. So did the airport cop. On the superhighway he realized at the last split-second it wasn't Krystina and pulled away. I've got to nail him now. But you're right. I've got to have someone alongside of me he'll think is Krystina."

Four young couples poured out of the Hotel Savoy chattering

506

gaily. As they came alongside, Arnold mingled with them, Scott, after a second's hesitation, joined him.

The Croisette hookers were out, wearing preposterously lowering platform sandals and tiny shorts, a grudging concession to the local definition of the minimum decency.

They called to Arnold as he passed. They sensed he was looking.

"Bonsoir," one of the girls called. Arnold had noticed her before. She was built vaguely like Krystina, the same height. And it was all on display, like those cheap restaurants that advertise *prix fixe* menus, no surprises. "Ah, Sylvie," Arnold called back.

"No, monsieur." The girl smiled, she couldn't have been more than seventeen. "I'm Jackie."

"Of course. Jackie."

"Monsieur is lonely?" Jackie asked hopefully.

Scott, a few meters ahead, examined original paintings a young bearded type showed him, ghastly abstractions made with sequins and turned out by the dozens in some hidden studio in the hills, then peddled to tourists.

"I am lonely," Arnold said, "but you're the wrong color hair."

"What color is that?" Jackie asked eagerly.

"Copper, shining copper."

"If it is that you need," Jackie said sympathetically, "it can be arranged. If it is only the head hair you wish?"

"Only the head."

"I have many wigs," Jackie said excitedly. She knew Arnold was rich, she'd heard of him. But he looked so strange she was suddenly frightened. She must have had several bad experiences. Sado-maso the girls called them. "That is all you want? The color hair? Because I don't do specialities."

"I understand," Arnold reassured her, "no specialities."

507

Jackie hesitated another moment, then as Arnold was about to go on, let him take her by the arm.

"We'll cut through the garden of the Grand Hotel."

"But it's so dark there," Jackie hesitated again.

"It is simply that I don't wish to be seen."

That must have sounded reasonable to her.

Scott followed them, he was a lousy tail. He stopped when they did. Jackie almost sensed they were being followed.

Arnold and the girl disappeared into a shabby apartment house not far from the Grand Hotel on the inland side.

Jackie's apartment was a one-room studio that had been converted into three rooms. A loggia had been built with a huge bed, a kitchen and bathroom installed. It was stifling hot and the lights flooded in from the neon sign of the bar across the way. The wooden shutters kept out all fresh air.

Jackie quickly slipped out of her cork platform shoes, zipped off her tight thonged shorts, tossed them to one side with relief.

"They bind," Jackie turned so he could see her bare belly and buttocks. "Okay?" she asked anxiously in English.

"Great," Arnold said.

"You would prefer the other color there too?" Jackie asked nervously, his manner was not reassuring. "If you wish to be a regular client I can have it dyed, what is left of it. We must shave for these new-style shorts."

Only a wisp, a smudged brush stroke of pubic hair, very black, streaked her underbelly. Arnold shook his head no, it was fine the way it was.

"I'll get the wig." Jackie was beginning to have after thoughts, she definitely found Arnold's manner disturbing. "Although it is a very hot night for a wig." Arnold nodded distantly. Bare-assed, Jackie twinkled up the staircase, returned a moment later with a copper red wig. She'd taken her blouse off, was stark naked. There were pink welts under her breasts

508

rom her bra. She adjusted the wig, turned and spread her
rms wide in hopeful offering.

Arnold would have liked to tell her she certainly didn't
ave collars and cuffs to match but he didn't know the French
or cuffs. Besides it would have been a betrayal of Krystina to
se her joke. At that moment, Arnold felt compellingly close
o Krystina.

"Get your clothes on," Arnold handed Jackie a five-hun-
lred-franc note, which the girl took uncertainly. Five hundred
rancs. A considerable sum. This man was strange.

"Not here?" the girl asked in dismay.

"Not here."

"You are the writer," the girl said suddenly.

"Yes, I am the writer."

"Remind me what your tastes are"—Jackie didn't move—
'and if it is not too bad we can do it here."

"What tastes?" Arnold said. "I wish only for you to put
n the red wig and come for a ride with me in my car. I will
give you another five hundred francs." Now Jackie was really
rightened. "I'll tell you the whole truth. My wife has a
rivate detective following me. I have just been with my
nistress. You will slip into my car with the wig, he will
ollow us and when he sees the color of your hair, he will be
sure he has made a mistake, he will think I have been with
ny wife."

"He will remark the color of the wig at night in the car?"
Jackie asked.

"He'll see the color in the passing light. Then he'll give up
and think himself a large fool. He'll be back of us, remember." Arnold was impatient, irritated by her questioning.

"That is all you wish?" Jackie asked. "And a thousand
francs for that?"

"Yes. It's worth a thousand francs to me. It's my marriage.
Now come on. We must go immediately. And I'll give you

the other five hundred when we return. It will only be for a few minutes."

She finally agreed. He told her, explaining carefully, where the Monteverdi was, gave her the key, showed her how to open the car and slip in calmly. He would join her a few seconds later.

Outside, Arnold waited, watched Jackie disappear through the gardens of the Grand Hotel, carrying the wig in a paper bag.

Scott came to him quickly.

"I want to take another crack at talking you out of this," Scott said. "Get back to the goddamn yacht and wait until morning. Those two kids of yours are bound to show, the way they did after the other unsuccessful attempts. You'll talk to them. They'll have to call the nut killer off."

Arnold's eyes were wild. "I told you. You don't have to come along. Pull out."

"You're out of your fucking head."

"Go back to the apartment," Arnold said coldly. "Telly's waiting for you. No hard feelings."

"Shit," Scott said with passion. "You saw the 604. You saw that murderous hulk sitting in it. He's been sitting there for hours. He must be as crazy as you are by now." Arnold remained rigid, uncompromising. "Okay," Scott said finally. "I'll get Telly's Renault. It's parked not far from here."

"I'll wait with the girl in the Monteverdi until you come up. But stay far enough behind me so the 604 will have a chance to cut in."

"Where will you go. Do you know?"

"I'll play it by ear," Arnold said.

Scott shrugged and yielded.

They crossed the dark Grand Hotel gardens; the automatic shop illuminations had turned themselves off.

Arnold moved fast, down the stone stairs to the Croisette, past the Festival Café, and into the rue du Canada so that he passed the 604.

Jackie stood mutely before the Monteverdi. The outline of the 604 could be seen dimly.

"Put the wig on carefully first so you will not be seen doing it." Jackie did. "Adjust the wig before I open the door."

Arnold went over to the driver's side of the car. The light sprang on, those very bright interior lights he'd had specially installed, made Jackie's wig show up bright red. The light jumped off as Arnold shut the door, seated himself behind the wheel.

In the rear-vision mirror, Arnold saw Scott almost get himself run over as he crossed to where the Renault was parked. Arnold started the motor, was reassured by the arrogant explosion of power.

"It's been like this ever since the *crise*," Jackie whimpered.

"Like what ever since what crisis?" Arnold demanded. He must keep her calm, she was more frightened than he'd anticipated.

"The world *crise*," Jackie said bitterly. "All the girls have remarked it, many more clients are asking for unusual services."

"What sort of unusual services?" Arnold watched Scott in the Renault approach and caught a movement in the 604. Orville-Billie had started the motor. They were on their way.

"Being put in chains, whipped or whipping them. I thought it would interest you as a writer, for they say you write about such things." Jackie saw him watching the rear-view mirror. "Will we be going far?"

"Only until I am sure the detective sees us."

"I'll give you your money back," Jackie made a sudden move.

511

"Don't be stupid." Arnold switched on the light and drove slowly past the white car.

"I'm frightened," Jackie said.

"There's no cause for fear," Arnold said. "Fasten your seat belt."

"I can't find it," Jackie said hysterically. "Why fasten a seat belt? What is it?"

The Monteverdi shot out while she fumbled for the belt.

"There's a traffic light ahead," Arnold said, "if it is red, it will give you time to put the belt on. If it's green put the belt on at the first red light we hit. It's now the law to attach seat belts after ten o'clock at night."

"There's something wrong, the man will know I didn't come with you."

"There's nothing wrong," Arnold said sharply.

They changed directions over to the ocean side. A car intruded momentarily between them and the 604. The light turned red for the left-going traffic.

The cop directing traffic at the intersection gave them a friendly salute. Arnold waved back. Jackie's fingers were clumsy with the belt. Arnold reached over and pulled the belt across her chest, as the intervening car disappeared.

In a crazy reflection of light, Arnold caught a quick glimpse of Orville-Billie, his bulk leaning over the wheel, he looked more than ever like something that came out of a wrecking yard.

"It is the man behind us, the detective?" Jackie asked.

"Yes."

"Then he's surely seen us. We can stop soon?"

"In a few minutes."

Jackie slumped down in the seat frightened.

"Sit up straight. My wife does not sit that way."

"It's because of the bullets."

"There'll be no bullets."

"Please stay on the Croisette," Jackie pleaded, "there is illumination."

The traffic light went green and they swung left.

"What are you going to do to me?" the girl asked strangely resigned.

"Nothing, nothing." Her air of resignation infuriated him.

There was another light at the intersection with the rue d'Antibes and it was green too. The 604 stuck close to them, Scott in the Renault close behind. The rue d'Antibes was crowded. The cinemas had just ended their last show of the evening. The street was jammed with pedestrians and cars come to pick up the late moviegoers.

It was hard keeping Orville-Billie in sight. Jackie had her feet braced against the floorboard. Arnold was sweating.

"Relax," Arnold commanded.

"I am relaxed," Jackie said, terrified.

"Because he'll get suspicious if anything about you makes him feel you're frightened," Arnold barked. "You're supposed to be my wife."

The traffic finally unscrambled as the parties of moviegoers called gay good-nights to each other.

The lights in the shop windows went off. Rue d'Antibes slowly grew dark.

Arnold made a sudden turn off right, north. Jackie went rigid.

Orville-Billie in the 604 clung to them a few cars behind.

"It's so dark. I'm afraid."

"Sit still."

"We're on the autoroute," Jackie's voice had a shrill edge. "This is far enough. He's seen us. Please let me off."

"He's following us. Can't you see?"

They were on the crosstown overpass and there were few cars. Arnold had about a kilometer of unencumbered road ahead.

513

That would be the killing ground; but the 604 had suddenly sensed something and whipped over to the left. Arnold slowed down abruptly. Scott in the Renault had to brake to avoid a collision and the 604 now was certain something was wrong. He roared off.

Arnold let the Monteverdi go. She darted out like a snake's tongue, was immediately alongside of the 604, who tried desperately to escape. Jackie screamed as Arnold swerved viciously to the right, forcing the 604 to swing wildly. But Orville-Billie was trained for this kind of emergency. He locked the wheel firmly, his tires screeching, but Arnold sideswiped him relentlessly. Jackie screamed again. Orville-Billie showed a fantastic virtuosity, almost managed to maneuver himself out. Arnold gave the Monteverdi her full power pounding the 604 toward the concrete railing. There was a crashing sound as metal was crushed and glass shattered. The 604 rammed to a collision halt against the concrete railing.

Arnold pulled up in such a way as to block the shattered 604 if by some miracle it could still move. Jackie whimpered in shock.

Scott whipped to a halt. Arnold rushed over to the 604, pulled on the mangled door, opened it, yanked on Orville-Billie, whose head was cut and whose face was covered with blood. Orville-Billie tried to stand, kept moaning words Arnold could not hear, then tried frantically to crawl away, he was only trying to put a distance between himself and the car. Then Scott moved carefully to the battered 604, got in, came out with a can.

"Jesus," Scott said in awe, "he had a can of napalm in there. He was going to set you on fire."

Arnold opened the back of the Monteverdi, pulled out a heavy wrench, hurried toward Orville-Billie.

Scott grabbed him. "Get back in the car."

Arnold swung at Orville-Billie with the wrench, but Scott managed to deflect the blow. Scott shouted something that Arnold didn't hear at first. "A murder rap," Arnold finally realized Scott was saying.

Arnold suddenly saw the wrench, Scott, the half-conscious Orville-Billie. A strange calm descended on him.

"It's all over," Arnold said to Orville-Billie. "No special hard feelings even though you almost killed my friend's girl, my wife and me. Tomorrow morning you'll be put on a plane bound for wherever those shit kids of mine are sending you. Now hear this, Orville-Billie. I've got a standing contract out on you. The minute you get out of line, we'll pee in your pool, do you read me?"

"I'm an American citizen," Orville-Billie mumbled. "I got my rights."

"You got shit," Arnold said, "The Mob is in on this now. You're on parole to the boys. Don't fuck around. From now on, stick to movies. Strictly a stunt man, okay? Now, how much did my kids give you? The money you got for your first payment you hand over to me. My kids robbed that money from me. The boys'll let you know where to pay. You don't want the boys sending a special collection agency after you now, do you?"

"You're with the Mob," Orville-Billie said bitterly. "I never figured the Mob was going to get into this. Shit, man." Orville-Billie went to pieces. "All I got was twenty-five g's, I swear. That's all the fucking jewels brought. Minus what I had to put out, legitimate expenses."

"Okay," Arnold said. "Pay back everything that's left. They'll let you deduct your legit expenses but don't try to pile it on. I don't go for that kind of shit, only transportation and living, all the rest goes back to me."

"I never crossed the Mob my whole life." Orville-Billie expressed an article of profound personal faith.

"You did this time. Napalm! As a hit man you're a first-class asshole. Don't try anything like that again as long as you may be lucky enough to stay alive."

"Fuck," said Orville-Billie dejectedly.

"You said it," Arnold said as he walked toward the Monteverdi.

An ambulance and a police car came to a halt before them. "Next time it'll be a hearse," Arnold said as he got back alongside of Jackie, who was frozen in shock.

A cop came up, saw the can Scott was still holding.

"We thought we might have to smash the car door to get the man out." Scott made an explanatory gesture with the can. The cop nodded dubiously.

Another black Peugeot skidded to a halt and Bellarosa came running over. He was haggard and drawn. He'd obviously passed a sleepless night.

"It's all right," Arnold said numbly. "Krystina and I are not hurt. There he is, your 604 maniac."

"What madness," Bellarosa said. "Considering Krystina's condition, perhaps she should go in the first ambulance?"

"Ambulances frighten her," Arnold said. "I'll take her to the yacht and have Dr. Jean-Louis look her over."

"All right." Bellarosa was trying not to see Jackie. "Get Krystina home. We will take care of this."

Arnold started the car. It shifted easily, raced away. The Monteverdi almost came out of it unscathed.

Bellarosa moved away to Scott. Orville-Billie, bleeding, seated himself on the curb.

"It's understandable why he doesn't want an ambulance," one of the cops said to Bellarosa. "He had a prostitute in the car."

"There was no prostitute," Bellarosa said flatly.

The cop hesitated a moment, shrugged and walked away.

Bellarosa indicated Orville-Billie to Scott. "That one was on the yacht last night."

"Monsieur Elton wishes him out of his life," Scott said. "Without the inconvenience of publicity."

Bellarosa looked at Scott sourly. "We'll think of something. Reassure Monsieur Elton."

Arnold slapped Jennifer's face hard with one hand, then he other. Her head bounced from side to side. She tried to over herself with her arms. Arnold pulled her hands away.

"Why?" Arnold punctuated each slap with the question, "Why? Why?"

"Keep your hands off her, you lousy creep," Robbie said.

They were in the Villa Lou Soleillou living room. The shades had been drawn as though the house were in mourning.

Arnold turned from Jennifer and slapped Robbie, who made no defense, not even trying to shield himself. Arnold hit him harder until the boy's nose started to bleed.

Finally Arnold saw the blood on his hand. He had a fleeting image of Adelheid, stopped hitting Robbie, hit Jennifer again. "Why?" She seemed not to bleed so readily.

"You dirty bastard," Jennifer mumbled from swollen lips, "you made me have two nose jobs, two fucking nose jobs. The first wasn't good enough for you."

"I did that for you." Arnold, aghast, hit her again. "I wanted you to be pretty. Goddamn it, everything I've done is for you."

Jennifer's face suddenly went slack. Arnold recognized it as the look he put on when Mama Henrietta went to work on him. Goddamn, everywhere he struck he saw himself.

"I loved you," Arnold exploded.

She suddenly sat down on the floor her legs extended like a child's. Arnold was forced to get down on his knees so he could continue hitting her.

Robbie, holding one hand at his bloody nose, pulled urgently at Arnold's sleeve trying to get him away from her.

"Why? Goddamn it, why?" Arnold shook her in a fury.

"I let you buy me gifts," Jennifer said numbly in between blows, "I let you give me money, I let you buy me a car, I let you take me all over and what the fuck did you ever do for *me?*"

Arnold, about to hit her again, dropped his arm, looked at her in utter bafflement.

"All you had to do was give us the bread," Robbie said. "We had everything set—Jennifer was going to produce and I was going to direct." The blood spread over his denim shirt. "We had all the stars lined up, half the money. All we needed was that shit money from you, a lousy eighty thousand dollars."

"You asked me for a hundred thousand," Arnold said.

"You told us, Always ask for more," Robbie said. "We would've come down to eighty."

"Maybe even seventy-five," Jennifer said.

"We would have made it goddamnsonofabitchenbastard," Robbie said with deep passion. "We'd of been on our way, we would of made it, made it, made it. Fucking trust fund you gave us, we don't touch any of the capital until we're forty, ready for the shit wagon."

"Hold your head back," Arnold said. "You're bleeding all over the fucking carpet." He handed Robbie a handkerchief. The boy leaned back holding the square of linen to his nose.

"Basically it was just another hustle," Robbie explained.

"Another hustle." Arnold moaned, hunched over, pounding the floor with his blood-smeared fists.

Scott was right. If you could fly your dentist from Beverly Hills, why not Dr. Braunschweig at a moment like this?

Although the climate was quite like the Southern California Braunschweig had known for some thirty-nine years, another

518

Braunschweig had blossomed. The shawl-draped brooding Olympian distance had been replaced by a sporty, casual elegance. Perhaps Europe was his element after all. Certainly the luxurious sea-front suite at the Majestic Hotel in Cannes was a fine setting for him.

"I have always tried to impress on you what you have known instinctively as a writer, how very subtle and complex is the human soul." Arnold was shocked. Was it possible Braunschweig always had such a thick accent? Or was it because he was in Europe, or because he'd aged and no longer made the effort, permitting himself the soothing comfort of his native Austrian accent? It was a trick of memory, for as Braunschweig spoke, it became slowly apparent he'd always spoken that way. Braunschweig came into sudden focus as foreign, Germanic.

Braunschweig stood at the window and enjoyed the view of the sea, the palm trees, the color of the garden below, the bathers splashing in the pool, the parade of elegant guests. "Every schoolboy knows today that what is considered abnormal, psychotic, is an extension of the normal. I have thought deeply about this unhappy episode with your children. We must regard it finally, and it is the only way we will live with it, as the ultimate flattery. They have tried to be like you so much they have carried this imitation to its absurd and tragic extreme. Like you, they went after what they wanted with everything they had.

"But murder?" Arnold said. "And you're making it sound like my fault."

Braunschweig made a quick soothing gesture; after all Arnold was paying for this lovely and unexpected treat. "There is no need for guilt. For you yourself are a reflection of the reality in which we live, *nicht wahr?* And what they have done has taken them into an impermissible, totally unacceptable world, beyond civilized values. But here we

approach an area which is not mine and into which I do no
venture, the world of so-called moral values."

Nonetheless, Arnold got from Braunschweig that somehow
it *was* his fault and that he had no real right to be angry.

There was a tennis club not far from Beejay's hotel. It was
the soft part of the fading afternoon. From a bench Arnold
and Margaret watched the play on the red crushed-tile court.

"This has to be the weirdest tennis match of all time,"
Arnold said.

"I don't see anything weird," Margaret said. "They play
real good and they look real nice in their tennis clothes."

Scott and Telly were playing against Beejay and Robbie.
The balls were hit hard. They were all excellent players.

On the other side of the court, neat, pretty, subdued and
docile in her tennis whites, Jennifer sat alone on a bench, her
head swiveling as she followed the doubles.

"But they're not playing for fun. They're all trying to kill
the ball. They're playing to win," Arnold observed.

Margaret didn't understand what he meant and continued to
look on with almost maternal admiration as Robbie hit the
ball hard to Telly in the mistaken idea that she was the most
vulnerable. Telly smashed it right back to Beejay, who took
it, having anticipated it accurately, then drove it deep into the
back court to Scott. He cracked it back with a slightly clumsy,
but mighty two-handed backhand. Scott hadn't taken lessons.
His game was not as clean and precise as the others' but more
interesting. "If I had played tennis, that's the way I would
have played," Arnold thought.

Beejay and Robbie almost collided as Scott's ball whizzed
into dead-center court. At the last moment, Robbie instinctively
pulled back and let Beejay kill it.

"Good shot," Robbie shouted.

"This is a nightmare," Arnold said.

"Where I live," Margaret said, "and I don't mean your house, I mean where I *live*, happens all the time. Nothing special, fathers killing their children, mothers killing their children, their children killing them, only when it moves from our backyard to yours it's *special*, like it don't really count when it's us."

Beejay and Robbie won the match and openly enjoyed that too. They played well together. He was his mother's son.

Scott and Telly walked off to the other side of the court, and Jennifer started to play with Robbie. They played silently, warming up, hitting long, clean, swift strokes. Jennifer was surprisingly graceful on the court.

Beejay came over to Arnold and Margaret.

"Well, I don't know what else we gave them," Margaret said, "but they sure learned how to play tennis."

She got up, moved away to another bench.

"Tennis usually gets rid of it for me," Beejay said, "but I guess this is a little too deep for tennis."

She dabbed her face with the towel. It was hard to tell whether she'd wiped away sweat or tears.

"You talked to them?" Arnold asked.

"They've agreed to an institution in San Francisco."

"Agreed? Who the hell are they to agree?"

"You want to keep this away from the authorities."

No, her tone was not accusing. Arnold sat numbly and couldn't answer.

"I'll see them whenever I can."

"You seem to be able to forgive them," Arnold said.

" 'Forgive.' I try not to think in those terms. I try to deal only with situations in which I think I can be useful. All I hope to do is patch them up so there's a small chance they might make their lives have some value."

She rose abruptly and walked away.

Arnold watched her—trim, well-muscled, strong, tanned

521

arms, the hair still golden—and for a fleeting capriciou moment, wondered what his life might have been if they' stayed together.

Beejay joined Scott and Telly. The three laughed togethe They formed a world of their own, one Arnold would neve enter. A *pic* and *poc* sound filled the court as the two youn people drove the ball back and forth with disciplined ferocity

That morning Wacszinski had called. Hume had arrive and read a statement Arnold had prepared. A meeting o Associated stockholders was scheduled for two weeks fror today.

Reilly had phoned from New York, everything was copace tic.

It was already known that there would be a new board wit Arnold on it and that something would be worked out wit Hume. The stock was rising steadily. It was all workin, exactly as planned. Except it would all go to Uncle Millie.

5

"Broken homes is what did it," Krystina said to Arnold as they sunned themselves on the deck of the *Delphi*. "We mustn't ever ever ever let our home be broken." She leaned across her deck chair and lifted the huge straw hat that hid Arnold's face. It was hard to tell whether he was asleep or awake. The hi-fi was playing soft music, something from Schubert. The *Delphi* rolled gently like a cradle. "Arnold, if you think there's a danger we might not stay together, say so now. I'll have an abortion."

With the hat now covering his entire face, Arnold reached out, found Krystina's hand. She clung to it, trusting.

"We'll never have a broken home," Arnold said.

"And you'll have to take time out for the baby and me," Krystina said. "Go out together, trips together, be interested in him, Dr. Jean-Louis thinks it will be a boy . . . I mean children really have to be worked at."

"Sure."

"You agree with me, don't you?"

"One hundred percent."

Krystina sighed, reassured.

"Love you."

"Love you." Arnold realized he could just as easily have said "Have an abortion."

"Just about now you usually say it's the most beautiful hour," Arnold prompted Scott. "Blake used to say that too."

"Blake? Lawrence Blake?" Scott said slowly. "Do you know he died two months ago? A great talent unrealized."

"Tough."

From the *Delphi* deck they watched the quay as evening moved in like a guest who's a little late but doesn't want to disturb anyone. On the breakwater fishermen began to dismantle their rods. The Mediterranean would yield no more of the two-inch fingerlings it gave them when they were lucky.

"It *is* the most beautiful hour." Scott sipped his vodka and tonic, watched Krystina and Telly at the other end of the deck talking animatedly. "But I wasn't sure you'd feel it that way today."

Arnold said defiantly, "What am I supposed to do, curl up and stop living? I've got too much going for me. We should fly back tomorrow. You'll be especially useful to me right now."

Scott thought a moment, then fumbled in his pocket, pulled out the scrap of paper, studied it wistfully, looked up to see that Telly across the deck was watching him. She flashed him a smile. "I won't be flying with you," he said as he handed the tattered paper to Arnold.

"What is this? Have you thought about this carefully? Do you realize what you're doing? This'll never happen to you again. Look, don't be a horse's ass. I want you with us. If you're worried you'll get lost in the Arnel setup forget it. You won't be on the twenty-four-hour merry-go-round. That's for no-talent schmos like Reilly."

"No," Scott said. "What you really want I can't give. It would be a cheat."

"For a year? For a few months?"

"I keep hearing my grandfather quoting the much-maligned Clausewitz, 'Honor can be lost only once,' I don't want to sound pretentious but I think I would be selling what my grandfather would define as my honor. What's the matter?"

"You want the last question to stand?"

"I withdraw it."

"Hey—are there tears in my eyes?" Arnold asked.

"I think so."

"Then move your chair so Krystina and Telly won't see me." Scott shifted so he was between Arnold and the women. "If Braunschweig is right, that's an improvement. I'm crying externally. Means I won't have asthma. What are you going to do now?"

"Write. Go somewhere with Telly, somewhere not too expensive."

"Lucky bastard," Arnold said wistfully. "I envy you going off any goddamn place you feel like."

"You envy *me?* What's to stop you from doing the same thing?"

"What's to stop me?" Arnold demanded indignantly. "What have you got coming in? Eighteen? Twenty thousand dollars a year? I've got millions each year. How can I take a vacation? And now I'll be on the board of Associated."

"Okay. I see that. It's only logical. You make millions every year. You can't take a vacation."

Arnold sighed.

"I'll tell you what's running through my head," Arnold said. "A German folk song my grandmother used to sing." He began to recite.

"I bought a piece of cloth, from which I made a coat. When the coat wore out, I made a tie—" Scott was watching Arnold curiously. He wondered what Arnold was leading to. Everything Arnold did had a purpose.

"When the tie wore out," Arnold went on, his eyes fixed on some distant spot on the Mediterranean horizon, "I made a buttonhole and when the buttonhole wore out, I had a nothing." Arnold stopped, looked over at Scott. "And from that nothing I made this song."

"And from that nothing I made this song," Scott repeated softly.

"How about you writing a book about what just happened to me?" Arnold suggested eagerly. "My publishing house would bring it out. It's a cinch to be a bestseller."

Telly and Krystina looked over anxiously but Arnold flashed them an excited smile. They leaned back relaxed reassured.

"We'll make a shitpot of money on it. I couldn't write it—You understand that, don't you?"

"Sure," Scott said.

"You won't come right out and say it's me," Arnold had worked himself up. He was again vibrant, pulsing with energy. "Besides, readers want to be teased, they love to guess. I'll wangle you an advance—nothing spectacular, ten thousand. I might even convince the company to go as high as fifteen. Maybe twenty. And the paperbacks—we'd really do a campaign on the paperbacks. We'll exploit hell out of it, the elements are all there. Use it all, everything that happened. Scott, I'm offering you my life. What do you say?"

"Your publishing house won't like it Arnold," Scott said. "Not the way I've been writing it."

BEST OF BESTSELLERS
FROM WARNER BOOKS

SCRUPLES
by Judith Krantz   *(A96-743, $3.50)*
The ultimate romance! The spellbinding story of the rise of a fascinating woman from fat, unhappy "poor relative" of an aristocratic Boston family to a unique position among the super-beautiful and super-rich, a woman who got everything she wanted—fame, wealth, power and love.

LOVERS & GAMBLERS
by Jackie Collins   *(A83-973, $2.95)*
LOVERS & GAMBLERS is the bestseller whose foray into the world of the beautiful people has left its scorch marks on night tables across two continents. In Al King, Jackie Collins has created a rock-and-roll superstud who is everything any sex-crazed groupie ever imagined her hero to be. In Dallas, she designed "Miss Coast-to-Coast" whose sky-high ambitions stem from a secret sordid past—the type that tabloids tingle to tell. Jackie Collins "writes bestsellers like a female Harold Robbins."
                                                    —Penthouse

THE WORLD IS FULL OF DIVORCED WOMEN
by Jackie Collins   *(A83-183, $2.95)*
The world is their bedroom...Cleo James, British journalist who joined the thrill seekers when she found her husband coupling with her best friend, Muffin, a centerfold with a little girl charm and a big girl body. Mike James, the record promoter who adores Cleo but whose addiction to women is insatiable. Jon Clapton who took a little English girl from Wimbledon and made her into Britain's top model. Daniel Ornel, an actor grown older, wiser and hungrier for Cleo. And Butch Kaufman, all-American, all-man who loves to live and lives to love.

THE BOYS IN THE MAIL ROOM
by Iris Rainer   *(93-676, $2.95)*
They were at the bottom rung of the ladder, but not so far down that they couldn't see the top, lust for the glamor, covet the power, hunger for the dolls and the dollars. They were four guys with a future—baby moguls on the make in Hollywood.

BEST OF BESTSELLERS
FROM WARNER BOOKS

THE CARDINAL SINS
by Andrew M. Greeley   *(A90-913, $3.95)*
From the humblest parish to the inner councils of the Vatican, Father Greeley reveals the hierarchy of the Catholic Church as it really is, and its priests as the men they really are. This book follows the lives of two Irish boys who grow up on the West Side of Chicago and enter the priesthood. We share their triumphs as well as their tragedies and temptations.

THE OFFICERS' WIVES
by Thomas Fleming   *(A90-920, $3.95)*
This is a book you will never forget. It is about the U.S. Army, the huge unwieldy organism on which much of the nation's survival depends. It is about Americans trying to live personal lives, to cling to touchstones of faith and hope in the grip of the blind, blunderous history of the last 25 years. It is about marriage, the illusions and hopes that people bring to it, the struggle to maintain and renew commitment.

To order, use the coupon below. If you prefer to use your own stationery, please include complete title as well as book number and price. Allow 4 weeks for delivery.